THE MASQUERADE

I0692899

Also by Remi Shitu

Brotherly Shackles

THE

MASQUERADE

Remi Shitu

Illuminating the
Literary World

LUMINAIRE

First published in Great Britain in 2012.
This paperback edition published in 2012
by Luminaire Publishing Ltd,
Ground Floor, 2 Woodberry Grove,
North Finchley,
London N12 0DR.
www.luminairepublishing.com

Copyright (c) Remi Shitu 2012

The moral right of the author has been asserted.
This story is a work of fiction where all names,
characters, places and incidents are entirely of the author's
imagination or are used fictitiously. Any resemblance to
places, real persons, living or dead, or events
is entirely coincidental.

All rights reserved. No part of this book may be
Reproduced or stored in a retrieval system
in any form and by any means (electronic, mechanical,
photocopying, recording or otherwise) without
the prior written permission of the publisher.

A CIP catalogue record for this book is available from the British Library

ISBN 978-0-9571140-0-5

To my loving children; All children!

They taught the world to mask
Yet the world has masked better
Light and heavy.
Masquerade, how did you mask
Have masked
Will mask?

They taught the world to dance
Yet the world has danced better
In colours and costume.
Masquerade, how did you dance
Have danced
Will dance?

R.S.

PROLOGUE

November 1760 A.D.

It was an all-male entourage of six trekkers. Two of them were the all-important guests, four their interpreter-escorts. They had done fifteen miles of the journey in total ignorance to the strangeness of the environment, yet they showed no sign of fatigue. Instead, their anxiety to dispose the next ten miles and meet their intended host, King Japeedoe I of the Ila Kingdom, kept them in clandestinely-high spirits.

The two guests, though united in a single sponsoring sovereign were, among other things, of different intentions. In this procession, the guests tried hard not to discuss their purposes to the level of the escorts' understanding. If such purposes had already been betrayed by the guests' appearance, they wouldn't know.

One of the guests – the leading who was also third on the track – wore a white, dust-browned robe whose length almost buried his grey trousers. In order to counter the absurdity of his robe, first he removed its top attachment, the tap collar, and then clutched it together with his small Bible. It left his other hand free to hold up the hem of the robe or adjust his brown trilby whenever the occasion called for it. The Bible was the only protector he seemed to want

1

anybody he would meet to recognise as such on him. He prayed he would not have to show anyone the first of the invisible protectors, a berretta pistol, rested together with a knife deep inside his pocket. He, Jamie Macdonald, was going to Ila as a missionary.

Equally, the brown toupee, the double pocketed khaki jacket tucked inside a belted knee-length pair of shorts of the same material, and a brown pair of leggings atop a black dusty boot, all on the burly build of the second guest, widened the difference between the two men. The protector he chose was of a different kind – a Doune pistol of Thomas Caddell's originality. He held it at the ready for any wayward hyena, a foolish leopard, silly cobra, or unfriendly native that would be so tired of living to the point of daring the entourage on its important mission. His manner of dressing notwithstanding, he was basically a chartered trader filled with some strange trade proposals. His name: Collin Mackinnon.

"How many more miles to Ila, any of you?" the man in khaki arrogantly asked the escorts after a while.

"Almost there," answered the escort immediately at the front of the Bible carrying man. "Can't you see the goats, the hens and the cocks?"

"Eh, why do you talk like that?" the trader snapped at the last respondent. Those who speak rudely least accommodate rudeness. "What about goats and chickens? Have I told you I am unable to see them, eh? They are not the men I want to see!"

"He didn't mean to be rude," his clergy colleague interrupted to save the developing antagonism. "He meant the sight of domestic animals and birds is an indication that we are near to the township." He would not expand into the type of men his colleague had in mind – slaves roped down for sale!.

"I see. That's what he should have stated clearly. Haven't we seen wild animals and birds sharing with the townships, and the townspeople sharing with the wild? Haven't we encountered numberless strange things since we set our feet on this part of the globe?"

2

Just then, two men heavily camouflaged with leaves and aiming bows and arrows sprang up from the Ila side of the moat. They were the elite frontier guards of Ila, already briefed to expect the group and allow it a safe border crossing. The guests realised where they were. The lecture they received during their departure from base informed them that the moat signified they had reached their ultimate destination.

For the guards, authenticating the genuineness of the guests was easy enough. Each of the escorts had a visible, royal messenger belt, the width of the palm, diagonally hung across his chest from the shoulder. The belt was of red leather with crown design beaded to its centre at a point. It was all a royal messenger of any of the adjoining kingdoms needed in order to safeguard his entire passage when carrying or delivering a message, even at the height of inter-kingdom hostilities. Only an animalistic war would not protect the sanctity of such an emissary. Not allowing such a courier to deliver the message or return to base after its delivery meant that war had already been declared on the initiator of the emissary.

The frowns on the faces of the moat guards became smiles; and the smiles friendly words to the escorts. "You all can cross and continue," one of them issued the permission.

"God bless you," the missionary said to the sentries, waving his Bible at them, and praying deeper down in his heart that the friendliness continued. His colleague felt relaxed too, that he did not have to go back to the pistol he just tucked inside his belt, out of the sight of the moat guards.

"Wait," the same guard ordered again. "Cross carefully from this side," he directed the group, pointing to the side of the bridge laid with true wooden planks.

When the crossing was over, Jamie and Collin were surprised to see that the sentries they crossed to were actually eight in number. And still more astonished were they when they looked back at the side they crossed from and saw a similar company which did not appear at all to them when they first arrived at the moat.

They eventually conceded a salute to the fortification arrangements of the kingdom a short moment after the moat when they were crossed by another company of a dozen mounted soldiers, well armed and shielded. The warning re-echoed in them, not to start an assault on their way to, and inside Ila.

With the moat five minutes behind them, they were passed through two large cotton farms, each about the size of three football pitches. Collin was particularly thrilled to see for the first time ever, cotton lint on the *gossypium* plants. To him the immaculate whiteness from the buds' opening resembled laughter of some sorts, one that varied from a serious smile, through a hearty ha-ha, and ending in side-splitting, saliva-dripping gusto. A quest for the successful negotiation for cotton trade was one of the many reasons he was in the kingdom. "Cotton and cotton plants?" he exclaimed to whoever would confirm his belief.

"Yes, clear enough, they are; aren't they?" responded the clergy.

"What a *fair big fairm*!" he qualified the very big farm in Glaswegian tongue. "What a beauty! I am excited."

"I knew you would be – just as I would be also, to have the souls of those women working on the farm saved for Christ," Jamie replied.

"And what a special energy, that could make people work happily under this unbearable heat and dust? They must have been exceptionally strong! Just like those ones shipped into Glasgow before we departed.

"Do they jointly own the farm?" This time Collin meant the question for the escorts; and the last one on the march volunteered the answer.

"It must have belonged to one of them, or to her family," the escort said. "This is a women's cooperative doing the picking. It is likely they will do the farm on the other side next if it belongs to one of them."

4

"Cooperative?" asked Collin. "What a novel idea in this part of the world! We must remember that as soon as we're back in Scotland. We could try something like the cooperative too, couldn't we?"

They passed other farms after the two of cotton, all of them vying to upgrade the visitors' inadequate knowledge of tropical crops and agriculture. So corn cobs weren't from the top of corn perennials! Besides the sword and green-eye, other types of peas existed! A wonder that peanuts matured in the soil but its plant flowered above it! And tobacco plants and leaves could be so pungent and abrasive! Cocoa flowers and pods on the stem! Yam, what yam – giant potatoes!

"And look at what's immediately ahead of you!" Collin alerted the escort at the front of the march. "What's the man doing on the date palm, fruitless date palm? How did he conquer the smoothness of the stem and reach that height? What's swinging dangerously under his shorts?"

"It is not a date palm," the escort at the back saw what the guest meant and answered. "That is a palm tree, the source of roofing, oils, candle, kernel and palm wine. He is the wine tapper, collecting the wine into the dangling gourd he has tied round his waist. He uses the strong creeper cord he locks round the stem and himself to climb and descend." The curious Glaswegians, still wondering, ordered they stopped to watch how the tapper would descend. It was an amusement which, instead of helping their understanding, actually added to the puzzle.

"How far more do we have to go, any of you?" Collin asked again. It wasn't that he was tired; but he was thinking of how they must spend time with the ruler of Ila and still make it back to base that day.

"Not far now," one escort replied.

After walking another ten minutes, the guests saw clearer reasons to reduce their questioning. First, the path tripled in width and smoothness, the growth on both sides having been cut down and

5

rested along the edges. Then, not only were there more goats and chickens and cocks, there were also sheep, rams, pigs, ducks, and more of them, all roaming about their businesses without one disturbing the other. The group were on a long, gentle slope and could see native houses, some of them emitting smoke from cooking, far away on the scattered hills. "Thank Jesus we are there, aren't we?" the clergy asked, wanting a formal confirmation from the escorts.

"Yes, almost there," the escort at the front replied again with an unpleasant exactness. His 'there' meant the precise distance and position of King Japeedoe's palace. What the clergy had seen were some roofs and walls of residential compounds scattered haphazardly, as allowed them by slopes and tree shades. Their actual destination was still well beyond what they could see. Scores of such compounds constituted Ila, and the palace they wanted was right in their centre. The path became wider, and, by the Scots' true assessment, a real road. It was partly paved and soon forked out. The prong they followed continued to meet and pass other convergences that sandwiched the walls of the compounds.

The local bungalows were mostly rectangular, the few round ones being the holding barns for food and harvested farm produce. Each of them carried a wooden door and one or two windows of relief carvings. The walls were layers upon layers of two feet wide continuous mud bricks that went round as perpendicularly as any other eye-gauged wall could be. For thatch roofing, meticulously woven sheets of palm fronds were reinforced onto straight wooden stem rods, using clay and ropes.

Most bungalows faced the road from the compounds, and had open, spacious verandas running their entire lengths. Under these airy places, the natives played, sat and professed their trades. These natives, Collin curiously noticed to be mostly women!

Unlike those in the town they had started their journey from, the natives were not frightened by the sight of the two white men. Their ruler, King Japeedoe I, had already passed word round

6

the township through his chiefs and criers that the guests were special albinos – to them, a unique creation of the gods and so, ordered to be honoured by the gods. Culturally, the albinos were believed to own the nights, when they were expected to come out; but this day, the physical presence of the royal escorts with them gave the citizens no cause for alarm. However, this special classification denied the Scots the chance of actually stopping too close to the natives in order to probe the weavers in a veranda, the dyers outside a compound, goat milking women under a shade, and women porters by a big furnace. All the same, the Scots were convinced excitedly that they were at the centre of a great civilisation, and that right before them were immense wealth, strength, a great religion, and a rich history, all overripe for exploitative exploration.

* * *

King Japeedoe's court was ready. It had the royal stool arranged backing the inner door, with three long wooden benches placed head to head on each side of the stool.

Ten chiefs, two of them women, filed in from the side door to join the royal guests. They were beaded in coral and glass, and clothed in heavy local cotton materials of varying stripes. Nine of them bared their scalps which were cleanly shaven and deeply oiled to produce light reflections that varied largely with the shapes of the scalps. Ironically the tenth chief, the only one with a tall red cap on his head was the most huge of the lot; with the cap he excessively confined his fellow chiefs to heights that were artificially about half his own. He was the most senior of them, the man the interpreter to the visitors readily called Chief Tantalo.

After the chiefs had taken their seats entered a palace maidservant. Compared with the two women chiefs', her beads would have been ordinary but for the fact that they were uniquely made from some birds eggs. Starting with the chiefs and ending with the guests, the maid passed round with half kneeling courtesy, the

7

contents of her crafted calabash – kola nuts. The guests hesitatingly took theirs, but could find no heart to do anything with what they took.

"They are fruits His Highness offers to welcome everyone here to this meeting," the escort translated for the spoken Tantalo. "They bring energy. They bring life – more abundant life," he added.

Still, the guests just held on to the fruits, fearing they could be stomach-upsetting. They leaned sideways and discussed what their response should be. "No, we don't risk these fruits now," Jamie whispered to his colleague. "Instead, get out one of the drinks for everyone to toast the start of the meeting with."

Collin dragged nearer to himself one of the cane baskets of gifts they brought with them. From it, he removed a three-litre bottle of Scotch whiskey that had come directly from a top Glasgow distillery. Then, the escort translated its designation as per Collin's instructions.

"The kola is from the king, and not from us," responded the senior chief again, after Collin's instructions. "So, your gift should go to him first, and not to us," he finished the point of correction.

Whatever the response the guests were going to give, the sudden blare of a trumpet from behind the inner door stopped it. The sound alerted every native in the court to stop talking, be upstanding, and look towards the inner door. The door opened, allowing in the king, his guard and his fanner. Amidst a short, rousing cheer, he took his seat.

"Thank you, Your Majesty, for welcoming us with the important gift of kola nuts," Collin eventually stood up, and greeted King Japeedoe. Then, he introduced his colleague. "My king in Great Britain also sends you this special wine, among other things. May your reign be long."

"I welcome you to my kingdom," responded Japeedoe I, turning lazily on his stool. "Welcome to the palace of the only death

8

of all deaths, the only light of all lights, and the only wise of all wisest.

"I thank you and your king for the wine. However, it is after we have talked that we will know if and how to accept the wine and the gifts. Besides, wine, assuming yours is as good as ours, is never appropriate for the start of a meeting because it creates blurred sight, blurred hearing and blurred understanding. Perhaps after the meeting, we would be able to share your wine and our own, oguro. Kola is for life and for energy; it is right for the start of an important meeting like this. First, tell me now, before my people, why the two of you are here."

Collin rose again, to explain their mission. They were from Glasgow; and had from and on behalf of the King of United Kingdom brought good tidings and friendship. They were happy to have come, and to have witnessed how Ila Kingdom was much greater than their king ever thought. They had seen acres of golden cottons smiling on their shrubs, the kingly tobacco dominating up-soil with its strong aroma, the precious corn cobs safely backed on the stalks, and the industrious, strong looking men and women of Ila working very hard on all of them. They had seen leather, threads and cloths being made and dyed with artistic exclusiveness, and had seen decorative arts and pottery being delicately produced. They had seen a strong and progressive kingdom the King of Great Britain would love to trade and be friendly with. That was why the king had shown his respects by sending through them, two baskets-full of special gifts. If the trade proposals they carried with them were accepted, his king had several lovely things he could use to pay the King of Ila. More importantly, if the King of Ila had a troublesome neighbouring kingdom to tame, or he wanted to expand the kingdom of Ila at the expense of the virile citizens of the neighbouring kingdoms, his king would join forces with Ila for free, to do so. "It is what other great tribes are already doing, more for the greatness of their kingdoms than for the value of the few materials and men they sold to us," he concluded.

9

So, Collin wasn't only the clever politician-businessman appointed as the head of the mission, he was also a soldier-combatant fully uniformed and licensed to defend the mission with his guns if need be, to seek to establish a trade that would include human cargo!

The clergy addressed the court next; and quite intentionally, the court misunderstood him. The court wanted the God of Jesus he talked about to belong to Jesus alone, and leave the people of Ila to belong to their gods, their ancestors and to King Japeedoe. Ilas, they claimed, had for ages been aware of such nonsense from the land of Pharaohs they emigrated from. If Ilas refused to compromise their great gods, kings and ancestors then, they were not going to allow anyone to sneak any of the Books into them now. The guests had no alternative but to agree to the stance – at least until trade, mostly illegal, would boom multi-directionally enough for the Bible to root. They were confident the last laugh belonged to them and to Glasgow.

CHAPTER ONE

The Arrival

November 2000 A.D.

As far as Victor was concerned, everything about the road he now led his friend, Kazuggi, on was normal and sober – in layout and occupancy. Whether it was because of the time of the day, of the backward position of the road, or of its obtuse left-right bend, he wouldn't know. Their current fair distance from the bustle of the town where they had their hotel suggested they should expect to see more of such a quiet road. The normalcy was so till the tourists approached its far end and everything started to change.

Victor was the first to notice the wane. He stopped and looked back at Kazuggi, his friend he preferred to call Uggi. He was unsure of who or what to hate: Kazuggi who had so fallen behind, or a good twenty steps Kazuggi had to nullify between the two of them. He reversed the gaze to the original direction they faced. Now they were at its junction end and he wondered alone why every soul was going right, rushing.

From his position at the corner, he threw a look to the right, focusing intently behind every passer-by, and then faster ahead of them. He could see the end of the march, a nearby point where it was met by a similar march coming from the opposite direction on the same road. A war charge of some sort? But nothing like physical combating was taking place and there were no displays of weapons.

11

Instead, the marchers, as much as their numerousness allowed them, thickened and funnelled into the road that was opposite the kerb on which he glued his feet. Now he realised he was on a wide, staggered junction.

"Come on, Mister Millipede," he looked back again and commandingly urged Kazuggi, who, though had moved closer, was yet to notice the environmental abnormality. "Come on Uggi. You should be explaining these to me!"

Kazuggi had nothing significantly different to explain to Victor about Ila town or its on-going festival. Basically, both of them, being first time visitors to Ila and the festival, only deferred in the depth of knowledge of the town's stories as told them by a common principal source – Kazuggi's father, Reverend Ali Jaiye, back home in Glasgow. He assured them they would meet many people, and that due to the festival especially, the journey would be full of fun, wonders and excitements that certainly dwarfed Rio de Janeiro's. They were both told how every year in Ila, Kazuggi's ancestral root, the festival would send the participants magically into an outright trance. Victor had already seen some pictures of the festival that Kazuggi's father hung on selected walls inside his house. Kazuggi's father had spoken to both of them about the pictures with burning passion, guarded pride, and on occasions, with concealed shame. "Such was how beautiful life in Ila was, and how it should be," he once told his son and Victor as he pointed at the pictures. "It is how people of your generation should meet, understand and maintain the culture," he added. The pictures were mainly monochromatic – of revellers, acrobats and fashion – and would have matched a modern Olympic march-past's had they been in colours.

It wasn't that Victor's dad, Ben Mackinnon, didn't speak about Ila to Victor. Privately, he discussed with him the business opportunities that Ila could provide Victor in the future. Ben had told Victor how Ila was once famous for priceless artworks than for its masquerades; and how it didn't appear so anymore. He wished his late father, Davey, had taken him along when he went there years ago; and wished he had directed himself to visit there since the time his father died. Now he was sponsoring Victor both to go and enjoy the festival, and at the same time study the genesis of the kingdom's current business abnormality. If Victor would continue in the family's faltering arts trade, directly establishing and restoring certain contacts in Ila would particularly be beneficial to Victor.

Both Ben and Ali back in Glasgow, got to know each other and develop their friendship through serious circumstances that were beyond their common membership of the cathedral. Inevitably, the friendship extended to their sons.

Victor held his friend's hand and pulled him along a few steps, safely and mindful of the fact that no one in this part of the world ever read meanings to an open man-hold-on-man. In fact, as far as the members of Ila community were concerned, such a hold denoted necessitated guidance, the exact type that long existed in Glasgow between the blind man and his Labrador guide dog. And if he still had his doubts, the sight on the streets of citizens paired up in all genders and ages quickly re-assured him. The tourists walked on, on their side of the road, and stopped directly opposite the space facing the convergence. It was a bigger thoroughfare, a human confluence they were ready to cross over to, and possibly follow through.

"Watch it," Kazuggi screamed at Victor, pulling him back with an extemporaneous force. The refraction and pull just saved Victor from being knocked down by the combined weight of a lone biker and the woman he crashed on. Kazuggi swiftly helped the lady back to her feet, mildly rebuking the biker.

"Where are the police?" Kazuggi asked, fuming. In a rowdy situation like this, he expected to see the type of uniformed tatterdemalions that were abundant in the Bilitie Hotel area of the town where they lodged. "And except madness itself, who and what on earth has permitted cycling in a place like this?" he added, before both Victor and the few men who cared to stop.

No one answered him, not even the fallen woman who was now realised not to be alone. Without waiting for more pity, she grabbed the left hand of the little girl who was on the spot while another woman took her right; and in a Y- fashion pulled the girl away with them into the busy thoroughfare.

"Where exactly, are you all rushing to?" Victor confronted the biker.

"What? Did you ask where?" the unconcerned and unrepentant biker asked Victor. He knew Victor and Kazuggi belonged to another planet.

"We are collecting together," a fat man volunteered an answer to the tourists' questions. To the two tourists, the answer was not only useless, it further compounded the complications already aground. "We are going to the collection point," he proudly added, to make himself clearer.

"Collection point?" Victor asked the man. "Has there been an outbreak of fire? And, are there enough firemen around?"

"Fire Spirit, not firemen," the volunteer corrected, inwardly losing his patience with who were to him, a bunch of deeply ignorant foreigners.

"What? I asked if you have the firemen."

The fat man saw no reason to go on with the tourists. He too was convinced that not only were Victor and Uggi from a different planet, but they belonged to one where its inhabitants were incapable of any form of inter-communication. How on earth could somebody in Ila not know it was the judgement day for Jacquensica, shortened Jacq, the big mouth? He dashed off, believing Victor must be a foreign, white fool.

"Well, Uggi, we better get back," Victor wasted no time to suggest as he remembered the advice of Uggi's father and the private safety tips his own father gave to him in Glasgow.

"To where?" asked Kazuggi.

"Where else? The hotel, at least." We don't know what the danger is, and whether these people have conspired to hide it.

14

Remember, your dad warned us not to be unwatchful and too daring about what we could not understand. Better we play safe."

"But when one is in a strange land, what can be safer than going the same direction as the locals? No stranger could ever know the direction more than the 'son of the soil'!"

"No, I beg to disagree; and there is no time to list my reasons. It can also happen that the guardian dog is herding the flock into the ditch."

"I don't think there's any danger. This appears more of a mutual convergence than any sort of heads herding. Why would so many women be in it, and for that matter, with their children – if there were dangers?

"Look," he went on confidently, "look at their faces, bright, anxious – happy! Yea, let's follow. Could be a quicker start to what we are here for."

Both men crossed over and mixed with other people hastening on along the road, gradually adjusting their pacing upwards to that of the flow. They went from fast to quicksteps, and to near stampeding, with no time to curse the dusts being thrown up by their shoed and shoeless feet, until they reached a large space the size of a football field, where the population of the people already there halted the race. Welcome to Kings Square, the cultural centre of Ila Kingdom that was purposely hidden inside the old township.

* * *

The sound of music that Victor and Kazuggi could not hear initially due to their previous preoccupations was now distinct. It was coming from the far opposite side which they were unable to see due to the rowdiness that matched that of a disputed football-match pitch invasion. The rhythm from the combination of its samba, tambourine, gong and drums was heavy and clear. The people around felt at home with it as shown by their necks gently swinging their heads. Others ignored it in order to concentrate on the more important reason that brought them to the square. The all-important reason!

Kazuggi went into a paternal adulation over his father's recent predictions about the visit they were now undertaking. How mostly correct they all seemed to be – at least, up to now! He was high on it when a loud hailing interrupted him. It was coming from the edge of the square nearest to them, and both men drifted towards it:

> *Face of the thief!*
> *Olè!* (Thief!)
> *Nose of the Thief!*
> *Olè!!*
> *Face of the witch!*
> *Àjé!* (Witch!)
> *Nose of the witch!*
> *Àjé!!*
> *Face of the thief!*
> *Olè!*
> *Nose of the Thief!*
> *Olè!!*

A black horse was being saddled into the piazza from the tributary road next to them. It was easy to see a mushroom-cloud of tall colourful feathers high above the horse. The feathers stem from the saddler's facial mask that allowed only his eyes and neck to be seen. Three other lightly masked men led the horse. Two of them were engaged in clearing the enthusiastic crowd along the path of the group, and the third sounding a huge wrought-iron gong at eccentric intervals. Each slow stride of the horse drew a cheer from the crowd nearest to it. The cheer vied with the audibility of the gong. As the short but rowdy procession passed by their front, the 'carriage' being dragged by the horse became obvious.

"Good Lord, what's this?" Victor screamed with fright. The sight of a most unusual object, not of the ugly mask of the horseman, had shocked him to his socks and pants. It was a woman, fully eagled out on her back and bound to a wooden cross with lengths of thick cord. The two arms ends of the cross were reined to the horse in such a way that the head end rested on the side of the horse while the legs end dragged along on the ground. Both the slow stride of the horse and the openness of its cargo enabled a rain of assaults from the most heartless of the spectators – and they all seemed to be – in the form of curses, jeers and spits.

A young woman surged out of the crowd, gave the cargo a dirty look and yelled 'thief' on her. She raised her hand, about to cast a stone at the roped when one of the guards at the front noticed and restrained her. But like a dozen others in that part of the square, she ejected a mouthful expectoration, which spattered from the prisoner's forehead into the vee of her semi-naked breasts. "Take that for a traitor," she cursed triumphantly, dodging the long whip of the guard.

In disbelief, the tourists watched the file of agitation move past them. Viewed from the back at that slow stride, the tied lady formed a cross near perfect to an ankh; at a fast stride, probably a St Andrew's. Slowly and intermittently, it moved further into the square and stopped by an arranged spot the tourists believed was the gallows. There, with the assistance of the three leading masquerades, the cross was detached from the horse and dropped like a sack of potatoes. Then, with wicked vigour, they lashed the crowd off the middle of the square, to the four sides that made it.

Victor was becoming dazed. He wondered if the warning of getting tranced given by Kazuggi's father pertained to the bizarre and criminal behaviour of the natives of Ila or to the temperature of the carnival. His mind went to the Roman film he once watched. It was a historical depiction of what happened in Rome about two thousand years ago. The Romans of old, led by one Emperor Titus, were a blood sucking, wicked lot. In performing a *humiliores ad bestias*, a defenceless plebeian was thrown into a large arena. One man, laughing dryly with delight beside the caged lioness he manned, released the lean beast into the same arena, forcing the

17

plebeian into a hopeless flight towards its opposite end. The run was just what the second animal keeper at the opposite end needed to release his own lioness; and again, forcing the plebeian to run from one beast of death to another. Instantly, the beasts competed for the flesh, blood and bones of the man while the spectators grinned with barbaric cheer of satisfactory amusement. But this wasn't an era of old, but two millennia after the time of Titus, and more than four decades after the wars. It was neither a Roman film nor was the prisoner Roman. The perpetrators too weren't anything Roman, but heartless, self-proclaimed Caesars of the primitive stock in a world called Ila, a world in a faked semblance of modern living!

The post-clearing minutes threw out another pair of masquerades to replace those guarding the prisoner. They emerged from the pack standing on the far opposite side to where the tourists stood. The pack had their faces netted under the masks and headgears that challenged each other in eccentricity and intimidation. The clearing gave the tourists a better view of the space that was left of the square. It was largely grass-less, sun-hardened, and randomly 'pebbled' by balls of hard goats' dung. At the prisoner's, the guards sheathed the cutlasses, and jointly hung upright her cross. Victor and Kazuggi suspected the arrival of the actual time for the decapitation of the prisoner.

The spot where the prisoner was dumped wasn't the exact centre of the piazza. It leaned to the only side where some spectators were specially seated, their multiple rows of seats sandwiched safely between the gallows to their front and a very large building, the symbolic main of the square, to the back. To ascertain the prominence of the dignitaries seated on this side, beautiful leaf and textile canopies were erected above the seats. The gloating calmness the tourists noticed of those seated suggested they were the ones the show was primarily meant to appease.

The left side, next to the canopies, started with a cluster of more masquerades and ended with a mixture of spectators farthest from it. The spectators continued into the square's next two sides, the last of which both Victor and Kazuggi stood and watched in disbelief.

Those of the spectators who were strong enough but were unable to secure a good view of the stakes took to the top of shaded trees in the periphery. Still, others, most brainless either out of personal savagery or induced brain blockade took to the balconies of a few single storey buildings which, though were around the square, were cut off for a view of the focal point by the ring of people. This was how every member of the beastly crowd took his position, with no regards to height, size, age or sex.

"What is going on here, would someone tell us?" Victor restlessly arrested two men hurrying past both him and his friend.

"Festival, sir...of judgement," one of them stopped to answer.

"Festival of judgement? What's that?" he asked him.

"E e e r, judgement; judgement of festival."

"Still, don't understand."

"Well, today, here at the Kings Square, the Almighty will deliver the judgement on the sinners." He dashed off to a fresh position, avoiding an ill-timed nuisance to what he had come to the piazza to enjoy.

The hurried conversation left Victor still confused. He began to wonder if it's a carnival they came to see. "Which Almighty was the man talking about?" he asked Kazuggi. "Is the biblical God openly visible here? And which sinners? Is it a church congregation we are here to see?"

"I too am not sure. I have never heard of The Creator inviting all the creatures to assemble for an open judgement. As far as I know, none of the scriptures taught that."

"Anyway, didn't you once say the world started here in Ila – that God lowered the first man down here, using the magical thread?"

"It's dad who told me so. And that God lives in spirit here more than anywhere on earth – inside their newly imported mosques and churches, as well as in their shrines. But he said nothing about any judgement of sinners, or of the righteous for that matter."

"Well, you might have something to tell him when we get back."

"O yes, that's sure." He raised his black SLR Konica camera and snapped away rapidly. "We need some snaps of all these to back it up."

"Go on then. Start with the gruesome; but with none of us appearing with them."

They changed to a more advantageous position. Kazuggi added more clicks.

"Are the snaps good?"

"Trust they are; and hoping the flash won't make them too light. We could try moving a bit more forward for even better pictures."

"No way," Victor flatly objected. "This spot we've arrived at is just good enough. Can't you see what you want us to be nearer to?"

In horror they looked at the two sturdy poles sunk at a distance of a football goalpost. Another wooden beam having a hangman noose round it was tied about ten feet up across the sturdy poles. On the dusty floor between the two poles were a set of three logs arranged one atop two, and laid parallel to the side canopied for the dignitaries. Indeed, gallows tree and guillotine combined!

The dignitaries themselves were relaxed. Three maids were going round them, pouring $\grave{o}g\grave{u}r\grave{o}$, $pit\acute{o}$, the local wines, and $\grave{o}g\acute{o}g\acute{o}r\acute{o}$, the local gin, into the mugs most of them held.

"Already this is neither a holiday nor a carnival to enjoy, but an execution we are not supposed to witness. We just have to leave now. No, we mustn't get involved." Victor was frightened.

"Okay, just one more snap," Kazuggi said, giving in. As he did so, he depressed the shutter release button rapidly again, setting off the flashes, and sharply capturing the prisoner at the centre. The pseudo distance covered by the emission from the flashes actually went beyond its intended object – into the eyes of King Japeedoe sitting majestically under the canopy and surrounded by his queen, children and other dignitaries.

"Call that man immediately – the white man with the camera," the king wasted no time ordering the guard on his right. Victor, for the colour of his skin, was the easier for him to see even though it was Kazuggi who took the pictures! "Bring him and his friend," he added, unable to hide his fear of the snoopy cameras. Experience had taught him that white cameramen loved to focus on the ugly instead of on the beautiful sides of events; and that they usually pretended by starting with sharp-shooting when in fact, their true intention was trouble-shooting. Almost all the ten white men who attended his carnival two years ago carried a camera each. Not even one in their group made a complaint, but still, they did not stay to see the finale as they earlier promised to do. After they were gone, some subjects revealed to him why they stayed only three of the seven proud days: they were horrified by the offhandedness of the masquerades and their male escorts. They used the cameras to capture scenes of masquerades inflicting privileged floggings on the people, as well as of masquerades forcing money and gifts out of those without a trace of wealth in their standing. Then they carried the pictures back to Glasgow and used them to dissuade other white men from ever coming to Ila. He was sure the same blackmail was being re-enacted by the snap-happy tourist; and that this time the effect could be more negatively serious on him and his entire kingdom.

"Come," the king re-ordered the same guard who was just departing to Victor and Kazuggi. "Your hand! Where are you going with that? Were you born with it?" he angrily queried the guard about the cutlass in his hand. It went straight, handed over to the guard behind the king, leaving the guard free to race through the short crowd to the pair of Kazuggi and his white friend.

21

"My king wants you," the guard eventually delivered the oral invitation to Victor, remembering to bow a courtesy even though he was in great haste.

"Me?" Victor asked. "Who is your king, and where is he?"

"Yes, the two of you. He wants you – over there. Come with me."

"We are coming nowhere with you," Kazuggi told the guard. "Tell whoever sends you that. We haven't come here to see anyone personally."

"Come quick," the king summoned the guard on his left on suspecting that the first guard was having a problem with the tourists. "Run down and tell the two of them I want to see them." He could successfully read the argument that was going on among the three men. "That I guess they are here for the festival and that I have got some seats for them…that we are friends and we mean no harm!"

In the end Kazuggi was the first to change his mind. As soon as he did, he assumed from the guards the persuasion of Victor. He suggested that going over to the king would present an opportunity of discovering more of what was happening in the square, and another of intervening if needed be.

"Hello friends," a deep voice greeted them from under the fringes of a special headwear. "King Japeedoe the Sixth is speaking to you. Welcome to our kingdom and to our festival. I did not realise we have important guests like you until I saw the flashes, otherwise I would have seated you earlier. Please bear with us for two minutes for your seats to arrive. They are already on the way."

* * *

Victor and Kazuggi were relieved the king did not order their camera impounded or its film confiscated. They assumed he was a man even though his style of clothing allowed no part of his body to be visible.

22

Externally, everything visible of him was truly earthen in colour. His small cad was of intricately tacked, polymer clay beads of various thickness and lengths. The fringes were closely set; as they dangled they covered the whole of his face and neck. From under the fringes, beaded chains totally covering his chest and shoulder hung down. The garment, though heavy for that hot evening, was made heavier by being fully ornamented with beads.

The tourists were however convinced that going by the sparkling English coming out from under the fringes, he must possess some elements of enlightenment, the barbarism on display notwithstanding.

The tourists were uncertain about the type of chair he sat on though. It was covered round by the extension of his big garment and so, impossible to see. But whatever type it was, it was probably backless, set to the comfort of his knee-bend, round, and rotating. Each time he turned on it, he did so with the ease of one on a barber's chair. When he stopped, the triangular totality of his shape, starting from the head to the points the broadest part of the garment touched the ground, made him look like a huge tropical anthill.

Two servants rushed in two stools – round headed, probably like the king's – and rapidly re-cleaned their shining leather tops to reconfirm the cleanliness to both the requester and their intended users. Then he ordered them positioned together to his right.

"Yes, my friends," he addressed the tourists still standing, "for you." He pointed to the stools. "Nearest to His Highness, The Mightiest, Japeedoe the Sixth."

The tourists thanked him.

"Now, my friends, what are your names?" he asked when they were seated.

"Victor."

"Have you ever been here?"

"Err r no, sir."

"And your friend?"

23

"My name is Kazuggi. You may find Uggi easier to pronounce. It is the shortened form."

"O ho, really?" the king straightened up and faced Kazuggi. "Interesting, my friend, you're really Kazuggi?"

"Yes. Are you surprised, Your Highness?" Kazuggi asked.

"Never mind that for now; we shall talk about that later. You are both together I suppose. Correct?"

"Yes, we are, Your Highness," replied Kazuggi.

"And you are from where?"

"From Glasgow in UK," Victor replied.

"Aha, Glasgow, in England? That's interesting."

"Yes, you can say that," answered Victor who saw no need in dragging words with someone he couldn't even see his face.

"Many of you used to come to our festivals; the last group came two years ago. But I was disheartened that none of you came last year. That we have the two of you here with us now will make us feel proud again. We have proof from the time of my ancestors that our good friends, people of Glasgow, used to visit Ila. Interesting, isn't it?

"And your name," he addressed Kazuggi, "it's our native name, a fine name that combines royalty with a good hunting skill."

"Hunting skill? What type of hunting?"

"Gaming – big animals like lions, elephants, giraffes, hyenas, tigers, gorillas; big birds like eagles, hornbills, peacocks and ostriches; and big snakes like python and rainbow, can I say. Only the bravest of the braves and the wisest of the wise could do it. You can imagine how rare those types are. That name your father gave you means you are one of the rarest, of the bravest, of the wisest. Were you from here then?"

"My grandfather, Jaiye senior, was. He left from here as a child."

"Incredible. Interesting. In full that name is Ologbonjaiye, meaning the wise one who knows how to manage life. I could feel the blood! You only have to hear *Jaiye*, and the stuff you are made

24

of becomes known. Our historian-elders shall check our history and know exactly who he was." the king said excitedly. "*Kú àbọ̀*, do you understand that, meaning 'you are welcome'?"

"Yes, Your Highness, every child in my family did the lesson in UK."

"Interesting. You understand what *Ọdún Egúngún* is then?"

"Yes, Egúngún Festival, or Masquerade Carnival, my father told us."

"Correct of him. That will make you and your friend to enjoy what is happening here now, as we go along with it."

"Thanks sir," Kazuggi cut in. "But we would not be able to see more of it. Our laws forbid us from seeing this sort of thing. We are also tired, and must go now."

"You don't mean that, my friends. This comes up once in a year, and you are just lucky to be timely. I want you to stay today, and stay the whole period. We have just five more days after today."

"But Your Highness, do you mean we should stay to see another woman tied up and brought out here? Is something like this a part of your carnival every year? And is each one of the remaining five days like today?" Kazuggi poured out the questions.

"Oh no, my friend," the king answered, struggling to dismiss what Victor and Kazuggi had on their minds. "Each of the past years was excellent. This is the first time there is a big troublemaker; but it's going to be excellent too. Each day is different and interesting in a special way. But today is most significant; five days time is the finale no one should miss. Today I want you to be patient and see everything from this vantage point."

"We believe what is happening here now is private to your community," Victor stared to give excuses. "It is what we don't what to be involved in whether tomorrow or today. And if I may ask you sir, why is staying today most significant? Why can't we go and come back tomorrow if we wish?"

"Interesting. Exactly because I want you to see it all directly – without anybody telling you. Telling you about it now will kill the excitement and reduce the value of seeing it.

"Besides, after we leave here, I want you to be my guest and watch this annual festival till its end on Saturday. Two years ago I had no chance of sitting down with those from Glasgow. The presents I had for them are still there – wrapped." He clearly wanted to go on, but then, the sound of a flute horn prompted a guard to come over to him. The guard handed his whip to one of the king's guards, paid his homage and whispered some words into the king's hearing. Then he rose, took back his whip and returned to his point of departure – the prisoner's. The king was prepared for the final act.

The horse was dark brown. With its rider, it moved past the prisoner to the king and dismounted. His robe was danger red, with the sunshine rendering it visually redder. It was complemented by an ugly, whitewashed wooden mask made more frightful by the red lines and spots drabbed all over it. The tourists wondered over the significance of the funny clay pot he carried on his head above the mask, but not about the sword he hung on his waist. Then, another clearer-masquerade walked to him with a bottle in hand, poured some of its content in the pot and lit it up. "So this is the Fire Masquerade, the Fire!" the tourists exchanged the rude discovery. His homage to the king was brief in order to compensate for a longer time he would require to drag the prisoner to the king and then return her to the execution logs. On his way back to the prisoner, he drew out his blade, a hydra-headed sword whose naked sight alone was enough to kill the faint hearted.

The tourists were now able to take a closer look at the female prisoner. What they saw made The Crucifixion and its preparation a set of most decent acts. Starting from her clothing, what she was wrapped in from the chest down to the waist was in shreds. On some parts of it, and on other parts where the rope was tightened round her, she was soaked in blood that ranged from fresh

26

to red-baked. To the tourists, wrapping the ropes round her waist before passing them diagonally in the front to go through the two breasts on to the right side-neck was a deliberate act of her captors to debase her womanhood. One side of her face was black, swollen and bumpy; and so was one half of her head that was shaved clean to debase her even further. Layers of sands that patched on her head and face further thickened those parts of her body.

Neither Victor nor Kazuggi could imagine the type of willpower that could keep a woman still breathing under such condition. They saw no justification whatsoever in subjecting a prisoner, talk less of a female one, to that level of indignity. They felt the frontrunners of this crime were deliberately hiding behind the masks. Overtaken by anger, Victor turned to Kazuggi. "Who is she?" he asked him.

"You ask me again," was the only answer Kazuggi could murmur.

Even if Victor wanted to re-ask, he found neither the time nor the patience. "Your Highness," he said, leaning across to the king and having been pushed by Kazuggi's burning question, "who is this woman and what is her offence?"

The faceless mould was not surprised at both questions coming from the tourists. He believed where the tourists came from was a kingdom notoriously full of unguarded talkative idiots. It was the first time anyone would openly suspect and question his judgemental act. He knew that while the tourists could ask him, none of his subjects would ever dare. It was the first time an offender was being publicly punished, the first time that the level of such punishment ever reached that of an open, capital one, and the first time such punishment was being carried out at a time of masquerade festival. Normally, an unpardonable enemy of the kingdom was supposed to be just removed forever from the face of the earth by *Orò,* the executioner of criminals, in the middle of the night. He would not allow Victor's questions to fault his plan and timing which had successfully attracted a large number of

27

spectators, and would teach potential troublemakers how to keep quiet.

"My dear friend," the king replied, "hear Fire Spirit? He will tell you who she is, what she did, and all other things about her that the two of you might want to know.

"O yes, he wants to start now. Let's all listen."

"Fellow Mighties and brave citizens," the flame-carrying masquerade started to address the crowd, "my respect and greetings to you all in the name of my Almighty." He dazzled his hydra-headed sword, unsheathed in his right hand.

"To a large extent, all that this woman did was already known to you. She defied us all and defied our ancestors. She insulted us and insulted our ancestors. She started a war – the type no one, not even a man – has ever started in the history of the kingdom of Ila.

"My Almighty, the Mighties and friends warned her, but instead of making a change, she got worse and dragged her stupid husband into it. How can a woman this devilish ever fit a decent society like ours? She even attempted to seize the collective responsibilities of my Almighty and the Mighties, thinking we are all soft, stupid and easily misdirected like her soft and stupid husband.

"In the end," Fire Spirit ranted on, "the gods and our ancestors charged my Almighty to take action and save them from further humiliation from this woman. That is what is being done here today. From here, she will be sent on an endless journey that leads her to our ancestors. But before she commences that, her closest friend in her time of sanity will come out and bear open witness to what she did. This will save all of us from any guilt before our ancestors now and in the life beyond."

The lady friend promptly identified herself. The Queen – sitting next to Victor! She rose and took a regal walk to the prisoner, guarded.

"My dear friend," Queen Azzanaite addressed the prisoner, "that it comes to this is sorrowful. But you know, as your friend of many years, I warned and warned – until you were directly caught in an act that almost cost me my life too. That was when I had to bear an open witness to all you said. Remember, the witnessing is and was never false, because I do not want to incur the wrath of our ancestors. For now, I pray that the gods you betrayed give you another opportunity to learn when you are with them."

There was a short silence.

"Thank you, our dear Queen, and mother of Ila. Both our forefathers looking at you from beyond and my Almighty sitting with you thank you for your contribution. To you it may be small, but to them it is much. May none in your lineage ever turn the way of this one."

"She spoke well, didn't she?" Fire Spirit turned to the crowd again as the queen was leaving the central stage. "The prisoner is going to have the last opportunity of seeing her softer-than-woman man, the lily-livered man who has disgraced all men – together with the small devil they are both rearing as a daughter. My Almighty has told me not to deny her that last chance."

Another horse rider set out from among the masquerades. He was dragging a tightly bound man with him, towards the erected gallows. A lady holding a small girl of about five walked along, beside his horse. Both the lady and the child walked at the speed of the horse, ignoring the apparent tiredness of the little girl.

Unless one was able to identify the man before the start of his ordeals in the hands of the masquerades, it was impossible to know who he was now. A long period of torture, which included thorough beating, and imposition of artificial baldness by rough shaving, had inflicted on him a physical transformation that was brutally total. He was naked except for the underpants. All parts that would have normally contributed to a man's handsomeness – mouth, nose, eyes, ears and limbs – were bruised, swollen and bloodied.

29

Were beauty competition synonymous with men, he would have lost his deposit against the Incredible Hulk.

If the female prisoner was aware of the presence of her husband and daughter, she was too weak to show it. Even when Fire Spirit asked for her last wishes to the two prisoners brought to her, she opened neither her mouth nor her eyes.

"The mentality of these bastards now before you," Fire Spirit resumed "is like that of the thief. Do you all know what the general mentality of the thief is? Listen, I will tell you.

"The thief plans how he would not be caught in his usual act. So he chooses the dark nights to rule and plunder. He forgets his victim needs just one night to get him caught and deposed. Isn't it so?"

"Yes, mighty Fire," led a loud masquerade, followed by others.

"The thief could choose the night to plunder, but he must remember that when he is caught it's the day men who will pass a sentence on him. In that way, is the thief not foolish?"

"Yes, he is!" the same masquerade led answering again.

"And further, for all of you: My former neighbour had a son he named Never-You-Die. But the poor neighbour himself is dead now; and when will Never-You-Die too not die?"

"He will! He will! Surely! Die! One! Day!" shouted another masquerade high on top of others' voices.

"So, this is why we must be careful in whatever we do. Where care is disregarded, care also disregards the careless. Such is the case with these bastards here before us today. They thought they could secretly betray us endlessly without being caught. That they could, without shame, spread words to destabilise our community, stir the spirits of our ancestors and get away with them. They forgot the end of secret sin is open punishment. That anything born will die. Together they sinned against us; and together we, on our side, will give them the punishment they deserve. Isn't it so?"

"Yees!" the spectators screamed out the passionate affirmative, having been totally convinced the prisoners were guilty.

"They have done no wrong," a lady quietly voiced a disagreement to the man she was sitting with, just behind the tourists. Their position suggested they were privileged spectators. "How could they all turn round and accuse them now? This is never a true judgement of Ila, or of our gods. How can they ever defend bringing kid princes and princesses here to watch executions? How could friends so betray friends? This is sickening, unfair."

"Hush," the man quickly whispered. "I warned you to keep that thought of yours to yourself. The king could call his kids to do the executions if that is his wish. Does the tiger not start teaching its cub how to tear an animal into pieces from the day it's born?"

"But they are not guilty. They never committed the sins and acts of betrayal they were accused of. Queen Azzanaite could be my sister, but it's her who should be ashamed. She should, together with Sese, for their falsehood against their friends. They were the ones who were betrayed."

"Look, Bambo, we'd rather leave than you put us both in trouble. Learn to close your eyes and let go. You don't see anyone appealing against the verdict of the Mighties and Almighty. Before someone hears you, please drop it. We shouldn't be the ones to complain so openly. We shouldn't."

The debate caught Victor's attention. "Did you hear that lady?" he asked his friend. Kazuggi didn't.

All the same, the strong dissent of the lady with the panic in her husband's reactions was indicative of some indisputable injustice. Fire Spirit did not say clearly who the prisoners were, or what specific sins they committed. The prisoners were gagged, and the beatings they had rendered them too weak to speak at the stakes. At the start, the crowd was sceptical as shown on their faces, but now they supported the sentencing. Yet a couple among the VIPs-in-horror saw no justification, but went along with it for the fear of Fire Spirit and the king.

"What do you think about all these, Uggi?"

"Bad. And I dread the worse."

"Do we ask him? We should. Let's change. Move over here."

Among the few who noticed the exchange of seats was the king himself. He was about to ask the tourists the reason behind the change when Victor fired the first question at him: "Your Highness, who are these?"

The king was short of words. "Did you listen at all to that masquerade, the Fire Spirit?"

"Yes, I did. He didn't say who they were or what were their offences."

"Did you listen very well? No."

"Yes, I did, Your Highness. Fire Spirit seemed to direct all accusations – albeit without specifics – to the lady. And the poor lady was not allowed to reply and defend herself, because you already put her in great pains."

"I had the same thing in mind, Your Highness," joined in Kazuggi. "I too, am lost."

"You are not lost," the king responded directly to Kazuggi. "That is why you are here, in a town of your forefathers. Pray that you will never get lost like those two lost sheep that are lost forever – lost forever together with all members of their family. When both of you were expected to listen very well to the mighty Fire, you did not do that. Listen again is what I can advise because his explanation still continues; but it will not go on forever."

"The whole town has decided today under the Almighty, isn't it?" Fire Spirit went on.

"Yes," the crowd roared even though there had never been any formal meeting, talk less of an agreed judgement.

"That we give a judgement that is total?"

"Yes!"

"That will stop this once and for all?"

"Yes!"

"And forever saves us from further confusions from half measures?"

"Yes!"

"That the witch woman meets her gods today?"

"Yes!"

"That the gods receive her sinful soul."

"Yes!"

"Am I right and correct?"

"Yes. Right and correct!"

"Thank you all. As we talk now, fire, the type bigger than what you now see on my head, is already set and burning down their home, the home of sin. After burning, the whole compound will be knocked down, and both ashes and the immediate earth they fall on scooped away.

"On that plot will be a new hall of the masquerades, one that will improve the standard they plotted to destroy.

"Carrying out this judgement is the only way to please our gods and ancestors who were already angered by them. It is the only appeasement that will bring back the Birds of Fertility, the Rainfall of Healing, together with all the masks that had deserted our kingdom due to the abomination of this woman and her household."

"We are not unmindful of their daughter. The Almighty spares her. But she will not be allowed to continue the generation of the sinners. She will live as a slave in the palace, forbidden to ever have her own children. For her foolish husband, he is already made a slave; next he will be made a eunuch. Do I speak out what you all want?"

"Yes, our Mighty!" led the masquerades, enthusiastically followed by the crowd.

"Thank you, all."

Four masquerades set out for the centre, obeying the call of Fire Spirit. They were to assist him in despatching the prisoners appropriately.

33

"But, Your Highness," resumed a frightened but more determined Victor, "the Spirit tabled no single offence, yet, he passed a death sentence. Who are they, and what wrongs specifically have they done? And who is the man dictating death under the cover of fire, too cowardly to show his face?"

"My dear friend," the king, angry now, responded, "if you have never known you will never know. Why are you so ignorant and concerned about people who damage their own people? People who are *Mr Know-all* and *Mrs Know-all*, *Father Know-all* and *Mother Know-all*, who have even got a *Daughter Know-all*?" he squealed. "Don't you have your own spirits in Glasgow and England? You already told me yes. Do you disrespect them, and do your women disgrace them?"

"Excuse us, Your Highness," Kazuggi came in to ease the burden off Victor. "Glasgow is a big cultural centre with regular exhibitions, while London's Notting Hill Carnival is second to none in the whole world. They also worship spirits in Americas and Europe…"

"And in none," Victor hijacked Kazuggi, "did we see anything like executions, roping people down and so on. Two years ago, our friends came here and went back totally horrified. It was not easy for Uggi's dad to convince us that yours was a better carnival; and that's why he made us to come, to be able to confirm it to our friends that all is well."

"Yes, Your Highness, he convinced us; and then, we convinced our friends. We still want to convince them more – that the kingdom and its culture are truly as beautiful as they were already made to believe."

"But they are your subjects, aren't they? Can't you forgive them? You surely can. We appeal to you to set them free."

"Before now they were mine," the king was resolute. "Now they are subjects of their own downfall, and the food for the gods. They stopped being mine the minute they were caught plotting against other subjects. They are rotten. If you don't remove a rotten toe, the rot extends to the head." He was firm and angry. Nobody has ever questioned his wisdom, except of course, the prisoners who dared, and would never have the chance to dare again.

"Well, Your Highness, we are leaving," Victor resigned. "Our intention was to enjoy your kingdom. But now, we have seen enough. We shall not be a party to this crime. Good luck, Your Highness.

"Come on, Uggi."

Kazuggi sprang up as both anger and surprises jostled for prominence on the king. He was ready with his last words with King Japeedoe.

"Your Highness," Kazuggi addressed him with the type of bravery and crispness none of his subjects could ever have imagined, "I must tell you now, that I feel ashamed that we are witnesses to this, that you punish humans in this manner, and that you so refuse to show mercy. Foreigners will refuse to watch your masquerade festivals from now on, because we are going to make these known in Scotland, and in England. We will blow it all up."

The king's immediate reaction was pure fury. Even though the tourists could not see his eyeballs, his reaction said it all. He spun rapidly on his stool towards them, as if the next he had in mind was to jump off it and descend on them with his fists. Then he stopped, with his pride dropped together with his invisible face. He shifted the confused look across to the masquerades who were already rejoicing at making a scapegoat of the trouble-shooters. He realised he had a difficult choice to make.

"Okay, my friends, what do you want from me?" he asked with total dejection as he again looked across, this time at the spectators eager to see jungle justice inflicted on a woman-led gang they believed had insulted the spirits of their ancestors.

"To forgive them, your Highness," Victor wasted no time to answer.

"Just like that? How about all the Mighties and our citizens here today, how are they going to feel? How about all the friends

35

they betrayed through their treachery? Did you not just hear one of them?"

"Your Highness," Victor countered, "the lady we heard was not a friend. She could never have been, and no one would have liked to have one like her," he added bluntly. "Friendship is better shown when the other person is down, out or just going out. She did the opposite; she could never have been her friend!"

"Or, at most, we plead again," Kazuggi added, "give a lesser punishment if your subjects won't allow an outright pardon. They have already been punished enough – especially the lady. It's not beyond you if you mean to do it."

The king breathed a heavy relief and adjusted his weight on the stool. One thing, he felt happy that the beaded strings hung down his crown covered his face. Effectively, they allowed none of the visitors, the masquerades or the spectators to see the shame and defeat that engulfed the face as he succumbed to the pleas of the tourists. He believed the nets and gauzes on the faces of the masquerades would serve them the same way.

"Okay, my dear friends," he started to make a concession, "the best I can do for you is to postpone the carrying out of the people's sentence on this gang till tomorrow. The woman you pity most is the particular devil and gang leader who does not deserve to live. But you are invited to come and see me tonight for some talks. I can assure you that after our talks you will change your mind about these sinners and agree with the verdict of the people. Here is no place for further talks on this case."

Pure joy! Victor and Kazuggi were unable to stop its radiation passing from their minds onto their faces where it was exchanged. It was not solely for winning a round, but for the unexpected way it was won. The radiation was jointly beamed at the king, even though they doubted if the king reflected it back at them. "Thank you, Your Highness," Kazuggi added to the smile.

"That's kind of you," Victor added. "Where do you expect us?"

"Here, at the palace. Before you go you will be shown the entrance to use. Remember I did what you asked. The final sentence will depend on the outcome of our meeting."

"And one more thing, Your Highness: how are we going to know it's you when we meet you – you don't show us your face?" asked Victor.

"That is simple, my friend," the king embarked on answering yet another question he believed was a wayward one. "Where do the ordinary people see the face of their king so cheaply – except in England where they see it so commonly and consequently disrespect it? When you arrive they will take you to no other person but me. Secondly, even though you do not see my face, you have heard my voice long enough. The wise recognises people through other means than the faces."

It was as if the breeze was waiting for that moment of agreement. As the king turned his head back and forth, it gently pushed the crown strings the opposite directions to reveal a rare smile. The masquerades and spectators who caught a glimpse could not at first believe what was happening – that their Almighty had vetoed a reprieve for the beasts threatening the culture of the people of Ila! They wandered if the tourists who were nearer saw the smiles, which to them, were a spontaneous acknowledgement of something destructive for the kingdom.

For those who did not catch it, the confirmation began to unfold immediately when the king sent one of his guards to both Fire Spirit and a guard of the prisoners. They were to cut loose the female prisoner from the cross, but still leave her, her husband tied hands and legs. In that position, the guards should assist Fire Spirit to pack them to the palace dungeon, together with their little girl.

"Lucky them aren't they?" the same man turned to the woman.

"I told you they are innocent," the woman replied. "It is all victimization and nothing else."

37

"Look, Bambo, it's you only who knows it as that. A single woman can't be larger than the kingdom. She could be your friend, but she went beyond what's expected of a sane woman living in a kingdom of men. We all know that too."

"Now tell me, would you as my husband have thought the same of me if I were to be in the same problem? Would you, Silas?"

"Well, may you never be. Never."

"Anyway, I know they will eventually triumph over their wicked colleagues," she added grudgingly.

"If you couldn't keep your mouth shut till we are out of here, keep your voice down at least."

"Colleagues? Are they colleagues?" Kazuggi asked the lady. He was attracted by the spontaneity in the man's utterances and the resolve of the woman to disregard her husband and talk on.

Silas pinched his wife to stop talking, and followed it up with a staring look when she still showed no sign of compliance.

"If you are ready my friends," the king finally turned to the tourists, "follow the guard to show you how you will come. Six o'clock." The king rose, about leaving, two guards packing the long tail of his attire.

"Thank you, Your Highness," responded Kazuggi, "Victor will follow you to see." Kazuggi wanted to stay behind.

* * *

Kazuggi could scarcely wait for the king's entourage to reach a safe distance from him. He was eager to get the couple, Silas and Bambo, to talk.

"I am a friend. Now, tell me. Are they colleagues?" he directed the question at Silas.

"They were. We all were." Bambo snapped before her husband would retract the neck he stretched out to see off the king.

"That is only as far as you will know," Silas interrupted angrily. "And don't blame anyone if what you know now lands you

38

in trouble. You must learn not to know even when you knew. That's the root of the matter!"

"Indeed the root of the matter...which is the trouble with you, our men here! For me to pretend? Never. What's the point? Why do you know? It doesn't hurt to say what one knows, does it?" Bambo returned a shouting match and anger.

"Nonsense," Silas was not going to back down. "If that's truly your belief, then follow the king and tell him so – before he goes very far, you have a direct access to the palace. But I won't follow you. I won't lose my prestige and privileges over this."

Kazuggi was sure there was fear in the husband who continued to gag the wife. "Please, gentleman," he addressed the husband again, "what is this fear all about? Are the prisoners colleagues of yours, of the king or of the spirits?"

"Look, man, keep me out of it I say."

"Yes, mister," answered Bambo. "They were all colleagues, special colleagues. We all were on this side of the Square."

Kazuggi prodded Bambo on until she volunteered a summary of what she and her husband knew but which he was afraid to talk about:

The woman, Jacquensica, is the wife while the man, Nek, is her husband, and was one of our chiefs. Dancemaster masquerade was the spirit from the chiefdom of Nek's grandfather. It started like other masquerades of the time – maintaining discipline among the people of the chiefdom, praying for their progress, and carrying their gifts, prayers and wishes to and from the spirits of their dead ancestors.

During the reign of Nek's father, Dancemaster's dancing steps grew so popular with Ila. The women did not mind that it was a male spirit; they constantly flocked his processions and learned the latest in dancing from him. The thicker the flock, the more the donations they, naturally as women, gave. It was the start of the trouble.

39

He refused to use on any of his teeming followers, the cutlasses and whips he carried; and this bred more of them, especially the young women, behind him. The masquerade would dance from early hours of the day to late ones of the night during the annual festival, radiating an all round happiness among his followers.

When five years ago the father died, Nek was installed the chief, and he took over the control of Dancemaster. The father's burial was in the morning; and was followed by Nek's installation in the afternoon of the same day.

The family spirit wanted to use his renowned dancing to welcome the reign of the new chief of the family. So the spirit danced vigorously and hyper-obediently to the command of the new chief. The citizens too would not miss the chance of respecting the chiefdom that made them happy through Dancemaster, the happy spirit that allowed their prayers to be heard by the heavens. So, there was a great dance of respect, sorrow and joy, which was followed by huge donations in cash and kind. Nek had never in his forty years seen a crowd as big as that, and has never seen a donation as much as that given to any spirit, the king's included.

Nek, the new chief and chief mourner, rose to dance with the family spirit. In an unprecedented act, he beckoned to the crowd of mostly women to join him on the dance space. To allay their fears, he personally removed the belts of idle cutlasses and whips that hung round the waist of his spirit – forever! The spirit danced close to the people and the people close to him. He became the first to ban any form of intimidation, which to Japeedoe and some chiefs, was a familiarity allowed and carried too far. The king accused him of systematically cheapening the supernaturalism of spirits in Ila to please women followers his wife, Jacquensica, led.

And last year, Dancemaster refused to take donations from the citizens, and yet, all prayers through him were successfully delivered to, and bountifully answered by our ancestors. Mischievously, the king and other chiefs who Dancemaster used to supplement with gifts and donations accused Dancemaster of keeping the gifts for himself.

Next, there was a double murder a royal masquerade committed, and then sought Nek's protection. Jacquensica learnt of it and prevented her husband, Nek, from playing such a role. The king was angry that Nek denied the masquerade the 'institutional cooperation'. He was mad when his queen and friend of Jacquensica revealed to him that an order from Jacquensica had prevented Nek from shielding the murderous masquerade. It meant that Jacquensica had taken over her husband, probably with her charm or the help of juju. It meant Jacquensica would soon be seen openly running the male chiefdom of the Dancemaster. It meant a most serious abomination that needed a swift cleansing had occurred in the kingdom of Ila.

The king and his gang also feared that Jacquensica's small daughter, if allowed to grow will do worse than her mother...that the gods and ancestors were angry that evil had grown in limbs and bonds in the linage...that they must destroy the evil once and for all by publicly executing the unofficial leader of the chiefdom, Jacquensica.

That is it, the injustice, in the most concise form I can think of. They forget that the spirits of our fathers neither sleep nor fail to dispense true justice.

Oh, do not say I told you – plea-ea-se.

CHAPTER TWO

The Bargain

What exactly the matter was with the mentality of Ilas, the tourists still didn't know – except that the grey matter of every citizen seemed somewhat infected. It was barely six hours since the members of Ila community were emboldened to watch an open execution and serious abuse of persons. So soon, and everything appeared to have been forgotten. The streets were full of gaieties; the masquerades were ripping the citizens off their possessions, and the Kings Square still proudly retained the gallows in the front of the canopies set for the beastly dignitaries. "What's the matter with these people? What's wrong with their king and the entire leadership?" Victor and Kazuggi exchanged these questions severally on their way to meet King Japeedoe.

"Gentlemen, we are here by appointment to see the king," Victor told the two spear-armed guards at the side entrance to the palace. They were the same ones the king had sent to bring the tourists to the royal canopies earlier in the day.

"Too early now," one of them replied.

"Too early?" Kazuggi asked unbelievably. "The king expects us now," he protested. "And you were both there when he gave us the time," he reminded them.

"No," the other guard said. "He expects you by six o'clock exactly. That's when he told us you will arrive and we must lead you to him. Sorry, we must not disturb him until that time. He already warned strictly how there's always a purpose for time and timing."

A dejected Victor looked at his watch. Six minutes to six. He calmed himself and Kazuggi that the time which remained was never going to be as long as that they had been waiting; and that it would be useless explaining any further to the gatekeepers. By their job culture, all they ever understood was the initial 'start' or 'go' order, and never the subsequent 'stop' or 'come back' – just like a fresh army recruit!

Six o'clock was self-certified by the second guard. "Grekko," he called out, "get them in. Six has reached."

They were on the move when he further asked his colleague: "You know where, don't you?"

"Yes, I do. Lion."

"Wait," Victor sought a fast clarification." Is Lion your mate's name or we are going to the lion?"

"Yes and no," replied Grekko, "'Lion' is the hall where the king will meet you."

They walked through the courtyard, some sections covered and some open, until they reached a large, wooden double door which Uggi and Victor guessed must be their destination. Each door leaf carried a wide strip of lion skin. Mounted above the door was a carefully skinned and preserved head of a lion, complete with its nose, eyes, ears, teeth and mane.

Grekko noticed the hesitation of the men he had with him. "It's nothing to worry about: there is no animal in the hall," he assured the king's guests.

"But do you have to do this to a lion?" Victor asked Grekko.

"My hand is not there. So, don't include me." Grekko began to exonerate himself. "Do I look like one who could kill a lion? But then, isn't it better done to the lion than for the lion to do it to someone? Ah, God forbid a bad thing." He unlocked the door and

43

let them in, asking them to choose their seats. They took the sofa nearest to a corner as the guard returned to the gate.

A quick opening of the similar door on the opposite side interrupted their immediate moment on their seats. A man, loin-clothed, marched in. "The king, my Almighty, welcomes you," he said as fast as he entered. "He said you must feel at home," he added, and marched out through the same door.

But then, another man burst in, carrying a wooden table. He had weird make-up in the thick, single red beads that pierced his ears, pounding his cheeks; and another in his lower lip, beating his chin. He gave a short, sour grin that was not accompanied with a single word of greeting. He set the table down and hurriedly arrested his falling loincloth, re-tying it as he marched out.

Through the same door, and with the promptness of a hard-pressed man rushing to enter a loo, barged in yet another servant. He held the door open to let in the same weirdly beaded man who, this time, was carrying a large wooden tray. The carrier was visibly trembling due to the weight of its contents. Delicately, he put down the tray on the table and grinned out again, slamming the door after himself, and leaving the one who had opened the door behind with the tourists.

"The king, my Almighty, welcomes you," the earlier door opener said, rolling and tightening his loin cloth. "He said you must feel at home." His message was not only delivered tone for tone, but also word for word like the earlier man's. He however made three additions: the king said all the drinks and beverages were for them; that they would best enjoy the clear wine in an unlabelled bottle he raised up and called *ògógóró*; and that the king would soon be with them. Then he gave an expansive grin that was made even wider by the mammoth size of his mouth.

Victor and Kazuggi had expected the king himself to enter immediately after the departure of the last man – perhaps in his loincloth too. After all, everything, from the start of their day on the streets to the present time, had been fast paced. Five minutes passed, and no one entered. Nobody would in the next thirty. This presented the first opportunity for the guests to relax.

Kazuggi surveyed the pots, mugs and bottles on the tray set before them. Slowly, he opened the first pot to see its content; it was tea. He opened the second: tea. The third: fresh milk.

Next, he turned round each of the four bottles of Scotch whisky that came with the beverage in order to read the picture and name. There were two horses for *Whyte and Mackay*, a single horse for *White Horse*, an integrated hand bell for *Bell's*, and bag pipes for *Grant's*.

"Everything here is funny and eccentric," Kazuggi said as both men started to gain a clearer view of what surrounded them.

"If they are to you, what do you expect them to be to me?" Victor responded.

"Oh no, Victor, I can't answer that for you."

The dark green settee they sat on was comfortable enough. There were many of them, all set end to end around the over five hundred square feet of space the large parlour occupied. Their continuation was interrupted by each of the four doors leading into the hall from each of its four walls. Without the interruption though, the continuation would have not been monotonous. The settees were new, and the piles of the covering velveteen material so short that they gave the settees a dusty look at the slightest of touch or rub. A length of thick cord derived from further twisting together of single orange and white cords marked out each seat of the settees. Even though there were no arrests, the shine and glitter presented the eyes with a clear demarcation of how much of it a normal-size, single guest should occupy. The newness of the settees contrasted clearly with the shabbiness of the walls they skirted. Patchy areas of peeling blue paint stood out irregularly like ringworms would on a young, dirty human head.

Large framed photographs adorned the walls. They were of kings and queens, princes and princesses – dead and living – with their names printed at the bottom of the frames. Apart from the names, nothing else identified the personalities due to the heavily beaded coverage of the faces they were meant to portray.

"King Ja-pee-doe, Princess Ai-min-natie," Kazuggi was up, reading out the names on the two pictures above Victor's head. He pronounced them boldly as if he knew them better than when he learnt about them from his father in Glasgow, and as if their significance to him had been boosted by the sight of the photographs. "Oh, King Ole-di-ran too!"

"Oh come on Uggi," Victor stood up and silenced Kazuggi from the meaningless enthusiasm that wouldn't give their sitting presence some peace. "What's special about them? Who are they that you won't let people rest?"

"Who are they? Can't you see?"

"But seriously, can you? They are all bloody the same. Faceless. That's all there is there to see. The same body could be carrying different names in different postures, who knows? Daft, isn't it – that they could spend money to make big pictures like these only to deny them identifiable faces? Bloody daft. Everything!"

"Oh well," was all Kazuggi could say. He returned to his chair, feeling guilty of a sin he did not commit, of comments he had meant to be appreciated.

"Is that all you can say? It's beyond 'oh well', Uggi. Look at the walls – less than half a century old perhaps; but look at their state – grossly unpreserved since. Look at the mini football pitch of a hall we are in now and compare it with these bloody windows that are smaller than a Black Maria's. With the winds of civilization blowing round the world, why do those of oddities still nest here?"

"Oh Victor," Kazuggi called out in total agreement, bursting into laughter that dragged both men into mocking their environment even further.

They noted the ceiling, dirty, cobwebbed and spider infested. It looked down directly on to a floor that was fully covered with linoleum of square blocks design and a spectacular four-crown print at the exact center.

They believed the two double and two single doors were far too many for the hall, that they made an excessive perforation on the walls. Perhaps, they thought, it was why the windows were of insignificant, small sizes. And neither did they see the artistic relevance of a large, wood-carved lion placed behind a similarly sculptured kneeling lady by each door. Was it to warn women like Jacquensica of the fatal punishment that awaited any woman who would dare instigate a rebellion in the kingdom?

Even the styles of reception and entertainment – their interpretation of punctuality, the rushing in and out on guests, the offer of drinks without food and that of tea without end, and the lack of female maids in a typical royal household to serve the table – were all weirdly to the tourists.

Victor and Kazuggi did not see any sense in all the men shaving their heads. It showed not only an unpleasant assortment of colours of the scalps, but also of the size and rotundity of their heads. They wore nothing except pilgrim-white cloths wrapped round their waists to reveal a varied degree of floppiness, protrusion and hanging of their chests and stomachs.

"Since we have arrived in Ila," Victor summarized, "everything has been too funny for words, as if this is not a part of the same world."

"Yes, and weird too."

"What should we expect of the king?"

"Some oddities too, whatever the degree."

47

"Right, Uggi. If every subject and everything in the palace is odd, we must expect the king to be also."

* * *

Victor and Kazuggi laughed loudly again, terminating the laughter forcefully when one of the double doors was opened.

Two men carried in a large chair of polished wood. It had a large lion head carved on the back, and a small one at the end of each armrest.

"If trees were lions," murmured Victor to Kazuggi, "the people here would have long felled them to extinction."

The men were stressed but sufficiently focused on what they carried as if they were made of lead and decorated with glass. They slowly set its legs down beside Victor and Kazuggi and stood by it. They were recognized as two of the guards who were by the king at the square. Victor and Kazuggi knew the king was about to come in.

A small, fully beaded, fringeless diadem on his head; a white net vest over his body, a long gold chain, and heavily ringed left fingers distinguished him in the group that entered next. As soon as he entered, he directed the flash of his white teeth fixedly at his guests. Then he shook their hands very warmly, roaring the earlier message he sent to them: "You are welcome; feel at home."

With a backhand, he directed where he wanted the chair positioned. When the two guards had complied, he waved them to leave.

"You saved the idiots today. You are not only their angel, you are their god, their good luck and their re-creator," he said with all seriousness.

"Thank you, sir," and "very kind of Your Highness," of Kazuggi and Victor were simultaneously emitted. There were smiles all round – genuine on the guests' and false on the host's faces.

"But I mean, I mean not yet…or, or…," the king stammered.

"What does that mean, sir?" Kazuggi asked.

"Oh, that they are not totally saved yet. That is what it means. Or, what else, my friends?"

"Are they still being held?" Victor asked.

"Yes, my friends. I told you earlier they couldn't just go like that. Not until we have talked. Is that not why you are here?

"But feel at home first," he sang the usual line, "and enjoy your drinks. Then, I can show you round the palace. Then, we can talk about the criminals. Then, the talk will determine what will be my final recommendation to the kind people of Ila. Then, they can go free, or not go at all." His words signaled to Victor and Kazuggi that more would have to be done before the prisoners would be released, that the host was not as kind as he had pretended to be.

"In that case, Your Highness," Victor said, "let us discuss their freedom first. First things first."

"Oh, don't worry, my friends. Though their case is serious, we shall resolve it – together. It must not spoil your time with me. Feel at home."

"We have a short stay, sir," Kazuggi said, reinforcing Victor's suggestion, "and another day is almost gone. We are already at home with your kindness. But like my father used to tell us in Glasgow, the guest does not put the welcome before the objective, else he ends up like the tortoise."

"Like the tortoise?" the king quickly sought clarification. He was amused at the unexpected mention of the tortoise, and more so at Kazuggi's intention of linking a story with it. In his domain, most stories of cunningness and trickeries and frauds were wrapped round the tortoise. So, the culture of Ila covered areas as far away as Glasgow! So, the greatness of the kingdom went beyond producing the greatest masquerades to supplying intelligent tales to the wider world! He urged Kazuggi to please share the story of the tortoise with them.

"The tortoise had an important function to attend to the next day," Kazuggi began the story, "but had neither a befitting suit to wear to it, nor the money to buy one. He knew his friend had one, so he went to him to borrow it.

"By luck, the tortoise met his friend at home having his dinner of porridge, a favourite menu of the tortoise himself. Before his friend could complete extending the invitation to dinner to him, the tortoise was already at the table sharing the dinner with his friend.

"The dinner was going on when another friend came. He too was after the same suit the tortoise had in mind. As usual, the common host invited the new-comer to join the table.

"'Thank you very much,' said the new entrant, 'but could you please lend me your suit? That's why I have come to seek you. I want it for an occasion tomorrow.'

"'No problem,' the host replied. He interrupted the dinner to fetch the suit.

"'But, friend,' interrupted a worried tortoise as the suit was fetched and was being handed over to the last entrant, 'that's why I am also here – to borrow the suit!'

"'That can't be why you are here!' the host retorted. 'If it is, you wouldn't have chosen the porridge first. And I have just this one suit.'"

"Brilliant!" exclaimed he king. "You and your father even told the story better than I have ever heard it told by my own people here. Maybe sooner you will invite me to Glasgow to hear more of these stories, and in their better fashion too. Or, won't you?"

"If that is your wish, sir," Kazuggi said, "you are welcome at any time. But please let's discuss the prisoners first."

"Alright my friends, about these criminals: why at all are you bothering to save them? And if you would, why so early? Why? Why? Dangerous, isn't it?"

"We want you to pardon them now, Your Highness," Victor replied. "Now won't be too early. Like in the same Glasgow, Your Highness, we are taught that 'the quality of mercy is not strain'd..., is enthroned in the hearts of the kings..., an attribute of God himself.' That's Shakespeare, you've heard of him, haven't you, Your Highness?"

"Oh yes," he replied loudly, laughing. "A good man. A clever man. A truthful man. You need to 'shake' these criminals quickly and 'spear' them, before they would 'shake' and 'spear' you dead yourself!

"But seriously, my friends, these ones are different. You see, they wanted to drown themselves, to commit suicide; I didn't have a problem with that. They included their own daughter in it; I didn't have a problem with that. They could wake up their dead ancestors from their graves and include them, and I won't have a problem with that either. Then, they wanted to rope the people of Ila and my humble self into it. How could we ever agree to that? How could I agree? My friends, you too must not agree. If anything, we must assist them to drown themselves."

"Your Highness, this quality of mercy..."

"Look, my friend," the king cut Victor short with all seriousness, nodding his head, "they should have thought of that before. Well, if both husband and wife – and daughter – could not know that it is an abomination to commit suicide that is just too bad. And if we must save them from drowning themselves, we must first allow the water to fill their silly stomachs up to their throats. If we don't, they will take us down with them. You now see why I say you don't have to save them. If you must, now is too early."

As the debate went on, King Jap was particularly adamant that until a victim was completely down he would never know the true value of mercy and relief. He explained how he had lived long enough to see and know many of such victims. Usually, they misused the opportunities, undervalued any help rendered to them, and found time to criticize their helpers. Instead of being grateful, they used the time to lay false claims to the help they themselves could never and had never rendered to any other soul.

"How many days then do you recommend we should wait, Your Highness?" Victor asked in order to cut short the king's story time.

"Days? We should be talking of months or years, the exact number they used to prepare their crimes. And my friends, they are many."

In that case, sir," Kazuggi said, "can you allow us now to see them where they are being held? That would show us they are still alive. It should not affect the time you would set them free."

The king wasn't keen at the suggestion. He was of the opinion that it was far more important to use such time to see how beautiful his palace was. When he eventually agreed to their request, he added the conditions: the visit must be brief, no conversation was to be made with the prisoners, and a guard would accompany them to ensure that the royal instructions were obeyed.

"What's your name?" Victor, in order to break the silence, asked the servant as the three of them walked on along the corridor. Since the king left them in the hall they had spent three minutes together without any of them uttering a word. They had seen sculptures and decorations they wanted to ask about, but the servant just walked on in silence, feeling unconcernedly.

"Friend, what's your name? I am Victor," he slowly repeated himself.

The servant stopped and looked back briefly. "No talking. That is the instruction from the king," he reminded Victor who was right behind him, "and my job is to see that it is faithfully obeyed."

"But you are not the prisoner," Victor responded. "The rule is about talking with the prisoners."

"No," he countered with displeasure at both Victor and his interpretation. He felt offended that Victor wanted to show he understood the king more than himself. "It is about no talking. We go straight back if you don't agree."

They walked through an open space into a covered corridor, and then through a back door into a large garden walled to the back of the palace. An area of this garden looked like a small, loose zoo – of about a dozen goats and a lone antelope. The garden separated from the palace, two bungalows, each about four times longer than its width. As they approached the first, they could see its four doors ahead of them. One huge man sat under the faint light in its front, his white loincloth giving him away as much as near-darkness would a ghost in white.

The man sprang up at once from a fair distance. He pointed a huge arrow at the group; and without regard to the similar loincloth their escort had round the waist, ordered the approaching trio to stop.

"Me, Glawanu!" The silent escort shouted a self-identification at once. "On errand from the king!" He would allow no personal carelessness to send to him an accidental arrow-discharge from his fellow guard. "The visitors from Glasgow are allowed to see the prisoners for a second."

"Aha, Lawanu," Victor muttered, "not for a second. His Highness didn't tell you one second."

"Please, don't call my name," Glawanu responded. "That is the time you are allowed. Or is it the whole night you want?" Glawanu was angry and sarcastic. "Thank your stars you have a whole second."

The exchange attracted another guard out from the central room of the block. He was also huge. At first, Glawanu's quick hello to him was returned with a cold stare and no verbal acknowledgement. Clearly, he showed himself as the boss of the armed guard.

"Why leaving it till this time, when tomorrow will soon come?" he asked Glawanu at last.

"If you are the other king in the palace," Glawanu replied, starting to laugh, "then, be brave enough to ask the first king why he has sent me here by this time." It was a brief joke not meant for Victor and Kazuggi to participate in. At its end, the guard dipped his hand under his loincloth and brought out a small bunch of keys. He handed it over to Glawanu without bothering to follow him to the adjoining block where the keys would be needed to see the prisoners.

They all ended at the last room of the building. A room? No, it was a cell. No, it was a latrine, a dump, a sty – a hell! It was all these combined. Its lone occupier, with barely any clothes on, sat down on its bare floor resting her back against the peeled patches of the wall. She was the lady prisoner. Automatically, she had been taken over by an environment that had converted her to itself – to a cell, a latrine, a dump, a sty, and a hell. As if the door and the bars on the tiny back window were not enough to keep her in the room, a chain about two meters long, secured her left ankle to a log.

The visitors were stunned.

"So, Uggi," Victor started to lament, "the king has actually increased her punishment. Did he not say he was going to be lenient? Did he not promise?"

"Yes, he did. My dad told me how promises and the like meant nothing here. He used to prefer not to talk about such things; each time he did, the pain showed on his face."

"But these things need talking about," Victor said, raising his voice. "She is a human being, just like her jailers who refuse to recognize that." Getting angry, he faced the lady prisoner, "young lady, are you okay," he asked her, and immediately felt the ludicrousness of his question. "Oh, my God. Poor me…blind bat." He slapped his own head. "How could I even ask her that?" He was still angry with himself. "What have they done to you?" he asked as a correction. "Don't be afraid. Tell us."

"No questions. No talking. Understand?" their escort warned.

"You are the one who didn't, and couldn't understand," Victor snapped angrily. "Not any of us but you. We are going to make her tell us what you lot did to her."

A moment of silence followed; it ended in the lady slowly turning her bruised, battered and sunken-eyed face. Like a tilapia in its final breathing struggle after being fished out of water, she opened her mouth. "Glawanu," she spoke in a voice barely audible, "have you killed my daughter and my husband? I heard their screams. Wait no further to kill me too."

"Have you really?" Kazuggi asked the escort.

"No questions. No talking. Enough," Glawanu reminded them again.

"Listen, man" Victor yelled, "the laws of your chief apply only to you and to others like you – others who are robots, dummies, wood-carvers, carved woods, or whatever. Do you understand that?"

"And look, Glawanu," Kazuggi complemented his friend, "the fact is that if you don't free this woman and her family, we shall make sure you all are in trouble too. We are from Glasgow, and we promise we shall make war and have all of you locked up in the prison. Do you understand what that means?

"Make no mistake. 'All of you' means we are going to start from you Glawanu who forbid the prisoner from talking after you have tortured her and locked her up. Then, we shall go on to your two mates who ensured they stayed locked up. Then, to your king himself. It is he we will eventually force to identify who the stupid masquerade we saw during the day was. Now we are witnesses to everything. You understand that?"

Glawanu felt a surge of anger inside him. It was brought about by both the genuine fear of repercussion the tourists threatened him with and by his own bruised ego as an officer of the kingdom. He twisted his face and curled up his nose like a boxer about to deliver a killer-punch. Then he hesitated and shifted the fear to the reality of some truth in the superior status and war waging ability of the men from Glasgow. He was aware of how it was already news that the prisoners were spared during the day only due to the intervention of the two men, and the fear the king had of their abilities.

"In that case, you are not good witnesses," Glawanu started to protest. "Did you see me arrest them? No. Drag them? No. Cell them? No. You can't be good witnesses. I didn't even put her here."

"But we were with you," Victor took over, "when you prevented the prisoner from talking to us, and we to her, wasn't that so? You didn't allow her to talk so that your crimes would remain covered. And she asked you and nobody else, if you had wiped out her family. She will testify and implicate you when that time comes."

"Besides, Glawanu," added Kazuggi, "if you are really from this place, Ila, you should know what the people believe – that in a stealing operation, the thief who assisted to lower the stolen item to the ground is equally as guilty as the one who lifted it from the loft. Is that not so?"

Glawanu clearly understood the facts of his involvement as presented by Kazuggi and Victor. He became unsure of what to do – to allow them to question the female prisoner or not, to allow her to talk or not. And with Glawanu's protestations of innocence, Kazuggi believed the guard was fast cracking up.

"Do you still insist," Victor quickly followed up, "that we must not ask, and she must not talk?"

"Yyess," Glawanu was emphatic. "You must not. She must not. But, I can do it, if you will keep it. In that case, nobody in the palace will bear witness against me. But you have to promise." He searched their eyes to see if he was leading himself into trouble or to salvation.

"We can't," Victor responded. "Not to your sort, Glawanu. None of you in this kingdom knows or respects promises. So, why should we give one? There is no point doing that."

"All right, Glawanu," Kazuggi quickly came in. He had already heard stories of how heartless the natives could be, and he did not want to miss what looked like a rare opening. "Suppose we promise you, will you set her and her family free now?"

"Oh no, I will not do that," Glawanu admitted. "But if you promise, I can let you know all you need to know that will help you, and whether the king will set them free or not."

"Tell us now?" Kazuggi asked.

"Some now, some later, because there is no time now to tell everything."

"It will be too late, and will be of no use."

"It will not be too late. That guard, Sam, who gave me the keys, is very dangerous; and he is looking and listening. Two years ago he reported the man you saw with the beaded chin for whispering on the kingdom; and the king ordered his tongue cut and his lips padlocked to prevent him from ever talking again.

Sam carried out the 'surgery' on him. That was the primary source of the beaded holes on his chin and lip. We all reckoned chin-beaded, his name, Amadi, was lucky because the king believed that the best way to prevent the parrot from talking is not to throw a hood over its head but to remove its eyes and twist its neck. Since then, Sam has been made to render another servant dumb by cutting off his tongue. That was how Sam was promoted to become the Enforcer.

"Now, he takes direct instructions from the king and from Sese Abram, the king's special assistant on all matters. After the king had spoken with Sese, Sese instructed Sam where to lock them up and what to do with them later.

"I heard the king told Sese not to allow Sam to be too severe on them until after you have visited him in the palace and gone. He guessed you might like to see them, and he might like you to see them. That whichever it was, you must not meet them locked up in chains...that their punishment would continue after you were gone.

"He feared you have certain powers, and so, he would not take chances..."

"Which means Sam was responsible for the torture?" Victor wanted confirmation.

"With his boss, Sese," Glawanu readily confirmed. "...Oh no, excuse me; he's coming – Sam. I will tell you more later."

"What's taking you that long?" Sam shouted as he approached. "Haven't they seen what they came to see?"

Instead of Glawanu giving Sam an answer, he turned his back, pretending to be busy, faithfully carrying out his assignment. "Yes, that's her." He shouted for Sam to hear. "That's the no-good woman – wicked woman," he made a u-turn, pretending with his remarks. "What can she say? She mustn't say anything. She has said enough of trouble for everybody already,"

Glawanu continued with the verbal attack on her until Sam reached the three of them.

"Are they okay now, now that they have seen what they wanted to see?" Sam asked Glawanu.

"Yes. They are. They must be."

"No, we are not," Victor disagreed. "We still haven't seen the husband and the daughter."

"How did you know they are husband, wife and daughter?" Sam asked Victor. "Who told you?"

"We were at the town square you know," Kazuggi answered. "The couple near us confirmed they are. And so did Fire Spirit."

"Which couple? Do you know them or their names?"

"I don't know," Kazuggi lied.

"But you heard them, yes?"

"Other people heard them too. And she said it herself in her cell."

"So, Glawanu, you allowed her to speak?"

"She spoke from behind the bars," Glawanu started to explain. "You had the inner key; so, I could not reach her to cover her mouth."

"But," Kazuggi interrupted rudely, "but what's all this nonsense – that she mustn't speak, while only you can. Remember, if you are all a party to this, we shall make you all pay for this very soon. Do you understand?" he asked both guards.

"Yes now, that is it," Glawanu cut in, pretending to be angry. "You have heard and seen too much. That's why – why I said you would see only the woman criminal. No more of my time will be wasted. I am taking you back now. His Highness is waiting." He slammed the outer door, locked it and handed back the bunch of keys. The team walked towards the back door they had taken out of the palace, Sam stopping off at his office.

"I had to avoid suspicion. I hope you didn't mind," Glawanu apologized as they reached the door.

"We understood," Victor said. For the first time he showed he did. "But we expect you to tell us more."

"And listen, Glawanu," Kazuggi whispered loudly enough, "if you can help us in whatever way we want here, we promise to protect and reward you. We want to get all the prisoners freed. We need to know exactly what to do, who to influence, and who the important voices are. You will have some nice presents from Glasgow, and we may invite you to Glasgow itself."

"Okay, I will try," he pledged, even though he was unsure if he would actually be given that which would be due to him, a most privileged reward of his life.

Next, Glawanu gave the most helpful advice that time would permit: When they got back, they must first plead with the king. They must not believe him and his promises until after the prisoners had been released to them. If pleading failed, they should look him in the eyes and demand what they wanted. Even though he pretended not to fear them, he did. He feared anything connected with Glasgow. He did not want anybody to know what he was making through the masquerades and how he received and spent the booty. He hated women and believed they were like poisonous creatures whose heads and tails should be cut once and for all. But the tourists could stop him because he wouldn't dare fight with anyone from Glasgow...

"Are you okay with the doors?" Sam shouted from the distance of his office. He could see they were on the same spot for longer than necessary.

"Yes. Thank you, Sam," Glawanu shouted back. "The door lock was jammed but I have done it now."

Glawanu pulled the door open and led the visitors back to the hall. "Good luck. I am with you," he said. "And don't forget your promise." He was leaving them in the Lion when the king entered.

"I trust you are happy now that he has shown them to you," the king said with confidence to his guests.

"Yes, we saw them," admitted Victor, "but no, Your Highness, we are not happy," he disagreed.

"Eh?"

"We are not," Kazuggi joined in. "The state we saw her in now was worse than that at the square. You promised to be lenient."

"No, my friends the state was better. Must be. Or you saw different prisoners?"

"We saw only the lady," Victor replied, strongly tempted to ask if the palace was more of a prison yard. "She was in a dirty and over-fortified cell, yet her left ankle was chained to a large piece of wood-chop. She had on just what she had on in the square, which was almost nothing."

"No, no, no," the king poured out. "Can't be. Just can't be," he countered very strongly, and then paused, pretending not to know what actually was wrong. Equally, he hid his disappointment at Sese Abram who must have caused it to happen. "I will find out now, before you go. But was it the only woman criminal that you saw?" he further asked to find a way out. "Sure, it is not the same for the other two."

"We are not sure of that, Your Highness," Victor responded. "We did not see the other two. Your guards did not allow us to see them."

The king felt relieved, the outburst of Victor notwithstanding. In his heart, he gave credit to Sam for not showing the tourists the other two prisoners who must have equally been wickedly held. At the same time, he thought of Sese

Abram as being foolish and tactless for not delaying the heavy handedness on the prisoners until Victor and Kazuggi would have come and gone. He felt disappointed at how Sese's inability to gauge the present and the future was about to soil his own honour and integrity.

"I am very sorry that you didn't see them, my friends. I can assure you that they are okay, and are not in the same state. Sam will see to her immediately."

"And thank heavens we didn't see the rest of them. We didn't need to. If a poor female gender could be held so inhumanly, we can only imagine the state the husband is being held. And who knows, the daughter could be long dead and buried." Victor could not hide his anger.

The king was startled by the frankness in Victor's response. "How could you judge what you did not see? How did you know they are husband and wife – and daughter?" He laughed deceitfully.

"Your Highness, we heard it. We heard your subjects talking about them at the square, on the streets, everywhere, Your Highness."

"Like I told you earlier, they are disloyal subjects. Unpatriotic citizens like them are few, just too few to make me cough. The law abiding citizens of Ila see that family as unpatriotic, and an insult to them and their forefathers in heaven. So, they called for an appropriate punishment for them." He was worked up.

"Sir, we heard them say you should have been lenient with the wife because she is a woman, and with the daughter because she is only an innocent, small child. They don't understand your actions. They were even saying you should have forgiven the man because he was once your right hand man."

The king adjusted his chair. The gas of fury was spreading rapidly to all parts of his body. The smell reached his head and made an escape route via his mouth. "Woman, you call that a woman? She wanted to be more woman than Eve, the first. She is evil!

"She's evil in speeches," he went on. "She's evil in misleading her husband. She's evil in doing what should not have concerned her, what women are not supposed to do. She took up the role of a man without first returning to God for a rebirth or a sex change...!"

"But sir, it appears as if you really hate women. Do you, sir?"

"Oh my friend, you really want the answer?" He was extremely angry. "Then listen. I will rather choose women with their troubles, with their deceits, with their pretensions, with their satanic enticement, with their weaknesses in soul and physical strength. Yes – choose them instead of choosing your sort who understands not a single thing about women.

"Yes, the two of you need some lessons about them, and should have started by asking me why they are few in my palace. Or how many of them have you seen since you came inside this great palace? Do you realize that all of us, three men, sitting down here now are doing so because of the problem of women?

"Pleeese, my friends. Please, please, please."

"Your Highness, that would not be fair," responded Victor. "The assessment is wrong. In Glasgow women are duly respected, just like men," he said softly with a smile, the type used by a diplomat when delivering a sting.

"My friend, stop. Please stop there!" King Jap ordered in a roar that even though did not shake the floor they stood on, but definitely shook their cochleae through and through. In a flash, he was up on his feet and back on his chair. His skin ducts gave way to his sebaceous glands. He wasn't only in such a temper, he was the temper!

"One lesson: when next you go out to give a judgment," he roared on, "remember to carry your own court with you. And before you set the court, be sure the people will obey your ruling. Failure in any of these will more likely turn you into the accused and the guilty.

"You will not come into my palace and put the king on trial. You can not be allowed to issue a rude and stupid judgment.

"All the time you keep saying Glasgow this, Glasgow that. But here is not Glasgow. You are in Ila. It is not Glasgow where the son is allowed to caution his father not to be silly; or where the daughter can tell her mother to shut up simply because she carries the same properties on the chest and in the pants as her mother. It is not your Glasgow, where everybody is free and loose enough to talk nonsense inside all your Old Baileys.

"My friends, you know what? You must leave now – before my subjects put you on trial for international and cultural rudeness. This could come side by side with that of your criminal friends. This meeting is over!"

Within seconds of the loud outburst Sese came inside, accompanied by Sam, Glawanu, and Amadi, the chin-beaded. Amadi, a shining, large cutlass in his right hand, was shouting atop his voice that which fell outside any lingual understanding because he was only with teeth and cavity. No tongue.

"Are you threatening us?" Victor asked the king. "Why are we flooded with these people with dangerous weapons? Is this a threat?"

"No, it is the truth. Nothing but the truth," he barked. "Yes, Sese," he turned to the first man, "get Sam and Glawanu to see them out."

"Okay, thank you sir," Kazuggi told the king, "We are leaving. Come on, Victor.

"But remember, that we are witnesses to what we saw at the square and in the cells. If anything happens to that family, we shall surely testify against you, against the one you call Sese Abram, together with Sam, Glawanu and this nameless machete wielding mute. In fact, right now, a special report is being made. Your Highness, good night and goodbye." Victor and Kazuggi stormed out of the Lion and headed for Bilitie Inn.

It was just past midnight when Victor and Kazuggi arrived back at Bilitie. Inside Kazuggi's room they continued with the assessment of their performance at the palace.

They could not see why they should be blamed for the bad ending to the meeting with the king, except that probably, their tough reciprocity with the king as encouraged by Glawanu led to the disaster. In the end they agreed there was no way what happened could have been avoided. Overall, they were pleased with what they were able to see within the palace. They knew something about its layout, including the position of its dungeon. They knew the group of loyalists and servants the king relied on for carrying out his evil deeds on the kingdom. In particular, they knew the deadly quartet of the king, Sese Abram, Sam and Glawanu. Their discussion was interrupted by a gentle knock on their room's door.

When the attendant at Bilitie confirmed it was her knocking, Kazuggi reminded her that she had been told they would require no meal – it was too late for dinner and too early for breakfast. But she explained she wasn't calling for a meal, but to tell them two emissaries from the palace wanted to speak with them.

In silence they wondered what the king wanted. It could be he wanted to carry out his threat to harm them because they had disagreed with him. They would stay put, go nowhere and meet no one. It made no sense confronting an enemy at night in his domain, especially when you knew he was waiting for you. No, they wouldn't even go near the door.

A short moment later, the same attendant repeated the knocking. She had one of the messengers with her at the door she added. He would speak with them.

"Kazuggi," the voice rang out. It was recognized before it could introduce its owner. "It's me, Glawanu."

"What's the problem? Did he send you after us?" enquired Kazuggi.

"No, Kazuggi. What we brought from him is peace. Real peace. Two of us. Me, Sam and two horses to return you.

"But listen, I am at the door alone now; I used my sense to exclude Sam from following me to your room. Open for some quick hints from me."

They did as requested, and Glawanu wasted no time:

The king was sad they had parted as enemies instead of as friends. He blamed Sese Abram for the basic cause of the disagreement. Sese was not supposed to have held the prisoners in that block, and should have had more sense than to chain down the woman so soon after the events in the square. Sese must correct himself immediately by moving the wife and husband to separate but relaxed cells. The little girl should be put up with the palace women. All this must be, so there could be an agreement of friendship between them and him, which should happen before daybreak. He would not watch a lit fire beside his own thatched roof and go to bed. He earnestly wanted everything resolved tonight. A job one does appropriately at dawn would make one gain the whole day. They would get what they wanted from the king if they pressed harder with tact.

"Okay, for now, have something from us," Kazuggi said, pulling his chromed wristwatch off and handing it over to Glawanu. "Keep it. Many more will come, even after we have gone. We are taking you as a friend forever, can we?"

"Yes, friend forever."

* * *

The smiles that were exchanged among the king, Kazuggi and Victor were genuine enough when they sat together to tackle the main issue. The setting was more businesslike – no tea, no gin, no whiskey, no vodka. And there was a not-so-strange addition to the group.

"My friends, this is Sese Abram," the king said before his palace assistant could sit down.

"I want you to assume that you have never met him before. He too will assume the same about you. Why? Because the time you met three hours ago was a time of quarrel, red eyes and clenched fists. One must not remember a first meeting for any of these reasons because it puts one off the next. We must assume we are meeting for the first time now, at a time when we should give friendship to our enemies and forgiveness to our sinners; and of course now, the time of the great spiritual festival, when our great ancestors are happiest with us."

He went further, that they should have no suspicion over the presence of Sese. He was a good man whose poor look and humility hid his substance as a highly respected senior chief of the kingdom. He had invited Sese not only to contribute, but also to aid a faster and more balanced contribution among them, now that it was two versus two.

"Now, my friends," he finally came home, "be straight. Tell me, what do you want me to do about Jacquensica, her husband and their daughter?"

"Your Highness," Victor answered, "we want you to please set them free now."

"And we would not want you to attach any condition to it," added Kazuggi.

The king turned to Sese for his reaction, catching his face as it started to dodge his. "Sese, you heard them, their request. What do you say to that?"

"Exactly whatever you say is what I say, my Almighty," Sese responded straight away.

"Okay, my friends, if I say yes, will it make you happy, and make us friends?"

"Certainly, Your Highness," Victor answered again.

"Not only that, sir; we shall speak well of you when we go back; and you will be greatly respected," Uggi added.

"Okay my friends. To show you that I am honest about the well-being of the criminals, they will bring them here, starting from those you did not see."

"Just what we want, Your Highness," Victor responded.

Sese Abram departed. In five minutes, he opened one of the small doors and entered with the husband. "Long may you live, my Almighty. Here is Nek," he said.

"Nek for you here, my friends," the king pointed to the free man Sese had just brought in.

"Is this the same male prisoner?" Victor asked.

"Yes, my friend; the same one. His rapacious fascination to the exclusive possessions of a woman put him into this. Pray you don't have his type of mind – honest, but easily corrupted by every part that counts in a woman."

"What does that mean, Your Highness?" Victor asked again.

"There is no time for me to explain now, my friend; because the explanation itself is as long as the shore of the large sea."

Unlike in the earlier daylight at the Palace Square, Nek was reasonably clothed, albeit, in a combination of mal-sized clothing. He was holding on delicately to the belt of his loose, local trousers – apparently in pain. As he moved nearer, the uncovered parts of his body betrayed the treatment of hell he had been subjected to. When he was nearest, one could see that bruises and swells apart, that he was once a man of substance. He wasn't allowed to take any question; so, he never spoke. Within the two minutes after he was paraded, the king had managed to convince his guests that Nek was already enjoying the freedom he had promised.

"Thank you, Your Highness. How about the little girl?" Victor asked as Nek was being led away.

"Sorry, you cannot see her, for now."

"Any particular reason, sir?" Kazuggi asked.

"Yes, my friend, many particular reasons. She is a small child. She needs her sleep, and I have got her a better mother to ensure that. The mother sent her to bed early last night. Come and see her when she wakes up in the morning."

"Very well sir, and thank you," was all Kazuggi could say.

"My friends, you want to see the woman?" the king led.

"I was going to ask for that, Your Highness," answered an eager Victor. "What we saw of her earlier…"

"Okay, okay, okay my friend," the king cut him short light-heartedly. "Earlier does not matter now. Earlier has gone with the past where it longs and belongs, where it will ever remain. This is now. You want Sese to call her here, now?"

"Thank you again, Your Highness. It will be most appreciated."

Sese Abram went out of the hall through the small door nearest to them, and was back at his chair within two minutes – but with nobody.

In another three, adding new impatience to their original feelings of anxiety, the same door opened gently. The lady who entered briefly knelt to courtesy a joint greeting to the king and Sese Abram. She dressed simply in lightweight, three-piece local attire, if the floral scarf on her head was included. She was the first lady the visitors would see in close contact inside the palace, except of course, the animal-like one they saw rotting away in the cell. In their wildest dreams it could never be her – now properly clothed. Could never! Probably, she was a queen, a princess or one of those in the faceless pictures hung round the hall!

The uncovered part of her face showed no happiness, yet it could not be sworn, to be sad either. On her face was some fresh, heavy skin toning which blended successfully with the unpleasant hour of the night to deny the tourists the clarity of judgment over the effects of torture she had been through.

The local blouse she had on was not low, but the courtesy she made actually caused the eyes of all the men present there to be guilty of '*lookery*'. And the almost straight way the tips of what it covered pointed at them did not help the situation either. They were silently sure the bra was absent. They could see that clearly, as she remained on her knees about three yards away from them. The facial swelling had been patched up to restore a part of her past glory.

"My friends," the king called. "Why are you saying nothing now?" This is Jacquensica. Are you happy now?"

The beyond-belief, complicated, stunning appearance of the lady before them did not allow for an immediate answer from either Kazuggi or Victor. In fact, it swallowed any they could think of. They continued to gaze at her, even, up to when she turned to go, and until she completely disappeared. They saw her truly medium height now that she was not being made to crawl, the tired but feminine steps and swings now that both hands and legs are unchained, and the moderate fleshiness of the buttock now that the delicate wrap could be seen from the back. They also noticed certain things that were not camouflageable about her: the aloofness on her face and the limping movement she was managing. Truly though, she was beautiful.

The king noticed the look on the faces of his guests and instantly awarded himself a partial victory. "My friends, you still haven't spoken, now that you have seen Jacquensica," he said. "Are you sure, sure that it was her you saw in the cell?"

"Ah, our friends from Glasgow," Sese cut in laughing. "My poor self too wants to hear your answer to my Almighty. Isn't that so, my Almighty?" he added to louder laughter already coming from him and the king.

"Many thanks to you sir," Kazuggi finally found the dry answer, one that revealed his confusion as to the identities of the prisoner they saw in the cell and the beauty who had just limped off their sight. "What else can we say? You just told us that the word 'earlier' belongs to the past. What we saw now is more important."

"Are they free to go now, Your Highness?" Victor asked.

"Not entirely. However, I will free them. We have decided to free them without turning back or sideways. But there is only one small thing that remains. Very small." He stopped for Sese to say it.

"My Almighty wants you to enjoy yourselves and take part in the acts of the masquerades."

"That's okay, Your Highness," Victor said. "We don't have a problem with that. We are already here, and will stay to watch." Victor was yet to capture what the king and Sese were talking about.

"I want you to take part in the outing; I mean, each of you to carry a spirit," the king said.

"Spirit? Your Highness, what spirit?" Kazuggi asked.

"I mean your individual mask and costume, for your own separate crowd to follow you."

To the tourists, both the king with his proposal sounded starkly insane and strange even though they had not caught him sipping any alcohol in the last fourteen hours or so that they had maintained a sort of contact with him.

"My Almighty will give you the best masks, the best costumes and the largest followers."

71

"You don't mean that," said Victor. "It's crazy, I am sorry. You really want us to wear your masks and dance in them?"

"My friends don't let us go into this again because it will lead nowhere. I mean what I said, and you must let us know here what you mean, whether you are sorry or you think Ila is crazy."

"It is only a matter of exchanging the hands and hearts of friendship," Sese supplied a simplification, "which you promised to offer just a few minutes ago."

"Your Highness, we don't expect you to attach their freedom to anything or to something as impossible as this," Kazuggi protested. "We are visitors. Where do we start how to learn? How do we fit in? Where is the time? How odd would it turn out to be – for us and for you? The freedom should be tied to friendship, not to what you are asking us to do."

"Really, I have not attached it to the small friendship we ask but which you are refusing to show. If I had, I would not have allowed you to see them in the first place, or freed them as I have done."

"Yes," Sese corroborated. "My Almighty released your friends from the cells. He saved the woman from being executed. He saved the little girl from being de-breasted. He stopped Nek's punishment from extending beyond the castration which he already had. He stopped the family from being sold off as slaves. That is how important your friendship is to my Almighty. How important is the same friendship to you, I ask you?"

Still without waiting long enough for an answer, he continued. "My Almighty even planned to rebuild their house which was pulled down last week. The entire community did it in anger, at the indignity the family painted the respectable culture of Ila with. He planned to forgive their friends who misled them to commit the crimes against the kingdom. So, you have to show your friendship too – through the little he asks of you.

"Have no fear; I volunteer to assist you all through. This is the time that matters to my Almighty and his subjects."

Kazuggi and Victor exchanged a silent look of bewilderment at what they saw as clear but dangerous scheming where they were being used. They asked the king for time outside the palace and out of his and Sese's presence to consider it.

"Too long a debate over an action that needs to be taken means a loss on the time of its implementation. Take your decision now. Whichever you take, we are okay, my friends." King Jap was succinct in his refusal.

"If you agree," he continued, "the benefit is for all of us. Our masquerades will be more popular and more international. Ila will be more popular and more international. My chiefs and I will be more popular and more international.

"Victor will be more popular and more international. Kazuggi will be more popular and more international. Glasgow will be more popular and more international.

"In total, the four of us here will be more popular and more international. Do you hate that?"

There was a brief silence.

"Supposing we say yes, are you going to add other conditions before they are totally freed?" Kazuggi asked. He and his friend knew they were helpless, but not as helpless as the prisoners their succumbing to the demands of the king would save. "Will you release them at the end of the masquerade week?"

"We don't want to keep them and keep trouble," the king said. "At the same time we don't want them to be kept where our eyes will not be able to see them – where they will restart when we don't expect.

"My friends, you know what?" He paused and drew Sese near for a quick whisper, a privilege he had just denied his guests.

"You know what?" he said after he had interchanged the whispering with Sese, "I can give you the most dangerous of them, while we keep the lesser ones. How about that?"

"The most dangerous?" Victor asked the king.

"Yes. Jacquensica. We know the two of you like her, because you don't know her. We are releasing Nek and the girl to the palace, but to work. None of the family can return to their chiefdom because it is eradicated forever. Do you agree – to take her?"

"Yes, Your Highness. But could we then have the girl too?"

"You can't be serious. I have just handed to you a generous gift and you are demanding it must come wrapped. Do you think I was so foolish that I didn't know what I was doing? Let's cancel the deal now if you are not yet satisfied." The king was firm. He was running out of time. He had to attend to other issues inside the palace. Victor and Kazuggi grabbed the offer.

"Okay," my friends," the king finalized, "it means you must go away with her after you have carried the masks with us – at the end of the last day of the festival. She has to leave that day so that other women will have the time and the brooms to sweep her evil footsteps after her."

CHAPTER THREE

The Initiation I

Azzanaite saw the morning hours flying past and wished she could chain them down. Impatiently, she waited for Bambo, her sister.

Bambo eventually arrived at the palace two hours late. She displayed a mixture of furrows, twists and cracks on her face, prompting Azzanaite to wonder all a tactical defence to scare anyone, herself included, from querying the poor time keeping. Whichever it was, Azzanaite was determined to make Bambo talk.

"Why – your face, dear sister?" the senior asked, gunning for an apology.

"Why? What about my face?" Bambo snapped back.

"You have it all twisted," Azzanaite said jokingly, hiding the seriousness behind it. "Were you trying to frighten off the gatekeepers from stopping your entry into the palace?" she added, laughing. "Anyway, those ones are zombies of single track minds, incapable of fearing other faces or moods except the king's."

"I am sure they know mine. They always do, in their wisdom. But this is not the case now. "

"Then if it is about Jacquensica, just cheer up and forget. It is already a case of the dead, the buried, and the gone. You don't mourn them forever."

"Why not? What a complete contradiction. If one doesn't, there won't be this annual festival of the masquerades; we won't be preparing for the cemetery now, isn't it?

75

"And secondly, are you saying Jacquensica, Nek and their daughter are already dead and six feet under?" she asked Azzanaite, and eagerly awaited the answers.

"Bambo, this is a time for celebration and not for mourning. But all the same, let's cut it short. What I am saying is that it's unlikely the people will mourn anyone known to have died grieving over another dead person; it is a senseless suicide.

"For those three, we pray that they eventually survive. But right now, neither you nor I should be caught mourning over it."

"Really, sister, I wonder how you can see it that way. You and Jacq grew up together and were friends. For years past, her family related to yours more than to anyone else's!"

"But like everything with a beginning, that has gone the way of an inevitable ending now."

"Yes, inevitable indeed – that you should spill the beans on your friend, even when the allegations against her were untrue!

"You should be the mother of all the living mothers in the kingdom. Unfortunate that His Highness used you against a mother you should protect. Unbelievable…"

"Bambo, that's just enough!" Azzanaite screamed on her sister. "I have taken enough of your battering these few days. How much of the same accusations have you directed at your husband – at Silas you share your home and bed with? Was he not a confidant of the king in this matter? You should start with him, or probably, with the king himself now that you are in the palace. You should let me have my peace over this matter. Today, we are supposed to appeal to the spirits of our parents at the cemetery, to ask them to bless us; it should not be a day for a sisterly war."

The snooping appearance of Glawanu interrupted the two women. He wanted them to know he was through with his side of preparation for their journey to the cemetery. He'd overheard part of their conversation and was being careful not to be caught on the wrong side of their mood.

"I am ready Your Majesty," he addressed Azzanaite.

"How about the horses?"

"We are all ready, together with the ass, the senior ass. Ready."

* * *

Arriving at the well maintained cemetery in the middle of thick forest about noon time brought the company under the direct hit of the scorching overhead sun. Had the arrival been earlier as planned, just the pleasant rays of the sun forcing itself through the leaves would have been felt.

It was the largest of the four cemeteries scattered about in Ila. With the other three, its features were kept under specific but uniform designs. The assumed guards at its gate were relief sculptures of mythological imagery and contradictions. On its left side was depicted a horse-bodied angel in an upright, sprinting stride that covered the entire height of the door-less opening. Then its wings curved back over its head to the top left of the gate. Six other angels were plastered behind the first, each reducing in size the farther it was from the first horse and the gate.

The angel on the right of the gate was a lady. While her wings extended over the top right of the rectangular opening, seven naked babies sucked her seven strange breasts. The works of art were clearly recent.

As the three callers went through the gate, Azzanaite and Glawanu murmured some thanks and prayers. Bambo said nothing, and offered none.

Then, Azzanaite broke into a mixed song of praise and prayers for her dead parents. She was so carried away by the engagement that she failed to see the look of disgust on the face of Bambo, or that of rare amusement on that of Glawanu.

The party continued to the far end of the cemetery and stopped at a grave that was concreted all round the edges to leave a soft centre. This was the joint vault of the sisters' parents. Glawanu therefore put down his basket and returned to the animals for the second basket. Then he finally left the sisters alone.

The keen eyes of Azzanaite noticed two small weeds. They were on the headstone end of the grave, and had been missed during the intensive cleaning that was completed in the cemetery three weeks previous. Still singing, she pulled them off. It must not be the time for a weed to share the space with her parents.

"What do you think of the cleaning here this year? She eventually stopped singing and asked Bambo.

"Of the cleaning here? Nothing."

"I think it's better than last year's. Much better. Don't you think so?"

"Well, yes, much better," Bambo answered absent-mindedly.

Azzanaite still insisted on going on. "It's because the first rounds of the cleaning and clearing were completed almost a month earlier. They had enough time to dry up and be removed, followed by a re-cleaning where necessary.

"Look at the headstones and concretes. Aren't they clean and shining? Or, what do you think?"

Whatever was Bambo's thinking up to that stage, her sister's observation was correct. The senior masquerade in charge of weeding of cemeteries, ensured she and her observation were.

A month before the commencement of the festival, that senior masquerade had assembled all the young men from all quarters of Ila. They weeded, packed, swept, polished, painted and paved all the town's cemeteries. Headstones and other concretes were polished more than they'd ever been, while the non-concreted graves were kept with dignified simpleness.

Fencing was particularly improved. While the all round mild porosity was maintained, beautiful mats of woven palm fronds were secured at a regular distance all round it. Palm fronds, legendarily, were the leaves of heaven, perceived to be passionately loved by those who were already transformed from living on mother earth to living in the worlds beyond. Beauty Spirit used the leaves appropriately.

Beauty Spirit did not have to pay the young men for their labour. Mythological belief taught that the more fresh air their efforts gave to the graves, the more abundant would the dead reward them.

Besides, he told them that a better weeding of cemeteries would encourage a higher number of generous female relatives to come, seek and obtain blessings from the dead resting in their graves.

"Now, Bambo," called Azzanaite, "please set the candles and give me the matches."

Bambo opened one side of a basket and took out two silver candle stands and two white, foot-long candles. Azzanaite directed where she should put them – nearer to the headstone, on the two opposing, longer sides of the grave.

"Set the incense nearer to them please," she rang out a second instruction.

Bambo this time proceeded to the basket, rather sluggishly. "But sister, are all these necessary?" she asked.

"Look, Bambo," replied Azzanaite, trying to suppress her anger at the question before it could be visible on her face. "I have no time to answer that. You know the answer very well.

"It won't be here, before our parents that we will start to question how they wanted us to please them. Remember, we still have the market and the shrine to go to, and we are short of time."

"Okay, okay, okay," Bambo silently submitted. She knew it was of no use putting her views across any further to Azzanaite, who these days, took them as being rebellious.

Bambo also remembered it was just over a week ago when they had a violent argument on various aspects of the festival: the existence or non-existence of the spirits of the dead; the authenticity and spuriousness of the local spirits and their predictions; and the off-handed treatment of dissenters by the king and his lieutenants.

Bambo realised that despite her sister's early exposure to western education, her brains were still closed to advice and suggestions that were not from, or routed through King Japeedoe, her husband.

"Okay, what next?" she asked as she lit the last of the two candles.

"Good, now you are doing well," complimented Azzanaite. "Even the air around us now acknowledges that fact. It confirms they, here, are ready to listen to our supplications."

Azzanaite started another song, one of praise. It shattered the perfect tranquillity of the high noon. When she had satisfied herself, she faced Bambo now on the other side of the grave and asked her: "What do we want from them this year? Some things in particular?"

"I honestly don't know – if there's anything, or if there is a need to ask. That's how I feel."

"Well, you have to know. We have to ask.

"Have you forgotten so soon? Three years ago Jacquensica said she had nothing to ask when she was at her parent's grave, meaning she had all and knew all. Now that she wants to ask, the chance has gone, leaving us, her friends, to ask on her behalf!"

Centuries old tradition had taught them much about the dead, who automatically became extraterrestrials. There's nothing wanted from or asked of them that they were incapable of doing or giving. They, in fact, did not die. Not and never those of them who were mothers and fathers when alive on earth. They had no time to sleep or blink as they invincibly followed up and down the offspring they left on earth, guarding them.

The dead had long arms, infinitely long tentacles they could wrap round the off-spring whenever there were needs to pull them out of life's danger zones.

By mere pricking, they could warn their offspring of imminent dangers. When an offspring was insensitive, the ancestral spirit would appear to him in his dreams. Festivals like this were the only bonus times for the living, when the spirits of the dead could appear physically in the form of masquerades and dance with the living, speak with the living, and uphold the prayers of the living. It was the time when the spirits, through the masquerades, ensured their offspring were not taken over by Satan, the strongman of the crossroads.

The dead of the kingdom loved the worldly gifts even though they rarely asked the offsprings for them. Whenever they did, they were given without hesitation, without questioning. The more the offspring gave the more and the quicker his particular prayers would be answered.

Foodstuffs? Yes, especially the fresh and nutritious that were not easily perishable.

Drinks? Excellent. Readily welcome, especially if alcoholically very strong.

Cloth and clothing gifts? Optional – for as long as the supreme owner of the universe still spared the leaves, the stems, the skins, the feathers, the cowries and the paints. However, the citizens were astonished when, three years ago, the spirits of their dead modernized by unanimously demanding for gifts of materials of cotton, silk, damask and brocade. They even demanded for shoes and socks, without forgetting to add the sizes and colours! King Japeedoe claimed the ancestors made these modern wishes known to him; and he wasted no time in despatching his town criers to every corner of the kingdom to deliver the message.

"Give me your hands," Azzanaite commanded her sister. "Stretch them out that we link up over this everlasting bed the good heavens have provided for our parents."

Bambo complied.

"Alanie, dear father," Azzanaite commenced the call. "You are the guard with many guns; the brave with a thousand cudgels; the keen with many eyes. We thank you for your protection over us, the children you left behind.

"Lafia, our dear mother, you are the mother above all mothers; one with a brood more protective than the ostrich's; one

81

who milk-feeds her children and still has enough milk left for others'. We thank you for your protection over us.

"This year alone you both gave us good wealth in a size which no other person had been given. We had peace, which others didn't have. You protected us from the dreaded smallpox and *papa-pox*, its more dreaded senior. You banished measles, its sister, from our households. You allowed nothing to lock us up isolated inside our rooms. You did us favours too many to list.

"Please let these continue into another year, into other years. Move us into bigger homes of our own. Change us from four-hoofers to four-wheelers. Not the kind of rubbish wheelers though. We want the modern type – of diesel or petrol.

"Please enter the hearts of our dear king and his chiefs. Untie the knots they have against Nek. Let them set free Jacquensica. Let them show mercy to their daughter. Above all, let Jacq realise her sins and repent to the acceptance of this kingdom.

"We know the gifts you want from us. This evening we shall deliver all of them to the spirits at the shrine. Nothing is too much to give to both of you. Nothing will ever be too much…"

They were ready to leave. Azzanaite opened the other side of the basket and brought out two pigeons, both already plucked of their feathers.

"Your birds are here," she addressed the grave. "As their feathers grow, so we want our wealth and progress to increase."

Glawanu sensed the women were heading towards him. Their joyous approach was audible enough. He met them and collected the baskets, now empty, from Bambo. They mounted and headed for the market, just as two men surfaced from behind the fencing, unseen to the departing party.

"Thank heavens for another set of pleased callers," one of the men told his associate as he threw down some grains for the flightless pigeons.

"If those ones were not pleased callers, who else would be?" responded the second man, with a pen slung behind his back.

"Yes," upheld the first man, "it has been a day when most callers are pleased." He threw down more grains and proceeded to blow out the candles and disassemble the stands.

"It means a more bumper harvest and higher revenue for masquerades this week." As he put down his load he noticed something was missing from his associate. "Where is your own pen?" he asked him.

"Behind the fencing; too full to take more birds."

"You don't mean it. Supposing a woman caller sees it and disappears with it?"

"Come on, who will do that? Which man, talk less of woman will dare stray into the forests this time of the festival? And who will steal from the dead anyway?"

"Oh, simple. Any living being who discovers the dead to be that careless, will."

A sound interrupted the two men. It was of one piece of dry wood being knocked against another, and coming from a position outside the gate. They recognised it as the signal from their colleague who they hid on special sentry at the gate's approach. They grabbed the two birds and threw them into their pen containing six other naked birds. In a split second they were back in the hideout they came from, leaving the cemetery empty once again for the next caller. Who would say this year's improved cleaning of the cemetery was not producing commensurable rewards!

* * *

Ila Main Market was full of buyers and sellers, almost all of them in a hurry imposed on them by the special time of the year. As the most central and largest – five times the size of the Royal Market – a large population had descended on it from all parts of the kingdom. It's a day market.

No part of the market could be described appropriately in rows or stalls. It wasn't that it didn't have them, but because those it had were of no clear definition – in linage or distribution. Nor could it be defined in terms of cleanliness, which was just average. Everywhere in the market was a bit of every article relevant to the season – live animals, live birds, cloths and local produce of foodstuff. Such was the market this special and last day for buying the annual gifts for the dead, and delivering them through the Main Shrine.

Glawanu, however, knew which parts in the market he had to lead Azzanaite and Bambo to, and he wasted no time doing just that.

At first, Glawanu led them round the pegged goats as if searching for a particular one just stolen from them and brought in for sale by the thief. They stopped and touched physically and visually, feeling their sizes and temperament. They were by a big one, in the jet-black colour they wanted, when the animal raised its roped neck and bleated.

"This must be the one," Glawanu told the women. "It's the fullest goat we have seen in this market."

"Blah-ha-ha-ha, blah-ha-ha-ha," it went, zeroing its eyes on Azzanaite as she stroke its back. "Blah-ha-ha-ha, blah-ha-ha-ha."

"This is not for nothing," Glawanu eagerly cashed in. "Mama wants it. She is expressing her desire through the goat's bleating."

Bambo did not buy Glawanu's interpretation. She already noticed that the small trough of water serving the goat was on its side, its water already poured out. The goat must be crying for being thirsty, especially since the short rope noosed round its neck would not permit it to drink from other nearby troughs. It was begging for water! Bambo voiced out her interpretation.

"Tens of others we've seen had no water," Glawanu countered, "and yet they were quiet. This one, I am convinced, wants to come to mama."

"Okay then," resigned Bambo. She saw no need to further dispute Glawanu's deceit and pretence. She would end up being one against the two – democratically.

"Only that its fullness is of pregnancy, don't you think so Glawanu?" Azzanaite observed.

"We can never know for sure; and what does it matter? The spirit of your mama demands for a black goat, this is a black goat. Mama wants it to be the fullest in the market; this here, is the fullest. If truly, the fullness is due to a bonus of embryonic kids, it means mama would add extras to the blessings she meant for the two of you."

"No way," Bambo told herself. Goat or stud, she knew none would go to her dead mother or her spirit. She had no doubt that Glawanu knew this too, but was trying to fool them as per the instructions of someone yet unknown and unnamed to her and her sister. She wasn't surprised how, despite her vantage position in the palace, Azzanaite was foolishly ignorant of the secrets and deceits the king, through Glawanu, had strategized in the gifts they were at the market to buy. However, she was happy the goat, if bought, would not be slaughtered as was likely with a non-pregnant one. That instead, it would be shared out to a hardworking masquerade or chiefdom. In his days of authority, Nek, had many of such privileged shares, and trustingly shared the sources with Jacq who, in turn, whispered them to her, Bambo, as a friend. In fact then, such was the source of Nek and Jacq's large animal farm.

But now, Bambo's knowledge and suspicion didn't matter. They remained buried inside her while Azzanaite paid for the goat. Payment over, Glawanu grabbed the lead and walked the goat behind the women, to the part of the market selling live rams. Oracles had also demanded a bearded ram, a local impossibility, for Alanie, the ladies' dead father!

The women, accompanied by Glawanu, went from peg to peg looking for a bearded ram to buy.

"Have you got a nice bearded ram to sell?" Azzanaite asked a ram-seller. She was getting tired of wandering without a success.

"No, madam," replied the male ram-seller, "it's all sold out." As he replied, he wondered the type of fool Azzanaite was.

"Have you got a nice bearded ram?" she asked another.

"I sold the last one yesterday; but I will have two to sell tomorrow morning."

"Oh, God forbid. Do you really expect me, a woman, to come out tomorrow?"

"But you are a woman with a difference, a most privileged lady," he confirmed on recognising her and her company. He stopped short of thinking of her as a royal fool, or the foolish queen he believed she really was.

"That's why I must be careful not to behave as being above other women. Do you think I would be here now if I were different from any other woman? I am no different."

She still pushed on until she reached another seller. "Have you got a bearded ram?" she asked him with an anxiety that unsuccessfully concealed her frustration.

"You can wait here," he answered her. "Let me go and check for you where I just saw one." He walked off to a nearby shed where he met another ram seller. Both men had a good laugh at how the queen of Ila could be so ignorant. He then returned to Azzanaite. "Sorry, all sold out," was his disappointing message for her.

"This is frustrating," she said principally to Glawanu. She was unable to hide it anymore. "What else can we do? Why is it this scarce?"

"Because, it's the favourite of the spirits this year," Glawanu answered, feeling satisfied with his lies. "They've all been bought out by relatives who were faster than us."

Glawanu knew it would come to that. The king told him it would; and that he must reveal nothing to Azzanaite. Women of Ila, if unchecked, whatever their status, and however severe the deterrent they witnessed was, would behave like Jacquensica – as an antagonist of culture. Glawanu was now ready to provide the king's set solution. "In that case, you must buy two white rams. That's the alternative your ancestors dictated this year."

And so, Glawanu succeeded in making the women fall for his conspiracy with the king in the two key demands.

Buying the other gifts was easy and plain sailing. For example, foodstuffs were purchased in special measured units of *fingers and hands*. One *finger* was one piece, weight or measure of any item for sale, while one *hand* of it meant its five pieces, weights or measures.

They bought one *hand* each in tins of corn, rice, flour, soya-beans, cashew nuts and cooking-oil – all the non-perishable stuff that would last the dead for a long time without expiring before consumption. Glawanu loaded up his horse and the ass as much as he could. The ass was so over-laden that it rebelled, shaking off some of the load and refusing to move. In the end two extra asses were hired from the market.

Amidst a flow of other citizens, the sisters, together with Glawanu, made the pilgrimage in time to the Main Shrine, a large building of many hidden halls. There, they patiently waited their turn to carry their presents inside. Finally they entered through the left hand door reserved for the purpose. Once inside, they proclaimed their arrival in songs and words to the spirits of Alanie and Lafia, lamenting how the inner wall had physically barred them from the spirits of their parents. In self-glorification, they announced how the gifts they brought actually exceeded what they understood their parents demanded from them.

From behind the wall, the spirits vocally acknowledged the generosity of the latest gifts as well as of those they gave earlier in the day at the cemetery. They loved and wanted all of them. Azzanaite and Bambo should continue to be good and generous to them. The spirits guaranteed the sisters peace, happiness and protection forever. They should drop the gifts at the appropriate section of the shrine and dance out through the door on the right. And so they did, using solo praise songs as their source of music, and feeling happy that their dead parents still loved them.

* * *

It was pitch dark and all streets deserted when Sese Abram set out from the palace with Kazuggi and Victor on three horses, for the shrine. Sese was the trusted right hand man the king had told to supervise the tourists' initiation by the Chief Priest. It wasn't that Ila had no modern lights but they were all ordered switched off. Tradition demanded they were made so for the one week duration of the festival. While the dead could share the daytime with the living, night time was exclusively for the dead and their spirits. A citizen violating the night curfew was always charged for insulting the spirits. The king had also sent his town crier to go round and warn his subjects, using the modern loudspeaker he had just invested in.

The Ilas were always reminded of Tantalo, the Tiger, an arrogant, hefty chief known for his super strength and unsurpassable agility. He went out on one such night, wanting to know what the confinement was all about. He was confident his physical prowess as the kingdom's strongest man would handle any eventuality from any spirit or its medium.

The popular story was that Tantalo's dare-devilry didn't last. He did not come back alive to give a report of what went on between him and the spirits. It was believed that no sooner was he out there alone in the dark than the spirits surrounded him for his blood and flesh. Among the spirits were those of his forefathers and they declined to save him. They transformed themselves into a strong whirlwind and quickly blinded his eyes by filling them up with sand. Then the whirlwind lifted him up and threw him down over and over in violent tumbles before it finally lifted him away forever!

They were also reminded of the stories of some lucky men and women whom the spirits handed less-than-death punishments because they, the spirits, were satisfied these people were not out to dare them, but were forced out by some unfortunate circumstances. All the same, the men among them had their tongues pulled out so they would never be able to tell what they saw, while the women were turned into female antelopes that up to this day, roamed about in the forests of Ila. The beautiful antelope the tourists had seen in the palace garden was one of these. The stories were terrifying enough to deter anybody from researching into their authenticity.

The shrine's outer guard was waiting in expectation at the side entrance. As soon as he heard the clop-clop of the approaching horses of Sese's group, he alerted the inner guard.

At the gate, the guards wasted no time opening the large door. But Sese on the leading horse stopped, forcing the others to also stop. He turned his horse round and made it to march backwards inside. Victor first, and then Uggi did the same. After Uggi the guards slammed the door shut and locked it.

Inside the shrine, one man readily attended to the horses, allowing Sese to continue on foot with the visitors. He led them into a small hall that was red lit. They were the first lit electricity lights they saw since leaving Bilitie Inn.

"Take seat, gentlemen," Sese told Uggi and Victor. "That would be more comfortable," he added, pointing to the shorter of the two sofas nearer to them. It must have been made to sit two or three buttocks. "I will soon be with you," he added as he disappeared through the nearest door.

Victor and Uggi wished Sese didn't leave them. They found themselves feeling uncomfortable and goose-pimpled under the deep red light and strong smell of blood. The feeling was made worse by the presence of another man, a door minder. He sat with his back to them as if trying to hide his face. His next moves however proved this wasn't the case. Thrice he slowly turned his head round to the men; and on each occasion Uggi caught him in the act. Then he gave up and remained on his high stool until he had to perform a routine duty.

One by one, he went to each of the six lamp holders in the hall and lit it up, using the fire lighter from his pocket. Even though the new white flames appeared yellowish, it added a good brightness to the hall.

The visitors now had a better view of the lamp-holders. Each was about four feet in height, wooden and highly crafted, ebony black and well polished. There was a carving of a kneeling lady. Atop it was another of an elephant. Still on top was a brass tray carrying a small rectangular clay bowl filled with some thick red oil. A rope of cotton remained soaked in the oil with an end sticking out from a corner of the clay bowl. It was this end that was lit by the door minder.

They also noted the walls were covered with assorted drawings, paintings and carvings of animals and abstracts.

The minder had just re-occupied his stool when there was a knock on the door from outside. "Two guests!" the knocker announced.

He sprang up and grabbed a large fan of animal skin material resting on the wall besides him. He hurried back to the lamps he just lit; and with the combination of mouth and hand blowing, put out each lamp. He then rushed back to open the door for the new guests.

"Did he make a mistake at first?" Victor asked Uggi.

"A mistake? Of not turning on the white light, or of lighting up the oil lamps?"

"Yes, lighting up the lamps in the first place. Probably he should not have done it, otherwise why the rush to put them out because some guests have arrived."

"He must have lit them so he could see our faces or that we could see how beautiful his 'office' is. Three times I caught him spying on us."

When the door was opened three men walked in backwards. The one who led them in showed his two followers where to sit, then went out through the same door Sese had used.

"Probably this hall must be entered walking backwards, and in near or total darkness," Uggi suspected. Victor agreed with him.

The two new entrants did not have to sit for long when, came from a nearby room, the low but fast music of drums, gongs and bells. Then one man entered through the door Sese took out. His head was a desert of artificial baldness, and it shone orange under the red lights. So was his facial semblance indeterminable due to the white chalk it was crazily painted with. His loin cloth which also showed as orange was primarily white. Despite his appearance, Uggi and Victor did not feel intimidated; since arriving in Ila they had seen more intimidation and stronger causes for fear. He went straight to the last two entrants.

"Dauda and Emano, yes?" he bellowed onto their faces.

"Yes," they answered in unison, springing to un-soldierly attention.

"Are you ready – really ready?"

"Yes, we are."

"Then, come with me."

He led them to one of the doors and stopped to address them again. "Any clothes you have on, apart from your pants, let me have them. They are not allowed for now. I will return them later."

The men quickly complied, in a speed that suggested they anticipated the instructions. Each man handed to him his shirt, trousers, vest, shoes and wrist watch. As they complied, Victor and Uggi, watching from a fair distance, wondered if they would face similar orders.

The instructor had no time to fold properly what he collected from Dauda and Emano. He just rolled them together and threw them inside the big bag he had with him. Then, he pulled out from the same bag certain objects. "Here. You need these," he said, handing out two ropes of coral beads, each about two feet long, to each of the men. "And these," he followed up with two more ordinary ropes of similar length. "Tie one round every leg – at the ankle."

Emano, the faster of the two men just finished tying the coral round his ankle when the instructor noticed what he had done. "Oh no," he shouted at him, "the two together on the right ankle," he commanded.

When the instructor was satisfied the men had got the elements in the right places, he ordered them to stand side by side and face the door, while he stood behind them. He then extracted another affirmative to each of the same questions he earlier asked them in order to know if they were ready for the tasks that they were lined up for them behind the door.

"Do you remember you chose this and arrived here by yourselves?"

"Yes, we do."

"Of your own free accord?"

"Yes."

"Into this shrine of our ancestors?"

"Yes."

"So, be warned now, that going back is not possible – until after you've made your choice. And the choice now is between the comfort of the coral bead and the suicide of the rope.

"The door shall open now and you shall make your choices. I wish you good luck."

He did not allow the men to respond before he issued the next commands "Now face me and walk in backwards," he ordered.

Uggi and Victor watched the door slowly open behind the men and wondered if it would be their turn to be sucked inside. The instructor was the last to enter and he shut the door after himself.

"I believe that was a part of the initiation," Victor told Uggi.

"No doubt about that," agreed Uggi. "Perhaps, the beginning."

"But if a part or a beginning of an initiation is nakedness I wouldn't like to know what the whole or the end of it would be. Stark madness of the market-place, I believe."

A scream coming from the direction the stripped men went gave Victor no chance to finish his remarks. It was chilling enough even though both its distance and the walls prevented the tourists from seeing the face of whoever it was coming from.

"Oh, a barking one too," added Uggi. "Did you hear that?"

Victor did; and it spurred him and Uggi to stand and walk. to the door manned by the minder. "We need to get out for some fresh air," Uggi said on behalf of the two.

"You can't now," the man told Uggi. He promptly rose and stood between them and the door. "Please you have to wait," he firmly instructed them.

"Why can't we?" Victor shouted. "Wait for what?" He shoved aside the minder and seized the door handle while Uggi was forcing the latch and banging.

"Eh, what's going on over there?" a guard shouted from the other side of the door. He had overheard a part of the argument and was disturbed by the on-going knocks on the door. "What's banging? What's going on?" He double-checked and ensured the latch on his own side of the door was secure.

The answers came in a Babel of exchanges, more banging, commands and counter-commands, leading to the urgent return of two men, one of them Sese.

"You idiot," Victor swore angrily at the minder and rushed to grip him. The timely restraint Victor got from Sese's colleague even infuriated him more. It deprived him of fulfilling an absolute grip on the minder's neck. "You idiot," he repeated, spraying white foaming spit on Sese's face and chest. "Is this the plan – lure us here, strip us and have us imprisoned? Is that it?"

"Please gentlemen calm down and listen," pleaded Sese's colleague after persuading Uggi to let off the latch and stop banging. "We don't lure people here. In fact, every person you find here has begged to be allowed to come; it is a favour. And the king said you two volunteered to come."

"But for a long time Sese abandoned us and you people locked us up. We did not agree to come here and watch strip shows. That never was the agreement."

"That, we very much understand," continued the same man, "and we apologise if you have experienced anything strange. But please appreciate that although this place looks common it is an important place. It would therefore be silly to leave the doors unlocked at any time.

"Besides we were told the two of you are not just ordinary men – that we must give you double protection within these walls. The two of us were busy preparing a comfortable place for you. This was why we were away. The place is ready now. So, please follow me."

The passage was through another hall twice as large as the one they departed from. There, Victor and Uggi could see about a dozen men, but not a single woman. Every one of them was engaged in cutting into pieces, or cleaning slaughtered animals.

"Is here an abattoir?" Uggi stopped to ask. "So, this is where the smell of blood was coming from."

"Or is this a kind of central kitchen for Ila?" Victor added.

"Don't worry gentlemen," answered Sese. There will be time to explain all that. Later we are going to take you round every part of this humble complex. That will help your questions and make our answers easier for you to understand. So, wait and see."

Curiously the visitors followed them as they were made to pass inevitably by these dozen or so men. They passed by the bodies of three slaughtered goats carefully piled on top of similar number of slaughtered cows. There, they tried very hard to avoid stepping on the path formed by the streaming and coagulated blood of slaughtered animals.

They passed by three men sharing the jobs of skinning, chopping and carrying away into a large drum, the body of another cow. They noticed the drum was overfilled to the point of showing a hill of raw beef above its upper rim. To them, it confirmed the men had dealt with at least another animal in a similar manner before they entered. Yet in another part, two giant pots sat side by side on two local tripod trivets, one manned for frying, and the other for cooking.

The room they ended in was large and furnished enough for the temporary bed-sit it was meant to be. It had two wooden single beds complete with linen. The setting told them they would not be released in a short time.

Sese offered the visitors some food but they were in no mood to take it. The junketing of food and dead animals they saw had murdered their appetite.

Their arrival at the room also came at a time there was a scream, the second since they arrived, coming from somebody somewhere not too far away. Victor wondered if he and Uggi were now near to a torturing chamber and sought the source of the scream from Sese. Strangely Sese told them it was a moo from a cow yet to be slaughtered. For now, the scream and the answer even buried deeper, their appetite that was already dead.

"You will have to understand the masquerade which you are taking out," Sese began to prepare them for their mission. "There are a few rules dictated by our ancestors. Knowing them makes it easy to go out with the spirits."

"And what is the possibility of knowing these within this short time that remains?" Victor asked.

"Don't worry," Sese answered. "My Almighty has already bent some rules to favour you."

"But, how?"

"Don't worry, I say. We've found two surrogates for you. They are your perfect twins."

Uggi and Victor exchanged a look of ignorance, and Sese caught the exchange. "Means we won't put you through certain rites," he quickly added. "Two people are already mandated to do them on behalf of the two of you. They are waiting for us now.

"And ah, before we forget," added Sese, "my Almighty said we should let you know that your friends are also here," he teased the tourists.

"Which friends?" Uggi asked.

"Jacq and Nek."

"Really?" Victor asked. "Can we meet them?"

"Not definite. They are busy. What's the rush?

"Everybody knows they are going away with you soon. The ground does not get over-anxious to snatch the seeds of the ripening pod; sooner than later, and in whichever way, they are bound to fall on it. Anyway, if the king wants, you could."

Back at the red-lit hall two men were waiting. They were outside the same door through which Uggi and Victor saw the stripped men vanish with their face-powdered and bald-headed instructor. The only resemblance they had with the tourists was in their heights. One was as short as Victor while the other had the height of the much taller Uggi. They already had their heads shaved with a few grammes of oil rubbed on them. Sese led the tourists to them.

By the men, Sese ordered the taller of the shaven men to face Kazuggi and the shorter, Victor.

Next, each man in the opposing pair was ordered to put his left hand on the shoulder of the man he faced, while having the right hand raised and pointed to the roof.

"Uggi," Sese called the taller tourist, "from this moment on this is Uggi," he said, pointing to the taller of the shaven men. "He has taken over your name, body and spirit, till the rites are completed."

Uggi wanted to talk; but Sese, now in a hurry, was too fast for, and clearly uninterested in, any interruption.

"Victor," he went on to call the other tourist, "from this moment on this is Victor," he said, touching the shorter man. "And he remains Victor till the rites are completed.

"Anyway," he continued, scheming to ward off any question, "I will be with you or near enough to you both throughout the duration of all that needs to be done.

"I wish you well. And so do our ancestors who are giving you this opportunity today," he concluded the formal address.

"Now *Victor*, *Uggi*, are you ready?" Sese asked the first of the preliminary questions of the initiation.

"Yes."

"Yes."

"Yes."

"Yes."

"N n o o," screamed out Sese. "Only *Victor* and *Uggi* are to answer. Not all of you. I just told you that – just told you who each of you must be. I hope you understand now."

They seemed to. This time, only the shaven men responded to the repeat of Sese's question.

"Now, you will present yourselves to our ancestors the way you were born," Sese gave the next order.

The shaven responded by taking off their clothes, leaving on just their briefs. Sese promptly collected them and passed them to his assistants, who pushed them inside the sack he carried.

"Here," Sese followed up, handing to each of them, beads chains and two lengths of cord which the two men, without waiting for further instructions, tied round their ankles. As if they were special tags to prevent the men from escaping, Sese pulled each chain with his hand and felt satisfied it was secure. Then, he signalled his assistant to open the door before them. As soon as he marched himself and the four men in, his assistant shut the door behind them.

"*Victor*, *Kazuggi*, stop. Stop there!" Sese yelled out the first of his platoon commands inside the new hall. They were all about six metres away from a huge clay pot the size of one of those they had seen earlier in the kitchen. It was sat in the circular slot of a carved, waist high, wooden stool.

The four obeyed with varying degree of fright, those of the Glaswegians apparently being the most apparent.

"Move near that pot before you. When you reach it, one of you should lift up its lid. *Victor*, you do that."

Victor led the compliance, with the last steps being introduced slower than the previous.

"*Victor*, take off the lid," he repeated. "Use the white cloth by it to hold the lid's handle."

97

The short man moved forward and took a white piece of linen that was below the pot on the same stool. Frightfully, he stretched out to the lid.

"Move closer to him, all of you, so that you can see what is inside it."

In silence they obeyed, their hearts pounding and their legs wobbling. For the second time the tourists felt like retreating from the whole process.

As the lid was lifted, a thick vapour and sweet aroma followed it in hot pursuit, spreading out onto the faces of the four men standing nearer to the pot, the vapour preventing any of them from seeing what the pot contained. In another ten seconds it was clear enough, with its beefy aroma.

"What did you see, *Victor*?" Sese asked.

"Steam."

"I mean see in the pot? The two of you should take a look."

"A stew of meat," replied new Victor.

"Have you got a good sense of smell, *Kazuggi*?"

"Yes."

"How does the stew smell?"

"Sweet. Very sweet."

"Touch the pot, externally half an inch above the base, *Kazuggi*, and tell us how it feels."

"Hot. Too hot!"

"Yes, and do you know what that tells you? It is that for a pot to enjoy a nice stew, its base must first suffer from fire and heat. Now you want certain privileges, isn't it? You must pass the tests that go with them."

The tourists heaved a sigh of relief at knowing the objective of the pot. Had they not been gagged they would have condemned both the material and the illustration as being unnecessarily too long and perambulating for the point intended. That notwithstanding, Victor still managed to whisper to his friend: why couldn't he just say…?"

"Sh sh sh," Sese quickly cut in before Kazuggi could respond. "Stop it." At once he moved the group into the next room.

The room was about four feet wide and twice as long. A figure sat at its opposite end, apparently waiting for them. He was the Chief Priest, taking over the initiation for the remaining, more crucial stages. He was small, but the piece of white loincloth he had round his body bestowed on him a favourably exaggerated size as it radiated more white than the white lighting inside the room. Its wrapping passed below his right armpit before being held by two corners on the left shoulder with a wide armlet, the type he had round his wrists. His headgear was a tri-band of strung coloured cowries and parrot feathers reminiscent of a Zulu chief and an Appalachian Indian. The same were made into a long necklace that hung down to his belly.

The stool he sat on was about a hand higher than his knee level. He sat open-legged, resting his hands on his thighs.

A second stool by his right had arranged on it, a large gourd, a small one, and a calabash bowl with a lid. He stretched continuously and touched each of them with the whisk in his right hand as if warning off them, some houseflies.

His peculiar face competed with his personal presentation. Single rings of red, yellow and white paints were triangularly juxtapositioned round the right eye, the left eye and the mouth respectively.

Directly above his stool and the feather of his headgear was the base edge of a large cubical wall mounting. The front square of the mounting was a carved dragonhead. Two large eyes, one human-like the other owl-like, were hollowed out to allow coloured lights to glow from within. The glow, together with the largeness and the ugliness of the dragonhead, almost overshadowed the presence of the priest.

"I understand you applied to join in the race of the fast runners," the priest addressed them from his stool. "The gods have made me your chief inductor. If you pass the test you will be

99

welcome. If you try your best but fail, you will be re-tested. If you fail woefully you will be rejected. The speed with which you perform in your new roles will be most important; so we start with your speed work."

He stood up and carefully carried the small gourd first to the centre point between them and himself. Then, he poured out some of its contents, a white powder, onto the floor to make a small circle.

Next, he replaced it, swapping it with the big gourd he had brought to the circle. He tapped the gourd thrice with the base of his whisk while muttering some incantations. Then, he cautiously removed the lid. The tip of a flat object slowly appeared, and he quickly met it with his hand in the hollow of the gourd's neck. Live king cobra!

"Good boy," he said repeatedly as the massive creature coiled round his hands and was carried to his chest. Slowly he disentangled and settled it on the floor inside the circle he drew with the white chalk. "Good boy, my prince," he commanded it into position:

"The prince, with the pincer of the pins
Good boy, my prince,
The prince with the saliva that blinds
Be calm on your throne, my prince!"

Next, he carried the bowl to the centre, there took off its lid and dropped the chunk of meat inside it onto the bare floor less than a yard from the cobra. He reoccupied his stool while the snake rose from its stationary position.

"Now," commanded the priest, "whoever is *Victor* must go first. *Victor* will pick up the piece of meat before its guarding prince can stop him, and then, run across to me. Understand?"

"You can't be serious," the real Victor challenged him with fear and disgust. He spoke for the first time since the initiation began. "That is madness, pure madn…"

"Sh sh sh," Sese Abram stopped him as he did earlier to Kazuggi. All the same the short impersonator still proceeded, forward. He shook and twitched his spine like a body builder while at the same time marching up and down on the same spot. Like his colleague impersonator, sweat droplets merged into streams down his forehead. He was ready to have a go at the piece of meat. He inched forward, prompting the cobra to reduce its coil by gathering and lifting a substantial length of its body from the head. Its neck was flattened and there were angry hisses.

He moved forward and the cobra reduced its coils even further.

For the second time, the old man rose from his stool. He met the snake at the circle and hit the large gourd with the whisk a few times. The snake responded by re-coiling and lowering its body. The new Victor saw it as a rare opportunity he must not miss. He hardly waited for the old man to sit on his stool when he took the plunge – and the cobra its move!

More of a chew than a bite, the cobra locked both its fangs and expanded jaws firmly into the fleshiest part of *Victor*'s left arm. In his desperate struggle to free himself from the lock the snake put on more curls round *Victor*'s arm, flipping its tail angrily as it did so. In agony, *Victor* yelled out for help that did not look like coming. He passed out and fell – moments after Kazuggi, who could find no more heart to watch beyond the snake's initial assault.

Victor moved to revive Kazuggi. He pushed back Sese and his assistant at first; and wouldn't allow anyone in the room to touch his friend. He had no doubt in his mind that everyone in there was a part of the problem.

When Kazuggi opened his eyes he was still dazed. That moment Victor recognised that Kazuggi wouldn't be able to continue. "Please Sese, can you take him back to the restroom now?" Victor pleaded.

"Certainly. My assistant will do it. Aren't you going back with him?"

"No."

The Masquerade

To the old man, the dramatic scenes were nothing beyond ordinary. He initiated, saw, and controlled many of such every year. Calmly, he rose from his stool and went for the large gourd. He carried it to the cobra and tapped it thrice as if to announce his presence. Next, he undid the coil and pulled the creature. As it let go, he swiftly directed it back into the gourd and put on the lid. He returned the gourd to the stool.

With the snake caged, the old man went for the small gourd, principally for its white powdery content. He heaped some of it on the distorted incisions made by the fangs of the cobra on *Victor* and vigorously robbed it in, not caring for the painful groaning of *Victor*. He brought out a small white handkerchief from under his loincloth and poured out some quantities out on it. With the two men holding *Victor* down, the cloth was brought to his nostrils and rubbed over them severally until he began to sneeze. He sneezed uncontrollably until the force of the sneezing threw the kerchief off his nose. When it stopped every square inch of his body was covered with more sweat. Now he was extraordinarily conscious and his pains seemed to have gone or reduced greatly.

"Where am I?" he asked the priest, beaming weirdly. He turned his head as far right as it would go and return it back to go as far left as it would. "Where? In Paradise?"

"Yes, in Canaan; and in good hands," replied the old man who felt satisfied with himself.

"Where is our friend? Back to Glasgow?" *Victor* asked again. He was now pacing up and down in a mood so brainless that he couldn't see Kazuggi sitting and resting on the floor.

"Don't worry about him; that's him," Sese calmed him down, pointing at Kazuggi. Sese knew the drug and spell were working well, and that the danger from the bite was gone.

"Would you get him to the restroom now, please?" Victor asked Sese again for Kazuggi.

"Yes...well. And I asked if you would be going back with him."

102

"Yes. And I answered 'no'. I am definitely continuing with you." Victor was determined to do anything to free Jacquensica. He was sure, that had Kazuggi been well enough, Kazuggi would have loved him to continue at whatever cost.

"In fact," he continued, "here and now, give us back our names and personality. I was born Victor and I am Victor. He's Kazuggi and will ever remain Kazuggi.

"We are here to free some people from their sufferings; and we're not going to pass those sufferings to other people. It will be unfair.

"Retire these poor men; and I, Victor, will continue for the two of us." He was already taking off his clothes.

"But you can't do that," Sese said.

"Why not? I am doing exactly that," asserted Victor, holding on to the clothes he had already removed.

"Let him do it for both of us," cut in a weak Kazuggi. "I will join him later if I can."

"Then on one condition," said the old man, "that you agree to start with the snuff, right here."

"And what else?" Victor asked, nodding his consent to the term. "And who wants them, these clothes?" he further asked, stretching them out to Sese. Except Kazuggi who was resting, sitting on the floor, everybody stood still looking at Victor. He was raring to go.

"Take the clothes from him," the old man directed Sese. "He is a brave man. Return Kazuggi to the restroom."

"And is there any bead or rope, or both for my ankles?" he asked Sese as Kazuggi was helped up and led away by Sese's assistant.

"Don't worry about them," the old man assured him. "But you will take the snuff as a starter. I am satisfied you are a determined man."

Victor was; and the priest was inwardly thrilled about it. He was the first white man he would initiate.

103

The Masquerade

Within minutes of Victor inhaling some of the same white powder and rubbing some on his face, he was sweating and sneezing. When the sneezing subsided, he was smiling – endlessly. In this state the priest took him into the Chamber of Stings, leaving behind every other person.

There he took his time to dust Victor's body with yet another powder, this time a yellow one. When he had finished, he hinted to Victor as to what would happen:

Victor would remain on a stool he would put him to sit on. Certain elements would come out in their thousands to examine and welcome him on the stool. While they were out on him, he must not attempt to see or to hear them. The cotton buds, he would put in his ears. They would block the ears adequately and prevent him from hearing the song they sing. Some buds too, Victor would have in his nostrils to forestall inhaling any unwanted odour. But it would be Victor's own willpower that would assist him to keep his eyes and mouth firmly shut whatever the temptation.

The priest could see the strong determination in Victor's eyes as he led him into the small hall and sat him on the prepared stool. Next, he went to a side of the wall having a blue round patch the size of a football. In its centre was a double penny-size diameter pipe driven through the wall. He made the usual muttering and removed the plug on the pipe.

Within seconds, bees swarmed out through the hole and fought ferociously for places on Victor's body. At first, Victor looked like a tail-less baby cow with spots of flies it had neither the tail, nor the strength, nor knowledge to expel. Then he looked like a body of big spatters of reddish mud on yellow. When every space on his body was occupied, he finished blackish brown. They were on him for a good quarter of an hour throughout when the priest was singing a ritual hymn. When he stopped he changed to more straight instructional incantations to the insects.

The swarm started to rise and return to the adjacent room through the same hole it came from. When they were all gone, the

104

priest replaced the cover at the end of the pipe and got Victor out of the hall.

Victor came out with only swollen lips and the priest was happy for him – and for himself. It indicated Victor was loyal to King Japeedoe; and that he was surely one of the rare ones who deserved the honey and not the stings of Ila. If Victor had been a citizen, his recommendations on Victor would have qualified Victor for a lot of booty from the king at every festival.

"You have done well, and passed well," he commended Victor. "Just one more and it's all over.

"You are loyal but we have to make sure. May the gods and our ancestors make the last test easy for you."

"Thank you, priest," Victor responded, now under a reduced spell. "What's the next test?" His smile was of personal confidence.

"Enter the oath box in the next room," the priest commanded Victor into the adjacent room. The box was a topless glass enclosure, of a three feet square floor, and about seven feet high. Ten swords, all unsheathed and shining, but of assorted colours, lengths, curves and thicknesses, dangled blades-down lowly and directly above the box from the ceiling. Victor was marched in through the fourth and only open side of the box.

Once inside the box, Victor was ordered to turn round – to face the open side he entered through. In this position he also faced the disproportional statue of a king on horseback. The priest moved aside to let Victor have a clearer view of the statue. Next, he produced two more swords and shared them into Victor's hands. Then, he commenced his last set of commands:

"Stand upright...Face the King properly...Hold the handles firmly and cross the blades on your head...Say loudly and clearly after me...:

I, Victor from Glasgow
Standing inside the Oath Box of Ila
Hereby swear my pledge to you King Japeedoe
That my eyes see only what you want me to see

My ears hear only what you want me to hear
My mouth says only what you want me to say
My nose smells only what you want me to smell
My legs go only where you want me to go
My hands take only what you want me to take.

I accept the cut and curse of the swords
When my eyes see beyond yours
When my ears hear beyond yours
When my mouth speaks over yours
When my nose smells over yours
When my legs go beyond yours
When my hands pick above yours
Amen, amen; so must it be.

"Now kiss the swords and lay them down before your feet. Walk over them and come out of the box.

"Congratulations. Now, have this before you step out of this room; add it to what's round your neck." He handed him a silver pendant. "It is a gift from King Japeedoe, to only those who merit it. It is what others will identify you with in times of trouble. Welcome to the full membership of the *Order of The Eagle*."

Victor carefully opened and locked-on the pendant – of a spread eagle – round his neck.

"The king wants you to be a good eagle of Ila. Know when to grab the chick off the mother hen. Know when to disappear with the chick and make a total meal of it. And know when not to disappear with it, when not to fly too far before you return a chick unharmed to its mother. Never are you forbidden from grabbing a chick."

"Thank you very much," Victor said happily as he stepped out of the box. "Can I have one for Uggi also?" he asked the priest.

"He did not take the oath."

"But I did it for both of us. He authorised me to; and you approved it."

"Are you going to explain the oath to him then?" He handed Kazuggi's to Victor, knowing Victor was technically correct.

"Yes, I will, will explain all," he could not be happier to promise.

"Sese is here now to return your clothes. When you are fully clothed, you can attend the dawn meeting. It is a brief one. There you shall meet other friends you have not met before. After it you can return to the guest room to assist your friend."

When Sese entered he was with Kazuggi, now half naked. He had recovered enough and had compelled Sese to return him to take over the performance of the rites by himself.

"Why?" asked the priest, astonished. "You still come back?"

"I said I would if I could. Didn't I?"

"But your friend also told you he would do it all for you. So he has. Just collect the pendant from him and attend the meeting to know who your friends are. Then, go back for a rest. Only a very short rest."

CHAPTER FOUR

The Initiation II

Within seconds, Victor and Uggi recognised this hall of the Main Shrine more than faintly. They had been there before. The last time, it was near empty and held none of the mixture of weird and intimidating objects that now filled it up. Though it was still quiet, the poses of these objects made the hall appear loud and living.

The objects were masks on their own, masks with costumes already attached to them, and decapitating implements. They were not arranged in any particular order, their varying sizes and shapes disfavouring such an arrangement. These physical variations notwithstanding, they were reasonably spaced out – propped, seated, or hung – to allow adequate free passage round each of the nearly one hundred that were displayed.

They recognised the hydra-headed sword at once. It was the one Fire Spirit, the fiery masquerade, was brandishing about in the town square five days ago – the exact sword he was about to use to decapitate Jacq. It was still unsheathed but was delicately suspended among a carefully arranged group of two-dozen other knives, swords, axes, spears, cudgels, bows and arrows.

"We saw this before, didn't we?" Victor asked Sese, pointing to it.

"Could be," answered Sese Abram faintly, not keen on commenting any further.

108

"Yes, we did," corroborated Uggi. "We clearly did, at the lady's execution."

"That is not correct," countered Sese. "because there has never been any lady's execution."

"Well, Sese, that is not all that important," said Victor. "But do your people know you have all these here?"

"O yes, very much so. My Almighty makes sure our kingdom has them – masks, weapons, tools, all"

"And what do they think about them?" Uggi asked.

"That they are necessary, and useful to the kingdom," Sese started to to lie. "That without them as combined physical deterrents, some people would attempt to destroy themselves and destroy the kingdom. The people know them and when to use them. Patriotically, they always choose which of them is appropriate for the criminal. They were happy to do the same in the case of Jacq.

"Our citizens also do treasure their history – history of when those implements helped us to win inter-kingdom wars and preserve our kingdom. Our people know all that."

"So, the king uses them every year in the square as we just saw?" Uggi asked again.

"He never uses them personally; but may order them used on the people for the people. When he inevitably has to, it is only to seek peace and maintain order; and not to have a cupful of blood to drink. Are you satisfied now?"

Angel Eagle, as it would be called later by Sese, was at the front position, scare-crowed on a chest-high stand of a strong base. It was a wood carving of a large eagle in an intimidating full flight posture. Its base was hollowed out to sit comfortably on the head of the would-be carrier. A male suit with facial netting to allow the carrier the vision was attached around the sculptured crown.

The type of eagle it was could neither be ascertained at all by the tourists, nor reasonably by its creators. The feathers carefully stuck on it were of about a dozen eagles'. Both legs and the beak had rings of brilliant blue and white painted round them. The tongue was red, out-dangling like a hunting porcupine's, while the eyelids were also rounded with rings of yellow. All these punctured any perfect semblance to an eagle – or to a bird for that matter – that was ever known to the knowledgeable Attenborough or any other great conservationist anywhere.

"Whao-o, Sese!" Uggi exclaimed. "What a beauty! But of what specie is it? Any peculiarity with Ila?"

"What is 'specie'?"

"Type or breed," Victor explained. "What type is it?"

"Yes, it is a special eagle," Sese replied. He was pleased the tourists started this round with admiration of what they saw. He called it Angel Eagle, and launched into a full and weird description of the sculpture: The eyes of Angel Eagle were able to see all planets, and the tongue able to speak with the dead in all the languages of the planets. As for the wings, Angel Eagle could use them to commute between the living and their dead ancestors in order to take and deliver inter-planetary messages. Angel Eagle, being supernatural, could see deep, speak deep and fly deep.

"That sounds crap," Uggi countered this time.

"What is scrap – a sheet of metal?"

"No," Uggi replied boldly. "Some expressions that are not and can never be true."

"Now you are the one delivering the real scrap, the type unexpected of one who is true to his oath and to our Almighty. So soon?" He hissed and shook his head, surprised at how a black man could so rubbish a custom he was expected to revere – how Uggi could behave like a local bastard who preferred to use a stick instead of his finger to point at his family home! Disappointment glaringly wrote itself all over his face. Victor moved an agreement with Sese's rubbish talk, saving Uggi from further highlighting other aspects of the sculpture's defects.

They all halted at the next mask, a more complex wooden figure of five animals. Its base was a round, darker tray, about two feet in diameter. Four carved animals – a tiger, a leopard, a lion and a lioness – were seated, with the first backing the second, and the third backing the fourth. In the centre, a three-quarter body of a long horned antelope leapt skywards without the sculptor having a preference for the direction it faced.

"A mini safari! This is a nice pack," Victor commended and admired the delicately painted spots and stripes applied on them to distinguish two felines into leopard and tiger respectively. "Has it got a name?"

"Catcher, that's the name. I expect you to guess that before I even told you. Can't you see it?"

"Yes we can," Victor answered. "A reindeer catcher."

"Not exactly – it catches more than reindeers," Sese quickly embarked on an explanation. "It catches the sneakers, priers and evildoers. When someone denies an atrocity, he is brought before Catcher to swear. Where he is adjudged to be lying, Catcher imposes punishments, usually in fines for the first time, a period of servitude for the second, and a curse that will get him torn into pieces for the third time. No liar has ever walked past Catcher uncaught in the over a hundred years that our ancestors had sent it down to us."

"Over a hundred years?" Victor asked, unable to believe the mask was that old.

"Okay, your observation is right. This one is actually five years with us," Sese made a u-turn. "It replaces the former that existed for over a hundred years before it accidentally fell and broke at the end of a dance. Now, instead of a replica with three beasts, we have with four, with the fifth as the prey to feed on."

Very clever, the tourists silently agreed with Sese's self-satisfying claim. They saw the truism being depicted by the Catcher mask: same cats don't prey on each other but on other weaker animals. Here is a gang, a bloody gang of oppressors, comprising of the king and his associates, harassing the ordinary people of Ila. What a powerful lord, what a weak set of lorded!

111

"The clothing is attractive," Uggi said of the blue-red pinstripe cloth sewn to it. "But would it not be too heavy for the wearer?"

"Yes, it is nice and new, to be used for the first time. It won't be heavy at all. During the festival, the magic of our ancestors together with the efforts of our priest and our Almighty provides the wearers with extra strength. A wearer who could barely move is given enough strength to jump and run, once he is in the attire."

The next mask they stopped at had its bigger eye closed and a smaller one opened. The tourists perceived it as being too ugly to comment on.

"Won't either of you say something about this one?" Sese asked in order to break the silence.

"What else can one say about it?" Uggi asked him. "It is too ugly to be neared for any assessment or comment. Has it also got a name?"

"That is Mercy-eye-shut, one of the most important spirits in this hall," Sese said. "It carries out both the interrogation and the punishments of common offenders. The closed eye, eye of mercy, is totally blind. It used to be a kind and gentle spirit when it first arrived on the soil of Ila. So, his first assignment was to look after the sick, the distressed and all those in need of care. He would watch over them without blinking. It continued until one day an aggrieved ingrate whose sick wife he was watching over died. The man pounced on Mercy-eye-shut and plucked his right eye. When Mercy-eye-shut recovered from the ordeal, other spirits, deeply aggrieved, changed his duty – to containing the troublemakers. He continued to handle the job efficiently because he assumed it was the 'eye of mercy' that was plucked, to leave that 'of wickedness'. That was how the spirit got his name. The mask is always firm but just."

They stopped next at another double mask. Instead of a pack of animals like Catcher, it had two faces – of a woman. The faces were upright and back-to-back on a hollowed yellow wood base.

"A beautiful piece you must comment on," Sese recommended to the tourists before they could even have a close look. He wanted them to recognise and praise the artistry of the three men who had been working on it in the last two days and nights. Even though the work on it was yet to be completed, he wanted Victor and Uggi to laud the exceptional sanding that gave the faces a lotioned look, the blue eye lashes trimmed with golden stones, the hairs of wood parted into three main hair ridges on each of the faces, and the rows of black and coloured stones that were laid to form yet smaller ridges on the main ones. Sese also wanted them to spot and shout about the glaring, constructed difference in the look of each face. "It's excellent, isn't it?" he impatiently asked both men.

"Yes, Sese, the smoothest and most beautiful we have seen here," Uggi responded as the party walked round the wooden sculpture. "But why two faces, one pleasant, one triste?"

"Oh, the faces? They are not two for nothing. The two faces as a pair is the female of Jemba Couple. It's the female of the special emissaries our ancestors just sent down to us in Ila. The male of the pair, we shall soon see. Three men are putting the finishing touches to it. When completed, the happy face will be painted white, and the angry, red.

"The spirit will use the happy face to bless all those who respect motherhood. The twisted face she has for those who are against sweet motherhood, and are to be cursed. The male of the pair is similarly for sweet fatherhood – those for and against it. Each will be clothed in a way that the carrier can turn it round to see through the white face to bless, and through the red to curse. My Almighty expects the two of you to make use of the faces accordingly."

"The two of us? How?" Victor asked.

"He expects you to carry the pair at the finale on Saturday. He has reserved them for the two of you. They are called Jemba Couple."

"But they are still not ready," Uggi observed.

"Right. But there's plenty of time and hands to get them ready. More decorations in colours, beads and small mirrors and clothing will be added today. You see, my Almighty wants them completed last so they don't get soiled. He wants them clean enough for both of you to use on Saturday. By carrying the Jemba Couple on Saturday, you and the masks are starting a sweet, special history."

Sese was unable to go further into how Jemba Couple would make the sweet history. Without admitting it before the tourists, he knew that his knowledge of the history of Jemba Couple was shallow. King Jap had intentionally denied him the full knowledge:

The king silently conceived their existence four years back. He believed that creating and adding a new set of masquerades would boost his intake of personal gifts at annual festivals. At the time the tourists arrived, the masks were neither finished nor earmarked for a particular carrier. Jap therefore instructed Sese to show them to the tourists and cleverly prepare their minds towards carrying them on the last day of the festival.

Finally, the three men arrived at the male of the Jemba Couple mask. It had two faces, one white with a bit of smile, the other red and twisted; two caps, each beaded in white and red; and two towering abstract arches, partly beaded, painted and glazed, atop the caps. The tourists had already heard so much about it and so, had no questions for Sese.

Two weavers and a third person who was more of a craftsman than a local tailor, were working flat out to beat the deadline set by the king for the completion of the attires. The looms in use were locally made ones; one was wide, and the other, narrow.

When Sese and the tourists entered that workshop section of the shrine, the three workers in there were quite busy. The woven pieces were almost completed as evidenced by the nearly depleted warp stocks on both loom beams, and the large quantity of new fabric pieces, especially the narrow ones, being joined together. The user of the narrow loom performed the shedding and beating-up with all his hands and legs, forcing some sharp noises out of the loom. The noises were rhythmic and they drew the tourists cautiously closer to this operator who, still, was not looking in the tourists' direction. Instead, in addition, he was singing atop the sound of his loom. The song was being complemented by the weaver on the second loom, a much wider one, of lesser noise.

"I told you they are busy and far with it," Sese bragged as they stood by the singing narrow loom operator. "In another day, you won't know anything ever went on in this room, and on that pair."

"Yes we won't doubt that," Victor agreed on behalf of the two tourists. "Not at this speed of work."

Actually, none of the tourists had ever before seen the type of looms being used by the weavers. The nearest to them they ever saw producing cloths belonged to a class too complicated for a meaningful comparison. It was years ago, during their primary school days, when their class had seen calico and *hodden* cloths weaving at the Municipal Textile Mills in Glasgow. The factory was such a noisy place – so noisy that when one of the pupils dropped his ear plug, the noise in the mill would not allow anyone to hear the pupil's scream for help. Help to him had to wait until he was eventually seen covering both his ears with his hands. At another point, two pupils had raised their hands to ask some questions about the wonders of weaving but were signalled to reserve the questions until they would all be back in the small, noise-proof hall at the end of the looms shed.

"But...but..." all of a sudden, Victor was searching for words to describe what he just saw.

"But what, Victor?" Sese wanted to know. "Did you see something?"

"But did you all not tell Uggi and me that women are banned from inside the shrine?" Victor asked Sese. Judging by the dressing, Victor had believed the third worker he could now see more clearly was a woman. She had the hair platted as was customary of Ila women; and her chest had a pair of nipples almost touching the near edge of her sewing machine table. "A woman?"

"Yes, you can find a woman inside the shrine," Sese told them. "But it would be for a purpose, and the woman must be special," he added, laughing.

"How do you mean?" Uggi asked Sese.

"I mean, just as you have seen her doing a typical job normally reserved for people of her sex. You will see more when you go for your meals. They are born to serve," he said with despise, still laughing. Then he told his inductees that the worker was a man dressed like a woman, that men could dress up in any attire of their choice during the time of the masquerade festival.

"I hope you do a superb job," Sese reminded the tailor. "What you are doing now are for these two important men. You still don't need their measurement, or, do you, now?"

"I told you it is not necessary," the tailor replied. For the first time, he stopped the feet he scattered peddling the machine, and his neck that was dancing like that of Nipper, the gramophone dog, as he pushed forward what he was sewing.

"Sese, those masks' measurements we already took had served our purpose," the tailor added. He wished they hadn't come to disturb him.

Sese made no further effort to doubt the royal tailor. In the past, he had fitted clothes on various sizes and shapes of masks, men and even, spirits. He had cleverly used materials that varied from heavy to light fabrics, from tough beastly skins to the lightest of cellophanes, and from hardest tree barks to the most delicate leaves. Locally, he was most respected in this craft of using foot-pedal sewing machines, crude bodkins and thread needles of the finest gauge.

"Can we have a look then?" Uggi wanted to know. "Can we, if what he's making are for us?" Uggi moved to the tailor before anyone in the workshop could invite him or accept his request.

He paused at two piles of cloths, the nearest to the tailor. They were about a hundred pieces, each about five feet long with both ends turned and stitched down to prevent unravelling. "Are these forming a part of the costumes?" Victor asked.

"Yes, a part of them," Sese answered him.

"How are they going to be worn?"

"You have to wait. You will understand my explanation better when the bases are finished, because these pieces you see are going to be worn on top of the bases. The base costumes, as you will see next, are almost finished."

The second pile contained the two unfinished base costumes. How the tailor eagled them one on top of the other on the floor beside him showed they were meant for human species all right. They were both all-over striped, tubular, high-necked, headless, sleeved and under-legged. One attire was very much larger than the other in size; and for each pair, one arm was particularly longer than the other.

"Why are the arms not of the same length?" a curious Victor asked Sese.

"Why? You should know that – that no limb in a pair is ever long the same. Never. Usually we assume they are because we fear the embarrassment that would come with the proof. Now we are talking of the spirits; you don't expect their arms to be ordinary, but extraordinary.

"But seriously, it is because of the duties each arm is going to perform. The shorter one is going to be busier, and it will be complemented with a hand glove."

"Duties? What duties?" Victor asked again.

117

"Well, I might as well tell you since you are going to be the ones to perform them," Sese went on. "The one much longer than the wearer's arm allows him to hold the whip firmly and comfortably. The shorter, that will wear a beautiful glove, receives the gifts from time to time. The glove prevents the smart Ila donors from knowing through the palm marks, the identity of the man in the costume."

"How about the two pairs of legs? Or, are they also going to collect gifts the same way?" Uggi asked.

"My answer is basically the same – plus another simple question. Are the two of you of the same height? No. Anyway, we have got knee length socks to complement the under-legs."

In the end each of the tourists made his final choice of suits from the unfinished two and tried it on for a preliminary feel and fitting. Each man made suggestions for more comfort to the royal tailor who accepted them without a single objection.

"I wish we were a pair of Neil Armstrong and Buzz Aldrin in these suits." Victor joked with Uggi.

"Yea, Victor – indeed, or of Victor Gagarin speaking with Neil Uggi on the surface of planet Ila!" Uggi mocked as both men got themselves out of the headless costumes. "With this type of suit, I am not even sure if we can achieve mere hops, or any of the mad runs the king expects us to do – until after the tailor has completed the amendments."

"What are hops and Gagarin?" Sese asked the two laughing men. No answer ever came; but he felt contented with the silence. He preferred to continue with his busy schedule. "Now we must go for our food, and a break after that," Sese told the tourists.

With its white painted but black-smoked ceiling, a once-upon-a-time white painted wall, a large dark-oak assembled dining table, poor ventilation and poor lighting, this shrine's dining hall would almost pass for a massive photographer's dark room. Six other men were already there with the servers when Sese led the tourists in. The men were busy chatting and eating, apparently unperturbed by their stuffy surroundings. But because the group just arriving was Sese's, its members were accorded special treatment straightaway.

"Now, gentlemen," Sese called on the tourists, "you can go to any of the manned pots and ask to be served whatever you want."

At first the tourists were unsure of what they wanted. Even though they were hungry enough, the unhygienic condition of the hall gave them no corresponding appetite. Sese, on the other hand, would not miss the opportunity of the heavenly VIP treatment. He moved quickly from one server to the other, piling his large wooden plate with food.

There were twelve pots of food spaciously paired about, with each pair manned by a man. The tourists eventually headed to one of the servers they judged to be the most decent of the lot. He was the only one not momentarily tasting of what he had to serve while waiting to serve.

"What would you like?" the server asked Uggi at the lead, flashing his toothy smile and holding a large wooden plate in one hand and a big serving fork on the other. His grip on the utensils was so firm that it raised the threads of muscles and veins around his wrists and backhands. He was genuinely enthusiastic about pleasing the tourists.

"Wait a minute please," Victor interceded. "What exactly do you have here to serve?"

"This one," replied the server, putting his fork on the metre diameter and metre high open pot, "is sauced beef. This other one," he landed the fork on it next, "is sauced antelope."

"Is that all you have?" Victor asked again, fighting to believe his ears.

"Oh no. Over there," he pointed the fork at the next server and the pair of pots before him, "we have a pot of grubs and mushrooms stew, and one of *tomato-ed* and seasoned python."

"Anything else?" asked Uggi, now becoming sick of the strange foods. The whole set-up was becoming crazier to him. "The next pot must be one of stewed mosquitoes and elephant tails, isn't it?" Uggi mocked angrily, his question coming as Sese was heading back to them.

"Here, nobody ever dreams of eating those you just mentioned," the server immediately objected on top of his voice. "You don't say because the mosquito sucks your blood you must do the same to it – the efforts just won't be worth it. Also, you need to know that the majestic king of animals, the elephant, is the symbol of our Almighty Majesty. It is sacred to us. We don't eat it here."

"Gentlemen, is there a problem?" Sese intervened. "You have been moving slowly, if at all you were moving." Sese was already done with the gathering of what he wanted on his plate. The tourists could see that his plate was trying hard to accommodate a meandering stew of grubs, python and mushrooms atop boiled rice and potatoes. "Go across if you don't like this stand. Pots of goat meat are still virgin, with nobody touching them yet." Then he returned to the other end of the table for more chat with those he was with before.

"These are a sinful, wasteful lot, aren't they Victor?" Uggi asked. "They make no sense at all – twelve huge pots of food for just the few people who are here? They should not have taken in so much food, and should have instead returned so much."

"But that's what the citizens love."

"No, don't make that conclusion. It can't be what they love. Only those of them who could just seize and eat, cook and eat, serve and eat, and profit from it one way or the other, would love this."

"But we saw many animals being led here together with ferries of gifts – all with songs, meaning they love the culture that way."

"This is silly, Victor." Uggi was getting angry again. "Silly indeed."

"It is not. But your complaints are. You complain more than those you regard as being denied and cheated. If the crane does not complain of the weight of a load why should its driver? How are we sure more people will not be coming here tonight for free meals? Let's face our own project, conclude it, and leave!"

"Okay Victor, no problem. I can't believe that you are now turning your eyes and ears away from the wickedness of Jap and his men. Daddy told me about all these – hunger and thirst in the midst of plenty, servitude in the midst of freedom, and exploitation in the midst of poverty. He told me long before we left Glasgow. Had there been a practical scale we could use to compare and contrast the weights of those inside the shrine and those outside it, you would have agreed I am not just complaining."

"I am sorry, Uggi; the project must still remain our priority." Victor was unrepentant and unyielding. "Jacq is still there on death row, Jap still reigns supreme; so, no arguments will count until she is freed."

The more Uggi listened, the more he was convinced that something was already wrong with Victor – with his latest line of thinking. Uggi believed they must tackle the obstacle before the two of them, but that unless they were careful and observant, the kingdom would create more obstacles for them in order to hold them forever. "Could this bloody man have secretly influenced Victor?" he wondered as he saw Sese heading back to the table he occupied with Victor.

"At this speed," Sese started another, but this time, serious joke, with the tourists, "you won't have enough to eat before all the pots are empty. It is a sin to go hungry inside the shrine."

"How can the pots be ever empty?" Uggi grabbed the chance to reopen his recent argument with Victor, with Sese who he already assumed to be a master in the sinners' group. "I can't see that ever happening with twelve large pots!"

"Yes, it can – and likely will – though not due to your slow type of help and helping, of course. In the shrine, once prepared, you don't keep the day's food beyond midnight. After midnight, whatever food remains yet unconsumed must be thrown away. That is the command of the gods and of the spirits of our forefathers. It is a taboo in the shrine to eat any food prepared the previous day. With drinks it is different because they ferment and get stronger with each day."

"So you see what I was talking about, Victor. There's too much waste here, because all items came in as gifts."

"Waste?" Sese could not understand how. "But we are talking of only a period of one week."

"Yes," said Uggi, "one week of this year, and one of every year. This means a whole year of waste in every half a century!"

"Century, what is that?"

"Anyway, so much for that," Victor intervened, quickly forcing a wink at Uggi. "What next is to be done after food, Sese?" he asked.

"But wait a minute," Uggi interrupted before Sese could answer him. He had just seen four kids collecting food in the shrine. "Sese, why are those kids here? Didn't you say children must not be seen here?"

"Well, you have seen children. They are special children – children who are above children."

"What puts them above others?" Uggi asked again.

"I can't tell you. You have to ask the king and others who own them. We don't have much time." He wasn't prepared to discuss the privileged children any further.

"Alright, what next?" Victor asked again?

"The next is to take some important notes of what else you need to know. It is best done while we are still here."

"Like what?" Victor asked.

"Same foods and drinks. The masquerade never eats or drinks in public, and rarely during an outing. The only times he can eat or drink – and to his tummy's swell – are before he steps out of the shrine and when he is back at the shrine."

"What if he is hungry, thirsty and tired during the outing?" Victor asked.

"He has to fill up properly before. Have you not heard of what the camel does before he starts the journey of the dunes? But if and where he indeed needs a refill after taking off from here, we have some mini shrines about town."

"With all this eating and drinking there's bound to be a lot of pissing. Have you considered that?" Uggi asked Sese another question.

"Not only considered that, we have experienced it."

"So, what did you come up with? Are there sufficient numbers of toilets about in the town?"

"Toilets?" Sese was surprised. "What do you need toilet for, Uggi? If you don't see masquerade filling up, then you must not see it discharging. Never!

"Anyway," Sese went on after some laughter, trying to allay Uggi's fears "the same mini-shrines will take care of that. Seeing a masquerade eating or drinking in the public will expose the spirit to be human after all.

"And I have another joke for you: Even without the mini shrines, pissing will not constitute a problem for a masquerade. You see, here, in Ila, people worship the masquerade so much that had it not been for the fear of the masquerade getting discovered as human, a masquerade could order the people to open their palms for him to discharge on them, and the people will gladly oblige. Anyway, the guide will arrange it whenever it is required."

"The guide?" Uggi wanted an explanation from Sese.

"Who is the guide?" Victor asked Sese first, before Sese could provide the explanation Uggi wanted. "Or, do you mean a guard?"

"No, not a guard. He is much more than that. He is the pilot to the plane of the masquerade, the director behind the masquerade. As such, he shows you your routes and the sequence you must ply them. He manages the protection of the masquerade by controlling the crowd at the immediate environment of the masquerade. Among the followers of the masquerade, the guide aids the social cohesion with the masquerade by making the band play the appropriate music, and by suggesting appropriate songs to the followers to sing. Above all, he knows better who does or does not donate a present to the masquerade, and he receives the present – be it material or monetary – for the spirit."

"What you have listed would make the masquerade look like the monkey working for the baboon to feed on," Uggi breathed out his conclusion. "Well, the guide might as well carry the mask. There is nothing left for the masquerade to do!"

"Far from that, gentlemen," Sese started another round of explanation. "Without the masquerade there is no guide. For a special purpose, the masquerade conceives and gives birth to the guide. So, the guide can never outgrow the masquerade. Without the masquerade there is no crowd; and without the crowd, no gifts to collect because there will be no remembrance. However big, small, enticing or fearsome his mask is, and even when he has no mask at all, he is what the single man and the entire crowd want to celebrate. He is ever more important than the guide. The guide himself recognises his own limit. Afterwards, he hands over all the gifts to the masquerade at the end of the outing.

"My Almighty," Sese continued, "also wants me to know some aspects of your dances and prayers, consider them with ours, and see which of them you could perform on Saturday. This is important because Saturday is mainly for dancing and prayers. And if we could start with dances, can you tell me about them – how many there are in Glasgow, and which of them you will be prepared to do?"

"That's nice, Sese," Uggi remarked. "There are beautiful dances in Glasgow, all well mastered from special schools and dancing clubs.

"O yes, five, if you don't mind. We can do *basket, figure 8, kissing, allemande* and *circles*. Victor, you are a better dancer; so explain them to him."

"*Basket* is built around two couples. That is, two men and two women. The first man uses his right hand to hold his partner's waist while the woman puts her left hand on his shoulder. The couple then close in on the second couple who are already holding themselves in the same positions. Next, the women rest their free right hands on the men's left shoulders, and the four dance round.

"*Figure 8*: One couple stands apart while another couple dances a figure eight round the man and woman. Usually the woman, or the older of the couple, dances first.

"Now, *kissing* dance…

"Okay Victor, thank you, is that a dance as well?" Sese stopped Victor, fearing how dirty and ugly the dance he would next describe would be.

Sese also felt even though he had listened intensely to the reels of the different types of Glaswegian dances, he could not understand them. And if he could not, no dancing group in Ila would ever. He was particularly irked by the mention of 'kissing', an unsociably labelled act that was publicly, strictly forbidden in Ila, and a behaviour Ilas believed was synonymous with sexual promiscuity. Sese believed that even if the kissing dance was not what he believed it stood for, how about all the others which the tourists said were to be done with men joined with women? How was he to recommend that the superior male spirits should hold the women and dance with them? Which woman would even wait, after seeing what doing something lesser did to Jacq?

"We may not require you to do any of them," Sese finally told them. "But thank you all the same. Our people prefer a dance they can master and partake in without being embarrassed." Then he rounded up with a story on why the Ilas may never need a dance from Glasgow in the end:

"All dances were born in Ila in the first place. When the big God sent the first set of gods from the sky to the earth to increase the beauty of the earth, they danced all the way down and arrived first in Ila. There, they turned the natives, their animals and plants to an exceptional beauty, and then danced back to the big God to tell Him they had dutifully completed the assignment.

"'First, sit beside me and let's watch if the creations are truly beautiful,' the big God told the smiling emissary gods.

"When they had obeyed, He had another question for them: 'What do you think?'

"'They are very beautiful,' they jointly replied as they watched Ila humans, animals, plants and insects moving about."

"'They are not,' the big God disagreed. 'A truly beautiful creation shows it on its face and in its legs: it smiles and dances. None of them is doing any of these because you forgot to teach them. Now, go back and add smiling and dancing to their lives; and then you can come back and finally sit down with me.'

Sese said the gods ran back to Ila and there successfully gave the lessons to all creations that breathed in the kingdom. That was how Ila became the origin of dancing, singing and smiling. These gifts were always radiated by citizens of Ila whether they were happy or sad. Equally they were by their horses and donkeys with or without loads on their backs, by fishes and reptiles in and out of Ila waters, by plants and trees when being planted and uprooted, and by insects of Ila whether at biting or stinging! Principally, the annual festival was an opportunity for everything to dance, and dance – from the reserve they had kept from the previous festival. Sese concluded Ilas' was therefore a superiority the tourists could never match. Instead, Victor and Uggi should learn and do the dances of Ila.

"But how could we, within two days and two nights that separated us from your finale? Uggi asked. "It's impractical."

"Simple, you can. You can..."

Had Victor not followed Sese's assertion with a clearing of throat, Uggi would have commenced questioning Sese's sanity ever before Sese would go any further with his inspirational belief.

"Through the voices, limbs, and drums of Ilas you can, and will. Just watch how they sing, move and dance, and copy them as much as you can. Any further balancing or addition that is required will be spotted and done for you by the guides."

Sese was confident their movement would be adequate enough for the occasion. He even warned them never to over-dance once they were in the costumes of the spirits, because the costumes automatically imposed certain mystic powers of skill and energy on the wearers. Dancemaster overdid it and it ended in his self-destruction! They must keep a safe distance from their followers so that no form of dangerous familiarity would occur. They must not allow the women to rush them with gifts, as the women could use the ploy to get dangerously familiar. They must always remember they were the spirits.

Next, Sese took up the lesson in prayers with Victor and Uggi.

"As far as prayers and supplications are concerned," he started, "my Almighty wants you to know that our people are always full of their personal wishes. That includes me, my Almighty, and the spirits of our forefathers. My Almighty always arranges how these wishes are passed to their intended heavenly destinations, while I humbly assist him in some other small ways towards achieving this. He is happy that you have fitted well, more than anybody else, into this aspect of Ila culture. He knows you have a local language in Glasgow, and that there is nobody here who understands it. At the top of your prayers for the people, and at the highest of their gifts, use the language passionately."

"You don't mean we should do some pattering, or talk in tongues to them, do you?" Uggi asked.

"Exactly what they want! When you talk in tongues and tones, they will believe you are a super spirit who can guarantee a faster delivery of their wishes to their forefathers. They believe the language of the ordinary is to the ordinary, of the deep is to the deep, and of the spirits is to the spirits. They will believe that your Glasgow dialect, for being beyond their understanding, is all that is needed to speak directly with their dead forefathers. They will also believe that will save them from waiting endlessly to see their forefathers in their dreams."

"But I still don't see the point," Uggi insisted, "because none of them will understand the patter or the prayer."

"The point again? It is that wishes, assumptions and hope are the core of prayers. Pre-understanding any of those only cheapens the prayers and put them out of respect. Even where people are cursed in tongues they don't understand, they are happy to assume they are being prayed for – and therefore shout AMEN!"

"So, does it mean nothing will be in your local dialect?" Victor wanted to know.

"Of course, there will be many – some of which would equally sound like tongues to you. They have their special powers that we have benefited from over the centuries. You will be taught their generic basics. From where you stop, the guides will take over."

"Interesting, can we also have a bit of them now?" Victor asked.

"They are about acquiring cheap monetary wealth, good luck, victory over opponents, escapes from dangers, discovering rebellious cover-ups, finding love and suitors, safe delivery of pregnancies, peace in the homes, and bumper harvest from the farms. Also in these modern times, it is about graduating from being bike and horse owners to car and lorry owner-drivers. Something in that order, each with unlimited depth and width."

The tourists derived some amusement from what they saw as the idiocy of typical Ila prayers. They agreed to learn them, and eagerly asked for some simple recitals.

"Lastly, Victor and Uggi, my Almighty wants you to know that as the star spirits of the finale, individuals and groups would approach you to arbitrate in quarrels. They believe you have all the wisdom to do everything. If they come, don't bother to analyse the disputes. On an important day like that of the finale, you don't allow any analysis to vie with the principality. Instead, just impose instant fines on the parties – for damaging the special day of their ancestors. The fatter-cheeked, more pot-bellied, or the smoother-skinned of such a party must be ordered to pay the higher fine. Or you could order your guides to transfer the parties to Fire Spirit."

* * *

Early morning of the finale, and the two horses provided by the palace for Victor and Uggi for another market, the Royal Market, were ready. It was a market much nearer to the palace than the Main Market. They had a full couple of hours to see and study firsthand how the masquerades, as the spirits of dead Ilas, normally put into practice the type of comprehensive training the two of them were given inside the shrine.

As they cantered down the streets, the tourists cherished their new but purposeful esteem, however vain. Most distinctly, the presence of the duo of a white and a black man riding high along the streets showed them off majestically.

The streets were exceptionally clean, and so were the users very gay. Many doors, windows, animals and trees along the streets had colourful cloth strips and ribbons tied on for the great day. Everything around the palace and the square was in a festive mood.

"Why didn't they show us these at the beginning? Uggi asked. "Why that horrible experience first?"

"Well Uggi, today is a special day," Victor replied, "and we could only look forward to it ending beautifully."

"Yes, we deserve it; and I hope they know we do."

Victor and Uggi approached the market from the palace direction. At the entrance they dismounted from the horses, tied them to the posts, and walked into the market.

They already learnt the market was as old as the palace itself, and that it was initially established to make shopping for food easier for the members of the royal family and their friends. Why it wasn't called the more deservedly Women's Market they wouldn't know. All the stall owners, and almost all the shoppers they came across there were women. Its individually roofed and open sheds notwithstanding, the near planlessness still buried it in a slum category.

The passages around each shed were very narrow. Those of them that were neither tarred nor well prepared had their surfaces hollowed down by inevitable, same-spot, footsteps. The deeper the foot valleys, the more the shoppers rubbed their bodies against each other as they slid past.

Each stall accommodated a maximum of two tables standing towards the passages. Depending on the type, the foodstuffs were displayed either directly on the tables, or in-trays on top of them. The displays were such that they allowed the browsing or actually buying shoppers, as well as the dusts and flies, to partake in the touching as much as they wished.

Two men held up the foot flow about a dozen densely packed bodies away. With their backs turned to the approaching Victor and Uggi, the men appeared quite ordinary. Because the line was packed, the tourists were unable to figure out in the first instance what was happening around the two men to cause the long bottleneck that originated from them. The tourists could however notice a directionally uniform gaze that each passer-by made at them, with each gaze slowing down further the movement of the marketers.

Five standing bodies away, the tourists could hear the men croaking some prayers to the stall owner they faced. Then they realised the croakers were junior masquerades. Each of them wore a wooden, butterfly-carved facial mask that allowed vision through two small piercings. One's was yellow, the other's blue. The prayer rained persistently until the stall owner, a woman, had to ask them which of her food items – dried peas or rice – they wanted as a present. The one with the yellow mask pointed to the tray of peas while the other pointed to that of rice. She gave each man a measure of his preference and received a payment of more prayers.

At the end of the prayer, the tourists were surprised to see the masquerades specifically turned to them. "Hello, our visitors from Glasgow," one of them greeted. "Do you want all or some of the gifts?"

"Oh no, and thank you for the offer," Victor responded. "And felicitations for the day and season!"

The masquerades were pleased with the refusal. With competitive rapidity, each one shoved the kilo weight grains into his prepared body pouch and moved on to the next stall.

The next set of junior masquerades they encountered dressed perfectly like women in purdah. Like those of the first pair, they were full of prayers in songs. But unlike the first, the songs were in terrible squeaks boosted with double sambaing and light footwork.

"Felicitations, our fathers from heaven," the stall owner greeted them, even though their squeaks and way of dressing presented them more like women. "Thank you for stopping at mine this year. Which here is your item of choice – cooking oil or fresh eggs?"

"Aha," one responded without pre-offering some thanks for the offer. "Your fathers in heaven would want none of them. They have already got them in abundance. They want money. Just money."

She dropped a note and some coins into the palm of each masquerade; and more prayer songs followed as the masquerades closed their palms and moved on.

All these got Uggi more curious. "Victor, are we supposed to be doing all these?" he asked. "Is this the type of behaviour Jap and Sese wanted us to come here to see – and learn, and do?"

"No Uggi, I don't think they expect us to do any of these. These must be for smaller masquerades only."

"But then, if the small masquerades must and could insist on taking away personal items from the poor market women, how far would big ones like we are going to be, go? Do we just pack all their wares on their donkeys and take off with them? And if they protest, do we threaten them with the whips and machetes that are a part of our attire?"

"Of course, we won't do any such thing, Uggi. Just the appearance, dancing, and a few words. As Sese promised, good guides are going to be with us."

"Anyway, cutlass and whip are not for me," Uggi said. "That's one thing I have thought over and decided against. What if one should fall in an accident – and fall on one's own blade? Good Lord forbids."

"Come on, Uggi, all those are standard part of the attire; and are especially complementary to it. They should be the least of our worries today. We haven't seen anyone misusing them, have we?"

"Yes, we saw Jacq almost put to death with a machete."

"No, they were going to use either a rope or a pyre."

"So what are you saying, Victor? Evil is evil, whichever way it is defined. I am not allowing any of those items with my attire."

Victor successfully pleaded caution for the sake of their anticipated objective. They agreed to ditch the machetes and leave the whips on, just when a bugle call started from the palace, and was being repeated in the market.

"Tu tu tu, ta ta ta…!," it went on up and low, hard and soft, but all the same, purposely piercing, and sparking off a rowdy pack-up, lock up and mass flight among everyone in the market. The call was a last one, ordering them to vacate the last market session of the last day of the festival, if they were yet to do so. The market was supposed to be used early in the morning; and must, for whatever reason, be well over before the sun would be overhead. The wise buyers and sellers were long gone before the bugle, or were packed up and ready to go at it.

Within minutes, a swarm of junior masquerades descended on both the market and the remaining market users. Though the masquerades were lightly attired generally, their appearances were more intimidating and their behaviours very violent. Victor and Uggi were sure they did not see any of the masks or attires they wore among those displayed in the hall. Perhaps, they thought, it was because they were not as important, or that there's no space for them. As they ransacked all passages, stalls and fleeing market users, the small bells of metal and local pods they had round the wrists, ankles, waists and necks emitted harsh noises that caused more confusion, which the masquerades happily fed on.

The tourists watched unbelievably how a fleeing lady had to buy her exit from the masquerades with some money; how another had her sales tray full of corns wrestled off her and the corns carried away by the masquerades; and yet, how a third with a large basin full of live catfish had to throw it away together with its fish in order to escape being caught and beaten up by two masquerades who were chasing her, her wares being their main target. They saw the two masquerades terminating their pursuit to gather the two-dozen or so gasping-for-breath fish that were scattered over a large area of the bare floor, and carrying them away. The high noon of the finale had arrived, and with it the spirits of the dead ancestors of Ilas, with all the violence and naked robbery they imposed in the name of culture.

CHAPTER FIVE

The Finale

When King Japeedoe made his entry – certainly, his most triumphal ever – into the square, he was greeted with a frenzy that grew even higher the moment he got off his horse's back.

The entry party, a mixture of humans and spirits was modestly large. Most notable among the humans was his queen, Azzanaite, also riding side by side with him from the palace. She was flamboyantly decked with beads and gold chains, and heavily bangled on her wrists and ankles. Planted stone studs glittered on her eyebrows, atop her upper lip, and round her ears. Hers was a deliberate show of rare gemstones whose excavation was exclusive to Ila. So soon, her sacrifices at the cemetery to her long dead parents were yielding handsome dividends!

The staff bearers, all palace servants, were also an important part of the human group. Each of them, in double loin cloths wrapped round his waist, carried an insignia of King Jap's authority – a large bow and arrow, a tall staff with a beaded crown top, a large white calabash with lid, and a gold blade that was too wide, too long and too expensive to fit for a fight. What each of them carried was more important than the bearer, even, to him, the bearer. Therefore, he moved carefully to avoid a fall, while at the same time acting as a friendly guide to the royal group.

The accompanying band was made up of trumpeters, flute players and drummers, some of who managed more than one instrument as they marched along. The sound from the band boomed beyond being loud to being deafening; it rose above the frantically thunderous noise of the mammoth crowd.

Wisely enough, both King Jap and his queen did not allow the rhythm to madden them. They curtailed their dancing to within the galloping on their horses, royally shaking their heads on their necks, and their legs in the saddles, as their animals made majestic strides into Kings Square.

Getting the royals off the horse was a drama of amusement in itself. It happened just as the party were at the canopied side of the square. The four heftiest slaves in the group did it, beginning with the queen. When these perfect lifters raised her into their arms, Jap's face showed no jealousy at the men who had to cuddle his queen unavoidably in the process. The king knew none of the men had a chance of advancing any amorous thought his action could stir, since he was nothing but an overfed-for-strength-only palace eunuch, one who could go no further with a woman, even in the most private section of darkness. Next, they moved over to King Japeedoe, carefully entangling his massive parachute-like garment, before gently putting him down like a two-year old baby some ten feet from the royal chair.

At first, he drifted towards his seat, a distinguished wooden carving of very loud self-projection. Its backrest depicted a crown; its armrests, an elephant each; its seat, two-inch thick wood; and its circular stem, a set of figurines of kneeling women and children. The entire stool, with the exception of the seat's thickness, was painted golden yellow. The thickness was painted black, allowing the sets of objects it separated to be easily viewed. Queen Azzanaite's stool, though similarly constructed, was smaller and less striking.

The masquerade, Fire Spirit, was already in the square awaiting the arrival of the royal train. With a few other masquerades, he occupied the opposing side to the royal seats. There, as the most senior, he was supreme. If he wasn't, the glowing flame on his head, with which he dangerously jumped and danced up and down like a mad idiot, and his occasional stops to do some magic acts or watch his junior masquerades do some, forced the crowd to recognise his supreme seniority. Throughout the time their acts lasted, his junior masquerades paired up in turns to stand guard over a small, domed canopy placed over a spot on the ground. The guarding became more intense when the king arrived and Fire Spirit and other masquerades already in the square had to switch to dancing down to welcome him.

Only King Japeedoe knew he was not going to take his seat yet. Going by the age long tradition, he should take it straightaway. That tradition, he had decided to change for the day's occasion. First, he had arrived earlier, ahead of every senior masquerade except Fire Spirit, because he had his new masquerades to show. Secondly, before the senior masquerades would arrive, he wanted to warm himself into the hearts of his subjects by dancing to the four sides and corners of the square.

One of the servants, a fat one, quickly went to Jap's designated throne and sat in it, barely touching it with his buttock before shooting up again. Mysteriously, it was done for the imagined safety of King Jap. If for any reason an unknown enemy of the king had secretly planted some evil spell on the chair, such evil would prey on the servant who first sat on it. For the same reason, bringing the chair from the palace and returning it there after use was made the responsibility of a special team headed by the same fat slave.

"This way, and good music!" King Jap commanded his train, his white teeth brilliantly flashing what looked like a spotty extension of his white crown. Then, the music roared to set him loose for the first ever pre-commencement royal dance. With him giving the direction, his party had no option but to follow him round in the dance.

Intoxicating music had its birth in Ila; and the band wasted no time in starting to celebrate its birthday. So, off went the music, with the leading gong talking drum thundering:

Father remains father
Whether you throw yourself down further
Out of jealousy
And break your neck.

Father remains father
However much the child is a puffer
You are the father of Ila
Whatever anyone may want to say.

"I have never seen our Almighty dance as happily as this in this square," an excited lady said to her lady friend. She frantically tiptoed to gain enough height for a clearer view from her position behind the first row of the crowd.

"But why are you surprised?" the friend asked her.

"Oh, well, not any more now. But what happened to the new masquerades they promised us last festival?"

"Last festival? No, the promise is three festivals late and stale now. May be it will eventually come; may be never."

"Really?"

"Well, going by what had filtered out, it was rumoured that Jacq wouldn't let the king."

"But how did that woman grow into such a monster? Can anybody imagine a mere woman denying our population the chance of having a new masquerade? It is something that not even her husband had the power to do. She is definitely more than a normal human being – she must have been a spirit disguised as a woman."

"No, she is not. If she is, she wouldn't be caught at all, and wouldn't have remained in her current situation.

"But then, why should any woman pity her? Her behaviour has put every woman under suspicion. Thank God that she single-handedly over-beat her drum to a note of burst."

Just then the king's musicians changed their rhythm and notes:

Who will ever attempt crossing your path?
Only the foolish crawler-plant
That would dare cross the elephant
And give the elephant
The chance to trample on it and devour it.
Almighty King Japeedoe, who?

On arrival at the domed canopy, the king's party gently slowed down – and stopped – for Fire Spirit to take over and make his speech.

"My dear Ilas, your attention, please!" Fire Spirit screamed out. "When a date is given, however far away, it will surely come. It will, because no mortal has the means to delay or imprison the movement of the sun, or of the moon, or of a day. For a couple of years, we have been expecting the arrival of the greatest ones our ancestors promised us. I am delighted to tell you they have arrived. Today therefore, on this spot and now, you will join my Almighty to welcome the spirits of the spirits, the Jemba Couple, into our midst."

A short burst of musical response where every instrument around partook instantly greeted the end of Fire Spirit's last sentence. The end of the burst synchronised itself to terminate the very moment Fire Spirit, assisted by two of his masquerades, removed the canopy that was placed over whatever it was above. Then, with anxiety, it was all silence again.

"Won't you clap to welcome the Jemba Couple?" Fire Spirit shouted again, charging the crowd to recognize the feat.

The crowd's response lacked a clear definition. Two masked heads on the bare floor? But they were turning – turning two full opposing circles each – stopped – facing the crowd – really... really!

"Fe-li-ci-ta-tions. Fe-li-ci-ta-tions," the masked heads shrieked on the floor in strange, extraterrestrial tones of spirits that had never visited planet earth before.

"Now, won't you clap?" Fire Spirit asked again, this time with frenzied passion.

It was unthinkable, and had never happened before, that a bodiless spirit visited a known kingdom. Now it is happening in broad daylight inside the Kings Square of Ila! In the past were stories of the powerful Aroso mask appearing without a carrier to some citizens; but then, in nightly dreams. A few people, at first frightened by what was happening inside the square now, felt like fleeing. But then, King Jap who they would have run to for protection was right there with them! Everybody and every instrument, without an option, started to 'clap'.

"What is unfolding? And what will, next?" the tiptoeing lady asked her friend.

"Well, you are now asking questions after you have given the wrong answers. You spoke too early."

"Now, I believe I did." So did most citizens – silently or vocally. "This is unbelievable. It is pure magic!"

Swiftly in the heat of clapping, Fire Spirit deployed a shield of six of his junior masquerades round the heads of Jemba Couple and himself. The actual shield was of the tabard of dried hide which each of them wore on top of his basic costume; it kept Jemba Couple completely away from the public glare. Then, Fire Spirit and two of his junior masquerades pulled Jemba Couple up the hidden steps in the ground, out of the hole they were delicately placed earlier before the crowd gathered in the square. A good landing on the surface of the earth had now been accomplished. As soon as their feet were stabilised on the ground, and before the members of the joyous royal party would start dancing back to their seats, twelve Dane guns were fired into the sky to welcome the spirits. Then, the drums broke loose:

> *Welcome to earth, great ones,*
> *Welcome to Ila. Are you well?*
> *Give me not out of your food, 'cause it's worms.*
> *Give me not out of your drink, 'cause it's muddy water.*
> *Welcome to earth, great ones,*
> *Welcome to Ila. Are you well?*

"But where is heaven?" the tiptoeing lady asked her friend yet another question.

"Why? Do you want to go now?" her friend responded.

"No, God forbid; I prefer my earth! I only want to know the direction – whether skywards to which we pray, or to below the ground from where the new spirits have just risen."

"Better you return with the new spirits when they are going back. They have at least shown they know one of the directions!"

> *Welcome to earth, great ones,*
> *Welcome to earth. Are you well?*
> *Give me not out of your food, 'cause it's worms*
> *Give me not out of your drink, 'cause it's muddy water.*
> *Welcome to earth, great ones*
> *Welcome to earth. Are you well?*

King Jap soon arrived back at his seat after a dance-round with Jemba Couple, Fire Spirit and his original party. As he fly-whisked in all directions, his seat carrier repeated the earlier sitting ritual. The king, satisfied that he had adequately greeted those present, occupied his 'golden' stool.

At first, Jemba Couple had their stools specially positioned beside Queen Azzanaite who separated them from the king. As they gazed at each other through their facial nets, the ironies of their current position came pouring into their minds. Five days ago, the atmosphere was tense; now it was relaxed. Five days ago, they were mere foreign tourists, but today, most special native masquerades. Then, the king's face was covered; today, it was theirs that were. Then, both the king and Fire Spirit dominated the gathering; now, they, the tourists, were sharing the prominence with the royals without anyone recognising their faces and voices. A great transformation indeed!

On the other hand, they felt lonely. Most of the faces around them were new. They wondered why Sese Abram was not in the current royal group, keeping their company and taking care of something for the king. The last time they saw him was hours back when they were putting on the attire of Jemba Couple. Then, Sese had assisted them with the fitting; and reminded them to carry along the whips if they couldn't the machetes. Uggi, the male of the couple had repeated how unnecessary that was – that the whips would make them appear cruel. Sese had countered him in turn, drawing an example from King Jap who was noted for only carrying the sword to demand fear and respect, and not to carry out an execution. He had repeated that even if an execution had to be carried out, the king never drank blood! The couple must therefore carry the whips not for any other thing than to gain fear, respect and space, irrespective of how efficient their guides were.

* * *

At first it was two men, each with a long cultivated plant whip in hand, who chased each other into the middle of the square. There, they stopped and commenced lashing ferociously at each other's naked body. Next, four more from the second road into the square joined in, in the same fashion. Then, about ten each entered from the third and fourth roads. Within a twinkle of the eye, more of the naked-to-the-waist men had invaded the square from all directions and were fully engaged in the vicious battle of the body lashing, pain and endurance. The spectators clapped and roared with pleasure as they waited eagerly to see which of the combatants would be the first to drop or withdraw due to torn flesh or blood spillage.

Victor twirled and wriggled in imaginary pain as whip strokes whistled round the bare flesh of the competitors. Soon, he adjusted himself imaginatively to absorbing them. The situation was now fully arena- and gladiatorial-like again, backed by satanically intoxicating music. He was however pleased that each of the floggers was equally equipped, unlike what it was five days ago, or in the Roman film he once saw.

After a long, tough twenty minutes, King Jap signalled all music to stop for the royal band to lead the applause for the combatants. His instruction was being obeyed when he rose and slowly waved his whisk at both the crowd and floggers. He was highly elated that another first was being recorded during his reign. The annual whipping had lasted longest, and without any of the young participants dropping out or dropping dead. It signified that his young men were the bravest in the generational history of Ila and its immediate environs. It meant he now had among them, enough to promote into the rank of junior masquerades that would hide around to snatch offerings at cemeteries and shrines, plunder the stubborn market women, and ruthlessly carry out the job of policing during cultural celebrations. He would have no trouble in selecting the best and bravest of such junior masquerades into the rank of the exceptionally daring men allowed to wear the highly privileged senior masks and costumes.

All of a sudden, the tempo of the music was increased, and it sent Fire Spirit into the centre again. He marched round menacingly to the king and knelt down for a long courtesy. When he rose, he continued to the whippers and gestured a stop-and-dismiss order to them. While being slowly obeyed, he announced the arrival of the acrobatically multi-talented eléwe masquerades, to a change in the source and type of music. Eight new masquerades, two from behind each corner of the square, and a single band for all of them, danced in. Like the Jemba Couple, their attires were new all through, and the design motif on each of them different. Each main cloth was a medium-weight piece simply covering the head to the waist, with side slits to reveal the forearms down to the hands. Another slit coarsely netted across the position of the eyes, was long and wide enough for easy vision.

The back part of the waist above the buttock had five belted rows of palm-size, leather-covered lightwoods. The belts smartly tucked away the loose end of the attire. The covering leathers were of very bright colours and perfectly geometric, bodkin-crafted designs. At the lower end of each covered lightwood were attached six equally bright coloured, woollen tassels which beautified the dangling hang-down.

The shorts were Bermuda styled, stopping a couple of inches above the kneecaps where tens of small bells were attached. After the bells and below the exposed knees, as well as on the exposed lower arms up to the wrists, were single wraps of leather gaiters. The masquerades wore neither shoes nor gloves; but each held a rectangular hand fan woven of bleached jute.

The common band had six members including a six-year-old boy. Each talking drum, *bàtá* type, was long, round, hollowed and double ended. Because the circumference of one end was much bigger than that of the other, the overall shape cut between being conical and cylindrical. Each end was leather-membraned and heavily tinselled round. A wide leather belt attached to both ends of each drum allowed the drum to be hung down frontally round the drummer's neck. The length of the belt was adjustable to positions where the drummer could comfortably palm-beat the bigger end and at the same time leather-beat the smaller one.

The guide to the eight masquerades signalled a snap stop to allow his spirits accord the king the annual, customary respects. This was followed by one of them song-praising the king with a solo that was being momentarily authenticated by the leading drummer's short bursts of drumming. The guide signalled his masquerades to start their act; and this prompted the *bàtá* music to resume with fuller force and the people to go wild with excitement:

> *Masquerades, masquerades, watch the ground*
> *Spirit, spirit, watch the ground*
> *Caution, beware, beware*
> *Be careful!*
> *Caution, beware, beware*
> *Be careful!*

In a flash, the eight masquerades broke into two opposing groups, with each group standing about twenty feet apart. Starting from one group, one masquerade made an exotic dance across to the other side. On reaching the other side, he turned round and returned to the side he started from in fast, multiple acrobatic somersaults. Every masquerade performed this feat flawlessly. After the eighth, the leader of the drummers changed the rhythm to a danceable one:

> *The enemies prayed we wouldn't arrive*
> *When, already, we were on our way.*
> *It's the good fortune that joined us on our way*
> *That had caused a bit of delay.*

> *Almighty, your enemies prayed you wouldn't arrive*
> *When, you were already on your way.*
> *It's the good fortune that joined you on your way*
> *That had caused a bit of delay.*

The tail end of the dance drew out Fire Spirit again. Without endangering the masquerades with the flames on his head, he carefully partook in the dancing. Next, and to the displeasure of the crowd, he drew the acts of the eight acrobatic dancing machines to a close. After the stage was cleared, Fire Spirit announced the king was happy enough and ready to address the festive assembly of Ilas.

"My dear sons and daughters!" King Japeedoe shouted, upstanding and puffing.

"Yes, Your Highness!" the crowd thundered back.

"I call you again – my dear sons and daughters of Ila!"

"Yes, Your Highness!"

"Do you recognise and trust me?"

"Yes our Almighty, owner of all, second only to the Creator." Customarily, the citizens had memorised and reserved that chorus for any reigning monarch of Ila.

"Thank you and congratulations. Congratulations several times over, and happy festivities to you all.

"You heard what the drummers of our last performing spirits just said – that our enemies prayed we Ilas didn't arrive. Rightly too, not only were we on our way, we are now home with all the good luck that teamed up with us on our way. It is the enemies that we did not meet at home; because like water, they have dried up or guttered away forever. Isn't that so?"

"Yes our Almighty, very much so!"

"Two years ago, the cloud of hatred was heavy on me, you, and on our dear kingdom. This time last year the cloud was even heavier. And today, our ancestors have made it disappear. They have blown it away to the scorching sun; and the sun has consumed it without the slightest bit of upset to its stomach. Now the liars and segregationists are gone forever.

"What is better celebrated than this beautiful festival of our ancestors? And how is it better done than with welcoming to our soil, the arrival of Jemba Couple, the two new representatives they have specially sent down to bless us. Soon they will take to the floor, listen to you, and dance with you. They will allow you to make your supplications with hope and assurance. They have no problem understanding any language signed-spoken or speech-spoken in this world; the only language they don't speak is the one that has never been formulated.

"Very soon, your other big masquerades – Kaka, Worshipper and Aroso – will join in. Since after midday, they have been on the streets with their people. We are grateful to our ancestors who enabled you to glorify them more this year. The glorifications in gifts are so much that some of them are already arriving here ahead of the donors. I urge you to continue the generosity when all the spirits are finally assembled here.

"Because I, your Almighty, don't want my dancing to outdo my glorification to the ancestors, I am donating those six goats, six baskets of hens and six sacks of grains over there, before the next dancing starts. More will follow from me when all the spirits arrive here. For the love of your ancestors you must also do the same, and give much more. It will not matter whether you have already made a donation at the cemetery, at any of the shrines, directly inside your compound in the past week, or it was just a pledge you have made.

"Congratulations again, my sons and daughters. Have I spoken well?"

"Yes, our Almighty, owner of all, second only to the Creator!"

Kaka and Worshipper, two of the masquerades being expected arrived about the same time. Worshipper, his group approaching from the first direct road into the square, was the first to arrive within its five hundred yards. His thunderous drumming notwithstanding, he could hear Kaka's drums loud and clear coming from one of the other roads into the square. In order that he would dance first at the square, he despatched across to Kaka, an emissary asking Kaka to tarry a little before making his entry. The emissary emphasised to Kaka the facts that Worshipper, was almost inside the square, and he did not want to dash in and dart out for his dance.

Kaka was angry at both the message and its sender. "I, Kaka?" he breathed out loudly before his followers. "I won't say 'over my dead body,'" he retorted. "I won't, because we are both heavenly spirits who can never die. The worst that could happen would be for one of us to go back on an extended stay with our ancestors. So, please tell him, Worshipper, I don't intend to go back; I have covered a longer distance to arrive here. Tell him, I deserve to enter and dance first. Tell him he has to dance after me."

"Why is Kaka now talking of distance when we should be talking of the traditional order of appearance and dancing, which are most relevant?" Worshipper reciprocated in more anger, through Kaka's emissary. "That is tough luck for him. What's distance compared with prompt arrival? Don't they say 'first come, first served'; and that 'the early bird catches the worms…?' All these are of course, if we should brush aside my natural seniority."

"Which only leaves us to meet at the centre and fight it out!" Kaka instantly concluded, boiling and stamping his foot on the floor, and his inner group members and drummers waiting for a call to fight.

"Yes, that's what will happen," Kaka had no illusion about it as he fumed. "Worshipper should admit that his earlier arrival was due to lack of enough people and admirers in his territory, and along his route. If they were there – like they were in ours – collecting their gifts, respect and worship would have delayed him too. What use is his barren area and empty route to our Almighty and the kingdom, what use?" Kaka marched in and beckoned his group to follow him.

His band of six musicians was closest behind him. They were ecstatically playing their aerophones of side-blown flutes and horns, slit down idiophones, and a European whistle. They were almost naked, with only their short knickers on. Some lengths of young palm fronds were tied round the knickers while some more, in combination with long but single upright feathers, were made into tight-fitting head tiaras. As they swerved their heads pounding away, the scenario of a disturbed formation of soldier ants was readily created. The head drummer seized the instigative opportunity to push his big masquerade. He descended his gong on his drum's membrane and changed the tune and the boast:

The Masquerade

> *Mountains are mountains*
> *But no two mountains ever peak the same*
> *We are the higher*
> *The very highest.*
> *They are the lower*
> *The very lowest!*

Kaka's head was frightening enough on its own. It was of two masks. One was an abnormally big head of a buffalo he carried on top of his head, and the other, a large six whiskered human face masking his own. The foot long buffalo horn of juju he held out was red, and its open end covered with black material to which cowry shells were tacked. He made two heavy steps forward, stopped and swerved the mask to the right. He made another couple of steps forward, stopped and swerved to the left. Then he repeated a right and a left step four times with corresponding right and left swerves, and stopped. Next, he ran a few mad steps forward, stopped and repeated the whole sequence menacingly. As the drums boomed, so his followers including his junior masquerades chanted, spurring him to lead them. Thank heavens that the eye slit on his facemask was so narrow that the redness in his eyes and the bulge of their balls were successfully concealed.

The comportment of Kaka's leading guide was quite untrue to custom. It was disappointing of someone in whose hands were entrusted the all-important job of directing a senior masquerade. From head to toe he covered himself in charcoal paste; and had young palm fronds tied round his head, arms, waist and legs. One eye, the left, was pasted with a ring of red, sandwiched between two of white, rendering the eye bigger than actual when compared with his unpainted right eye. He carried with him the second of the pair of horns his boss had. Then, and again, the drummers changed their words of enragement:

> *Which fire is in enmity with the rain?*
> *Do you understand?*

Let it appear if it is brave enough
Do you understand?
Appear if it is tired of glowing
Do you understand?

But Worshipper understood, and so was he brave enough. He was not the bravest of the senior masquerades in performing feats and magical acts; but he was the most elderly and thoughtful, and regarded as being more powerful than Kaka. He understood the recklessness of Kaka, and so did his musicians who simultaneously led him into another part of the square with their own chants:

Despise the elder and abort your growth
Despise Worshipper and meet your doom.
Be wise and live
Be wise for health
Be wise for life.

King Jap recognised a perilous situation now in his hands as Kaka squared up to Worshipper in the open, for a heavenly duel for supremacy. It was still fresh in his memory how a similar duel between two senior masquerades set off a period of doom for his kingdom five years ago. Then, Dancemaster, from Nek ancestors, challenged and defeated the no-nonsense Fire Spirit. Dancemaster's victory, King Jap believed, was one of what emboldened Jacq to start imparting rebellious education on the women citizenry of Ila. And from then, till when Jacq and her husband, Nek, were captured and Dancemaster destroyed, there was a reduction in the volume of annual gifts the citizens offered.

Kaka and his group on one side barked and sneered angrily at Worshipper's group now in the counter-attacking position on the opposing side. Kaka was eager to make it a clear victory over Worshipper. Such a victory would guarantee him a better recognition among the senior masquerades, as well as give him the privilege of ever sharing more of the kingdom's booties. With his followers solidly behind him carrying every juju charm they could muster, he charged forward, ready for the war strike that was already being sung by the drums:

> *Let it tear if it will –*
> *Smash the big leaf, torrents, and*
> *Let it tear if it will!*

Five years ago, Fire Spirit was always the quick and aggressive masquerade – always quicker to attack than to reason. Since the time of his humiliation by Dancemaster, King Jap had assisted Fire Spirit to regain much of his pride, agility and special skill of understanding the language of drums. This particular talent of understanding surfaced him at once before King Jap.

"What are these spirits playing with, my Almighty," he howled?

"Spirit, I haven't got the time to give you an answer. Just go there at once, before they fully become infected by another type of Jacq and Nek virus. I am sorry to mention those vile names again. Go. Go at once, please!"

Fire Spirit was successful. He started by chiding the provocateur musicians of both sides, and went on to calm down the two main masquerades with the threat of immediate and everlasting royal sanctions on them should they move any closer to each other. Next, each of the groups should dance swiftly past the Almighty and then return to the corner allotted to him. There, he must wait until called upon to do his main thanksgiving dance. These instructions were being obeyed when the sound of the music of another senior masquerade, Aroso, rented the air.

By classification, Aroso was regarded as the strongest and bravest of all the masquerades in Ila. Because other masquerades duly recognised his supremacy in charms and magical powers, they never dared him – at least, never singly. A few times in the distant past, the story said, he surprised a formidable gang that mistook his humility for weakness and challenged him in the open. Then, he used his magical powers to control the enemy's consciousness, to hypnotize the gang members collectively. He then sat them glued to the bare floor in the open for seven days. There, he ensured the sun, rain, hunger and thirst beat them into a disgraceful submission before he succumbed to the pleadings of the townspeople and restored their senses.

The story of his magical powers was also connected with a wild beast. It dated back to the time of the mask's first carrier who lived three centuries ago. A brave hunter, he was on a night hunting expedition in the jungle when, all of a sudden, a large female tiger leapt on him from behind, knocking his poisoned bow and arrow off him. He managed to turn himself round and put up a brave fight against the beast. His magical incantations came in handy; with them he dazed the animal of its strength and consciousness. Then, he removed the dagger he belted to his waist, and with it, killed the beast with a single thrust to its heart. When the animal was eventually skinned full length, its skin was attached to the back of his attire forever to show his bravery. The whole attire, the skin included, was removed for cleaning when the tourists were inside the masks hanger three days ago.

On a day like this, typically, he did not want to be arrogant. He would never be, before the ancestors he was duly representing. But he would remind the finale – humbly – what a powerful masquerade he was. Therefore, he did not mind his drummers leading his followers to give his strength a befitting definition:

We are on the march to the market place
Chorus: All marketers hide yourselves.
We are on the march to the market place
Chorus: All marketers hide yourselves.
Aroso is on the march
Chorus: All marketers hide yourselves.
The lion is on the march
Chorus: Tigers hide yourselves.
Aroso is on the march

The Masquerade

> *Chorus: Lesser spirits hide yourselves.*
> *Aroso is on the march*
> *Chorus: Stay clear, hide yourselves.*

Though none of the spectators or the other masquerades went into hiding, but they cleared off his path, allowing him with his followers to go and park on one side and await his turn to dance.

Jap directed Fire Spirit to call on Worshipper to dance first, being the most senior of the Ila's three senior masquerades.

Nothing was that charismatic about Worshipper's mask. Its first part was a circular light wood, three feet in diameter and six inches high. Blue and white cloths in wide stripes covered its flat upper and lower sides before the same were wrapped round the height to make the headwear a large turban. More than less, he looked like a trans-sahara swordsman on foot. One escort walked beside Worshipper, holding up as much as possible the extra tail of five metres extending from his turban's main wrap. The second part of the mask was a wide, white painted human face, well polished, and forever laughing.

Worshipper's followers were all men mostly dressed up like women and revelling among his swordsmen and musicians. Ironically, most of his donors were always women. He was always smart by forcing the women of his chiefdom to pledge and donate weeks before the start of each festival. Then he would collect all the gifts and promises in the first three days of the festival week and had his men carry them down to the palace at once. For Jap, Worshipper's collection usually served as a barometer with which the king guessed the current annual wealth of Ilas, as well as predicted the volume of gifts the kingdom should expect.

Kaka danced next; and his was devoid of the dashing intimidation of the immediate past when he had wanted to engage Worshipper in a fight. Instead of the old appearance of fear, the ringed eyes now showed as rays of coloured beauty. Before Jap, he collected an unprecedented volume of foodstuffs in baskets, and fowls in large wicker cages. He was particularly happy with himself when King Jap openly acknowledged his brilliance with a royal wink.

When Fire Spirit signalled Aroso next into the square to dance, Aroso entered with the largest ever number of fans to follow a single masquerade – up to that time. King Jap was quick to note the pressure this powerful and sociable masquerade was putting up with, in mixing his dancing with collecting and transferring of incoming gifts. So, he mandated Fire Spirit to allow his junior masquerades to help out Aroso, and himself of course.

* * *

When next came the expected prayer and thanksgiving dance with Jemba Couple, it was a woman from the ring of crowd that led it. She danced towards Jemba Couple whose seats were now moved out into the square, directly before the king. The initial steps of the woman were wobbly because she had to cope with the he-goat she neck-roped and leashed, as well as with a year old baby she strapped to her back with a piece of heavy fabric. The more forward steps she made, the higher her spirit became, and the more commandingly she managed her act. Each time she wriggled her body sideways in obeisance to the drums, the he-goat rebelled frightfully and walked to the opposite side, while the baby on her back shook in both ways. Interestingly, the woman coordinated both baby and animal with short steps that were graceful enough to show her brilliant artistry. No sooner was she about twenty steps from her take-off point than she was followed by scores of other similarly dressed women of her group. Unlike her however, no other person in the group carried a visible gift.

"What is it that you want from the Spirits?" Fire Spirit asked the leading woman on behalf of Jemba Couple. Simultaneously with his question, he signalled the music to dampen down. "Your ancestral fathers want to know."

"Good children," the leader answered on behalf of the group, with other members standing behind her. "Good children who will outlive us, who will bury us when we are dead. This is what we ask of you. It is this blessing we want from our forefathers."

"But can we ask you in particular, what you already have on your back?" Victor, the female of the couple, with a shrieking voice that was truly celestial, asked the woman. "Your forefathers want me to ask if you are not getting greedy."

"Great heavenly spirit, it is a boy I have on my back. He is not mine, but my neighbour's. My love for children put him on my back."

"Oh nice; that's nice. Your forefathers acknowledge you as being very kind. They thank you for knowing that your own child does not have to come from your own womb. And because of your kind heart, your forefathers have upheld your prayers. In addition to the one on your back, we, Jemba Couple, the special emissary from beyond, will deliver you of a baby boy before the next festival. The same will be for every member of your group.

"We will dance with you. But let us deliver their special prayers to you first. All of you must kneel down where you are and listen."

Uncharacteristically, silence engulfed the women and the music, allowing the disguised speeches of Victor and Uggi to take over. Their speeches, already scripted, were taken in turn line-by-line in two distinct, highly guttural voices – one coarse and masculine, the other faint and feminine. Twice, one spirit called Jackal Masquerade and standing by interrupted the lines with a loud "Hahaha, hahaha!" which Victor and Uggi discovered to mean "amen and good luck".

Uggi, in the male outfit started off the incantatory prayer:

Uggi: Barrenness is now banished from you all –
Victor: As it is from $ẹdá$ rat of multiple births.

Uggi: In multiples ever are the grains of maize plant;
Victor: In multiples come the tubers of a cassava plant;
Uggi: Multiple is the number of eggs in the fish row.
Victor: Never, never do you find it –
Uggi: A barren banana plant by the riverside.
Victor: This time of next year without fail,
Uggi: You will all carry to this piazza,
Victor: Before the spirits and forefathers of Ila,
Uggi: Your new babies on your backs,
Victor: With more foetuses in your wombs,
Uggi: And your generous presents in your hands.
Victor: So shall it be;
Uggi: So we have destined –
Both: Destined, destined, destined!
       Destined, destined, destined!!
Jackal masquerade: Hahaha, hahaha!

"So, rise now and dance well like the maggots," Fire Spirit, taking over at the end of the prayer, commanded. "But don't go away yet. The spirits have to sprinkle you with the heavenly water of fertility as you dance past them. Then, donate well and pledge well as you dance out, so that the water may stick permanently to you, and you shall be more grateful this time of next festival.

"Now, you, their leader, stretch out your hands and open your palms."

The woman obeyed without fright. The palms were touched by the Couple's wet-ended whisks repeatedly.

"Rub your palms together and then rub your face with them," Fire Spirit further commanded.

She complied, extending the rubbing to both the face and the skull of the child on her back.

"This exactly is what all your members will now do," Fire Spirit instructed loudly. Then he beckoned to the band to resume the music.

"*Child, child, oh child,*" went the head drummer with his talking drum. The message was instantly caught by other drummers in the band as well as by the child seekers. They already knew how it went and ended:

> *Child, child, oh child,*
> *Love you so much*
> *To have you, the true clothing.*
> *Child, child, oh child*
> *Love you so much*
> *To have you, true human existence.*
> *Child, child, oh child*
> *Love you so much*
> *To have you, true family continuity, post-parted.*

The Couple responded by standing up to dance with the women. Their steps were heavenly – truly beyond King Jap's wildest envision. A much carried away Fire Spirit turned to out-stage the two guides he assigned to Jemba Couple by transforming himself into a dancing and gift collecting guide! As the couple from heaven danced with the women of the earth, they dipped the tips of the two whisks they had with them into a bowl of water carried by a special appointee and sprinkled the water on the women. In turn, the women danced madly to receive it. Next, their men on standby, danced in. Each man led a live he-goat – intentionally not she-goat – to show how badly each woman wanted a son. They eventually danced out with their women through the special side exit prepared to receive such gifts. In their minds, the special atmosphere had confirmed their forefathers would grant the favours they all sought.

More groups appeared before Jemba Couple as scheduled by King Japeedoe through Fire Spirit. Each was happy, hopeful and generous over its aspirations: want of husbands and wives, big houses, jobs, better jobs, victory over known and hidden foes, and want of lorries and cars, the new wonder gadgets taking over Ila township.

At the turn of the group seeking husbands and wives, Fire Spirit urged them to donate generously from the bottom of their hearts and the depth of their pockets. He allowed them a longer time of intimate dancing, with the calculation that it would spark off an early, natural acceptance of their prayers by the spirits – and guarantee more lovely presents come the next festival.

Good and better luck seeking group. That was the group that last took to the stage before Jemba Couple, as the sun was beginning to set over Ila and the year's festival.

The group, in all actualities, was beyond one. That it was the largest – so large that the number of its devotees was uncountable – presented it as a population. The style of its call-out style was so gripping that King Jap himself stood up, wanting to join it. The sight of a rain of visible and invisible presents, and the diligent speed with which they were being carted away by Fire Spirit's appointed aides were not enough to make Jap realise positively how lucky he was already. For the first time in his reign, he got enough of good luck to thicken his thinking. He waved his flywhisk wildly at the crowd, eased himself out of the royal chair, and was on his first steps to the group at the center. Greedily, he became a thieving ruler searching for more luck!

At this point in time, Fire Spirit commandeering a sharper sight and a faster speed swiftly arrived at King Jap's and reminded him of his position in the kingdom. He was the one and only Almighty of the kingdom, the real good luck, who mustn't be seen asking for more, but for giving some to his praying subjects!

At that moment, it served no useful purpose pitying some masquerades that were deserted by their followers joining the good luck prayer group. Some masquerades had actually joined the group and enjoined their defecting followers to donate generously to it. It was so riotously revelling that as soon as a part of the group had finished praying before the Couple and moved out, another group or part-group immediately replaced it. Again, King Jap, sensing the danger being posed by the prevailing scrambling, ordered Fire Spirit to act.

"Space! Create space!" Fire Spirit yelled at the four guides – the original two now doubled – now serving Jemba Couple, and struggling to cope with the high volume of incoming gifts. His flames too had extinguished; and moments ago, he had cleverly blown some of the toxic drugs used for the tourists' initiation to the faces of the Couple, slowly intoxicating them.

"They will choke you up, my spirits!" Fire Spirit shouted the warning to Jemba Couple. "Clear them off – with me!" He was sure his drugs had taken the Couple over.

"But how?" Victor shouted from under the female costume. "We don't have lashes!"

"Your whips! Your whisks! You have both; use them! Don't hold the rod and give the dog a chance to bite you! Use them!"

Now, Victor his senses already lost to the drugs from Fire Spirit, obeyed madly, and without suspecting who Fire Spirit truly was. Not satisfied with using his whisk to beat away the crowd around him, he snatched a long whip off a guide and lashed ceaselessly and mercilessly at the crowd, scampering them and cursing them with Scottish phrases.

Uggi, on the other hand, least affected by the drugs, was surprised to discover that the devilish goad was Sese Abram whom both him and Victor had wondered where he was since the start of the festivity.

"So, you are Sese; and haven't vanished into the heavens!" Uggi expressed his surprise.

"Yes, I am. Just as you are Uggi."

"Then, stop the lashing!"

"No, you should join it, and prevent yourself and your wife from being choked. You should lash to create your own space. It's the only thing they understand! She's coping well – can't you see that? It's only canes they understand!"

Uggi realised that his friend had been taken over by some evil forces, that he had to race up to free him from the spells of Fire Spirit as well and from the lashing he was blindly giving to the generous donors.

"Stop Victor or I scream," he talked crisply to Fire Spirit. "You are turning the dancing into stampeding. This is not a collapsed Spanish bull ring. Stop him now or I scream your name – scream who you are; and disrobe you." Uggi's whispered threat was clear enough to Fire Spirit.

"Go on then; and you will be the first spirit to openly die again. You understand that?"

Uggi, totally disgusted at Sese, realised the wastefulness in continuing with the verbal exchange – Sese and his junior masquerades were already smelling cannabis as well as drenched in $ogùro$ and $pitó$, two of the most wicked of Ila alcohols. To his horror, he discovered that Fire Spirit and his men had successfully got Victor heavily intoxicated!

As fast as Uggi could, he wriggled through the agitated crowd and caught up with Victor as Victor dished out more lashes instead of collecting the load of presents the people were still competing to give to him. Uggi could neither think of nor find the answer to why the generality of Ilas, the people of his roots, were so senseless at giving, at taking!

"Stop it, Victor, and remember who you are," Uggi shouted as he struggled to seize the long cane now in Victor's hand. "You are Victor and must behave like Victor. You have been behaving violent, even more than Fire Spirit! You are Victor – Victor Mackinnon, and not any Jemba. Stop it Victor!"

Uggi's words forced Victor to apply the break, which Uggi made permanent by holding him and finally wrestling the whip off him. He urged him it was time to quit the stage.

Obviously too, to the brainy organizers of the most successful festival in Ila, the current happenings were signs of the time to end the carnival. They had achieved enough good luck, and the people could return to their quarters and hope to be followed by what they had prayed for but were yet to receive. So the crowd dispersed from the square with their senior masquerades, to their quarters. There, they continued the revelling late into the night, boosting further the inflow of donations into the pockets of the masquerades. For King Jap, time to stock the bountiful harvest.

* * *

King Jap's proverbial barns were at a great overflow due to the best ever harvest from the finale. They were so full that he wanted a repeat cultivation that would commence immediately and continue into the next festival. He realised that for such a cultivation to happen and end in another good harvest, Jacq and her family must be held for another year, for the next festival. King Jap immediately sold this to Sese and all his other senior chiefs.

"Jaquensica is gravely ill," King Jap welcomed Victor and Uggi with as soon as they arrived for her on Monday morning. By their agreement the king ought to have released her to them immediately at the end of the finale late on Saturday. "She has been ill, in bed and can't be disturbed."

"Strange, Your Highness," Victor responded. "So, what do you want us to do?"

"Nothing," Uggi started to answer before King Jap would, "nothing but to take her with us now and care for her." He was hiding his anger and disappointment.

"You can't now," the king said. "Chief Priest is already seeing to that. He expected her to have fully recovered by Thursday."

"But we have the plan to depart from Ila with her tomorrow," responded Victor. "Can we see her to assess the situation?"

"No, you can't. It is pointless."

"Alright then," said Uggi, unwilling to play into Jap's trap, "We shall wait till Thursday and come for her."

"You won't even have to come, my friends. I will send her to you at the hotel on Thursday," he promised what he wasn't going to do on Thursday, perhaps, never.

The tourists, not sent Jacq on Thursday, returned to the palace on Friday.

"Come to think of it now, my friends," Sese started the bombshell at the tourists, "we have changed our minds. We will not release her to you because we don't want her dead. We learn that extreme cold regularly kills in Glasgow; and we don't want her to be a victim. So, she is not coming with you. She is remaining in Ila."

The tourists could not believe their ears. They had danced brilliantly and kept their own side of the bargain in order to forestall such a decision. Why should Jap or any of his chiefs suddenly care that Jacq they slated for execution would catch a cold? It was now six nights after the festival, and both Jap and Sese are now back-tracking from a pact that was jointly made. Instead of Jacq the only thing Jap had sent to them had been some unimportant gift items – small masks, costumes, beads, diamonds, money, and drinks – that Victor, under the spell of drugs, had demanded from Fire Spirit. Irrelevant gifts!

"Sese, you can't be serious," blasted Victor. "You can't be! With all we have done for you and your kingdom because of Jacq and her family!"

"Look here, my friend from Glasgow," King Jap cut in angrily, "it would be better if you stop this, your nonsense. You did nothing for no one but for yourselves. As far as the business was concerned, we both agreed before we started. And now at its end, we have paid our own price honourably. You opted to accept as a final settlement the best of our costumes, money and wines; and all of these we have promptly delivered to you at the hotel. We did this without minding some terrible atrocities you performed when dancing at the finale. Honourable enough on our side, isn't it?"

Victor and Uggi gave no answer. They did not understand Jap's question or any of his expressions before it.

161

"You know what my friends?" Jap went on, "Since time immemorial when the spirits descended on Ila, no one has ever whipped the citizens of this kingdom as much as Jemba Couple did at the festival. And by Jemba Couple, we mean the two of you. Therefore, my friends, if you want your criminal friend to come with you, visit us this time of next year and we can consider it. And that of course, will depend on whether Jacq herself wants anything to do with you. For now, you would be surprised that she doesn't. Understand now?"

Somehow, Uggi had suspected this all along. His father had warned him about how leadership, reliability, greed and corruption were all ill defined in Ila; and how he must be on his guard during his stay and when mixing with the masquerades at the festival. His father once went as far as likening the Ilas to a people more cursed than cultured. And for Victor, even though he was well aware of the warnings and other stories related to their holiday destination, he least expected the scale of devilry Jap and Sese used to trap him and Uggi. Both men now realised that Sese and Jap had smartly shifted to using Victor, and snubbing Uggi immediately they suspected Uggi was becoming more uncompromising.

Impossible, Uggi also wanted to believe, that Jacq would prefer to remain and die in the murderous and corrupt community of Ila, one that wanted to execute her. He wanted to believe that Jap and Sese had said that about Jacq in order to discourage them from taking her away to her freedom.

He didn't doubt it that Victor had unintentionally soiled himself. By their home standard, Victor's lashing at the finale, his intoxication, and his demand for, and acceptance of gifts on behalf of the two of them, could never be justified. But all the same, he would oppose the king exploiting this to go back on their joint agreement. Happily, Victor's current state of soberness, together with his solidarity with him, was good enough ammunition to fight Jap and Sese with.

"Exactly what I expect from the two of you," Uggi slowly but clearly said to his hosts.

"Which is what? What is it that you expect?" Sese asked with eagerness.

"My father warned me and my friend about what could happen to us here," answered Uggi. "He warned me that Ilas don't honour agreements. And for your information, we got things pre-planned, and are fully prepared for it. You think you can blackmail us through Victor, but no. I knew all along, and arranged with someone who took some photographs and carried away the films he used to safety. The pictures are already out of Ila and are already on their way to Glasgow. So, you can do what you like with us. If you like, you can cut our throats and drink our blood; it does not save the situation. Instead, we want you to realise, and before it is too late, that you have to release Jacq, Nek and their daughter to us, as was in the original agreement. Real trouble will descend on this kingdom if you don't. Full stop."

An affront – one to King Japeedoe, the Almighty of Sese and the Kingdom of Ila! An affront before mighty Sese, the kingdom's human and spiritual chief law officer! What a compound sacrilege!

"Shut up your bitter tongue!" Sese shouted and rose, drawing out from under his garment, a long knife, the apparatus he was synonymous with, and which he always carried about. "Shut up with your threats and arrogance now or I remove that tongue of yours here."

Both Jap and Victor rose simultaneously, Jap struggling to pull Sese back to sit down, and Victor shading off an unperturbed Uggi from a likely attack from Sese. In the end, both parties realised the danger and moved from their two extremes to the centre of the negotiations. King Jap had to bring Jacq out before the tourists to ask her if she wanted to go with them.

"Absolutely no," Jacq replied to Sese's question. "I just don't want to; and I will not," she further affirmed.

163

"So, what next?" Sese asked the tourists. "You have heard clearly what her answers were."

"That's not a problem," Uggi said. "We heard her and would believe her after one thing – just one thing. You have to excuse us and leave her with us for about ten minutes for her to assure us freely. After all, you have kept her with you for a much longer period."

"Are you asking me and my Almighty to vacate this room for you, and let you abscond with her? What a mad joke!"

"Don't worry," the king prevailed. "Where could they ever run to? That would be silly. We give you ten minutes with her, from now. No more. If you try to abscond you won't go far.

"And, Uggi, one thing I have not told you from our findings about who you are: Your great grandfather betrayed the kingdom and had your grandfather smuggled out of Ila as a child. You or your friend must not follow that footstep because you won't go far."

Quite sluggishly, King Jap and Sese cleared themselves out of the hall, leaving Jacq with the tourists. As soon as the door was shut after Sese, the last to disappear, Victor embarked on the persuasion talk with Jacq. "Do you know Jap will execute you if you remain in Ila?" he asked her.

"He would have done that if he meant to do it," she was sure. "He had all the powers, but he didn't do it."

"He had his reasons," Victor said. "And we here, together with the pressure we piled on him, have been those reasons."

"Who can stop any execution or punishment he orders?" Jacq asked. "I know him; no one can." Since the night she was dressed up and brought out to the tourists, she had started to see her reprieve as an act of genuine mercy which Jap would soon extend to her daughter and husband. "Then, he was free to kill me, but he changed his mind."

Uggi felt sorry that Jacq was ignorant of the temporariness of her freedom. The unawareness didn't offend him however: it would be absolutely impossible for a convict already hooded at the gallows to know how his neck was saved, he thought. "We pleaded seriously with him for you. He gave us two conditions the second of which we have fulfilled. The first has to be fulfilled with your cooperation."

"The first condition," Victor started to count and detail, "is that you are banished forever from Ila. For him to be sure, he wants us to take you away with us to Glasgow. It is either he destroys you or we take you away forever to a place that will make him and the kingdom to feel safe. This is the only way he believes you will not again stir up trouble against the state. You have this minute to agree in order to save your life."

"No one will ever take me or sell me off as a slave, if that is what this is all about," Jacq innocently protested, the criminal trade she learnt about in school coming to her mind.

"We are not slave merchants," Uggi assured her, "and we have laboured and risked so much to get to this stage."

"Okay, you are not slave merchants; but has either of you got a wife, a child, a town, or a social environment of your own? What do you call a person who forces the other to abandon all these? King Jap can as well go ahead and terminate my life instead of selling me off. He might as well add my physical execution to the mental and spiritual executions he already carried out on me. I will not leave Ila alone and alive, without my daughter and husband. Only death will make me do that."

"We understand your feeling, Jacq," Uggi continued. "We have also heard some of your people's private comments about you and your family. You staying here to perish will not guarantee the life and safety of that family. But if you come now, you will stop being his hostage and he will not be able to execute you. That could give you a chance to fight for your family."

"Besides, Jacq," Victor added, "the king has allowed us to come back next year. Then we shall plead for freedom for your husband and daughter. But you must agree to save your life first before those of your family can be saved. If you agree now, we shall come back next year."

"Do you promise that?" she could only ask, realising she was between hell and fire.

"Yes, we promise you that," Uggi replied. "And one more thing that time has not allowed us to do: tell you our names. My friend is Victor Mackinnon; I am Kazuggi Jaiye. My father's ancestry was from this kingdom, but long settled in Glasgow. This should assure you we want to help you genuinely. But I am afraid the time King Jap gave us has expired. Have you changed your mind – are you coming with us?"

Just then Sese, the king behind him, violently pushed open the door to the hall, his face still carrying the abhorrence as to how the tourists had made him and his king leave the hall about ten minutes ago. Jacq did not miss the enormity of the hatred on Sese's face. Remembering how powerful Sese had grown in King Jap's command, she realised that the look clearly represented the actuality of what was behind King Jap's calm face. "Your Highness, I will go with them," she said.

CHAPTER SIX

Inside Glasgow I

Actually, Jacq saw her own new era starting at the very point her winged big bird took off in Africa and she was being observed delicately by her rescuers. Before she could comprehend it fully, the overwhelming force of the change dazed her into sleep.

The part she recognised came later in the plane. It was through the strangeness and weight of additional clothing being put on her by Victor who, fearing the effect on her of the cool in-cabin temperature, had wrapped his coat round her chest. It was not that the chill was drastic, but it could certainly be uncomfortable for a first time flyer going from a warm, to a cool temperate zone of the globe. Victor put it over the small blanket she was already served and covered with on her seat.

"What is this?" she softly asked the men she sat in-between.

"My coat," Victor replied. "It should be getting colder for you, and you will need it."

How truthful Victor's assertion was, Jacq didn't know; so, she didn't contest it. As far as dressing was concerned, she was yet to see a sane woman putting on a man's clothing and vice versa in Ila. The only chance was occasional, occurring where and when a few men-masquerades would appear in women attire for laughs.

Equally, she would not contest the assertion now that a sort of slavish mentality had overwhelmed her. As members of very few enlightened citizens of Ila, both she and her husband knew about the animalistic slave trade, which happened between the Ila of old and some other nationalities across the seas. She learnt such nationalities included the British and the Americas in particular. She thought because her and her husband's great-great-great-great-grandparents were in it, the gods must have been visiting its sins on her and her husband as a sixth generation, and on her daughter as a seventh and the last. She was certain that her daughter, Sariya, now in the king's care as announced at the venue she was to be executed, would eventually be killed. She would be, if only for the king to ensure her lineage did not continue. Without being roped, chained, and dragged in and out of the carrier aeroplane, she had become a lone slave. She must ask no questions. It was largely so until they finally disembarked at Glasgow Prestwick International Airport, and were inside Revals, a spacious women boutique at the arrival hall.

"Now, try this on," Uggi directed her. "Let's see how it fits. It should be your size." He was already removing the brown coat on the display rack from its hanger.

"Yes, it should be fine on her," said the female sales assistant who had moved up to them in her course of studying them. "But what size is this you have on?" she turned to Jacq to ask directly.

"I am not sure," she replied. "I don't know my size in European clothes."

"I think that's 12," said the assistant. "Let me get you size 12."

"Thanks," said Victor. The sales assistant returned with the size 12 and handed it to Jacq, exchanging it with Victor's coat which she'd been wearing since the plane journey.

"What a perfect fit for a good, warm *hap*!" the saleswoman complimented the wrap of the merchandise. She added her smiles and nods to show that she was not just acting to boost her sales commission. "Does it feel comfortable, darling? Move near the mirror to have a look."

Sheepishly, Jacq obeyed – too ignorant of Western attire to know how well it fitted, how it hung on her body, how it was paid for, or how the three of them left Revals.

Once she was led into the house she was to share with her rescuers along Whitevale Street, she was shown and left in her room. After they were gone, she had the time to admire her new coat. She gazed at herself before the round mirror of the dressing table in the room she was allotted, and admired her transformed self in the coat. The upper part of her body from the hip up showed in a beautiful curvaceous way she had never seen it before. She made one step back and the lower part bounced back a similar reflection at her. Then, she spun around. The exercise confirmed to her how now, and so soon, she was already a new woman in a new era.

As she appreciated the coat, she thought of how many squirrels and foxes the manufacturers must have killed to produce the outerwear. The number must have been in hundreds, and enough to threaten the existence of these animals and deny future generations of good meat. And high as that number could be, it could only be for the cream and brown furs of the coat, leaving the source of black, its dominating colour, still unknown to her. She had never seen a black fox or a black squirrel; so she believed the black fur must have come from mountain goats – from unfortunate hundreds of them, a number that equalled everlasting loss of a million gourds of rich milk!

She carefully removed the coat and hung it in the double wardrobe part of the dresser. As she did so, she felt the freshness of air – Glasgow's replacing the little sweat her overprotection from the cold had induced. Then, she embarked on other aspects of room management her hosts showed her how to follow. She turned the key and locked herself in for the first night in Glasgow, just two sunsets and one sunrise after she was taken out of Ila. How long, short, peaceful or terrible the new period would be, she did and could not predict. For the moment, and whatever would be that difference, she would switch off the lights and hope the resulting darkness wouldn't be a prediction of what was next in her life. She was ready to go to sleep.

* * *

When, the following morning, she had a knock on her door, it was from an unexpected quarter. She was already up from, in reality, a sleepless night where strangely, the fatigue of the previous day's journey had inflicted no effect on her. With caution, she had finished tidying herself up. She was particularly careful of the bath, as she had never used one before. Back home, her compound's source of water was a deep and ever water-filled well, which was classy as far as Ila was concerned. From the well, water was plumbed into two different heights of standing taps. Those within the first height, numbering four, were just high enough to allow bins, buckets and cans to stand under them for water collection. Those within the second height bracket, well over six feet tall, erected inside each of the three rooms they called bathrooms instead of shower rooms they actually were, were for performing bodily ablutions. She found it unhealthy to remain seated inside a pool of water into which she had scrubbed the dirt from her body, especially those internally from her midriff. Such dirt she trusted, her home shower would have blown down from head to toe without stagnancies. Having done what she could of the situation, she sat on the edge of her bed soliloquising. It was then the knock interrupted that her particular hour of pessimism.

"Oh good morning, Miss," the stranger she opened her door to quickly greeted her in a tone enthusiastic enough to rest her mind. "Do you know who I am?"

"No," she replied emphatically to a man who was clearly disappointed.

"And you have never heard of me?" he asked arrogantly as if to turn Jacq's genuine unfamiliarity to natural dimness. "Never?"

"No; never," she affirmed.

"Strange, that is – never heard of me." He puffed at what was to him, an impossibility happening.

Jacq wondered who this person could be. If anything, he must be a vain and conceited nobody. No truly important person would go and knock on a stranger's door to blow his self-importance. A chief of Ila would even do much better; he would rather summon somebody to his court well after a comfortable post-breakfast self-enthronement rather than ramming a stranger's door at such an early hour. Her eyes caught his bulging-faced wristwatch, which he intentionally flashed at her; it competed with his ugly and paunchy stomach, the type that unhealthily marked out a typical Ila chief.

"But who are you, sir? Would it not have saved time if you could just introduce yourself?"

Jacq felt no pity at seeing the visitor's face ruffled. The next moment, he forced on a smile to dust it. "Well," he said, "Ben; Victor's father, a successful dealer," he finally said, beaming and stretching out for a handshake which Jacq declined to take. "You must be Jacq. I have heard so much about you." He was still confident, her declining notwithstanding.

"Dealer? Oh, I see. Good morning, sir," she eventually responded as she regained her composure from the initial shock. She intensely probed the man with her look.

"They told me you put up a good fight, Miss. Now, I don't doubt that. We had a long phone conversation last night."

"I see," Jacq said, without thanking him. "And who told you what, sir?" She was beginning to show displeasure at the presence of an uninvited visitor who had surfaced to remind her of her horrible past. She was beginning to believe that just as, or more than Ben claimed, a full text of her biography had been released not only to Ben, but also to others she was yet to meet in Glasgow. She was appalled at how so soon on her arrival, Uggi and Victor could so spend the whole night stripping her naked. Painfully too she was convinced, her guests had not presented whoever they told with the true account of her story. If they had, Ben would simply not consistently refer to her as a spinster.

"What else did Uggi and Victor say about me? Was that why you came here so early?"

"Not to worry, Miss. What they said about you was not bad. It was all praise – the type that would make anyone want to meet you. I already planned to pass by on my way to work this morning. That's the main reason why I am here now. Anyway, this is my normal morning route, and we are likely to see more of each other. Enjoy your stay with us in our *Glesga*."

Jacq very much doubted Ben, but her basic unfamiliarity with him and the environment curbed her desire to speak her mind to him. She knew people hardly had time to praise someone or something from night to morning: they never found enough strength for that. Instead, they would rather lend their mouths to weeklong gossip. What plans, she thought, other than those of nose-poking and curiosity, would have pushed one out of bed at that early hour, veer one from one's way to work, and lead one to come and knock on the door of a complete stranger? She felt she was in a cage where anyone could come and stare at her as he would as a typical zoo inmate. So, as soon as Ben left her, she shut her door, completed her dressing up and dashed out again. The talking voices of her hosts suggested they were in the kitchen. She walked to them.

"Good morning Jacq," Uggi, the first to see her accorded her the greeting. "Your first night was nice and peaceful; am I right?" he added cheerfully.

"Well, yes, good sleep," she half-heartedly admitted, "but a bad awakening."

"How was that?" Victor asked her.

"How?" she snarled at what she saw as a clever pretension from Victor. "But what stories about me did you two feed your father with, within this short time of my arrival? He said he'd been told my life history."

"Victor said nothing about you Jacq," Uggi testified. "I was there when Ben arrived."

"How about in the night? He said he and Victor talked about me for most of the night."

"Well," Uggi continued with the exoneration, starting with himself, "I don't know anything about that, Jacq; but you should know that none of us would talk ill of you. You mustn't start to distrust us now. Breakfast is ready on the table. Let's all go and eat."

Uggi's responses were forgivably innocent. He wasn't aware of how long the conversation he knew of went on between Victor and Ben. He wasn't really sure of what the conversation was about. He could remember Victor's response of silence, yeses or noes which were indicative enough for him – that either Victor, his dad, or both, wanted him excluded from it. He was too tired to bother about it anyway, and was pleased Victor chose not to disturb his sleep with it.

In that conversation, Ben wasn't going to laud the rescue effort of Victor and Uggi in Ila. Ben believed it started well with their plea for the release of the prisoners, continued well with the securing of their release, but ended foolishly and immaturely on the tourists' part with the bringing with them to Glasgow of Jacq and her troubles. Ben told Victor it was nice enough for them to isolate the problem, risky enough to assume it, but totally idiotic of them to take such an incautious dive into tackling it. At worst, they could have returned with the little girl instead of with the mother; and by so doing, left the gravest in the community problem for the community to solve. Ben shocked his son when he claimed to know how passionately protective of their subjects every Ila king used to be, how recently such protection had turned into the complete opposite, how the citizens had been coping sheepishly well with the problem, and how the dogs would have better been left to devour the dogs. Ben shocked Victor even more when he claimed to have mastered the belief of the people of Ila that a person's heart could be read through his gazes, facial construction and palms. His late

173

grandfather who taught him added that the readings had to be in the early hours of the morning when the mats or bed linens would have rubbed off any facial chalk an Ila person might have slept in the previous night. It would therefore be necessary for him, Ben, to come over first thing in the morning to apply the tests on the unknown and unknowing Jacq, and determine the type of person she was. Then he would be able to determine if Victor and Uggi deserved any praise at all for bringing her over.

* * *

Just the way Ben's visit planted some elements of distrust in Jacq, so were the food items prepared as Scottish breakfast and set on the table by Victor and Uggi. And like in the aeroplane, to be on her safe side, she silently went for those she was familiar with – tea, and two buttered slices of bread. She wouldn't touch any of the toasted slices: she could not stand the agonisingly piercing noise they made when broken with hands, torn with incisors, or pounded by the molars. She wouldn't touch the oatmeal: it did not appear as though it was going to be smooth enough in the mouth or comfortable enough in its passage down the throat, unlike her smooth corn pap back home. She wouldn't touch what they called *paps*: they were fattened, sugared rolls and completely different from Ila's thick paste of fine grains. She wouldn't touch the boiled eggs either: they might be only half boiled with both the white and the yoke remaining in a sickening, semi-liquid state, like the egg fit for a thieving snake to break in its throat and swallow. She was slow and careful.

"Later today," commenced Uggi on noticing Jacq's difficulty, "we should take a stroll to Barras to shop for more foodstuffs and items of clothing, and for Jacq to see some other parts of the city."

"But we can't go because it's Monday and Barras is only for weekend shopping," Victor reminded Uggi.

"Sorry, I have forgotten that. I will go to the corner shop to get some emergency stuff while we leave Barras for the weekend. Tomorrow we can use to show the city to Jacq."

"Oh no, please," Jacq objected. "Seeing places today or tomorrow is not for me. I am still very tired and could be so for another week. For now, I will be contented with the area I can see from the windows and doors of this house."

"That's equally fine," Victor supported. "You can have your rest. There will be plenty of time to see both the old and the new Glasgow. Here in Whitevale Street, we are in the old Glasgow."

"Old Glasgow?" Jacq suddenly jumped.

"But why such a reaction Jacq? Is anything wrong?" Uggi asked her.

"Nothing really," she replied deceitfully. "But the old section of a city?" she could not help continuing. "Oh, nothing," she forced herself to stop.

Jacq was not going to expose the negative feelings she had always harboured against the old part of a town. Old town, the typical, wicked old township! A place not meant for the normal citizens but for the oppressors of the community! It was from such part that the well fortified community dictator, using trusted and sadistic brotherhood, terrorised the entire community. A smaller but stinkingly rich area, with its wealth ill gotten by milking the larger, new township! The part of a settlement where, just like the fetish the cat practised was aimed at catching the mice, the various weird rituals and idolatry sacrifices it carried out were to whip the larger township into fearful, silent obedience. When a citizen in the old township dared a rebellion, however rudimentary, he was expelled to the new town after being treated to an out-of-proportion deterrent. Such disproportions ensured the larger community remained blindfolded from knowing the exact size, ugliness and arrogance of their torturer. A smaller section which, fearing the intrusion and destruction of its myths, would unleash all it could in order to cow the larger new town into submission! To her, a typical old city was

175

the palace, the Kings Square area of Ila. It was from there the then reigning monarch granted favour to her great-great-father-in-law and moved him to beyond Bilitie area of new Ila to wear and manage Dancemaster. It was that favour her family still kept up to the time of her imprisonment, when the privilege was withdrawn by the powers from the old township. The new city area of Ila was bigger, cleaner and more buoyant, but the shots usually came from the old sector. She believed that as it was with Ila, so must it have been with any major settlement, old Glasgow included. Her fear of the part her hosts called Glasgow Green started at once.

"Come on, Jacq, your 'nothing' sounded quite loaded," Victor remarked after a while. "Why don't you offload it on us?"

"There's nothing to load or offload, Victor. It is only that I am not keen now. Maybe that will change by next weekend. Then we can see the old first, to tell me something about the new, and whether I should continue. But I am not promising."

* * *

The first Saturday after their arrival in Glasgow saw Victor and Uggi take their guest out on the excursion. The hosts were confident the outing would cheer her up and prepare her for any future plans they might intend for her.

Convincing her for the outing was not easy. Endlessly, and with hyperbolic and graphic description, Uggi and Victor jointly and in turn presented names and people in the metropolis to Jacq. The more she tried to escape the repetition from Uggi, the more she fell into Victor's. Already sensing the obstinacy in Jacq, both men intentionally sang and chorused everything forever: St Mungo, St Mungo, as if Oduduwa didn't exist; Clyde, Clyde, Kelvin, as if Òṣun, Oṣin and Òròkí were already dried up; palace, palace, Peoples Palace as if she had never seen and been to one, however crooked; Kelvingrove, Kelvingrove, as if Ila never had its own upper-river, high brow area of beautiful mix of houses and forest; Celtic, Celtic, football, as if she did not once lived behind the Kings Square that served well the wrestling, horse-racing and other sports needs of Ila. She wondered if the names would actually be relevant to her beyond the sort of imagination a theoretical geography lesson could impact on a student of map-reading.

"Buchanan," the first woman to climb into the single deck bus told its driver her destination and offered the fare without the driver's asking. She took the ticket ejected by the driver's *Bell* ticket machine, thanked him feebly and walked to a seat.

"Buchanan, two," and "thank you." Two other ladies completed their tickets purchase and walked on to take their seats.

"Buchanan."

"George Street," and "thanks."

The moment the passenger to George Street walked to her seat, Jacq made a u-turn from the assertion she harboured of the Glaswegians since stepping out onto Whitevale Street a few minutes ago. "So, they do talk," she informed herself inwardly. "Or, do they talk around this hour – only to bus drivers?"

The distance of about a hundred and fifty yards from their home to the bus stop on Gallowgate was not short of Glaswegians, mostly women on both sides of the road. Singularly or paired, meeting up with or meeting, they were too serious-minded and too self-concentrating to talk to one another. Jacq viewed it as an illness badly exposed by the comparatively better road mannerism of Ila.

"Why, as humans were they not saying 'good morning' to each other?" she asked herself. Back where she came from, people meeting on the roads were bound to exchange greetings by the hour, event or no-event. More for decency than impolite snooping, her people would always find an appropriate greeting to pick from *good morning, good noon, good afternoon, good blue sky, good evening, good night*! They would compliment deeds from among popular phrases like *welcome, well done, well said, well blinded, well idiot, well all!* Only on rare occasions, when time forced a curb, would two Ilas meeting on the street and not extend the greetings to *how are you, how is your health, how is your wife, your husband, your*

177

children, your household, your dog, your horse, your cat, your vest, your petticoat, your...?!

If it had been the people's walking that had prevented talking, how about the silent stance of the six women they met already sitting down at the bus stop? Probably Ila had more accommodating and friendly vocabularies than Glasgow! Had this not been so, all the women seen on the streets as well as those met at the bus stop would have found something to cheer each other up with. Some of them would have preferred talking to each other to smoking their cigarettes. Anyway, Jacq contented, it was places they were going to see – not people they were going to converse with. And where necessary, talking with Victor and Uggi would just be enough.

"Buchanan," and again, "thank you."

"Day travel cards, please," Uggi leading the trio asked the driver on his turn.

"For which buses: *First, City, Arriva* or *Harte*?" the driver asked Uggi even though his was *First* bus company's

"*First,* please. Three – one for me and one for each of my two friends behind me."

"But why is everybody except us going to Buchanan – or George Street?" Jacq asked Victor as soon as they took their seats. "You didn't mention any of those places to me?"

"Both places are by each other, in the city centre," Victor explained.

"We talked so much of George Square, didn't we?" Uggi reminded her.

"Hmn...yes," Jacq agreed, uninterested in arguing with them.

"Now we are here at last," Victor proudly announced. They were in Cathedral Square, having walked across from the bus stop on the High Street. "The exact source where the great Mungo discovered her. The nucleus, the source!"

"Really?" teased Jacq with all seriousness. "Mungo Park's source of the Niger?"

"What?" snapped Victor. He couldn't make a sense of Jacq.

"You just talked of the source being founded. Was it River Niger's by Mungo...em...Mungo Park – or the Nile's by John Speke?"

Victor and Uggi were both at sea. Neither of them knew anything about River Niger and its fellow Scot discoverer; so, they could never have known about the Nile and its English finder. Uggi, wearing a distinctive idiotic frown on his face, spoke next. He demanded to know what Jacq was talking about, and if she was with them in mind.

"Simple physical geography! Mungo Park from Scotland here, discovered the source of the River Niger; John Speke, an Englishman discovered that of the Nile," she lectured and joked. "Is that valley downhill the body of any of the rivers?"

"Oh shut up, Jacq," Uggi forced himself to laugh. "Victor meant Saint Mungo and the origin of Glasgow!"

"So, you are not only advanced in geography and the Bible, you know a lot of history too!" Victor praised her. "But the source we are talking about is that of Glasgow City. The first settlement started with this cathedral; and it was led by St Mungo. That's his bronze depiction at the top of that lamp-post," he pointed.

They walked to the nearest of the two lamp-posts in the square. It was about ten feet tall and curved two feet forward at the top. Under the curve dangled the circularly crafted, two-foot diameter emblem of the saint and the borough. A powerful bulb in its holder shone brilliantly under the emblem.

"That's him, St Mungo!" Uggi said, joining Victor's enthusiasm, and pointing to the figurine crafted uppermost in the emblem. Other depictions inside the emblem included two fish, each with a ring hooked in its nose, a tree and a hand-bell. "He's the holy St Kentigern."

The Masquerade

"St Kentigern?" Jacq asked. "Perhaps like how you made George Street to be the same as George Square a short while ago?"

"That's the name he was known by when he first arrived in virgin Glasgow," Victor answered. "The people's love changed it to St Kentigern after he'd performed spectacular miracles among them." Then, both men joined in telling the full story of the saint:

The king of Strathclyde had an adulterous wife, Queen Langeoreth whom he patiently sought to catch and punish. His chance came when he discovered the queen had given her wedding ring as a gift to her lover, a young palace soldier. The king arranged the ring stolen from the soldier and had it thrown into the River Clyde. Thereafter, he turned round and accused her queen of adultery. He would not believe any of her stories and would punish her with death unless she could show him the ring within three days.

Under the cover of darkness, the queen went to St Kentigern, confessed her sins and begged for his help. The man of God, agreeing to help, despatched one of his monks to the Clyde on a special fishing mission while at the same time he commanded a salmon in the river to seek the ring, swallow it, and jump into the monks' net. At the monastery, the monk recovered the ring from the fish's stomach and handed it over to St Kentigern, who handed it over to Langeoreth, who showed it to the king. In turn, the king had no alternative but to return to loving his wife forever.

"How about the bird on the tree?" Jacq wanted the amazement to continue. "Did it also recover something hidden in the branches?"

"It is not in any way like that, Jacq," Victor answered her. "The bird, a robin, was the favourable pet of St Serf, St Kentigern's teacher. Fellow pupils of St Serf, jealous of the special treatment St Serf gave to Kentigern, wilfully twisted the bird's neck three hundred and sixty degrees and blamed Kentigern for it. Miraculously, Kentigern brought the bird back to life.

"For the same reason, fellow pupils put out all heating and lighting on Kentigern and the congregation when St Serf was away

180

on an evangelical tour and Kentigern had to take over the church activities for a whole night. Kentigern turned a branch of the hazel tree to matches, and its leaves into a heater which he used to restore both light and heating. Such was his power.

"And the bell, before you ask, was the evangelical gift the Pope gave Kentigern when he visited Rome."

"In Ila, there are also some people like that," Jacq responded, "people with great magical powers – like Ajagunla, Great Warrior. But I refused to believe them because I was never presented with good proof."

"No, Jacq, this one was different, being a miracle permitted him by Jesus Christ," Victor explained with biased classification. "Ila's must have been magic or voodoo.

"Also there are some things you don't have to prove before you accept, or see before you believe. At times, proving or seeing could even be costlier. It's the end results that matter."

"And this time," Uggi took over, "one end result is the prosperous Glasgow, commanded to be so by the 'Let Glasgow Flourish' prayer of St Kentigern to the Lord Jesus."

"Hmn," Jacq sighed an acceptance to what she hoped would impose a stop, however temporary, to the story.

Jacq, now sandwiched between Uggi and Victor, was about to enter the cathedral by its main door to her left when she noticed a huge landmark directly ahead. It was separated by a park that sloped away from her at the door. She asked if it was a cluster of minarets that were there.

"That's Fir Hill," Victor answered behind her. "Glasgow Necropolis; and your minarets are tombstones of past wealthy merchants. For that, it is also called Merchants Park."

"The tallest," added Uggi who had now turned back from the door and joined the discussion, "is of John Knox. He was a great priest of reformation in Scotland and the cathedral."

"Was he wealthy too?" Jacq asked curiously. "Or why wasn't he buried by the church instead of among the rich?"

"Well, I can't say if he was rich or how rich he was," Uggi admitted. "But at that time, the rich merchants and the senior priests were said to be all united in political power sharing. John Knox's powers transcended that of any merchant, or of the reigning Mary, Queen of Scots."

At this point, Jacq changed course. She demanded they should see the Necropolis first, and then return to the cathedral.

"This is the Bridge of Sighs," Uggi announced as they were on the narrow, tarred antique ironwork in the valley between the cathedral and their intended destination.

"It served as the point of no return for both the body and the coffin, as well as where the accompanying mourners must physically express their grief if they were already not doing so.

"There was the story of a hundred mourners hired by the children of a deceased wealthy merchant. The mourners were to follow the coffin to this bridge and wail until their noise would wake up the dead merchant. The mourners wailed so loud and strong that ten of them actually wailed themselves to death. Fearing the exercise could end in more of them dying, the leading mourner prescribed laughter next. They laughed so loud that their horses joined by neighing, and the accompanying band, with music. Then, without any discrimination, all the corpses were danced across the point of no return, into the holes of Necropolis." The tale greatly amused Jacq.

As they spiralled up the wide and well kept path to the peak, Jacq was not surprised at the tranquillity that ruled Necropolis. Rather, she was of how the interned talked in tones of stones and concretes that varied between simple designs she admired, and bogus mausoleums she hated. What, she thought, other than silly waste, was the point of erecting a house that would soon crack up and be overrun by climbers and insects, as was evident? What was the point in erecting a building for a body that was incapable of rising up to maintain its cleanliness? She saw Necropolis as the birthplace of the tombstones idea that had spread to Ila cemeteries.

It was there at the cathedral that for the first time, Jacq encountered Gothic architecture at close quarters. As she admired the uniqueness of the building from the interior, she admitted that it was much better than any of the churches in her kingdom.

The presence with the trio of Uggi, a devoted choir member of the cathedral, made the tour of the building even simpler. Uggi also shared in the glory of his father, Reverend Ali Jaiye, the first black official with a senior rank in the House of St Mungo. So it was easy for Uggi to lead her with Victor around, through the stained glass doors and windows, arches, altars, reredos and vaults, until the unintended pilgrimage arrived at the tomb of the great saint himself.

"Don't go beyond here, the barrier," Victor cautioned Jacq principally.

"I can see the instructions, can't I?" snapped Jacq. It was fixed to the centre of a thick, tasselled cord hooked at both ends to two golden poles that were ten feet apart. "But then, why mustn't one go beyond the cord?" she asked Victor.

"You can imagine how short the tomb will last if all visitors – all with their different intentions – are freely allowed to it."

"To me that sounds rubbish, Victor," responded Jacq. "He was a saint, wasn't he – like St Mark, St Luke, St Mathew or St John, wasn't he? Does it mean he barred people from himself when he was living?"

"Of course, he couldn't have."

"And if the saint didn't bar people from himself when he was alive, why would any Satan bar them from him when he was dead?" she asked, laughing to lessen the effect of her tongue-lashing of Victor. She then moved forward and gripped a length of the cord with both hands. She closed her eyes, and unlike other noisy tourists with them silently engaged her heart with a minute of prayers.

Jacq believed in the powers of spiritual prayers – once upon a time. Her early school and church were founded by the same early English-speaking missionaries. The missionaries brain-washed them into believing in prayers, using the Bible. Her pagan-Christian father dragged her into the church choir which she still respected. She was married to another local man who was more a keeper of cultural and traditional beliefs than of the words of the Bible and the church. Then, like no other woman of her time had ever done, she watched and mastered the rare art of praying with strong native incantations. Her ability to combine this with her Christianity earned her the respect of the womenfolk, and the fear of Ila men. Throughout the time of her travail, she invoked the relevant names and verses, and only stopped when the severity of the torture that drained all her energy had forced her to stop. At that point, she was convinced all gods were either unreal or dead. But now, weeks after her 'resurrection', she could see how wrong she was about the deities and Jesus. She wasn't sure which of them led the tourists to Ila in time to rescue her and bring her to Glasgow, and to the shrine she was. Whichever it was, now that she was before a saint most revered in life and death, she would thank all gods through the saint and seek a complete rescue for her family.

Victor and Uggi quietly followed her lips as she prayed in her language. And so did another stranger to the group. The stranger was the only black man among the four full-time guides at St Mungo Cathedral. At the last but strong quiver of her lips, the three men jointly voiced out what they believed her lips must have said – "amen".

"Where originally are you from?" the black guide eventually asked Jacq as soon as she could see him as clearly as she heard his 'amen'. In the five years that he had been a guide, he had thrown the question at countless number of visitors to the cathedral. It was his way of making the visitors feel welcome to the cathedral; and he had never felt any guilt from the prying nature of the question. And if at all he would this time, Jacq's ready smiles told him not to worry.

"From Ila," she answered. "Apart from my friend and his father you are the first other black person I have spoken to in Glasgow."

"Yes? We've heard so much about Ila and her cultures. My father was from Trinidad and my mother from Virginia. Are you new here then?"

"Yes, one week; but my friends are natives."

"That's good. I know they are. You will like it in Glasgow. You will, if you can evolve and respect the culture of the Glaswegians more than you will of Ila's." He was clear and unapologetic, shocking Jacq. Jacq felt that even if any of the black attendant's grandparents was yet to obtain a manumission paper, he should be ashamed to put others' culture above his. But then, in reality, was Ila culture, as she left it, defensible? Must she be the rightful one to defend it? Reluctantly but realistically she admitted in herself, each answer was no.

"You will like it," he repeated. "Are you going to the museum from here?"

"Museum?" she queried. Her hosts had told her of many museums, but not one by the cathedral. "Which museum?"

"She meant the Cathedral's," Victor intervened. "St Mungo Museum next door. Yes, we are going in there when we leave here."

"Good, you will like it too. It is new; and the Black Culture Week is still on there till tomorrow. The young lady will find it very interesting."

Black Culture Week? The phrase throbbed in Jacq's head as she stepped out of the cathedral. How was the black guide sure she would find it interesting? Like a typical Ila woman that she was, the only people she recognised as being genuinely black were those from Ila and its adjoining kingdoms; and she doubted if a group of them was in Glasgow to entertain or be entertained. Not only that she didn't recognise those who departed her region due to slavery or other reasons, she hated all discussions about them as such discussions usually reminded her of her share in the guilt due to her

185

ancestry of ignorant slave traders. She assumed that those who left would have assimilated a new culture which must have expunged Ila's from them. Yes, the show at the museum could well turn out to be interesting. The curiosity pushed her forward as they followed the poster directing all visitors to the first floor of the next building, the museum named after St Mungo.

A combination of objects at the wide and open entrance to the temporary gallery suggested to Jacq she was right in coming. Right across the top of the entrance was a controlled white blimp with black and red scripts announcing the event and welcoming visitors to it. Below it, on the polished floor and central to the entrance, was a black and white polka-dotted podium. It was elliptical and the bright light being emitted from the dots made it appear larger than its two feet height and one foot width. The top of the podium supported a three feet, clear Perspex cube. In the cube sat the polished wooden bust of a god of Ila she knew and could never miss.

She couldn't miss *Sàngó* for any reason. He was the warrior-king noted for his oral cavity of flames and tongue of fire. He was the self-respecting god of thunder whose integrity every king, chief and commoner sought to emulate. His hairdo in delicate plaits was also unmissable as each plaited row curved rigidly to the back like the tail feather of a fully barbed cockerel, or like the sickle of a wheat farmer.

Equally prominent was his long, pitch black tabard. It was carved in a thick relief, complete with painted spots of cowries as well as real cowry shells. His symbolic axe was rested on him.

She moved closer and counted the vertical rows of the real shells, ascertaining in the process, the inequality in the number in each row. Then she looked on, to the base of the cube, and read the bold history of the god: "*Sàngó*: Devil god whose spirit is evoked to guard the large compounds during the nights..." Halfway into the reading, she stopped, curled and shook her head in disagreement.

Neither Victor, Uggi, nor the black youngster guarding the bust knew what Jacq was disagreeing with.

"Are you alright?" the youngster asked her.

"Well, not really," she answered, attracting her hosts' attention. "Not with the lines of rubbish posted about the god inside the cube," she added and moved on without looking at the three embarrassed faces directed at her.

Èsù, Ògún, Yemoja, Oya, Cliodna, Brahma – they were all there in cages, staring at her and probably remembering who she was. As a woman and an indigene of Ila, she never dreamt such a sacrilege to the gods was ever possible anywhere. To her it was a total disrespect to the gods and all the people whose culture respected these gods.

Jacq crossed to the centre of the hall, attracted by a huge truss system. Under a mixture of bright and coloured lights, the truss carried the picture photographs of Haile Selassie, Nelson Mandela, Mahatma Ghandi, Martin Luther King Junior, Kwame Nkrumah and Queen Elizabeth II. Jacq was not sure who some of them were, but was, that neither King Japeedoe nor Sese Abram was among them. She suppressed her tongue from asking if any of the organisers had never heard of King Japeedoe or Sese Abram, his hatchet man. Then she told herself that thieves and tyrants of the primitive intellect like the two men didn't often have international respect.

On the next side of the hall were displayed some home life materials: crockery, beds, mats, chairs and stools. Next, clothing items: modelled and pictured *agbádás*, kaftans, wrappers, boubous, hats and scarves – and English suits. Next, fashion accessories: jewelleries of metal, wood, leaf, leather, shell and textiles; slippers, stilettos, brooches, walking sticks, wrist watches and fans. Next, items of social inference: dancers, singers, flutes, guitars and drums. Next, weapons: guns, swords, bows, arrows, rubber slings, flame throwers, knives and machetes.

The last section was allotted to charms. It displayed belts and amulets of deeply dyed leather, metal and wood; leaf headgears,

187

horse shoes, horsetails, animal skulls and rosaries. The last of the rosaries was prominently treated. It was that of *Ifá*, the wise oracle, complete with divination tray, sands, stones and a kind description.

"Excuse me please," the white lady sitting by the inner reception table by the charms sought the trio's attention. Then, more for feminity, she faced Jacq. "Would you please mind to give your comments about the exhibition?" she asked.

"Who are the main exhibitors?" Jacq asked instead.

"Arts students of Glasgow College," she told Jacq. "It's annual, the first."

"For mine – I can't speak for my two colleagues – it will be oral if you don't mind that," she obliged, browsing through the pages of the ruled A3 book laid on the table for the purpose.

"That's fine," the lady agreed with Jacq who was ready.

"First," Jacq started, "the *Ifá* oracle part of the divination was good and correct – unlike the *Sango*'s at the entrance. *Sango*'s is untrue and misleading. It shows all of you know nothing about him.

"Then, if this is about Black Culture Week, why did you get things mixed up – like English suits among the blacks kaftans and *agbádás*, wrist watches and stilettos displayed together with African bangles and sandals, flame thrower with the African weapons, those sort of things? I call that confusion.

"Then, the pictures at the centre: they don't fully represent the black people – they don't.

"And lastly, about the gods and their stools: How you display the assemblage is totally without respect. Nowhere in Africa are gods just gathered for all eyes – good ones, wicked ones, evil ones – to feed on. Black kingdoms will do that only to objects meant to be sacrificed to the gods because they want the worshippers to see them first.

"Mark you, I am not saying the show is not good, only that it is misleading in one way and disrespectful in another," she ended brutally.

"Thank you for the comments," the only black man at the inner reception said to Jacq. "My name is Smith; and your comments are well noted.

"But we would also like our visitors to understand what the exhibition is all about," he continued. "We want the people to know the gods and learn about them. We want to dispel the myth with which the Africans mislead, misdirect and disrespect the people in the names of these gods. Only for a lack of true knowledge will anyone class that as being disrespectful to the beautiful gods.

"Then, to your question: My answer to it will explain all the other things you may wish to know. It was through temporary releases that we got the exhibits from their kind owners who are mostly white people. Others donated to the sponsorship of the Week. So, it cut across all people as it should. Neither the black man nor the black culture is useful in isolation. For example, look at both of us blacks, now in English shirts, and inside a Scottish building. Only a plague is good in, and for isolation. This is the only sensible thing to project now. Don't you agree?"

"Hmn, yes," Jacq sighed and agreed with the black man. For the first time outside Ila she suddenly realised the stagnancy and backwardness of her knowledge of the gods, as well as her closed mindedness on the full aspects of black culture. She realised her impromptu tutor had successfully seized upon her inadequacies to tell her diplomatically that she was not only ignorant, but she must be one of those misleading, misdirecting and disrespectful black people. Quietly, she stepped away, and out, followed by Victor and Uggi who were equally embarrassed by Jacq's remarks that had deservedly earned her the tongue-lashing. From there they walked the short distance to the nearby People's Palace at Glasgow Green.

Two photos of Jacq – one each with Uggi and Victor, and all after a lot of persuading her – were taken under the incredible forty-six feet height of the Doulton Fountain in front of the palace. In each of them, her face was as expressionless as the back she turned to the palace in one and to Templeton Carpet Factory on the

189

other. "Who am I sending them to; and what would be the purpose?" she kept asking.

"We can understand your feelings," answered Uggi, "but try to remain optimistic, Jacq. It's all a part of history, a passing phase. Soon you will look back and be very happy."

"Look back and be very happy?" she ruminated and asked herself soon after they eventually went inside the building. She fixed her eyes on the spottily positioned black female slave in the family picture of John Glassford, once the wealthiest tobacco, cotton and slave merchant in Glasgow.

The picture, delicately hung on the ground floor, shouted loudest. How could she look back and be very happy when she could read of the big pro-slavery fight jointly put up by Glasgood and the West Indian Association against anti-slavery Witham Smeal and company? How, when she now discovered that like her Ila, Glasgow was not neutral in the evil? How, when she could read that thousands of helpless Glaswegian women were shipped with their children to far away Australia as punishments?

"No," she said. "How does a slave look back and be happy – that he's shipped to a foreign land, that he's forcefully separated from his family and his familiarities, or that he's compelled to lose some years of fulfilment in his life forever?"

She believed that if anything, her own unsure plight would be worse than that of the black slave in the photograph. Tears dropped from her eyes, just as the spirit to continue with the excursion dropped off her body. She'd had enough for the day.

* * *

If anything, the visit to the Black Culture Week exhibition set onto Jacq canons of nightmarish bombardments from gods and masks. She believed the attacks were aimed by her spiritual assailants at sending her from her sleep to her grave. Her puzzle was how at critical stages in the dreams, some other spirits were always out in time to rescue her. The attacks – and rescues – occurred almost every night of the week.

The first attack on her took place on the first night after the city tour. She had hardly shut her eyes when one masquerade in a mask she saw at the exhibition appeared in her dream wielding a large nail-spiked cudgel. He seized her with his muscular arms and marched her to where Fire Spirit was waiting, holding a long sword in his hand. The two devils told her that her time was up on earth and she must choose from them which of the tools they held she would prefer to be killed with. She was still undecided when *Sàngó*, his big axe firmly in hand, appeared, roaring a bigger fire in his mouth. The two devils fled in the face of a superior fire power, while she woke up.

At the breakfast table the terror of her sleep filled her heart and destroyed her appetite. Prompted by questions from Victor and Uggi, she related the dream, blaming herself for partaking in the sacrilegious watching of powerful deities that were locked up. Her hosts, as summed up by Victor, saw it differently: She had been thinking too much about her experiences in Ila. Now that she was 4000 miles away from Ila she should shut her mind against those experiences!

She had another dream attack two nights after the first. There, she was walking home with her daughter from the Main Market of Ila in the morning when a black eagle flew low towards them from the opposite direction. It landed yards away from them in the middle of their way and began to sprout – before their eyes – to a mammoth size that blocked their passage. Then it swooped on her daughter, Sariya, and carried her to the top of the roof by the roadside. As she and Sariya screamed in fear for help, two other masks she had seen at the previous exhibition appeared and were jeering at them. Next from the horizon appeared *Yemoja*, the goddess of small rivers, in her immaculate white robe. She landed on the roof, rescued her daughter and carried her back gently. When Jacq related the dream to Victor and Uggi, both men insisted it was peace that Jacq hadn't allowed her mind that had gone into her dreams. They told her not to be bothered by mere dreams.

"They were not mere dreams," Jacq disagreed, "but warnings before they strike. I believe coming to Glasgow can't save me. In which case I would prefer you return me home – to die together with my daughter and husband. The two of you, please send me back now and let me have rest." Victor and Uggi thought she could be losing the plot.

In the third dreamt encounter, two other masks hung her, her husband and daughter by the legs on a tree branch that extended over River Òṣun while Jap looked on with amusement . They dangled and expected the water to rise and drown them. As soon as the murderous torturers went away, the river goddess appeared with four maidservants and walked on top of the river water to them. She ordered her maids to cut them free. It was so terrifying that again, she told her hosts.

"She needs to see a psychiatrist before she gets worse," Victor eventually told Uggi. "I will tell my father to arrange that."

"It looks like ending that way," Uggi agreed. "But let's tarry a bit for my dad to return by the weekend. He might be able to help when he meets her."

In the next attack, the fourth, Jacq believed she had lost her eyeballs. The same eagle had appeared and attacked her, picking and plucking them. As she screamed and struggled in self defence with the beast, her thrashing brought her back to life, to the realisation of just being in a terrible dream. She cupped her hands tightly to her eyes and cried the rest of the night.

"Morning Jacq," Uggi halted her inside along the passage and greeted her. "What's wrong?"

"Nothing; no problem; I am fine," she answered.

"Nothing? But I can see you've been crying your eyes out. You are sure you are fine?"

Jacq was silent.

"Still the nightmares?" he asked her.

She nodded.

"But Victor and I have told you what to do. Put your mind above your past and be strong. Turn yourself round and bother the bothers. In turn they will run away from you, bothered by the bother you gave them!"

"I have tried my best, Uggi; can't you see that?" She resumed sobbing. "Can't you see they are too strong for me to overpower?

" I changed my bed linen, slept in the opposite direction on the bed, laid down on different sides of my body, read Psalms onto my pillow – done all! What else is left – stop sleeping?"

"Okay Jacq, my father will return to Glasgow today. So this weekend you will have the opportunity to meet him. I know, being from the same place as you, he will be able to help you. He deals better with this sort of things. We all shall see him tomorrow if I can get hold of him today. He will sort it out once and for all." He hoped the following day would prove him right.

* * *

The setting inside Rev Ali Jaiye's house put his ancestral root over his secularity. From the moment Jacq stepped into the 4-bed semi, she could see lots of Africanism in full spread, and dots of Ila in broad artistic display. As much as time permitted her from her position behind Victor and Uggi, she glared at the walled portraits along the corridor. The portraits were of big cats in different packs and activities, some of which Jacq saw as equally cruel as the community of Ila she left behind. As if to dampen the biological ferociousness of the cats, smaller portraits of harmless giant snails and rodents were hung in dilution with them.

The hangings continued to Ali's large lounge where Jacq and her friends awaited Ali's appearance. There, they were replaced by those of professions and pastimes which any first time visitor to Ali's house would feel curious and ask questions about. They were of a woman weaving on a vertical loom, three groups of

193

masquerades, a female cotton picker, a male yarn pot-dyer, a palm-wine tapper, and a preacher on the pulpit. Three other pictures were in thick chrome frames. One had the picture of a boy of about ten in suit, another of the same boy standing in front of a sitting man and woman, and the third of a class of student clergy. Curiously Jacq suspected the preacher to be Rev Ali Jaiye; and expected the reverend to be one of the people in each of the chrome-farmed portraits. Anxiously, she expected him.

Jacq felt the genuineness of Ali's warmth as soon as he walked out to them, straight to her before his son or Victor. He stretched out for a hand shake. "Hello, my dear; very glad to meet you," he coupled with the out stretched hand.

"Good afternoon, sir," Jack responded. She knelt on her knees in a native cultural greeting she knew Ali would understand.

"Thank you. Rise and take your seat, my dear. As one of your well-wishers I welcome you to Glasgow.

"And please accept my sympathy for your ordeals. Take it that they are now over in the name of Jesus Christ. We shall discuss it after you and your friends have cooked yourselves something to eat. Jacquensica, isn't it?"

"Yes, sir."

"Please feel as if you are in your house, because you are."

"Thank you, sir," she replied.

"And now to you my boys," Ali turned to his son and Victor, "you are looking good, aren't you?"

"Thank you, sir," they jointly responded.

"I am happy Jesus Christ made your journey to Ila a success. Thank you boys." He then led his guests go into the kitchen they, excepting Jacq, were familiar with.

Dinner over, Ali resumed with Jacq in the privacy of his large study, leaving the boys in the living room.

"I am an Ila, just like you," Ali started his story in a fashion that would sooth and assure her. "Now let us discuss the problems your friends said you have. I suppose you won't mind me telling you a bit about myself first. Then you too can tell me a bit about yourself." He took up his own story, brief in the details:

Neither his grandfather he lived with nor his father had a chieftaincy title. They were denied titles partly due to king's persecution, and partly to the mistrust the king made the people of the kingdom to have for them for being the first natives to uphold and defend Anglicanism. Actually, the persecution started with my great-great-grandfather.

His father came to Glasgow due to the influence of his grandfather. When the old man was dying he asked of the Glaswegian priest he had served a last wish: the priest should please take his son with him to Glasgow to train as a servant of the Lord. In Glasgow a merchant friend of the priest, a man who was used to trading with Ila, joined hands with the priest to bring up his father. Thus, he, Ali, was born in Glasgow. But before his father died, he was happy to have him trained and continued in the priesthood. Now he thanked God for his mercies, and would forever be grateful to St Mungo Cathedral Foundation that paid for his upbringing.

He, Ali, did not miss Ila – the bad news that came non-stop from the kingdom ensured that. Instead, what he missed were his father who died five years ago in Glasgow, and his wife, Uggi's mother, who passed away a year after his father died. From the losses he learnt how both happiness and unhappiness forever interplay a game of displacements in human life; and how lives, as a field, must continually shift to accommodate the game in order not to become fallow. He already had a reasonable guess about how both elements had played upon Jacq; but what was of greatest concern to him was to know from Jacq how she had adjusted.

Jacq, responding, told Ali she was Jacquensica Nek, wife of Chief Nek, head of the chiefdom of Dancemaster. She grew up with two other girls, Azzanaite and her sister Bambo. Together they formed a lucky trio of girls enrolled for basic western education in Ila. They were inseparable not only in and out of the school, but in the Anglican church of Ila where their parents forced them to be active. As they grew into educated adulthood, a strong portion of the glue to their togetherness was melted by their individual desire to go into matrimony. Bright and arrogant, each of them went away with an elite suitor. Azzanaite made the biggest catch in the young and charming Prince Japeedoe, while the other two went with the heirs apparent of other Ila chiefdoms.

At that time, her dream of becoming a teacher superseded those of her friends who wanted to become good mothers or housewives. She was already married into the Dancemaster chiefdom of her husband, Nek, before she realised that her dreams were neither different nor superior to her friends' – that love could be stronger than personal aspirations. All the same, she managed to become the good teacher she dreamt of becoming. She loved her husband, his chiefdom and his masquerade. She also loved Christianity, taught it in the church primary school, and sang in the choir of Ila's small church. It was due to her experiences in the church and school that she asked the masquerades to be always fair and friendly. King Japeedoe learnt of her plea and arrested her and her husband, accusing them of spreading information that would turn the people against the kingdom and against the traditional way masquerade carnivals were meant to be celebrated. The king alleged her to be the rebel leader of her family and sentenced her to death. Both Nek and her daughter of five, Sariya, were enslaved in the palace, with a brutal castration for Nek as additional punishment. They were about to execute her when Victor and Uggi arrived and pleaded for her family. Then the king spared them but banished her forever.

"I am sorry to hear your terrible ordeal, Jacq," Ali said sadly. "Now you must put that behind you and tell me how you have re-adjusted. That is what is more important now."

"I have tried my best to adjust, but it has been impossible," she admitted. "Japeedoe and his masquerades still chase me about. Most nights they appear and trouble me in my dreams. Each time, they attempt to kill me, my husband and my daughter. Unfortunately

I am the only one of us in Glasgow. I want to return to Ila now and die with them." She bursts into tears.

"We shall get to that. But before then I want you to tell me more about these dreams – who or what you saw."

"Jacq," he called after Jacq had narrated what she could about her dreams, "dreaming is as old on earth as the first night of the first Adam. Therefore I saw nothing threatening you in them.

"I also agree with the Bible, that they are emotions which may need the interpretation of visionaries. But in your case they were all self-interpreting enough. That you and your family were regularly rescued at the last moment in the dreams signified you have triumphed, and will continue to triumph, over all evils."

"But they plucked my eyes," she reminded Ali.

"Look, Jacq, my dear, listen to me: No beak, claw or proboscis of Ila will ever be long and sharp enough to harm you – in the name of Jesus Christ.

"Your imagination was due in the first place to the respect you and your husband accorded masks and masquerades. The respect inspires you to see in them, the strength and supremacy, which of course, they don't have.

"From now, don't recognise them more than you will your non-living toys. Not more than that!

"You said you loved Christianity – and the Bible, didn't you?"

"Yes, sir. I did. I do. Each night I keep the Bible under my pillow to ward off evil spirits."

"Good. Keep one there. More important: always keep the true faith in you because you will not remain in your bed all the time. Use the strength of faith to pray; and you will discover that those masks and deities that trouble you now are weak, unlike those of the days of old when they were strong due to their truthfulness to the people. Will you remember and do that, my dear?"

"Yes, sir."

"Good. Then, I have three ideas that will keep your mind busy and developed. You said you were in the choir in Ila, didn't you?"

"Yes, sir, I was."

"Then, will you like to join the Cathedral's?"

"I will love that, sir. It will be a great honour." She was elated.

"Good. You can start tomorrow then. Victor and Uggi are enviable members. Come with them in the morning to the Sunday service. Today I will get your robes."

"Thank you very much, sir. And what is the second thing you will want me to do?" Her eyes trapped Ali's with anxiety.

"I will like you to develop your thinking – to enrol at Glasgow College when the term starts. You can do well in arts and Bible studies which, considering your background, should not be strange to you. Would you like that?"

Jacq couldn't believe her ears. "Well, sir, it is not that I don't like it, but how do I ever meet the cost?"

"Don't worry. That, I shall sort out if you decide to go for it. It's starting in March. Before then, you can keep yourself busy in the cathedral, and we shall see how we can help you.

"The third thing I have for you is about demystifying all masks before you. Have you heard of Venice?"

"Yes, one of the seven wonders of the world."

"Well, one could say so. The world has more than seventy wonders. But that is the Venice you mentioned – in the northern corner of Italy."

"The teacher talked to us about it in our geography lessons, that it was unique for being the original city built on the sea."

"That's correct, Jacq. The only addition – and one very important – is that it's also very unique for its carnival of masks and masquerades. The carnival comes up in three months time, in February. It presents first hand, how and what masquerades are supposed to be. It shows the true development in the co-existence

198

between man on one hand and masks, masquerades, statues and statuettes on the other. Would you like to see the carnival?"

Jacq was hesitant in response. She had just seen an exhibition of masks and gods at the Black Culture Week, with its horrific consequences still prevailing on her. She weighed Ali's claims against her own experiences.

"Will you go if I sponsor you?" Ali asked again.

"With you, sir?"

Ali could see her reduced enthusiasm. He believed it should not stop him from persuading her to go. Going would be better for her.

"No. With the boys. It's timely the college will be on break then."

"Okay, sir," Jacq summoned her courage. Approximately two weeks after the conversation – and after she joined the choir – she was on her way to Venice, sponsored with Victor and Uggi.

* * *

To both the sponsor and the sponsored, the going was a waste, a criminal tragedy that none of them would have normally wanted to partake in.

The arrival in Venice of Jacq, Victor and Uggi on Friday, the day before the finale, was a late one, compensated only by having their accommodation booked in Tessera, the village of Marco Polo, the airport.

Covering by road the distance from Tessera to Venice Mestre area the following morning was however delightful, betraying nothing of what lay ahead for the group. It continued to be so up to Piazzale Roma where they walked over the bridge and continued inwards on the choked Rio Tera Lista de Spagna, parallel to the Grand Canal. Now it all dawned on her.

Jacq remembered the geography teacher who taught her about 'wonder Venice' he himself neither knew nor dreamt of beyond mere fictionality. She remembered Rev Ali Jaiye, her sponsor, in his correct assessment of what qualified anything at all to become a world's wonder. A city with no cars, no car-taxis, no coaches, no delivery trucks? Only the unrivalled dominance of the canals and their assortment of boats – commercial, corporate and private! Just the hard narrow paths as streets with tall buildings chained up alongside them! It must be true that the world had more than a thousand wonders! Venice herself was holding a multiple of them! "Good Lord," she sighed out at last, "the whole of this world itself is a wonder!"

"How do you mean?" Uggi heard her and asked.

"I just don't know, other than that this Venice is all miracles in outlook!" She was strong, repeating the wonders she saw as they went among natives and tourists, shops and shoppers, masks and masquerades, on the streets and in the squares.

She had never seen masks as smooth, and masquerades as gracious. Seeing masquerades of women and girls in such a numerical domination and unceremonious normality in this archipelago was most unbelievable to her. In her Ila, which now was a damned place to her, apart from a few favoured men, only the male children of King Jap could wear masks. Sometimes, Sese's too. But never a female – whether old or young. The world had been turned upside down quite fairly, in Venice, in this Campo Dei Santissimi Apostoli where tourists gyrated side by side with a family of four masquerades, happily taking pictures with the spirits of the Venetians!

Victor and Uggi were convinced that Jacq was enjoying the experience, more so as she took turns to pose with the family of spirits. She loved the two kid-masquerades in the group. They reminded her of her twin daughters, Sariya now caged by King Jap, and Sariyu who died at birth and was hastily buried in a small hole, her body forbidden by custom to be seen by her. She wanted to round up with a special pose with just the kids and invited Victor with his camera. So, Victor obliged, focused and clicked away, only to catch the horrors of madly emotional Jacq tearing down their costumes and screaming "Sariya, Sariyu" endlessly.

Within minutes the police rounded up the three Glaswegian nuisances. Their journey to Piombi Prison was fast and free. It was made in another of Jacq's wonders, a police boat – over the Grand Canal. She was to rot in jail, but for the testimonies of Victor and Uggi about her problem of emotional instability. When they were released three hours later, the police put them on the next available plane. Good bye to Venice and her Carnival.

* * *

An afternoon it was, fourteen weeks after Ali Jaiye had counselled Jacq, and just one since Jacq, Victor and Uggi had returned from the carnival in Venice. Returning home from shopping for the house, Jacq had stopped by the display window of Toyland, the High Street toy shop between the supermarket and her home. She could not resist admiring two dolls made of porcelain. In turn they smiled to her from the clear side of the cardboard box that housed them as a single pack. Two of their features struck her: they were black, the first black dolls she had seen in Glasgow, and they were both dressed within reasonable similarity.

"Could the presentation be meant for twins as it would have been in Ila?" was the question that first came to her mind. All the same she bought the pack. Its content would comfort her by serving as her twin daughters – dead and alive. The purchase turned out to be a resounding reminder of the disastrous visit she had just made to the Venice Carnival.

Jacq returned to her room, to her dolls, after she had put her groceries away. She admired them endlessly on the mantelpiece where she finally sat them in their box. Her daughter – or, her daughters!

Her concentration was single minded. It prevented her from remembering to shut her room door. Normally she used to keep it shut not to keep out the unstoppable spirits but to checkmate the

201

sporadic incursions of Victor – and his father into her room. She believed the interloping traits in both father and son were the faults of the genes they both shared.

"How was the shopping, Jacq?" Victor's voice asked. "Are you back?" He was already entering her room before Jacq could move to shut him out. "How did it go?" he asked again.

"Alright."

"Oh," his eyes caught the dolls, "did you just buy the dolls?"

"Yes."

"But what for? Why do you need them?"

"What for? Why the questions?"

"Because I don't think it's a doll you need right now; talk less of two." He returned a look of hate at the porcelain objects. "I can understand if it's a teddy. I thought you have a phobia for things like these. Was it not just a week ago when such items caused a big problem for you, a problem you passed to us? We are still nursing the wounds!" He poured out the venom, crisp and straight, blaming Jacq and her terrible emotions for their deportation from the Venice Carnival.

"What are you going on about, Victor? Haven't you and your friend said enough since we came back? What have the dolls got to do with Venice?" She was raging.

"What have the dolls got to do with Venice?" Victor asked, unwilling to back-off. "Waste – they were both a waste. Yes, Rev Jaiye paid for the trip, but you have paid for these dolls out of me and Uggi, from the money we gave for the groceries. They are a waste which no student can afford. They are the price we are paying for your freedom, but to which you, the beneficiary, are yet to pay anything.

"It's time you started complementing our efforts. Do the right things. King Japeedoe swore to us you never did!" He slammed Jacq's door after himself.

It was happening too quickly – and too badly – for Jacq. In a fit, she pulled her door open and slammed it shut herself. She was frightened of Victor's affirmation of his and Uggi's believe in King Japeedoe. Perhaps they were communicating with the king about her!

She was mindful of Victor pairing 'price' and 'freedom'. She felt she was truly a slave. "But I told them not to get me out of Ila in the first place. I demanded that they sent me back since being here, and after Venice. But which master willingly frees a slave – without taking a price?" She was murmuring with anger; and Uggi had the misfortune of meeting her in that state.

"Thank you too, Uggi, I got the message," she welcomed Uggi with. "Your friend delivered it about an hour ago. He must have told you how well he did it."

"What message, Jacq? What is it this time?"

"Like always, it's everything – everything! Now, I know of your bad intentions – you and Victor's. The two of you had been expecting me to pay something for my freedom. Uggi, you must stop pretending. Didn't I ask you in Ila to leave me to my fate – that I didn't want to leave?

"Now, I purchased two dolls and Victor is making trouble. No doubt, you will, as usual, stand by him and condemn me. It is now apparent that I am here for enslavement. That must be why Victor told me that freedom was never free, that I need to pay a price."

Uggi was amazed and frightful at Jacq's apparent state of mind. He gently rose from his chair and held her hand. "Listen to me Jacq. You have to listen to me – and this time around, very carefully.

"We are for what will benefit you. I am sorry if Victor actually said something like that to you. We have never discussed depriving you of your freedom, or of demanding anything for it from you. This is not the era of the slave trade. The sort of slavery you mentioned died almost two hundred years ago. Wilberforce shot

203

it down and Mansfield paid the undertakers to give it an indecent burial. Here, in all its ramifications, it's criminal.

"About the dolls, Victor was right; and I support him, though for a different reason altogether. It's obvious you are yet to free yourself from the fear of masks. What then are you doing with porcelain moulds that could worsen your mental situation?

"And on your request to return to your kingdom now, what do you stand to gain from that? Would you prefer to go and fight to save lives, or go and surrender to be killed?

"What we are encouraging you to do is to develop stronger will-power and get your priorities right. Do these first, and you can pick what next you would like to do. Then strongly, we shall follow you to that 'next'.

"Next, to what next?" she asked, suppressing a laugh of scorn at Uggi's advice. It incited her to throw her bombshell – of finality: She wanted neither a next nor a follower. She would lead, go and follow herself at whatever cost. She had seen how the streets of Glasgow had peacefully accommodated all human faces; they would welcome hers too. She had seen women walking alongside men without molestation; hers would not be different. On the streets of Glasgow, she had seen the affluent peacefully coexisting with those that poverty accorded an outlook of insanity. She had seen how many poor people safely took up accommodation by the roadsides, the alleyways, and in the parks. She would rather be one of them – with free insanity rather than with sanity clothed in deep servitude.

"What 'next'?" she asked again. "That 'next' is that I am moving out now; and none of you will stop me. I have had enough of the two of you!"

Uggi could see the stubborn irrevocableness in Jacq's expression. It testified to what Fire Spirit said of her in the Kings Square – of what led her into the near-fatal trouble she was met in, in Ila. He believed it was useless for him or Victor to continue to plead with her. Instead, he contacted his father, Reverend Ali Jaiye, who she respected and who readily agreed to talk her into coming over to stay with him in his house.

* * *

Victor – and Uggi – could be right about Jacq's irrational behaviour after all, Rev Ali Jaiye thought conclusively that morning. Jacq was heading towards the door, going out to the college. Ali watched her probingly as her melancholic demeanour deposed any flash of a smile that accompanied her 'bye-bye' to him.

Five weeks it was, since Jacq had moved to Ali's, in the wake of her disagreement with Victor and Uggi. In that period, Ali could not boast of seeing the white of Jacq's teeth even once. Perhaps, he thought, it was due to the old problems in her mind. Perhaps she was still musing over her recent disgrace in Venice, perhaps over her past humiliations in Ila. Perhaps, it was due to anger from her self-eviction from the accommodation she shared with Victor and Uggi. Perhaps, he had inadvertently multiplied her woes instead of relieving them, in allowing her to come over and stay with him. Perhaps she did not like her college, Glasgow College, where she had just been for a week. But how could she not with the generous church sponsorship that came with it? For whatever reason, her continuous rigidity against a show of happiness – however momentary – was breeding unbearable pressure on him and the environment they both shared. Ali contended that if the combined youthful strength of Victor and Uggi could not please her, how then would his own older and weaker ever deliver her any contentment? Her stubbornness must have been one of the causes of the row Victor had with her!

With such a countenance as hers he thought further, how would she ever be able to think and see clearly? It was time he talked with her – before she would inflict more damage on herself and on others around her. Luckily, the evening of the same day presented him with that opportunity, just as she was about finishing clearing up after their dinner. Purposely, he stayed on, at the table.

"Please sit down, Jacq, and let us have a small talk," he requested of her.

She did, on the chair facing his own on the other side of the well-polished wooden table.

"You have been here for five weeks; and up till now, you've not cheered up a bit. Instead, you've continued to allow unhappiness to live with you. You've allowed sadness to shut you away from the world. I don't believe that's why you're here; am I right?"

"Thank you, sir; and I am sorry," she said after a silence which felt endless for Ali, prompting him to repeat his question instead of accepting a silent evasion from her. "The truth is that I find it difficult to concentrate because my mind is not here. It is always with my family. I don't know what has happened to them. Really, I want to return to them in Ila now. It is what will return my happiness; and I pray you help me, sir." Her eyes resumed their usual wetness.

"Look, Jacq,' Ali commanded as gently as he could, "from now on, I want you to think of the volume of salty water you passed as you flew over the oceans to Glasgow. Think of it and realise you don't need to shed more of the same.

"Secondly, I know you want to get back home; but, you have not prepared yourself for the return. Certainly too, this home you long for is not ready to have you back. Have you forgotten you're banished – and what banishment is all about?

"For you to force yourself on a place, the least you can do is to prepare well for it. You need to make good preparations before you can go and fight to victory. Good preparation is never cheap, never hurried. Does that make sense to you? Luckily, you have here my dwelling as a place you can use to prepare yourself."

"I am prepared and ready, sir."

"No, Jacq, you're not – because you don't understand Ila, talk less of Glasgow. You don't understand them; but it is not your fault."

Jacq felt that if there was anyone within that vicinity who needed to understand that topic, it must be Rev Jaiye; if there was another needing to be understood, it was herself.

"How else can I understand it?" she asked. "With what they have forced me through, and are forcing me through, the only thing I am yet to understand is death," she asserted, wanting Ali to believe.

"If you had actually understood all about Ila, the problems you had with it would have been avoided. Or, they would have come in a different way, and been solved with less persecution. But like I said, it's not your fault. Over there, those who were supposed to be the citizens' protectors did nothing other than preventing the ordinary man from knowing what was going on in the kingdom."

Again, she was silent – not accepting, not countering.

"Even now, let's assume you understood, Jacq; those royals of Ila, together with their so-called spirits understood far more than you."

"Well, sir, it was the opposite," she begged to differ. "That was what they thought. But they still remain a pack of ignorant pigs – pigs who believe in heating, beating and drawing the past into the present, their own twisted way. They were all wrong."

"Okay Jacq, can you now tell me what your offence was, detail of information you were accused of spreading, how it was they who were wrong and ignorant? I would like to know now. What you told me was a summary."

Surely, Jacq didn't expect the question. She remembered that Ben had already told her that Victor spoke with him all night about it on their first night in Glasgow. It was over ninety nights since then, enough time for Uggi to have also related or exaggerated the tale to his father.

"Did Uggi not tell you, sir?" she asked unbelievably. "Ben admitted Victor related everything to him before the dawn of the first night of our arrival."

"Well, that's Ben and his son. For Uggi, he has told me almost nothing about you; and you, very little about yourself to me. Instead, Uggi continues to accuse me of deceiving him into going to see the horror of a people and not going to see a good carnival. He claimed his only consolation was that he was there in time to save you from the hangman. He never said more than that about you. Neither has he listened to my full explanation of why I sponsored him on a holiday to Ila. So, Jacq, tell me more of what your offence was, and why those in Ila were the ignorant ones."

"They made no formal allegation before the arrest and trial," she said. "When they came, it was fast, and I was allowed no defence."

"How? I'm listening."

Jacq related how the first accusation she knew of was that of the kingdom accusing her of revealing to fellow womenfolk how the characteristic craziness and intoxication of the masquerades was always hemp-induced. What happened was that she once accompanied Azzanaite to the royal farm. There, she saw a large field of Indian hemp belonging to King Jap. Sese Abram was tendering to the plants and boasting that the farm had enough leaves of *cannabis sativa* to keep the masquerades high and happy for the next few years as well as for export to neighbouring kingdoms. After the visit both she and Azzanaite vowed to keep it within the two of them.

Her other problem she said started with Dancemaster, her chiefdom's masquerade. Originally, he was the god and masquerade of women. Later, it was upgraded to include that of the youth. Over the years, she had served him faithfully and had got the townswomen to do so more than ever. Being responsible for leading the women's dance to him, she persuaded him to shelve his canes when dancing with women. She, Jacq, couldn't be the one to lead the ever generous and happy dancing women to a lashing masquerade. Both the masquerade and the women welcomed the change as it benefited both parties. That the women could freely mix and dance with him was seen by King Jap as an undue and ungodly familiarity for which she was held responsible.

"The next accusation was the king accusing me of tampering with the women's donations that came in through Dancemaster."

"Were you putting aside some of them for your household?"

"No. It was because I once told some of the womenfolk that people didn't have to donate to the spirits before the spirits would answer their prayers."

Her last offence pertained to the attire of Yawa, the leader of the junior masquerades. On the morning of last year's finale, the junior masquerades carried out their usual ransacking of women and their wares at the Royal Market. In the raid, a market woman carrying her baby son in her hands fell while she was running to escape the raiders. Consequently both mother and baby died the day after the finale. Coincidentally, on the day of their death, she, Jacq, accidentally stumbled on Yawa's attire, carefully tucked away by her husband inside a room of their court. Of course, she promptly accused her husband, Nek, of the terror and double murder. She did not care if he accused her of clandestinely searching his room. Nek denied both charges but promised her he would sack the killer-carrier of Yawa masquerade. Next, she persuaded him to do more of atonement – to henceforth remove all junior masquerades attires in their home to either the king's palace or the town shrine. She learnt that the Main Shrine took them in, grudgingly.

So far to Ali, the story was a lengthy one interestingly shortened by its good substance. He wanted Jacq to continue. "Did you confront Yawa next?" he asked curiously.

"No, but the listening god, *Karma-phala*, the listening god of retribution, did. The man died of chicken-pox less than two months after the finale."

"Did you tell anyone about it?"

"Yes, only Azzanaite; and only as far as the attire I discovered. But later, every female citizen became aware of the atrocities of Yawa and the junior masquerades. It was a case of 'better not to perpetrate evil than to perpetrate it and try to hide it'."

Ali gave a big sigh, his stomach full of analysis, questions and answers, most of which, unfortunately, he could not bring up before Jacq. As a practising church officer, it was not that he was afraid to use plain truth to confront her. But in this case, any naked truth – or skimpily dressed one for that matter – would be more sinful than helpful. Though it might not result in the type of sin that could commit someone like him to hell with or without fire, but it would definitely be the type that would make anyone learning of it to adjudge he, Ali, was in a wrong profession. He would prefer to allow Jacq to understand gradually what she should have done, and should do.

"You've done your best, Jacq," he chose to compliment her.

"Thank you, sir. Victor and Uggi didn't believe that when they quarrelled with me."

"Put that in the past now. Not everything was their fault too."

"How do you mean, sir?"

"That I will tell you as we go along – if you merit it."

"If I merit it…?"

"Yes, Jacq. You need to pull your socks up or you will achieve nothing – about yourself, your husband, daughter, return, the new college, nothing. If you are out of your place only to continue to shutting your mind to people and crying all day, why would anyone want to waste his time with you? When I see you pull up is when I will talk of other things with you. Not until then, Jacq."

CHAPTER SEVEN

In Venezia

When Captain Piccioti's announcement pierced the cabin in Italian, Jacq did not have to wait until it was repeated in English or Glaswegian before it pricked her conscience. The time had come for her to make amends for her sin. Weather-wise, the harsh time of the year, the vast blue water of the lagoon on the Adriatic, the indefinable upper cumulus and the lower bluish white balls of fog, all seemed not to be on her side. She prayed that these elements would not combine their seasonal anger and direct it furiously at an aeroplane harbouring a spectacular sinner of her category.

Another look through the window, a last meanwhile, confirmed how her carrier continued its battle with these elements of nature as it struggled to land on the hydro-encircled Marco Polo Airport. She turned her face in and closed her eyes firmly, wishing feverishly the jerky approach would allow for a safe touchdown, a happy landing. By the time the relieving announcement to that effect came in English, she already knew and felt it – that they had safely landed on the Queen of the Adriatic. At last now, she sighed, she had before her the golden opportunity to purge herself of her sin against an innocent little girl at the same event, in the same Venice, a year ago. To her, this sin equally represented one she had committed against her daughter now languishing in Jap's dungeon back home in Ila, as well as against Ali who was sending her again to Venice after she had wasted his resources during the first visit.

Customs, then Uggi's luggage. Customs, then her own handbag. If up to those minutes, other controllers had executed their sniffing duties fast enough on other arriving passengers, what was this overzealous custom man looking for all that long inside Uggi's luggage and then, her handbag? With his smallish, dirty-looking sniffer-dog remaining quiet and composed, could experience and common sense not tell him to just wave both of them on, and prevent an unnecessary human backlog? Or was the dog just an ordinary pet, or one trained only to sniff contrabands that were Italian? She was becoming impatient, suspecting it was all deliberate mischief intended to terminate her determination to right her wrongs.

"It is looking better this time Uggi, don't you think so?" she asked as their taxi negotiated the first corner away from its allocated stand at the airport.

"Not only looking better, it is going better," Uggi complimented. "I only hope you keep it so, Jacq."

"Don't worry, Uggi I will. I trust I will – with your support." For once, her ebullient mood confirmed she meant her words.

Liberty Bridge: Jacq looked intensely at the two islands far away on her left; one of them, the bigger, as Murano.

She was not seeing Murano for the first time, having seen it from the same spot during the disastrous visit to the previous year's carnival. That time she had promptly remarked how elegant it looked afar off with its buildings of coloured bricks splendidly moated by the lagoon. Then, she had goaded the taxi driver taking them to Piazzale Roma first to address her curious inquisitiveness about the island and a few others sitting within swim lengths from it. This time, she was anxious to arrive there for the first time, at the Altamare Hotel they had booked from Glasgow.

"Oh, Murano, here we are at last," Jacq prematurely sighed this Wednesday mid-day. Their vaporetto called Uccello had just negotiated a clear right from Mirescodia Canal into the open New Fondamental, and breezed past another walled, small piece of built but forested land, an island in its own right, she would later learn to be a cemetery.

Unperturbed by the cold wind, and the hazy droplets being thrown up by Uccello, Jacq remained on her feet, her head among those of other passengers who had voluntarily tied themselves to the same position. Her small talk and photo snapping gave her out as a tourist ecstatic to discover the islands. Save only a first brief moment when Jacq summoned him to take her picture with the distant Murano as the background, Uggi remained seated on a near empty bench, minding their luggage and expecting the final *fermata* for them to disembark. It eventually came with a roar, followed by the silencing of the water taxi's engine, and finally, by its destabilising dance to the stub it was tied to. She – and he – had made it for now.

* * *

It was 8 0'clock on Thursday, the first morning after Uggi and Jacq had arrived in Murano. The dining hall they walked into was already full of other lodgers who had heeded the hosts' time-table with hungry punctuality. By fortune, Jacq and Uggi spotted a table of four chairs half-occupied by another couple sitting and facing each other. And more fortunate was it for Jacq and Uggi that as soon as the seated couple noticed Jacq and Uggi were heading towards their table, the male of the couple shifted to the empty chair at his left to allow them to sit beside each other. Within minutes, with the assistance of the waiters, Jacq and Uggi settled at the continental breakfast table.

"We arrived here in the same vaporetto with you yesterday," the older lady opened the friendly chat with Jacq.

"Oh, really? I didn't know that," Jacq readily responded.

"You would probably not," the older lady started to reason. "You were standing; and we, sitting on the bench behind your partner. I'm Patrizia, and he's Mark, my husband. You can call me Pat if you like."

"This is Uggi and I am Jacq. Nice of you to have created space for us on your table."

"First time you're in Italy?" she asked of Jacq the typical probing question an Italian would ask a recognised tourist. Jacq was hesitant responding.

"No. The second time," Uggi volunteered, covering the reason behind Jacq's sudden hesitation at answering Patrizia's simple question. "We were last year, and it's quite good and a reason why we're here again."

"I am not surprised," Patrizia went on. "Here, in Italy some cities are forever like that: when you visit them once, you always come back. Venice here, and Rome are among such cities."

"Yes," Mark added in concordance to his wife's claim and proceeded to explain the myth. "The proven story handed down to us was that both San Marco here in Venice and Fontana di Trevi in Rome forever control the lives, and thus, the movements of their visitors by means of special magical magnets. We too were here last year – and the years before that. And here we are again this year, pulled in by the magnet of San Marco."

"That's most interesting," Jacq said, responding to the couple's story which she found more amusing than odd. To her it wasn't any stranger or mystical than any of the thousands of who-will-prove-it stories that abounded in Ila. "Most interesting indeed. And from where do you frequent this place then?"

"From everywhere – far and near – should we say?" Patrizia replied.

"How is that?" Uggi asked. "As far away as Canada, or, as near as United States?" Judging by their guttural and nasal accentuation, he suspected they were from those parts of the Americas.

"Actually, my husband originated from Venice; and I, from the Cunni ancestry here in Murano," she answered, to the surprise of Jacq and Uggi. Then Mark took up the story:

His grandfather was a top Venetian glass blower with a big foundry somewhere in San Stae, along a place by the name of Fondamenta Rimpetto Mocenigo. There came a time when the city authorities, fearing the devastation an accidental fire outbreak from a foundry could inflict on palaces and light-deprived, crowded buildings, ordered all glass blowers to move to Murano. At first, his grandfather was exempted, having been backed by powerful men of surrounding churches that had enjoyed his free chandeliers and other religious glassware. Come the following year, and faced with the reality of the destruction an inferno could cause, the same backers withdrew. After his final plea based on his installing more hydrants along the inexhaustible water of Rio di Santa Sae was rejected, his grandfather moved with the foundry to Murano.

At Murano, he worked hard, prospered, and dragged him, his only son, into the trade. That's how he met his wife, Patrizia, for the first time, as a small daughter of one of his father's customers.

Fifteen years ago, he and his wife had a better idea: to sell up, leave the crowded archipelago, and move to New York which then had many glass buyers, and too few blowers. But they still kept in touch, as Jacq and Uggi could see. Except in the first five years of their emigration, they had visited Venice and Murano during every carnival.

"That sounds brilliant and interesting," remarked Jacq. "So now, you still blow, and she sells?"

"Yes, we have two medium-sized outfits in New York. One produces classy chandeliers and fancy goblets, and the other distributes them – funnily enough, to as far away as Venice and Murano!"

"Are the two of you in love?" Patrizia asked.

"We are just good friends, and both students in Glasgow," Jacq answered. "He's about to finish a clergy course, and I have just started a course on art and religion in the same college."

"How excellent!" Pat was excited. "You two have got a perfect combination of ambitions – one that could successfully lead you to do the exact opposite of what the two of us did to Venice, isn't it?"

Neither Jacq nor Uggi understood what Patrizia meant; and Jacq wasted no time in asking her.

"We emigrated, left Venice, didn't we – to a place we assessed to be more ideal to our jobs? In your own case, you are already in Venice, a city most welcoming to your fields of study; and you should just stay and grab the opportunities!

"You see, in the whole of Italy, when one talks of arts and religion combined, this region of Veneto, through its octupled archipelago of Venice, Murano, Burano, Lido, St Erasmus, Torcello, Sabioni Point and Cavalino, leads them all.

"Mark you," she sang along, "I am not talking of religion alone, because nothing will successfully displace the Vatican City in Rome."

Patrizia rolled her PR down the slope of practical and impractical areas of tourism in Italy, stopping only where she could to crown them with events and places around her nationalistic biasness. Except for admitting to the sacred inferiority of St Mark's Cathedral to the Vatican in Rome, Patrizia put her former locality ahead in all other good things in Italy.

Pat's trumpeting was endless. In displeasure it held down the staff of the breakfast hall, preventing them from performing their clearing duties. A lady member of staff moved from where she had stood speaking negatively about the lodgers and went to the group. "Sorry, *signori e signore*, we have to close now. We have been waiting for you," she confronted them with outward politeness.

It was already ten-thirty, and unbelievably, more than thirty minutes after the last breakfaster had left the hall! The chatting couples, clearly without a feeling of guilt towards the staff they held back, took their time to exchange more promises: in two hours time, they should knock on each other's doors and set out again in one vaporetto to Venice.

* * *

The two couples parted at Ca D'Oro stop, where Jacq and Uggi alighted, leaving Mark and Pat to continue in the vaporetto. They proceeded on the short road and then turned into Strada Nova. Their destination was the square of Santissimi Apostoli, the scene of the tragedy that befell their first visit a year ago.

All along the crowded road, up and beyond the Apostoli ground, the tourists saw no masquers, and therefore, Jacq's new brave resolve and boast of maturity at the sight of the masquerades could not be tested.

Shop 42 appeared the most special in the vicinity. At first look, the generous lighting at that time of the day projected a waste of lira – or of Euro, the new currency. The lighting beamingly combined with other seasonal articles that were spread behind the windows and outside the shop to attract tourists to stop and look inside. In this way it was satisfactorily paying for the waste, if waste actually existed. Among such enticed tourists were Jacq and Uggi. Their hearts convinced them that they were before the widest assortment of carnival articles Venice had to offer.

One blue hat with long green feathers at its back seen through the shop window forcefully caught Jacq's attention. It compelled her to pull herself and her friend inside the shop. Her intense enthusiasm at its physical inspection went on endlessly, until Uggi pinched her to stop and allow them to get out of the shop.

"What did you do that for?" a displeased Jacq asked Uggi as soon as they were outside.

"I could see that your excitement was already leading you to forgetting one important aspect of Venice dad warned us about – when in a Venetian shop, as long as you have the money you want to spend on you, learn to hide your true interest in whatever article or service you are interested in purchasing. In that way you have more of your money remaining in your pocket. The Venetian trader charges you according to your interest and personality!"

"That's true, Uggi. I got carried away. I am sorry."

They also reminded themselves of two other warnings that were applicable to their situation. One: Along the walk between the train station and the Rialto, there were more Basanios than Shylocks in the shops; whereas between the Rialto and St Mark Square, more Shylocks ruled the shops. Two: Price tag or no price tag, and as much as possible, haggle the price posted on any article you wanted until you were convinced the price was just.

Jacq had a vivid imagination of the masks and costumes she wanted for both of them, and for Uggi's father as well. In the end, their frantic search, up to the Rialto, proved purposefully useless, and they headed back to Shop 42.

This time the scenario they met on the grounds of Apostoli was totally different. A group of twelve masquerades, among them two children who were graciously sharing a photo session with some delighted tourists.

Uggi feared that another moment of disaster had arrived. He half-held his breath and closed his eyes for an impromptu prayer as Jacq rushed to the group. Though his eyes were opened too late to witness the kisses she planted on the foreheads and cheeks of the child masquerades, he was relieved to meet her on her knees between the kids posing for photographs. He was beginning to believe they would have better news for his dad back home in Glasgow.

Next, the Glaswegians watched two female masquerades in the group walking to the door of Banco Populare in the square; and its door was remotely opened to them. "Yes, most likely they've gone to withdraw some cash," Uggi remarked before Jacq who was already watching them could speak.

"Unbelievable," Jacq still managed to utter. "I am following them to see for myself. Are you coming?" She raced to the same door and caught up with them inside the bank. Smartly, she joined the queue behind them before Uggi arrived.

For the bank employees, what was unbelievable, as well as suspicious at first, was the intense gaze the two tourists directed at the masquerades as they counted and pocketed their cash. They watched Jacq clap wildly in surprise as she terminated her unintended banking transaction and pulled Uggi with her to exit after the masquerades.

"A rare world, Uggi, isn't it?" she asked.

"Yes, but in what sense this time?"

"When you were a masquerade in Ila, did you spend your own money or spend the money you were able to take from the people?"

Uggi produced no relevant answer. It was complex, implicating. "The shop!" he reminded Jacq. "We haven't got all day."

"Do you want the headgear now?" asked the shop assistant from his reception stool, on noticing the couple were back."

"Er em, yes," Uggi slowly replied. "But you will do us a favour – we need personal attention.

"*Certo, signori*," the shop assistant readily volunteered for any favour or attention they might need. He pushed in his drawer and moved across to the clients. "Now, the blue hat, can I take it down for you for a better assessment?" He actually did that ahead of an answer.

Calmly, the tourists turned it over and over again, admiring what were to them, its special decorations.

"These are peacock feathers on it, aren't they?" Jacq asked the assistant.

"No, *signora*, they are not," replied the assistant. "Peacocks are very rare and protected nowadays. They are just other big quills, bleached and carefully printed with the design of peacock feathers."

The Masquerade

The tourists were astonished at this imitation. About two dozen of the feathers were mounted upright round the back of its crown. On the crown itself, smaller feathers, probably of other birds, were set to compliment the big ones.

"Overall, the feathers are beautiful," Jacq remarked. "It reminds one of the beautiful peacock itself. Pity it is not real."

"Well," responded the assistant, "that is one of the realities we must accept – that at best a design can only resemble the object."

"I can see the resemblance being improved to make it look more like the real bird, if only you can add certain ideas to it," Jacq confidently suggested. "If you can, we shall have two – one as peacock, one as peahen – and pay you for them."

"Give us your idea then," the assistant requested from Jacq. "We shall make what you want in the shortest time possible. We are the best and biggest in Venice. We have enough expertise to implement any idea. That, we can assure you."

Jacq went on to describe the expanded picture of the design she had built up in her mind since she first saw the hat. For the peacock, she wanted its back to be extended so as to accommodate more of the spotted feathers from ear point to ear point. The feathers were to be rooted in a more erect form to look like the real train of the tail covert. The crown was to be fully plumaged.

"For the peahen," Jacq continued, "the plumage has to be more of brown. It should have a shorter train, earrings and necklace."

As Jacq went on with her description, Uggi's eyes caught a picture of the object she was building. It was a blooming peacock printed on a wall-mat souvenir. "Yes, she means like that," he said, pointing, while the others followed his direction. The assistant promptly brought it down.

"Yes, like this, with the bird's head, neck and chest blue," she agreed with her friend. "The head should be moulded, feathered and attached to complete it."

"And without making it heavy and uncomfortable," Uggi added.

"How heavy can feathers ever be?" Jacq asked her friend dismissively. "You can never attribute serious weight to feathers."

"Oh, don't mind her, my friend," Uggi jokingly countered Jacq. "She probably forgets that a man who is able to create peacock feathers from other feathers can also make the peacock feathers carry the weight of lead."

"Don't worry," the assistant assured them at the end of their laughter. "There's always a way out, once you can pay for it." He took the original hat from Jacq's hand and gently placed it on a headless model robed in a blue, flowing satin costume.

"Can I have the costume too?" Jacq asked. "Together with the lower gold ribbons and embroidery, but mixed with a bit of black and cream? And possibly with more sequins?"

Slowly, the assistant's thoughts peaked at the size and style of the orders before him. "Which family or group of Venice masquerades do you belong to?" he asked them. "Or, are you just assembling these for a group?"

"No, neither of those," Uggi answered. "We are taking them with us to Glasgow."

Jacq went on to list other things they would need with the headgear. One of them was a half-mask she loved for its triangularity and matching blue colour. "This is exceptional," she said. "I would like to add it."

"You can't have that, Jacq," Uggi objected. "No, you can't."

"Why not? All it needs is some good netting and it's ready."

"Netting?" the assistant intervened. "That won't be a problem at all. We have an abundant stock of high and low-density gauzes and nets from Torcello and Burano. They make better fashion with this type of mask."

The Masquerade

"Thanks all the same. We won't need them," Uggi insisted. It was an insistence Jacq strongly objected to – until Uggi temporarily excused the assistant and called Jacq aside to list his reasons.

"What works in Ila would never work here," he started the reminder. "Have you forgotten we are springing a surprise with our participation? The mask you want only goes with the net, and a net will betray our black lips, noses, as well as the colour of our eyes. We must first hide our faces as much as possible.

"Besides, this carnival, as we've been warned by dad, is synonymous with smooth faces. In Ila, we know it's with voices, bullying and cheating. Shaggy net will only render the face less smooth, and the wearer to resemble a caged animal."

Jacq understood and agreed with Uggi. She called the assistant and tabled her revised list. Prominent in it was a full facial mask lavishly ornamented with sequins and dust of gold, purple, yellow and blue. In a swift u-turn to what his potential customers wanted, the shop assistant witnessed that no net would go appropriately with the triangular half-mask!

Next, Jacq picked a pair of white, arm-length gloves from Murano, and the same colour of stockings from Torcello, together with two folding hand fans of imitation peacock feathers. Finally, they urged the assistant to meet the modifications listed so that a perfect king and queen of the birds would emerge. If he did, they would return to order two more outfits, one each for her daughter in Ila and Ali Jaiye in Glasgow.

The assistant assured Jacq and Uggi that by the following morning, Friday, the costumes would not only have been delivered to the shop from the factory, but he, the assistant, would have personally brought them to Altamare, their hotel in Murano.

"Appreciated, but don't worry about that," Jacq told him. "We would prefer to try them on here first to ensure they are what we ordered, and seek immediate alterations if necessary."

* * *

Both Jacq and Uggi laboured well with the preparation for Saturday. Until that day, none of them had known in detail, the full degree of each other's skills in masquerading. Uggi had never detailed before Jacq the rigours of the initiation and preparation for his outings in Ila. Jacq too had given nothing away beyond how Uggi first met her as a rebel about to be executed. But their individual skills began to manifest as both of them tried out the movements they intended to exhibit in two days time at St Mark Square. That evening, they were positive the costumes they had earlier ordered would safely arrive.

They set out early on Friday, because in addition to collecting the costumes, they had some light shopping to do by the Rialto. Principally, they wanted a hand sewing set that would contain needles of various sizes, threads of assorted colours, a thimble, and a pair of clippers. The set would be handy if, at the last minute before the outing, a minor tear or some loose stitches should occur. Such had happened many times with Dancemaster, and Jacq had done the mending in deals she kept between herself and her husband. After Rialto, they visited the bookshop in Salizzada where they shopped for colour-flashing stickers they believed would be handy for further ornamentation of their costumes. In all, Friday turned out to be fulfilling. They retired to bed early, in readiness for Saturday they expected to be busier and wishfully, most fulfilling.

It was time for breakfast on Saturday morning, the start of the day they all agreed to share inside Venice. Patrizia was the first to knock on the hotel room door of Jacq and Uggi. She was with Mark, and wanted to know if Jacq and Uggi were ready to come with her and her husband to the breakfast hall.

"Sorry, I can't open; Uggi is just dressing up in the bathroom," Jacq cleverly repelled her and her husband. "We shall join you very soon. Please reserve some lovely seats for us."

Very soon? Yes, if thirty minutes time lag fell into that category.

The Masquerade

And 'we'? Yes, if it would be applicable to a set of transformed Glaswegians.

When that 'soon' came and the Glaswegian tourists arrived at the breakfast hall of Altamare Hotel, Mark and Pat, like others in the hall, were stunned by the two objects that had suddenly appeared at the main door. Two gleaming masquerades, uniquely depicting a peacock and a peahen! Inevitably, their appearance hijacked the breakfast of every guest.

The sight was a joyful surprise to everyone. To the staff, it was a first experience in the history of breakfasting in that hotel or in any hotel in Venice and its environ. A junior staff member of the hotel actually sold it to her colleagues as a plan the management deemed too important to be leaked before its execution. To the senior management, it was most welcoming that they could take the credit for the exhibition they neither planned nor executed. Giol, the hotel director, was too excited when he joined his guests, called by his staff. Smartly he claimed it was a pioneering evolution, one meant to entertain them. He refused to let any guest with a camera beat him to photographing the pair for prints that would make everlasting witnesses on the walls of his establishment.

Then, in a pace that befitted 'their majesties' cock and hen, the two masquerades embraced and disengaged. Next, standing side by side, and facing the diners, they took the bow once before opening and closing their arms in simultaneous claps. The diners dropped their cutleries and followed the masquerades with their own faster, louder and more ecstatic claps. Drenched in the accolade, the two people behind the masks slowly pulled aside their masks to reveal no other persons than Jacq and Uggi!

"This is a fast one, a beauty you have pulled on everyone here this morning," Patrizia told the masquerades now seated on the seats she and her husband had originally reserved for Jacq and Uggi. "Truly extraordinary. How did you do it?"

"Well, thanks," Uggi acknowledged the praises. "But if you think it is fast, beautiful or extraordinary, wait till later today. Aren't you both coming to St Mark?"

"Eh, big mouth," Jacq shouted jokingly to quieten Uggi. "Supposing you have made a big mouth before today's breakfast, or at the time Pat was knocking this morning, would we have got this result?"

"It means you've got more up your sleeves, reserved for St Mark," Pat guessed. "Anyway, we've since yesterday, agreed to go to town together today, haven't we? Be assured, we can keep it between you and us. We are definitely going and returning together."

"Seriously, it is not a joke," said Jacq. "We already planned to get you involved. We intended to let you know before we leave the hotel for St Mark."

Though the time the four of them had before setting out for Venice was short, it afforded Jacq and Uggi the space for a post-mortem of their acts in the breakfast hall. Jacq was particularly hilarious. "So, this is what I have been missing – the skill you have failed to tell me about," Jacq accused Uggi, referring to Uggi's acts in Ila. Today wasn't the first time you would be a masquerade, isn't it?"

"Well, yes," Uggi admitted. "But that's quite different, Jacq. It's something I didn't talk about because I mustn't; something I didn't see because I mustn't; something I didn't hear because I mustn't.

"Besides," Uggi continued, "you already knew everything about masquerades when you danced with your husband, a senior masquerade. I believe you kept quiet because you believed you mustn't talk about it."

"But right now, there is one thing I would have loved: that Sariya is also here to feel the attires. That would have made my life. Mere wishful thinking, isn't it, Uggi?"

"It's still possible, Jacq. So, don't return again to that state of despair. You promised us you wouldn't. And, have you also forgotten you promised to dedicate the success of this to the same daughter?"

"Yes, and thanks for reminding me. It must be made to succeed – for her sake."

They were still in their masquerade costumes when, shortly after breakfast, Pat and Mark arrived at their room to enquire when they all would set out for St Mark Square.

"Thank you both again for the colourful breakfast," Mark reiterated. "We really mean it that we are coming with you."

"And you need to tell us what else will happen down there." Patrizia added.

"Nothing, other than that we want to show off our masks and costumes. We failed woefully last year; and that is the truth. Therefore we are making up for that this year – on the parade platform, right inside St Mark."

"Have you registered then?" Mark asked.

"Registered? For what? With who?" Uggi responded.

"Who else?" Pat responded. "*Il Comitato* of course."

"No, we registered nothing, with no one," Jacq answered, surprised but undaunted. "Who is *Comitato*, and where does he or she come in here?"

"*Comitato di arti di Venezia* or Venice Arts Committee. It is responsible for the A to Z of the arrangements," Mark explained. "You can't be allowed to join the procession, or be on the platform unless you register and meet its conditions. The farthest you can get without registration is showing your costumes to fellow visitors to St Mark."

Registration and *Comitato*? The two tourists from Glasgow hated the two words not because they made no sense, but because they suddenly put an obstacle before their intended goals. They didn't doubt it, that for an event like this to attain and maintain a level of success, it had to be qualitatively coordinated by a body. It just had to be that way. Jacq knew such a body existed in Ila; her husband was one of its senior members while King Jap himself headed the exalted body. Uggi also knew that when he was in Ila, only a handful of men were empowered to dictate to him and Victor what to do; and that it was these few men who were in charge of the festival adjudged the most successful ever in the kingdom. And in Glasgow, he knew his church had a standing committee for festivities, and that his father was pre-eminent in it. All the same, this time, the tourists hated the prospect of having to register or go through any committee.

"We won't register then," Jacq was adamant, "and we shall get to that platform and beyond it. We are optimistic."

"Well, it's virtually impossible," Pat negated, "because you won't know any of the conditions. Don't believe everything will be as simple as it was in the breakfast hall, because it won't be."

For once, Jacq was downcast. She recollected how impossible it was to meet such conditions in Ila, how it was an abomination to have a woman masquerade. "But why is it that everywhere has its silly conditions?" she asked Pat and Mark.

"Everywhere?" Pat wondered. "We are talking of Venice – unless you know of other places."

"Take it like this," Mark hijacked the talking from his wife before Jacq could think of an answer, or preferably maintain the silence as one. "Can you imagine what the place will look like if all masquerades from the entitled families or groups should appear at the same time inside the Square? So, the *Comitato* has to regulate in terms of families and groups representation, themes and depiction of masks and costumes, procession and order of appearances on the stage, balls and concerts, and pre- and post- carnival cleaning. Then it has to determine how the total cost of the festivity must be shared between the tourists and the Venetians."

"Oh good then," Jacq suddenly remembered, and jumped up. "The two of you visited the last twelve carnivals and many others before then, didn't you?"

"Yes," affirmed Pat.

"You both had your wealthy families and roots here, isn't it?" she asked again.

"Yes; why?" Pat responded again.

"If you could give us the right tips together with one of your family names which Uggi and I could jointly adopt in St Mark, then the problems are solved."

The smile on Pat's face showed that Jacq lacked an understanding of many aspects of the Venice carnival – that she failed to identify any of its basic obstacles.

"Alright," Pat faced Jacq and Mark, "supposing you adopt his family name of Ceriani, or mine of Cunni, how would you be able to use it among pure Italian-speaking Venetians?"

"But you are supposed to come with us, aren't you?" Uggi reminded them.

"Yes," agreed Mark, "but only up to immediately before the procession to the stage. The unmasked doesn't pass that point."

"Then mask up yourselves!" Jacq strongly suggested. "Mask up and join us to make the fun complete. Surely, that's possible!"

The two couples debated the possibility of the suggestion. They identified lack of time and money as its formidable foes. Pat and Mark would each need a complete set of costumes with relevant accessories, but unlike the Glaswegians, they had no reserve for a cost they did not prepare for. In the end, Mark brought up the idea of hiring, perhaps from the same Shop 42. Over the years, Mark knew the shop to be the most patronised by groups and families for the supply of masks, attires, and accessories for carnivals.

Jacq took it up with a phone call to the shop. She not only got a confirmation of the availability of costumes for hire, she was offered a discount because of the expensive purchases she and Uggi had just made from the shop. The two couples only had to set out early enough for Pat and Mark to pick them up and have them on.

Thereafter, they all would proceed directly to St Mark to confront the next obstacle they must overcome.

But time that they didn't have was the more devastating of their immediate foes. It rendered hollow Mark's next suggestion which though would be useful, couldn't be banked upon. Mark suggested he must obtain a copy of the day's programme of events which must have already been made and released by the *Comitato*. Laying his hand on one would make the most essential ticket needed to blend successfully into the programme of events in St Mark Square.

* * *

From the time the vaporetto departed Murano for Venice with the two couples among the passengers, the masquerades of Jacq and Uggi cornered the attention of other passengers. It was so for about five minutes when a new scene broke the monopoly: the vaporetto had stopped mid-water to allow a convoy of heavily decorated boats to pass to the island on its left.

Four gondolas to the front and eight bigger boats behind made up the convoy. To the heavy sound of tambourines, accordions, guitars and trumpets from two of the boats, every member of the regatta, gaily dressed and raising either a small flag or an upturned walking stick, danced without a care – not even for that of falling into the water of the archipelago.

"Could you tell me what this is?" Jacq asked Mark. "A regatta or a carnival without masquerades?"

"No, a special burial procession, probably of a jolly Sicilian," Mark replied.

"In Venice?" Uggi asked curiously.

"Yes," affirmed Mark. "The city has always boasted of hardworking and wealthy Sicilians. This procession must have been for one of their nobles. The lucky ones are buried on a people's day like this."

"Right, it must have been one of them," Pat agreed. "Both of you, take a look inside the second gondola," she quickly directed. "There is the coffin. Can you see it?"

"Oh yes," Uggi answered. "One partly covered with cloth?"

"Yes. Can you see its exposed half shinning brilliantly in this dull weather? It suggests it to be a special Veneto sarcophagus; and the covering cloth, a tussah baldachino from Mesopotamia or China."

"So, where will the procession end – and the burial done?" Jacq asked.

"Just behind the wall of this island here, by your left," Pat answered. "It is called San Michele, The Island of the Dead. That is the resting place of the powerful."

"Why is it walled?" Jacq asked. She knew the cemeteries in Ila were only fenced, with the belief that it would keep the dead together as friends in the world beyond. She also remembered the fences were made porous enough to allow easy grave plundering of the offerings by the notorious 'Sese boys'.

"No one has been able to give a single reason for the walling," Mark answered.

"Yes," Pat corroborated, "no one – either in Venice or in Murano. At first we were told it was to protect the epitaphs and their distiches from being stolen and resold. Others believed it to have been built to prevent the great goddess of the sea from carrying away any oversleeping dead. And yet later, we were told it was to prevent the prisoners locked up on the island from making escape attempts into the jaws of sharks and crocs."

"A prison built together with a cemetery?" Uggi wondered aloud. "That's most odd, isn't it?"

"Well, to you it might be," Mark reasoned. "It is certainly not, to the planners. How more balanced could it be? There is a monastery to maintain the tranquillity of the graves; and there is the Mauro Godussi church for all the tombstones to face, so that the souls of the dead will rest, awake and associate together in peace. Everything is thought of, and taken care of."

"Do they leave presents on the graves?" Jacq asked.

"They used to in the past – exotic food and drinks, gold, silver, perfumes, and even, coins – all that they believed the dead will need after life. But the activities of the grave robbers had stopped all that."

"So you have them here too!" Jacq wondered aloud.

"You mean 'they'" responded Pat, conveniently dissociating herself from her ancestry of grave and corpse looters. "Where else do you know that has grave robbers?"

"Oh it is nothing to worry about," Jacq smartly evaded. She wished the convoy would pass quickly for the sake of their appointment with Shop 42.

When it eventually did, and the vaporetto made its stop at Fondamenta Nuove, Mark disembarked to go and obtain an official programme from his uncle at the office of the *Comitato*.

* * *

Inside Shop 42, the catalogued list of the articles for hire was as long as it was elaborate. Extensive as it was however, they could not find any allotment for the Ceriani family they planned to adopt for their pranks. To their dismay, the shop assistant confirmed to them that the family was not participating in the carnival for that year.

"Have you got more of the peacocks then?" Jacq asked the shop assistant.

"Here, no. Yours were ordered specially. If what you want is for today, I am afraid, it is impossible."

"Alright then," Pat resigned herself. "We shall stay with what we can get. When Mark joins us here he will go along with whatever we choose for him."

"It appears that all the articles available to choose from are either blue or green." Pat sought the attention of the assistant. "Which of them is the principal colour for the year?"

"Both of them – mixed in any way and proportion you want. For the past two years, the carnival has saluted our soil and its fertility. This year, the respect is shifted to the blue Adriatic that continues to allow our merchant ships safe passage, our fishermen good catches, and our land to remain firm. Therefore, any colour, be it blue or green, will do. Mother Adriatic loves them both."

So, how Ila worshipped its land and rivers was fashionable by global standards, Jacq felt happy to discover. Probably more similarities awaited her. Probably she would stumble on live animals being displayed as offerings to the sea goddess or to St Mark!

The only outfits in the catalogue that made sense to Jacq and Pat were those of the Egyptian mummies. Jacq admired them because of the strong ancestral root that existed between Ila and the great Nile. Pat loved them due to the beautiful Egyptian history handed over to her generation through her past Roman ancestry who had been to Egypt. Finally, Pat held Jacq's hand and declared she wanted to have them.

"I wouldn't though, if I were you," Jacq responded.

"But why? You can't be me."

"Because you won't be able to ape the movement of the mummy. New York and Bawati are so far and unconnected!" she joked. "Besides why do you want to represent death and corpses now?" she humoured wickedly, successfully making Pat to change her mind. They all opted to see what other costumes the sales assistant had on the hangers.

Pat loved the final choice of the Vikings she made from the hangers for herself and her husband. She tried hers on while Uggi tried on Mark's in his absence. Then they all waited anxiously for Mark to return. It was two hours to the start of the procession, and the exact whereabouts of Mark, were still unknown.

"I am sorry, Jacq and Uggi," Pat apologised on behalf of her husband. "I can assure you both, that neither I nor Mark keeps the typical Italian time. I guess there are some difficulties out there. I want to suggest that you two go on while I wait for him. If there has to be any lateness, it won't be for all of us."

"That won't help matters," Jacq objected. "The problem of communicating in Italian will still be there. It's better the three of us go together. If he can, then he meets up with us later."

"Yes, that is a good solution," Uggi supported, "as long as we make the choice and the payment now. And since he knows his costumes will be here, he will come here first."

"How early before the procession did Mark suggest we should be there?" Uggi asked.

"Two hours, enough to study the field before we plunge in," Jacq answered. "Now we have less than that, and we are still waiting. We need all the luck and prayers."

"Hahaha, hahaha, hahaha," Uggi's rhythmic laughter caught both women by surprise. They saw the situation they were in as one of anxiety, not of laughter.

"Are you alright, Uggi?" Pat asked him after her initial astonishment.

"Yes, I am," he answered, breathing another, but quieter hahaha. "Some masquerades actually prescribed such laughter as prayers."

"Where did you meet such masquerades?" Pat responded, looking across to Jacq and expecting to see a similar strangeness on her partially unmasked face. Instead of her expectation, she saw only a half-smile and some nods she was unable to decipher. "Are you alright?"

Uggi gave no response but Jacq knew that he was trying to be Jackal, the funny masquerade of Ila, a masquerade with legendary laughter that brought good luck to the people. He was the laughing spirit created to cheer up the sad faces of the barren and the weak minds of the sick. She wondered no further, remembering

The Masquerade

Uggi was recently active among King Jap's masquerades; and that he must have seen Jackal performing his cultural duties. But all this, Pat had not the smallest chance of knowing.

"Unlike you Uggi," Pat said. "I feel like screaming at whatever might have held him. I know it won't be his fault. It just won't."

It wasn't Mark's fault, actually, but the circumstantial bad luck that forced itself on a man who hated 'no' for an answer, or 'fail' for an effort. When Mark got to Palazzo Otto, the traditional *Comitato*'s office he knew so well, it was empty, with the compound and the ground floor fully submerged in the waters of Grand Canal. Two big posters, one on the wall and the other on the main door, directed people like him to the new office, a long walk away, on Calle Larga San Marco, just behind St Mark Square.

"Stefano Massarani, can I see him please?" he asked the first man he saw as soon as he entered the hidden, new office of the carnival committee.

"Please, wait here for a minute," the man, glaringly confused, replied Mark. He disappeared into an office and reappeared almost immediately. "How do you know him?" he asked Mark, expecting an answer instantly.

"*Il mio zio*, my good uncle. But more importantly, I am yet to have from him, the carnival programme and order of procession as it affects the family. I am expected to have got them by now."

"Have you paid for them?" the man asked again.

"Yes, they were already paid for."

"Okay then," the man disciplined himself to be patient with the unsuspecting caller. "All copies are already distributed appropriately. Anyway, let me show you the one I have, for you to browse through if that will help. Then, someone will come and talk to you about our director, your uncle."

Mark thought of disappearing with the lone copy, but he dropped the idea when he remembered what its giver had said to him – that someone would be coming to talk to him about his uncle.

Why would his uncle not come out to meet him, or direct someone to bring him in, as was the usual with him? He went through the double sided sheets and saw nothing written there that resembled the traditional family name he planned to use.

"Was there an omission in it – in the name of Ceriani?" he asked the man as soon as the giver returned to him, leading another man.

"No omission. What it means is that the Ceriani family is not participating this year." The answer left Mark tired.

"This is what actually happened," the second man embarked on an explanation. "The family had stopped adopting that name for the carnivals since splitting into two family groups of Brozetti and Lentini."

Brozetti, Lentini? Mark quickly browsed again to ensure both were included, and to note their positions on the list. Before he returned the programme into the hands of its producer, as much as his brains would take, he committed the positions into memory.

"Now about *Signore* Massarani," the second man resumed with soberness and slowness. "He took ill three months ago. Unfortunately, two weeks ago, he passed on. As a mark of respect, and in recognition of his immense contribution to the Venice carnival, his burial was programmed to this great afternoon. It is going on now in San Michele should you wish to catch up with the family. We are sorry."

Mark wished he was in the group heading towards St Michael. He now believed it was the procession that crossed the vaporetto he and his friends took to Venice. He would have had the chance of delivering a befitting elegy by the grave side of a loved uncle. "Oh good Lord," he sighed.

As soon as Mark was out of view from the office of the *Comitato*, he paced faster with the fear that the vital facts he had laboured so much to collect could be rendered useless by his absence from Pat, Jacq and Uggi. The route he took to Shop 42 was through Campo San Lio which, though was the shorter from St

The Masquerade

Mark, was in complete parallel to the one Pat, Jacq and Uggi took about the same time to St Mark.

"They have gone," the shop assistant told a sweaty Mark who was trying hard to control his loud pounding heartbeat. "They left about twenty minutes ago, and left your costume with me. They have paid for the hire; and they want you to wear it and meet them inside St Mark Square. Can you please come with me to the costumes hall?" he requested.

"Hang your clothes there, please," he directed Mark to the long cloakroom of the hall. "You can collect and change back into them when you come back."

Flying through the streets, Mark's masquerade had no time to mourn about the impediments which the crowded presence of other tourists mounted along his way to St Mark. To most of those who saw him, he was the first running, and the fastest ever masquerade in Venice – and perhaps too, the first distressed one. On the one kilometre distance between Shop 42 and St Mark, he stopped not even once, except when one of his cuff buttons got entangled in the hand bag of a female tourist. It forced on him the first minute of rest. He wished the tourist he had got entangled with was Pat, Jacq or Uggi.

* * *

The large platform stood in the open at the southern end of St Mark Square, opposite to the campanile and the basilica. It was a temporarily raised one; two days previous when both of them were there after completing their purchases in Shop 42, the square was without a platform. Now it had one, covered with a velvet fabric which the ordinary eye could perceive from a distance as being totally blue because the dominating colour and the pile had jointly swallowed its small, round spots of white and red.

Jacq, Uggi and Pat entered the square from the same south. With great caution that relegated taking of photographs to the background, they proceeded through the crowd that separated them

236

from the back of the thrust stage. Their first point of stopping was the fixed, quad-stepped stairs that leaned on the thrust from their right. Watchfully, they walked round the long queue of the important masquerades that were about to ascend onto the stage. Now, they had a better view of the stage already surrounded by anxious Mecca of spectators who thickened about ten yards round the thrust before thinning to all other spaces in the piazza.

"Where can we stay that Mark will see us?" Pat eventually asked her fellow masquerades.

"With how things are now," Jacq answered, "better to think of how to be a part of this on our own. It's not likely we shall see Mark or that Mark shall see us."

"Better still to pray for good luck," Uggi added. "Hahaha, hahaha."

"Stop the nonsense, Uggi," Jacq, tense, yelled out a rebuke. "Don't be obsessed with that imbecile Jackal masquerade. We are not in that land of Satan. Real prayer would be more helpful than your funny noise.

"Ah," she sighed. "I just don't know. Now we must move back to behind the queue. Pat, you should lead 'our' Ceriani family – called out or not, Mark or no Mark." The secretary of the *Comitato* was now on stage, making announcements in deep Venetian lingua.

At each of the four corners of the thrust stage was mounted a pole carrying a cluster of light bulbs assembled in the form of a triangle. With the exception of the much bigger one at the apex of each group, the bulbs were of the same size. It was the four bigger bulbs the men directing the stage lighting started with, gradually dimming them while simultaneously lighting up the full colours of the small bulbs mounted below them. As the stage descended from artificial day incandescence to near darkness, and ascended into all colours of the full spectrum again, the chamber orchestra of about twenty members positioned by the walled part of the stage began to play.

"The girls, those are the girls," Pat rushed out the remarks as seven young women, responding to the commencement of the music, climbed onto the stage. They were in long, dominantly blue, frilled dresses. Their tiaras were of rhinestones spotted with blue leaf designs. They moved in measured grace round the stage and finally stopped at its strategic points. From their positions, they frantically waved their small vector fans to the ring of spectators.

"Which girls?" Uggi asked as the girls were being applauded and a man in suit joined them. "Do you do weddings as well on a day like this?"

"They are the young Venetian brides captured, enslaved and used by the Istrians," Pat explained.

"When? Since the start of the carnival?"

"Oh no, Jacq. It happened centuries ago. Then, Istrian pirates regularly raided Venice for its young women and jewellery for their personal pleasure. The Venetians, having decided they had enough, launched a successful counter-attack on the Istrians and set their captured women free. Next, they brought back the women to St Mark Square for all to see. This is its symbolic remembrance – to show how the Venetian women were freed from enslavement. The mode of dressing was to show regained purity from any forced violation their bodies must have suffered in the hands of their abductors." Jacq remembered the near exactness of the story with her people's Princess Moremi Ajasoro's.

"Hmmn, I see. Enslavement, enslavement – so women enslavement was and is still everywhere," Jacq thought aloud.

"But Glasgow women didn't suffer from any sort of enslavement, or did they?" Pat wanted to know. "I am sure Glasgow is more civilised than all that."

"Glasgow might not practise it now," Jacq replied, "but I read how they once expelled thousands of their women together with their babies to Australasia. Besides, scores of other places still cruelly enslave the women."

"Other places…like?"

"Oh Pat, let's get this over with first. Then, I will have time to list that." Jacq was sure Pat knew nothing about Ila and its neighbouring kingdoms.

"And the man who joined them, who is he?" Uggi asked.

"The secretary to the *Comitato* he must be," Pat was certain. "He has the order of things. He is the man to watch in the hours, minutes and seconds to come."

Finally, Jacq, Pat, and Uggi agreed on the end tactic: to wait around but near enough to the tail end of the masquerades' queue, listen to the family names of the masquerades being called on to the stage, usurp one of the families that has already left the stage, and claim late coming as the reason for not being with other members of the family masquerades when they were called.

Pat, Jacq and Uggi joined the last four pairs in the queue, putting themselves between the third and the last pair. Though both the intrusion and the resulting extension did not escape the secretary's notice, he continued with his call of the masquerades to the procession:

"Tazzetti!

"Pontiggia!

"Frigerio!" he called on the last family masquerade before it would be the turn of the gate crashers. Now, the three tourist-masquerades had no more place to hide. Their hearts pounded as the secretary halted the call and approached them on the queue. "Are you three together?" he threw the first of his questions at Pat, the apparent leader of the odd-numbered group.

"Yes, we are!" came a breathing answer from nowhere. Mark's! "We are four of us, part of the old Ceriani family, now in the new Brozetti group," the newly arrived Viking masquerade added.

"I just met you in the office about an hour ago when I came to see my uncle, late Massarani, to ask for our family's copy of the programmes."

239

Mark's words pulled the secretary to a halt, forcing him to look seriously through the face of the Roman Viking before him. He wished he could see more than the two shining eyes behind it.

"O yes. O yes, I am sorry," he remembered and apologised in a whisper. Time was unkind to the secretary; it left him no space to make a further verification of Mark's claims.

"Thank you," said Mark as the two Vikings, the peacock and the peahen climbed onto the stage en route to Palazzo Dona, the theatre-venue all the masquerades were programmed to end the parade with a competition and gala.

Suddenly the two women leading the quartet stopped at the end of the stage, short of descending its exit stairs, and consequently stopping the procession. The women turned back and faced both Mark and Uggi behind them, as well as faced the last pair of masquerades just climbing up to follow them. In a feat that was being performed for the first time in the history of Venice carnival, Jacq and Pat engaged Uggi and Mark respectively in a minute, jazz-wild dance before the crowd. As they did so, the last pair, unsure of what to do and how to walk past them engaged each other and joined the impromptu dance. As short as the dance was, the entire crowd wildly hailed a brilliant entertainment from the last six masquerades.

Once inside the theatre, Mark and Patrizia bombarded Jacq and Uggi with the *ad hoc* translation into English of events happening around them. Through pictures and lectures in her college back in Glasgow, she had learnt about theatres and stages including those in Italy. But which picture however clear, and which talk however factual, beat being physically inside a magnificent theatre like Palazzo Dona! Which theatre in majesty outshined Italian, outdid Venetian, outranked Palazzo Dona! The moment Jacq entered, its largely golden interior totally overwhelmed her – to a breathless loss of words. The floors of terrazzo and marble, the ceilings of vintage chandeliers and glasswork hangings, the walls of gold and silver, the scrimshawed ivory mountings, the colourful masquerades on their seats, the dazzling brass instruments, all combined to present her a rare world of artistic and architectural beauty.

"Listen, Jacq," Mark shook her gently to an attention. "We have been allotted our turn and time to dance on the stage – number 20. The announcement said there will be two prizes, one for the most beautiful, and the other for the best dancing masquerade or group. Then, the dinner where we don't have to mask up our faces." He remembered to add that the copy of the programme with him had confirmed the name of the announcing secretary to the *Comitato* as Alfredo Dotti.

A strong presence of arcaded designs boosted the marriage of the auditorium to the proscenium. The big floor space touching the near side of the rectangular stage was arched, just like the top of the two doors on each side of the stage. On this floor, the twenty-strong jazz orchestra arranged themselves semi-circularly, facing the stage. Behind the orchestra, the semi-circular floor line became raised and stepped up into a mini-amphitheatre that seated the dignitaries.

As far as Jacq was concerned, the style of dancing by all the ten masquerades that had mounted the stage in turn and danced was similar. Typical sequence: a paired adult appearing, one member of the pair gently pulling in the other through the doors on the stage left, slow moves and steps, a final disengagement, a visible bow, invisible smiles behind the masks, disappearance off stage amidst loud to weak clapping, the next pair appearing… So Jacq believed that the boring similarity would continue among the next ten masquerades that would dance before her quartet.

"Why are they injecting all this boredom into a big event, and in a place like this?" Jacq asked Pat and Mark.

"How?" Pat asked.

"Judging by what we have seen so far, would it not have been better if they had danced with different styles instead of every masquerade holding on and pushing each other around like in a light

Japanese sumo fight? Every masquerade has done nothing but used the entire five minutes he was allocated to kill the dazzle."

"What should they have done?" Pat asked again."

"Thank goodness anyway, that they are leaving what to do for us," Jacq answered. "And we shall do them all, in four minutes – with a minute to spare." Her friends, still fresh with the memory and basking in the glory of what she made them do on the outside stage, had no reason to doubt her.

Jacq was however elated that a free back passage connected both pairs of arched side doors to the stage. She could not understand why the carnival organizers had rigidly made the right stage for the masquerades to mount. She was determined that the call to the stage of her group, which was only eight minutes away and after just two more groups, would change that prescription. Her quartet would change it!

The pair of masquerades of Jacq and Uggi dashed on stage through the two stage left arches that had up to that time, never been used. Simultaneously the Vikings of Pat and Mark entered but through the normal stage right. Both pairs were ushered on stage by magnificent spotlights and the back cloth that had changed from blue clouds to a tropical forest setting. Then, in the booming of music the four masquerades stopped and sized up each other dauntingly, with Jacq facing Pat, and Uggi facing Mark. Each couple held hands between them and then raised them up in an arch as if inviting the other couple to a *Dip and Dive* dance. Next, they lowered the arches, broke up and stretched out diagonally holding and going into twirls of assorted speeds and heights.

Halfway into the five minutes allocated to her group, Jacq and Uggi broke up and individually took the way of opposing arches and steps down stage – to both sides of the musical ensemble. There, they went into another type of spin, while Pat and Mark remained dancing on the stage.

"You are doing just fine," a sweating Mark complimented his wife. "Continue to hold on that steadily." The encouragement came just when Jacq and Uggi exchanged signals that it was time to peak their acts. Each of them released the catch that kept his bird's "tail" together as an ordinary extension of the back. In a flash, the roots of the covert feathers webbed out and the train rose arrogant-majestically in rich metallic green, blue and brown hues with coloured spots, obtrusively angled to the body of the birds. The two blooming birds now danced gracefully besides the orchestra.

The spotlights did not fail to respond to the electrifying scenarios. From the moment Jacq and Uggi descended from the stage to the floor, the lighting tracked and highlighted the acts of every member of the quartet. Then, the back cloth behind the Vikings flipped over to a couple of brightly clouded sky-blue sceneries. Next to respond was the new, circumstantial orchestra-host to the peacock and peahen, and then, the orchestra. Its members rose and handled their instruments with rare madness while the birds refused to let it beat them into second place as they danced.

But one thing beat the quartet hands down – to beyond the second place. It was the delight of the cameramen recording a carnival that had just turned extraordinary. Uggi remembered he was in the same situation, taking the rarest of pictures, at the Kings Square of Ila. He however recognised the huge oppositeness in the eventfulness of the two sets of scenes.

Twenty minutes into their dinner, they were almost drowned lifeless by these cameramen and the press. Then an announcement interrupted the dinner to give the result of the competitions:

Best in dancing: No 20, Peacocks and Viking Group. Best in Costumes: No 20, Peacocks and Viking Group.

The applause due to the announcement rendered the quartet deaf, and its shock, dumb. The cameramen closed in and feasted on their faces and costumes as they received their prizes from the secretary and posed with him for the cameras and their blinding flashes.

"Why do they award prizes to the masquerades?" Jacq asked Pat and Mark moments after. "To bribe them?"

"No," replied Pat. "To encourage them for the next carnival. Remember how the masquerades worked hard voluntarily to make the people happy. For example, see how much of our private time and money that have gone into this."

"But then, the awards excessively out-paid the personal expenses, didn't they?" Jacq asked. "Surely, our expenses were lesser than a quarter of the awards."

"Well, no," Pat was adamant. "That will depend on how you make your calculation. By the way, does the carnival go without prizes in Glasgow?"

"Well, I leave Uggi to give you the answer to that," she said to the surprise of Pat and Mark. Jacq wanted to believe that Pat was asking about how it was in Glasgow, and not in Ila. Shamefully, she remained silent about the one she knew of, Ila's: extortion of prizes from the citizens by the masquerades, and the heavy punishment melted on anyone who dared to be a *Mr Objection* or a *Mr Too-know*. "Uggi, up to you," she summoned after her pensiveness.

Uggi gave no answers; he knew nothing much of Glasgow's. The extortionist-takes-all of Ila he participated in was something one should not talk about, even when one remembered.

"So you see, it makes sense to take it," Mark joined in. "We can give a quarter of it back to the committee as donation to the children's charity here."

Pat was satisfied with her husband's suggestion.

"Okay, Mark," responded Jacq, "if I agree with you, would you – and Pat, and Uggi – also agree with me further on the same argument?"

Mark asked what she had in mind.

"Since we never anticipated winning any prize at all, can we change the order of the sharing – take a quarter of the prize money and leave three quarters to that charity? That would make our day and week more fulfilled. What do you say to that?"

"Brilliant, Jacq," Pat rushed in her response before her husband's. "Mark – or Uggi – shouldn't object to that. They mustn't see it as women deciding for men. If they do, I believe they would be gentlemanly enough to concede to us."

The women won the concession. It delighted the secretary into announcing the kindest gesture ever made to the children charity.

The announcement barely beat Giol's protests to both the chairman and the secretary of the *Comitato* about who the prizes went to.

"I have two questions for you," the secretary told the quartet before they would leave Palazzo Dona, and before he would discuss Giol's allegations with his chairman. "The first is: what we can add in order to advance our carnival? You must be full of suggestions."

Mark, most surprised at the question, led in the response. He saw nothing practically or theoretically to add or criticise. "Perhaps Jacq would agree with me" he added. "Our winning was due to her vision and hard work," he commended her to the secretary.

"All of us had actually worked hard," Jacq humbly responded. "But as long as you put the well being of the people and of Venice first, and make the carnival open as it should be, you will always have the joy of the people to confirm to you that you are truly progressing. That is the summary. The details could keep us here all night."

"Thank you," said the secretary. "I will definitely meet the four of you in your hotel by noon time. Then we shall chat about the details.

"And my next question – or wish, if you prefer to call it so: In one single night, you have brought great Augustus back to Venice for a brotherly visit, brought Africa for a feathery

245

entertainment, and brought *Madre Teresa* for the kindest gesture ever; can you please join the membership of the *Comitato*?"

"We wish we could," Mark smiled in appreciation. "We really wish we could."

"But what stops you? It won't be me or any of my committee members."

"The problem," said Mark, "is that while my wife and I are true Venetians, we live in New York. Jacq and Uggi here, the two who did all the planning and directing, are from Glasgow. So, none of us lives in Venice, or in Italy."

Uggi felt humbled by the high praise from Mark. He seized the moment to advance them more appropriately. "Thank you for the praise Mark," he started, "but if I could tell you for the first time, Jacq here inspired me from the start and all along. And, she is not even from Glasgow; she is from Africa's Ila Kingdom!"

'Oh' of Pat, 'really?' of Mark, her husband, and 'no wonder' of the secretary clashed in response to Uggi's revelation.

"No wonder; is that so?" the secretary asked with eagerness for a confirmation from Jacq. "We learnt so much from Ila; but that was long ago. Our great-grandfathers who visited Ila long ago spoke of how they learnt a lot from them. I never dreamt I will ever meet someone from Ila this easily. By noon today, I must be with you in Murano."

Feeling thoroughly flabbergasted but satisfied, Jacq could only return a long smile as a response to the secretary's praise and promise. His coming by noon would be just fine by her. She would have enough time to see her friends' Viking costumes returned, have time to buy one costume each for Uggi's dad and Sariya, and would be back at the hotel to commence a 24 hour countdown to their departure from Venice.

* * *

The hard knocks on the door of Jacq and Uggi's room were loud enough to serve all the rooms along the same corridor at once.

It shocked them out of the bed, from the deep sleep that followed their packed, last twenty-four hours.

"Here, for you!" the panting hotel manageress pushed the day's *La Domenica Veneziana* newspaper into Uggi's hand. "Congratulations many times!" She was full of excitement.

Uggi took a cool look at it while Jacq moved closer and joined him in the newspaper gazing. Even though none of them spoke Italian, the front page of the newspaper before them had confronted them in a pictorial language they well understood.

"Or, is that not you?" the manageress screamed with emotions. "Yes, it is. So you and the Cerianis made it from Murano to St Mark – from my dining hall to winning trophies at the Palazzo Dona!

"Yes, you are having a special dinner on the hotel management this evening – all free with the best of our *bianco*! I must see the Cerianis too. Please come over when you are ready." She dashed off, leaving the newspaper with them.

At the dinner, the four instant celebrities pondered on why the secretary hadn't shown up as promised. Uggi believed he must have been too busy broadcasting the achievements as his own.

"That would be odd," opined Pat. "What would he expect us, the real actors, to do?"

"Do what you like," Uggi believed. "Should he care?"

"With all his kind words," Jacq came in, "I wouldn't believe he's a man like that. He looked nice and real."

"Well then," Uggi said, "unless he's being overpowered by what Pat mentioned to us some hours ago inside Shop 42 – the Italian time syndrome." They all laughed with Pat believing it would have been a syndrome carried into madness, one that would have set a record in the history of lateness anywhere!

When the secretary finally made the contact, it was well after the dinner. Instead of the physical presence he promised them repeatedly, it came as a phone call to Jacq. His words were incoherent and distressed. He managed to praise the quartet for their contribution to the carnival, and apologised that he hadn't been and won't be able to see them in Murano. But before long, he would see them in Glasgow, and in New York. He wanted them to leave Murano and Venice immediately. He had been in some sort of hell since the dancing ended. Some ingrates among the Venetians and in the *Comitato* were spoiling for a fight with him the secretary, and with the quartet. Among the trouble makers was Giol, the owner of the Altamare where they lodged, and the leading instigator of the trouble. "Please, leave now and don't ignore me," he finished off. He then set off for Calle Larga San Marco to attend the emergency meeting of the *Comitato*.

* * *

Despite the lavish decorations, the atmosphere in the room was damp – like the apparent mood of the three men and one woman who were already sitting there, waiting. None of the four people had expressed to the other words beyond the morning greeting of *Buongiorno*, and these were without the kind of warmth that should make the greeted feel the greetings were real and meant. Each person took a seat and adapted himself to the next difficult quarter of an hour when the clergy who summoned them would arrive. Each one of them had his anger carbonated and bottled inside him.

The loud noise from the summoner's hard soles battering along the wooden floored corridor announced his arrival tens of steps away before his actual appearance. Quite disappointingly, he was a small man, made even smaller by his all black priestly garb. His eyes were big and chameleonically revolving; they hung out enough to guide over the big mouth he would soon put into a commanding use that noon time.

Those already waiting deliberately avoided noticing the anger he equally packed in the eyeballs – they already had their own burning inside theirs. Neither did they acknowledge the pack of newspapers he was struggling to hold in joint mass inside his left armpit – whatever stories the pack contained would be scarcely different from those in the day's newspaper each sitting person had with him.

A quick and shallow blessing by the convening clergy was followed by a direction to everyone to take his seat. He went straight to the point: previous day's carnival – parade and dance.

"This meeting is not a substitute for the *Comitato* meeting due for tomorrow," he stressed arrogantly, "nor one for the monthly Venetian Council. Rather, it is an emergency one to repair the series of damages already done, to stop further damages from being inflicted, and to put in place a permanent system of damage control on the carnival. Can we start with the reports of the carnival inside these newspapers?" Apparently, he had four of the day's with him – one for each of his invitees.

Silently, the attendees restricted themselves to the front pages. Except for size, the pictures of the peacock and Viking masquerades they carried were similar. As for the captions, they eulogized the quartet in different directions – Brozetti Pea-kings! *Inghiltera Fantastica!* (Fantastic England!). Unbeatable African Dance! The Kindest Quartet! The newspapers also had carnival supplements but the invitees largely ignored them.

"Now that we have seen the newspapers," he resumed after a short moment, "what do you think? Should we now congratulate ourselves and the *Comitato*?"

"Both deserved to be congratulated," said the only woman at the meeting. "And tomorrow's meeting of the *Comitato* should do just that." She was the owner of Shop 42, and a special member of the *Comitato*.

"Do you agree with that, Stefano," the clergy asked the journalist member in their midst, the editor of *La Domenica Veneziana* that screamed "Unbeatable African Dance" as its caption.

"Absolutely," Stefano had no doubt. "All Venetians said that; and the newspapers attested to it. Absolutely."

"No, you are all wrong," the convener cut in with the crispness of a controlled anger. "And unless you correct your mistakes now, there will be nothing of it left to congratulate by the time we would sit tomorrow. There were so many mistakes. Didn't you all talk with the people? There were – mistakes!"

"There were, and were none," Alfredo, the secretary to the *Comitato*, seized his turn. "If there were, they were baseless. Did you, as the head of the committee, expect a project this massive to be completely murmur free? Father, it's impossible. This was the best ever!"

"I believe that too," said Stefano. "The people honestly expressed it as attested to by all the captions. The judgements came from individuals, and yet they're all the same."

"You all seem to forget that I constantly face bigger congregations," the convener reminded them with bias. "The members of my congregations are Venetians, not tourists. You are all taking sides with each other, as the flies would with an ulcerated head wound."

"Look Father," the fourth person, the secretary to the duke, broke in, his tone confirming he'd had enough. "You are not only the head of the Committee, you are a senior clergy as well. You are unnecessarily angry and insulting, and none of us can understand why. Why don't you humble yourself and be specific with what you found wrong? We might just have to leave if you don't. For me, I have an appointment with the duke in an hour's time."

The Father became quiet as the humble pie was forced down his throat. He took a big breath, eventually apologised, and attempted a restart. "Giol alleged that none in the quartet was a Venetian."

"The solution to that is simple enough, Father," proffered the duke's secretary. "Tomorrow at our meeting let Giol properly move for a ban on tourists to Venice; or better still, to Murano. He is a hotel proprietor, and we shall see who dies first from such a move.

Who argued that we didn't need more land and buildings for glass blowing in Murano? He, not any of us!"

For the first time, laughter descended into the rooms, onto the faces.

"Next," the convener went on, "he claimed that in order to compete, the four of them had adopted a family that wasn't theirs."

"Absolutely untrue," Stefano answered. "I verified that two of them still have their strong families in Venice and Murano. A true Venetian family had a right to design its costumes and invite whoever pleases it to carry them on its behalf."

"He said they were not good enough to have won the prizes – that the secretary influenced the decisions in order to favour them."

"Really, we have to move away from these nonsense," Stefano cut in again. "This man, a bad loser, does not constitute the committee, the tourists, or the Venetians, all of who witnessed the best ever.

"You saw them perform yourself, and you applauded them. They won the prizes and most generously left almost all of them to our charity.

"I was told how in his hotel at breakfast time yesterday, the quartet was almost deafened by the praises both staff and guests showered on them. That was where they lodged; and if they were not truly good enough, why did he and his entire staff toast them to the point of hanging their pictures all over the place so quickly? Please, please, please, can we move forward?"

"One last question please," the lady requested. "Why is the complainer himself not with us? Didn't you invite him?" she asked the Father.

"I did of course. Why he's not here I don't know."

"We have said it," the duke's secretary reminded the sitting, "Let's move forward."

The Masquerade

The progression started with a general acknowledgement of the carnival's huge success and the excellent contributions of the quartet to it.

Through his secretary, the duke enjoined the committee to make all tourists feel more welcome, and in future gave them more opportunities to take part in the fun. These the *Comitato* acceded to, but with certain definition pressured in by the Father. The definition centred on what they called basic rules, masquerades, and dances.

Under basic rules, no foreigner would use the masks to ridicule any noble or citizen of Venice. It had taken a long time to evolve from when African servants and slaves started the whole thing by disguising under masks and paints to ridicule their masters or nostalgically remember their roots. Foreigners and tourists must not be allowed to bring this silliness back to Venice.

Preferences of taking part in parades and balls would be given only to masquerades who could speak Italian. The masks had already disguised the faces enough; easy and direct communication among the masquerades would reduce the effects of such separation. There must be no mumbo-jumbo, and no one would be allowed to compare his deity chants with the in-church *latinus* tongues of Venetian clergies.

On the type of costumes allowed for foreigners, the meeting accepted that the Venetians were just lucky that the quartet came up with something beautiful and decent at the carnival. The committee must watch it that in the future, foreign participants wouldn't come up with weird ideas like carrying blood-drooping monkey heads, poison-fanged snakes, frightening dragons, ugly carvings or dreadfully painted faces. Shop 42 which was central to sales and hiring of masks, costumes and accessories must sell out only the beautiful and decent materials synonymous with the spirit of the carnival and the true beauty of Venice.

On dances, the *Comitato* welcomed safe innovations. African idolatrous ones like fire dance, blood dance, initiation dance, death dance, ancestors dance and so on must not be allowed to resurface. Venetians had seen them centuries ago in Africa, seen them brought to Venice, and finally banned these crude movements. They must not be allowed back into the premises of St Mark, or inside any of the Venetian palaces.

Lastly, the *Comitato* must continue to measure critically, the type of innovation the tourists would introduce, otherwise the tourists would end up claiming they built the Rialto, defeated Mehmet the Conqueror, routed Barbarossa, apprenticed Giovanni Bellini, inspired Carlo Goldoni, and built the gondolas!

"And one more thing," the lady interrupted the current light-heartedness among the attendees as they were about to disperse. "Since we accepted the quartet did well, should we send a special emissary to them in their hotel, to thank them on behalf of the Venetians?"

"Sorry," said the editor, "the news is that they have left – gone back to England and America."

"But why so soon?" the Father asked.

"Why not, Father?" the editor asked. "They took a quadruple precaution from the double threat you and Giol made to them. And two hours ago came the latest news: Giol had sacked his manageress for giving the quartet a free, congratulatory dinner on behalf of his management. He discovered the unauthorised feting when he was looking for the quartet in order to deal with them."

"I am sorry about these, and happy that all is well now," the Father said with all soberness. "We must find their addresses and invite them back – to thank them and show them the true warmth of the Venetians. They are the type of tourists we need, the type of artists we could share our knowledge with – in the *Comitato*

"Alfredo," he quickly turned to the secretary, "please do what has to be done"

CHAPTER EIGHT

Inside Glasgow II

As soon as Jacq and Uggi were safely airborne and away from what they believed was a Giol-led attack on them, they had agreed on how their experience would be related to Ali Jaiye back in Glasgow.

"My dad wouldn't believe our achievements – all we were able to do for the Venetians," Uggi told Jacq as their aeroplane stabilised after the take off.

"But will he believe they planned an attack on us, and that we were lucky to escape?" Jacq asked Uggi.

"Probably not. He has so much respect for Venice and Venetians. To him, they can do no wrong."

"So, which side of our experience do we share with him?"

"The positive, of course," Uggi replied.

"And leave him to discover the negative by himself?"

"Well, if ever he would. At least he won't start mourning another disappointment so soon. And if he ever discovers that it's not our fault this time, it will gladden his heart." The two of them were contented to let it rest at that.

At the airport in Glasgow, Ali saw both of them from far away. They were so busy chatting that they didn't notice his presence when they got to him.

"Needless to ask you how the journey was," Ali jolted them. "You are both chatting away happily. You must have had a nice journey this time around."

"Hello, sir," responded Jacq. "We are happy to see you again." She hugged Ali first, before Uggi did.

"We are happy, dad, especially after the long week," Uggi added.

"Long week? You've only gone five days! Felt long to you?" He hoped it didn't. Only a troubled experience would feel long in duration. He hoped that for staying all of the days they originally planned, unlike the first time they visited Venice, they must have had a non-disastrous sojourn, and return.

"Somewhat long," said Jacq, "But it doesn't mean we didn't enjoy the journey. Actually the experience was marvellous, one for life!"

"I knew it – that it was going to be a nice thing for both of you," Ali commended his own foresight as he drove them back.

"But you shouldn't have stopped at the tips," Jacq took over the compliment, "it would still have been nicer if you had come with us."

"I thought about that, Jacq, but for whom in the cathedral could I have left the holy days to manage? Good Friday, Easter Sunday, Easter Monday...have you forgotten?"

Ali compelled his son to stay the night with himself and Jacq so that Jacq and Uggi would continue with the reportage of their visit over dinner. They were just into the meal when Jacq and Uggi simultaneously took a 'one minute' excuse from Ali to disappear into Jacq's room. "We have to fetch your gifts, sir," Jacq said.

"Here, for you, dad," said Uggi, the first of the two to re-emerge. He stretched out two multi-folds of picture postcards to his father, shaking open the one depicting colourful Venetian masquerades.

"Isn't this beautiful?" delightfully responded Ali as he received the shaken-out fold. Then he had the second, showing popular landmarks of Venice.

"How about this then?" Jacq asked as she jumped out of the room, her face masked.

"This is incredible, Jacq!" exclaimed Ali. "I can't believe it – that you could be so brave to wear a mask, that you matured much sooner than you promised me. I must congratulate you, Jacq!"

"Thank you, sir," responded Jacq. "You showed me how to conquer fear. I would never have been able to do it if not for your encouragement.

"We have our own – the ones we actually use for our outings in Venice. So, this on my face is for you, sir. We regard it as the 'father' of the masks, one that's more important than our own." She removed it from her face and was tying it round Ali's.

By the time its fixing was completed on Ali, another surprise was already waiting for him in Uggi's hands. It was a set of costumes, complete with a tall hat and decorated walking stick, all complimentary to the mask fixed on his face. "Yes, dad, they are all for you, Uggi affirmed."

"Wear them," Jacq said proudly. "And later, you can hang them on your walls," she added.

"Yes," Uggi agreed, "like the management of the hotel we stayed hung pictures of our masquerades on their walls for all the guests to admire."

Ali broke off from both Jacq and Uggi as soon as he was fitted with the mask and costume. He walked to the tall mirror along the passage to the main entrance door and admired himself unbelievably. "*Il carnevale* is here with us tonight," he screamed with delight, returning to them. "Thank you, guys. Thank you very much." He returned to his chair.

"Did you not just say they hung some of your pictures?" Ali suddenly remembered and asked his son after he had sat and removed the mask from his face. "Won't you show me the pictures?"

"Come on then, Jacq," Uggi commanded. "Let's show dad the real thing."

Again, both Jacq and Uggi made another brisk trip to Jacq's room. They returned together with Uggi wearing the main costume he wore in Venice, and Jacq her peacock mask only.

Ali, himself a man of carnivals, could hardly believe his eyes when Uggi knelt down for Jacq to impose herself over him from behind. Then she released the catch to the tail feathers, allowing the peacock to bloom in full.

At first, Ali couldn't find an expression to fit what had just unfolded before his eyes. Both his father and grandfather, when on earth, were prominent men of masks and masquerades; and he grew to know them as such. Masks and masquerades were strong aspects of tradition and culture both men, though Anglicans, thought him to respect. It was out of his concern for the Ila masquerades going awry – cooked and falsely spiritual – that he made private visits to other carnivals across Europe, to verify if the Ila situation was intercontinental. In all these visits, he did not see a mask or a masquerade that was as beautiful as the one now before him.

"This is incredible; or what else can I say?" he finally pulled himself together to speak. "Absolutely marvellous – that two people could fuse so successfully to depict a peacock!"

"In Venice," Uggi took up the clarification, "we had a peacock and a peahen. We were onstage in St Mark and inside Palazzo Dona; and we collected all the prizes. It was all due to Jacq – all due to her. She was nothing but special."

"It was all due to you, sir," Jacq differed. "We donated the prizes to the children's charity, in memory of Sariya, my daughter, who we also got a complete costume for." She lapsed into momentary grief.

"Cheer up, Jacq," Ali consoled Jacq. "If you continue to be strong, she will wear them one day, and soon – in the good names of our ancestors in Ila and the pure name of Jesus Christ. Mark my words again, my dear Jacq.

"So, can you now see one of the advantages of my not accompanying you to Venice? You wouldn't have had the wisdom, freedom and bravery you applied to perform your acts."

"That could be so, sir, Jacq partially agreed, "but we would have been able to receive direct answers to certain questions we still have unanswered."

"You could have asked all those around you in the high places you operated. They would have been happy to please you."

"We asked, dad. We went as far as pinning down the secretary of the *Comitato*. We received nothing, unfortunately."

"From the secretary himself?"

"Nothing from him, dad. And there is no need to go further on why he evaded us and our questions. We wouldn't have had a reason to direct those questions to them if you were there with us."

"Alright guys, if you don't feel it's too late, you can still ask me; and I will try my best to answer them."

"It's too late now, sir; and we are all tired. We shall reserve them till another time." Jacq and Uggi had had enough for the day.

* * *

That Sunday evening, Ali Jaiye recognised the caller's voice straightaway. He had called twice before and it was Ali who answered him both times. His first call was five days ago, just two after Jacq and Uggi were back from Venice. He particularly wanted to know if Jacq and Uggi were okay. Then he strayed into asking Ali if either Jacq or Uggi had recently received any call from New York. The funny inquisitiveness compelled Ali to ask who the caller was even though the caller had reinforced the distinct, long distance, ringing tone of the phone with telling Ali that he was calling from Venice. He called himself Alfredo, but better known to Jacq and Uggi as 'the secretary'. "Call back for Jacq on Friday about this time," Ali had directed him, adding "she's sure to have returned from the college."

Ali recollected how dejected Alfredo sounded on Friday when Jacq wasn't there as was assured him; and how Alfredo had to leave him his number to pass on to Jacq and Uggi, hoping they would return his call.

Ali also remembered that Jacq was uncharacteristically dismissive of Alfredo when she, on returning home, was given Alfredo's number. "Hasn't he got something to do with his time?" Ali heard Jacq murmur against the nuisance. Now, Sunday, he had called again – unfortunately when Ali was expecting a church-related call and Jacq was at home. Alfredo must have been a prayerful man desperate to win a woman's heart, Ali had thought wildly.

"Jacq, it's the man again – the secretary. From Venice. He wants to speak with you."

Jacq knew she had to speak with Alfredo this time, otherwise Ali would suspect something. Worse still would it look of her should she request Ali to lie to Alfredo that she was not at home. She felt quite unfortunate all over as she eventually took the phone from Ali and uttered a hateful "yes?"

"Congratulations, Jacq," the voice on the other side contrasted sharply. "I have been trying to speak with you since Tuesday," he added, as if Jacq wasn't aware of his efforts.

"Why the congratulations, and why do you want to speak to any of us after pelting us with threats to our lives?" Jacq asked in a voice she lowered barely enough for Alfredo to hear. "Didn't you publish bad stories in the newspaper in order to turn Venice against us? On Thursday I got a copy of *La Notizia Venezia* sent by one of you; it was dedicated to insulting me and Uggi." She was finding it hard to control her anger now. She didn't want to continue with the conversation.

"Please, don't hang up on me," Alfredo pleaded with her. "*La Notizia Venezia* is only one of nine Venetian newspapers. All, I mean, the eight others, praised the four of you, and you especially, for your invaluable innovation and contribution. Even the fickle reverend head of the *Comitato* and the mischievous Giol, owner of the hotel you stayed, were both brought to their knees for being that unreasonable."

"Can you imagine how humiliating Pat might feel on receiving her own copy – originating from the town of her birth?"

"Jacq, I assure you, the story was false and unrepresentative of us. Just dump it into the waste bin where it belongs."

"It's already there, Alfredo." She was becoming calmer but louder now. "I binned it straightaway."

"That's good, Jacq. And do you know what Jacq? We want you to come back!"

"Don't you even talk about that. It will not happen. We've made two journeys to Venice and each of them had ended in serious problems for us. It could be different for Pat and Mark since they are one of you."

"Perhaps I should have talked about other things first – about how the special invitation came about."

Alfredo went on to say how it was Giol, the hotel proprietor who started the trouble. As the only committee member competing in the mask and costume events, he believed the judges should have favoured him to win the prizes. As soon as Giol discovered he had lost, he rushed down to him to protest that the judges had foolishly allowed a stranger's dance of no conventionality to triumph over loved traditional dances, and had thus brainlessly enabled the non-Venetians to go away with Venetian cash. By the time Giol sought an unholy rectification from the chairman at the Palazzo that night, Jacq's quartet had already donated the prizes to the charity. And instead of appreciating the kind gesture, the chairman in sympathy with Giol, took it as insulting to Veneto that the biggest ever donation to that charity had come from foreigners. But other committee members saw it differently and they strongly objected to his actions. Already, all the papers, except *La Notizia Venezia*, were against the views of the two corruptible dissenters. Before it was be too late for him, the chairman realised he would become a chairman without a member, a head without a body, and practically a clergy without a congregation. So, the chairman quickly toed the line and moved it that the committee called back the quartet to show the *Comitato*'s appreciation. They even discovered Giol sacked his manageress for treating your quartet to a dinner in his name. The *Comitato* had to force Giol to reinstate her, or lose his membership of the *Comitato*.

Jacq was attentive, and convinced. However, she still had one question for the narrator. "Are you saying that in the whole of your archipelago only two persons were against us?"

"True, only those two people. They had no reasons other than those of selfishness for one, and close-mindedness for the other. We couldn't even understand how the chairman was so narrow-minded. It was difficult to believe his subsequent admission, that he had heard of and exchanged much with your Ila. It gave us the chance to scold him for being that retrogressive.

"So, when will you be coming? We want you to meet the children you donated the prizes to. When?"

Jacq wished she knew the answer. She would be proud to have and to honour an invitation from the *Comitato* if only she could trust it. She would wait to receive the praising newspapers Alfredo promised to send her.

During that telephone conversation, Ali picked a few of the keywords. He realised that somehow, something negative had happened to Jacq and Uggi in Venice, their nicely painted reportage to him notwithstanding. He recollected that Jacq received by post on Thursday morning, a long, rolled item. He was happy the weekly bin collection wasn't due till the following morning. As soon as Jacq was on her way to the college in the morning, he would go through the bins and recover the newspaper to discover what Jacq and his son concealed from him.

The Masquerade

Ali was pleased he found the newspaper edition the following morning. His scanty knowledge of ethical Latin and Italian, together with his old English-Latin dictionary had made the modest translation simpler than he had anticipated. He kept the paper and awaited the after-college hours when as customary, Uggi on his way to the house he shared with Victor, would arrive together with Jacq in his house.

"The two of you are masking away from me something about Venice, aren't you?" Ali softly confronted Jacq and Uggi before Uggi would continue his journey home.

"What are you saying, dad?" Uggi challenged Ali, even though neither he nor Jacq was shocked at Ali's question. They knew it would come someday, sometime.

"Exactly what I said – that you are hiding something. And, may I add that whatever it is must be something so nice that you don't need to hide it. So, tell me with your own mouths!"

"Did you discover something then, dad?"

"Well, yes."

"Was there another phone call for Jacq or myself?"

"No."

"You must have seen the newspaper, sir," Jacq wanted to believe. "Did you, sir?"

"Yes. I found it and read it. I also guessed from a bit of your conversation of yesterday. Anyway, I recovered it; and I recommend you honour the invitation the secretary has extended to you."

"Please, sir, let it go back into the bin. The story was biased and untrue."

"Listen, the two of you. Wait first for the newspapers Alfredo would send. But you mustn't throw away the invitation. Someone or some people had engineered a failure for you, but you succeeded. He who says you won't succeed must always be the one to whom you should first display the humility of your success. I want you to honour the invitation and go back there, very soon. Go back there and identify the faces of your detractors from behind the masks that hide them. Go back and shine before those faces.

"It's then you'll determine whether to bin that newspaper together with the already exposed evil faces of your detractors. That's how I suggest you handle it, how you treat such crooked masks and masquerades. They're everywhere you know, and you can both stand and start to show them why they should change."

"Even in Venice?" Jacq asked.

"Everywhere, including Venice and here, Glasgow. You said you were at the cultural exhibition, didn't you? But of Venice, the good thing is that the crooked masks are very small in number, and unlike in Ila where they still dominate the carnival. I don't need to tell you more. You have seen both yourself."

"You need to tell us – to tell us more – dad. Why can't Ila adopt the ways of Venice?"

"Because the kings, the chiefs, together with their stealing instincts wouldn't let the kingdom," Ali replied. "But the irony is that it was Venice who used to learn from Ila of old."

"How?" Uggi, puzzled, asked. "Would that be why the secretary claimed to have heard of Ila?"

"Certainly, yes."

"But the same secretary confirmed that their leader in Venice swore not to welcome the ways of Ila masquerades, that he classed them all as stupid," Jacq reminded Uggi, and his father. "A newspaper also condemned them in the same manner. And honestly, I can't remember seeing a single ugly masquerade in Venice."

"They are there," Ali assured Jacq, "only that they balanced their appearance with beautiful attires and pleasant manners. You must know that it's the man behind the mask who makes the mask good, ugly or crooked. There, unlike in our Ila, no ugliness ever went beyond the actual masks."

Surprisingly to Jacq and Uggi, Ali went on to justify the fears of both *La Notizia Venezia* and the chairman of the *Comitato*. "It could be due partly to the natural pride of Venetians, or partly to their awareness of Ila's current ways of celebrating the masquerade festivals," he vindicated them.

"On the question of pride," Ali went on, "that's how they've always been. But then, they were adventurous, hardworking, and never vain. They once reached the Nile and its extensions which included Ila. They not only brought material wealth home from there, they also returned with rich, cultural experiences of those lands. Their war generals and clergy equally did the same – they, one time or the other, returned with human cargo in the form of gifts, servants and slaves. As these classes of travelled Venetians invented their own group and religious celebrations, they allowed their imports to entertain them as well as to remember their culture. Due to the superior beauty of the imported culture, these Venetians took it over and adapted it to what the two of you saw in Venice.

"True, Jacq and Uggi, which sane people will ever want to do the masquerade festival the way it's done in Ila nowadays?

"The protection it once offered to the people had been made to vanish. The communal unity it enforced is no more. The wealth of the people it ensured is now hijacked. All the goodness of the masquerades in Ila is gone – seized by the ignorant thieves and colourful robbers who continually pose as political kings, rulers or nobles united in the use of deadly intimidation to prevent the citizens from wearing their own masks, or from groping to know whose faces are behind the intimidating masks."

* * *

Two evenings after Alfredo spoke to Jacq, there was another phone call. It was from a different source, Ben, to yet another recipient, Victor, his son. Ben had called to know if Uggi had briefed him on how he, Uggi, and Jacq fared at the Venice carnival.

"Just yesterday he was hilarious about the visit," Victor told his father. "I didn't ask again, and was not going to. I am not eager; and sure you too are not, dad."

"Not eager to see any of you going," Ben responded, "but eager to know what happened to anyone that went – principally and including your friends – quite eager to keep a tap on. So, why was Uggi hilarious about it?"

"He showed me two photographs."

"Yes…of her on the Rialto, or of them doing a 'Trafalgar Square' with the pigeons of St Mark?"

"It's more than that, dad. They are photographs of peacock and peahen masquerades."

"You mean of carnival masks displayed in the shop for sale?"

"Of both of them in full costumes they wore and competed in, inside St Mark."

With Ben, the conversation soared into one he could neither understand nor judge anymore – partly due to the distance between their two hand receivers and partly to the apparent tallness of the story. Ben reckoned further verbal exchanges on this were better continued face to face with his son. He invited Victor to pass by his studio the following evening on his way from the college with the photographs.

"So, what were you telling me?" Ben asked his son. He struggled to be patient for Victor to take his seat beside him.

"Well, dad, look at them," Victor responded, handing over to Ben two photographs. "That was them in full peacock and peahen costumes inside St Mark. Uggi said they both won all the prizes and were toasted."

"Ha ha ha, boy," Ben laughed contently at what was to him a truly laughable matter. "I hope you are not already mercerised into the thinking pattern of a typical Ila person.

"Good artwork, yes. But whose faces were behind the masks, we need to first ask Jesus Christ. You must never fall for this sort of gimmick.

The Masquerade

"Do you think if the Venetians are desperate for masquerades, that the next place they would go would be Virginia, or more insultingly, to Africa's Ila?

"It has always been known that Jacq had phobia of the masks; how then would she had allowed a mask near her face? How would she had allowed Uggi to wear a mask and stand beside her? It's all just too unreal. It's only the pictures of the *golden oldie* that couldn't tell lies!"

"Yes, dad, she used to be mask-phobic. But after that first disastrous visit to Venice, Rev Ali Jaiye had sort of braved her out of it. This is a proof."

"Okay Victor, consider another question: Where would they have found enough time to make such flamboyant costumes?"

Victor could not find an answer.

"None of them belonged to a Venetian family or church – how could they have participated? None of them speaks a single Italian *parola* – how could they have participated? Where was the chance of any of those happening? Nowhere.

"And lastly, Victor, between you and me, I don't expect black people to posses the ability to make such beautiful masks and costumes. It's just beyond them."

"Well, dad, further argument would serve no purpose," Victor replied, preferring not to get into a race or colour debate with his father. "But I wouldn't be surprised if there were some truths in Uggi's claims. We saw fantastic masks in Ila. In Ila, everyone portrayed Jacq as being above ordinary. Same for our own experience with her here – she is so strong and brave that nothing could be put beyond her. Uggi even said they are returning to Venice for bigger masks, bigger costumes and a special carnival they have been invited to. He said the *Comitato* has offered them guest memberships."

For a while, Ben was silent, his eyes, gaping. His perception of his son's story was coasting from a horrible dream to a deadly reality, one that had positioned itself on the verge of

266

destroying the source of his family's greatness and survival. A lot to say jam-packed his mind, making it difficult for his mouth to pick what it should race out first. "I have always said this – and dreaded it," he murmured loudly with his eyes firmly closed, "have I not?"

"Said what, dad?"

"Said what?" he marvelled disappointedly at his son's mind of forgetfulness. "That she has the tongue of a conceited slave and the waywardness of a disobedient servant. You should not have brought her. Her type was one that was easy to export but difficult to import. Instead of her being a good slave and servant to you, me or Scotland, she is already a big trouble to everyone, to everything. Do you understand, son?"

"Whatever we are saying, dad, slavery and servitude don't apply, as they are two trades that were gone forever."

"Yes, gone forever and leaving this sort of confusion! If Jacq should move anywhere near the *Comitato*, have you thought of the terrible position that would leave us in?"

"Us?" Victor asked, unable to reach the depth of his father's thoughts.

"Yes, us – me, you…us!

"I am just imagining a black female convicted prisoner, together with a black, man influencing a major European arts policy. Crazy, wouldn't that be?

"From time to time, I make business exchanges with Venice; so, what will happen to the family business?

"She shouldn't and won't be allowed to partake in another show, or in the decisions of the *Comitato*. She must be prevented, blocked!"

"But why would anybody do that to her?" Victor, now becoming suspicious of his father's extremism, asked him. "Here, everybody is free to do as he wishes as long as no law is broken. Besides, she is doing it with Uggi; so, how are you going to block her?"

"Just warn Uggi to stay far and clear. If you can't, I will."

"But what if he's reluctant? We both promised to look after her; so, we can't both abandon her totally. We promised King Jap to keep her like he wanted."

"But you promised never to return her. So, what does it matter where she is, or what happens to her?"

"You are not planning to harm her, dad, or are you? Victor asked fearfully. "Frankly, dad, we should just leave her as she is. She is a free person here now though we shall continue to watch her."

"Free person my foot!" Ben turned and shouted at his son with a forward thrust that almost ended in a head butt. His son's stance had clearly sent him mad. "And it is entirely your fault – that she is not only full of freedom but she has extra to destroy my business with. I long recognised she is a bad omen, and can't believe you too refuse to recognise that. I believe you need to consider where your loyalties lie – with me in the family and the business, with King Jap in his jungle, or with a black convict you call Jacq. Now, you must take a side and let me know which."

Victor, terrified, was quiet. Loyalties? Yes, he believed he had them, though in different kinds, for every name his father mentioned. The oath he took stuck with him like a louse in an unkept head. He feared the curse of betraying King Jap. He feared the mind of his father. He saw the fears as placing him between further antagonizing and helping Jacq. But for whatever it was for now, he wouldn't harm Jacq – or Uggi.

* * *

More than for her blunt and strong personality, the sudden and overwhelming success Jacq experienced in Venice had started to influence pig-headedly, her relationship with both her course mates and her course work. On this Friday which would have been another normal one, one of the art teachers had come into her class and openly accused her of misleading some students subordinately, which she had denied and explained. It was outside the class, during an extended explanation to her mates, that a young man approached her group.

"Excuse me, the stranger called for Jacq's attention. "Are you Jacq?"

"Yes, is there a problem?" she answered and asked. Not that she actually suspected one, as assured by the radiance on the young man's face.

"None whatsoever," he confirmed. "I am Sam Mahoney from the department of geography. This is a note for you, from a gentleman who unsuccessfully tried to locate you. I offered to help him."

"Ben Mackinnon?" Jacq asked herself and the letter, quivering at the sight of a sender's name she was happy to forget, of a man she lately discovered hated her more than any other woman on planet earth.

The last time she set her eyes on Ben was a couple of weeks before her last journey to Venice. She was with Uggi and walking past the Commercial House whose uppermost floor, the second, housed his office cum studios. When they met Ben near the door, he had just lifted a large cardboard box by the straps off his car, and was carrying it towards the main door of the building. He had said a quick hello to them and struggled on as fast as he could before either she or Uggi could offer him any assistance. Both she and Uggi knew Ben did that in order to maintain his dislike for her and discourage her from ever coming to his office. Now a note from Ben – from Ben!

"What is it about?" she asked the courier as she held on to the white envelope.

"I don't know," he replied, backing off as if it's a timed letter bomb he had delivered. "You can find me in the department in case you have a note to send back." He was gone, before Jacq could open the envelope.

Quite unlike the purported writer, the note was polite. Very curious was it to her that the message started with a mannerism

269

synonymous with Ila – with a perambulation into enquiring about her good health before getting to the objective. It requested from Jacq, an hour of her help after her classes that day. The note said Victor was not in the college that day because the writer had sent him to a neighbouring town to collect some artefacts. Victor would return to Commercial House at 5 p.m. and the writer would be grateful if Jacq would assist Victor to stack and shelf the items he had gone to collect.

She browsed through it again, reading aloud the name of its sender. It was signed Ben Mackinnon! Ben of all people! She could not boast of knowing Ben's handwriting but the crookedness of the lettering added to her conviction that the note could be from Ben.

"Didn't they say a person's shape, beauty and mentality are easily given away by his handwriting?" she remembered. And what of the strange politeness for once? It could be the start of a behavioural turn-around by Ben who she had always known to be negative and rude! Victor's absence from college that day turned out to be true when she probed it. She wished Uggi had not left the college by noon after his last class; they would have gone together.

Jacq slowed her feet down to a halt outside Commercial House and looked round, wishfully thinking the friendly surprises would continue. Ben who had written that politely could equally be awaiting her arrival. And so could Victor – he could be waiting in his father's office on the topmost floor. She went in.

The large reception dominating the immediate entry into Commercial House was unmanned at half past five when Jacq arrived. The first time she had set her feet in the building, she was with both Victor and Uggi. It was about the same time of evening and both the lady receptionist and the uniformed security man assigned to that position were there, quarrelling. Because of the receptionist being between fat and huge, the uniformed man had cheekily asked her to search the handbag of one exiting, feared woman, while he attended to an inter-departmental phone call. The receptionist instead, was going to give the security man the benefit of her physique when the three of them entered and Victor had to pacify the situation.

The next reception on the first floor was also empty, enabling Jacq to attribute the emptiness of the building to the effect of Friday. Friday, a day most workers were likely to seize in part as the start of the weekend, and so go home early! She heeled up the carpet-insulated stairs to the next level and finally to Ben's office on the second floor. All through she saw no one. She was sure that arrogant Ben, anticipating the early desertion of the building by his slack workers, had swallowed his vomit and asked her of all people to assist Victor.

Ben's reception stared at Jacq with all its bareness as Jacq pondered what next she should do. The pondering was intruded by a squeaking noise coming from the partially shut and now wind-pushed door to Ben's studio and office. It was agape, and both the sound and the openness beckoned her to it.

"Ben! Victor! Are you there?" she called and knocked on the door. No response came. One of them must be far inside she thought, as she held the handle and pushed the door to peep. This time, the response came to her twofold, all lacking any form of pleasantry.

First was the shattering noise from the fallen objects behind the door which her push had caused. She was eager to ascertain its nature, so she allowed it to finally pull her in. She covered her mouth and shrank in confusion when she stood before a spread of broken china and glasses as well as two wooden carvings that lay haphazardly on the floor.

"Why on earth am I here, in this building?" she questioned herself. Why did she not go back when there was neither Victor nor Ben waiting? Why did she push the door? Why? Why?

"Victor, are you there! Why had nobody answered!" she screamed.

In panic, Jacq moved to do some as-far-as-possible salvaging and tidying-up. As she bent and stretched, she realised

271

how hopelessly impossible it was for her to find a point from where to start – or to stop. So, she rose and looked at the mess again, this time extending the browsing to the shelves, the floor areas, as well as stools and hangings of various Egyptian and other African artworks of wood, glasses, pottery and metals. She could see the large room she was in wasn't alone – that a second fully opened door lead to a larger hall she had neither the time nor the intension to enter. The two wooden carvings! She bent to sit up the first of them, just as she realised an intruder alarm had been triggered: the lit gunpowder had already reached the pellets!

Jacq turned back to the door into the reception. She grappled it, pulled and jumped out, knocking down some of what she had just stood upright inside the studio. She flew down the stairs.

"Stop there, you!" an ascending hefty man just two steps ahead of a woman on the stairs ordered Jacq before Jacq was midway between the second and first floor reception. Together with the woman, he blocked her flight solidly. "Who are you?" he asked Jacq.

"And where are you coming from?" the accompanying woman extended the questioning. "Can't you hear the alarm triggered by your forced entry?"

Stuttering helped itself to initiate an answer on Jacq's behalf. It couldn't finish it and Jacq returned to speechlessness.

"Where are you coming from? Can't you talk?" the woman shouted at Jacq. The shout added to Jacq's fright, extending the dumbness of her mouth. Now, she had no doubt she had foolishly stirred the wasps nest – she had walked herself into a defenceless and shameful criminality.

"Okay, turn round," commanded the man, "and we shall follow you to see what you have done."

She obeyed slowly, turning half circle to face the stairs. The conformity fooled the restrainers into believing Jacq was ready to comply fully with the twin instructions they gave her. She made only a step when, suddenly, she spun another half circle, ducked and shoved aside those behind her. She fled down the stairs, out of Commercial House, unto the street where her misfortune was reinforced by the presence of two policemen on patrol. After a chase helped by some good citizens on the street, she was apprehended and dragged back into the building – to Ben's studio door she had refused to return initially.

"Well, open it," said the first policeman. "Haven't you already forced your way in? Can't you hear the alarm your entry set off?"

"I met it open," Jacq offered her first ever sentence before her accusers, "I didn't force my way in."

"You must have," said the first woman to co-block her. "A secured door can't open itself, can it?"

"How did you get there? Who in the building allowed you in?" the second policeman asked again.

"No one. I saw no one at the reception and on my way up."

"Liar!" shouted the woman. "Liar and a sneak. You must be one of those who have been raiding this building in recent months. We were two at the main reception." Now the stark reality of the scenario dawned on Jacq. She was a thief – a robber caught in the act and still attempting to escape!

"Don't imply I am a thief or a robber, because I am not," she started to protest. "I have an invitation to come here."

"Enough of those nonsense," the first policeman cut her short. "You should have waited for whoever invited you. Your guilt made you flee. No one would invite you to break into his place. Anyway, let's see what you did inside the studio."

He led the entry, and was promptly confronted by the destruction. Instantly, the ugly lay-out ordered him what he must do. "Miss," he said firmly, "you have been caught in the act of committing burglary. We need to know your accomplices, what you have stolen and how much you have damaged. You have to come with us to Charles Street."

"Committing burglary...come with you to Charles Street?" Jacq asked as if her hearing was deceiving her.

"Yes, the police station. You are under arrest."

Marched down and out in clamps, and pushed into the waiting police van, Jacq had no doubt that for her, it was back on the arc of the same circle of encasement to continue in the same orbit of woe. Months ago, she paid for an accusation; now she was paying for another, though this time, a totally false one. Then, she was in ropes; now, in handcuffs. Then, she knew her accusers King Jap and Fire Spirit; now, they were more faceless than the masks. Then, she was lucky to be rescued; now, only a miracle could lower such luck to her and let her attract any pity from those who could help her – Uggi and his father.

* * *

A rustling accomplished the stiffness of the door when pushed by Ali Jaiye. It was about ten in the morning on Monday when Ali, just returning from a full weekend of evangelism, was about to enter his house. He guessed the ruffling must have been the sound of the letters delivered through the letter box; so, he entered cautiously.

The mail was certainly more than a day's delivery and Ali wondered why this was so. Of course, he did not doubt he was among the few individuals on his street who kept the postmen busy due to his religious activism. His chairmanship, secretaryship and floor membership of several groups in the cathedral ensured he had many letters daily. His local sorting office was so accustomed to his mail that its staff only had to see at the back of the envelope one of his non-Scottish names, or of his church – whatever the state of its completion or legibility was – and such envelope would be pushed through his letter box. He could also not remember the postmen embarking on, and so just returning from any of their silly strikes – like striking over management's non-provision of teacups, or for sacking a postman caught drunk on duty. In such a case, the immediate post-strike delivery to his box was always understandingly heavy, requiring pressing his door bell or banging the flap of the letter hole to summon him to the door to take it. He knew the pile represented more than a day's mail; and frightfully, that neither Jacq nor Uggi had been around to clear it from behind the door.

He walked over to his mail cabinet by the dining table; it was empty. He noticed the laundry Jacq had put out for ironing on Thursday night; they were still there. It was obvious that none of the key holders had been in the house for at least two days – that something was wrong!

Breathlessly, Ali fetched a chair to the door and was going through the envelopes, paying utmost attention to indicated senders and handwriting on them for some pointers. None came until a slip sandwiched between the envelopes flew out onto the floor. At once, the oddity from its orange colour and uncharacteristic size pushed Ali to pick and browse through it. Sender: Illegible signature but dated Friday. Origin: Charles Street Police Station. Message: A lady of black African origin by name of Jacquensica Nek in their custody had used Ali Jaiye as a referee. Special remark: Urgent. The slip made him sit up straight, forced him to look straight, but blocked him from thinking straight.

When Ali's central position to all that was unfolding forced him to regain himself, Uggi was the first person his mind went to. Why didn't Uggi trace him by phone? If he wasn't sure of his exact whereabouts why didn't he go to the cathedral to obtain the current phone numbers? Was Uggi also detained? Was Uggi involved in Jacq's arrest or crime?

And as for Jacq, had she responded in her naturally ferocious way to some expressed racial hatred, or become characteristically crazy at something to do with culture? The questions poured in. The immediate answers had to be at Charles Street. He jumped in his car and sped along, with the orange slip as his only companion.

"I am Reverend Ali Jaiye. Is Jacquensica Nek still being held here?" Ali asked the constable behind the polished oak reception desk, tendering the slip.

"Yes, she is," the officer confirmed after reading the orange piece of paper.

"May I see her please?"

"No, sir. But you may see the sergeant who signed the note. He will advise you on whatever is possible." Within minutes, Ali's initial waiting ended as the prosecuting sergeant called him inside to his desk.

"I am sorry, you are too late," the sergeant said firmly. "Too late to be of assistance to our inquiries. We waited two days for you."

"Really? Too late?"

"Yes, I am afraid so. Jacquensica has already been charged and will appear before a magistrate tomorrow afternoon."

"Charged with what, if I may ask?" Ali was now trembling, eager to know how Jacq had become a criminal. "Charged?"

"Yes, for trespassing, burglary and wilful damage."

"Where?" Ali asked, devastated. He was sure that the Jacq he knew did not have such traits in her. With the exception of the front and back doors of her house, no other door in the house he shared with her had a lock on; and yet, nothing had ever gone missing. Since she had moved in, she had honestly preserved all the household materials, money and valuables.

"She broke into Ben Mackinnon's arts studio, damaging some artefacts and making away with others."

Ali could hardly wait to respond as he straightened himself up in the chair. Ben's...burglary...artefacts...Jacq? A prank...a joke?

"Impossible, sergeant, that Jacq would do any of those. She had no reason to. Never, sergeant!"

The sergeant saw the defence outburst as being borne out of Ali's mediocrity in human behaviours. "The heart of the rogue is

276

bottomless," he started to lecture the clergy. "It is deeper than appearance, age, gender or physique. His only guide to the evils he performs, and which he rarely explains, is his own level of sanity during its performance. That is what I have experienced in my job. But all the same, we must leave this for the court to decide."

"How about Ben Mackinnon, has he said anything?"

"Well, poor Mr Mackinnon. What does anyone expect him to say after all his losses – other than volunteering to witness for the prosecution? Yesterday, he accompanied us to the scene of the crime for some finger prints."

"Well, I still don't know – except that there were more reasons why she wouldn't do that."

"Look, Mr Jaiye," the sergeant demanded, "I am not certain which of the two you want to do: whether to represent her yourself, or hire someone learned to do so." He told Ali he was a law officer and not the law court that Ali was apparently mistaking him to be. He wasn't ready to continue listening to any of Ali's submissions. "Whichever of them you want, better save the arguments for the court."

"Then, can you allow me to see her, and to apply for a bail on her behalf?"

"Very well, Mr Jaiye, you can see her, but not bail her now." She has already been charged to appear before the magistrate tomorrow afternoon. Then, the magistrate can grant that application if the case still continues, and if it pleases him.

"I will take you to her now and give you twenty minutes to be with her. After that, we all meet in the court tomorrow."

Jacq had experienced the worst of cells in her native Ila, so she felt no physical brutality in her cell at the Charles Street station. However, it was the first time she was being accused of a crime she never set out to commit. She knew she was neither a thief nor a burglar. If anything, she was only a foolish woman forced into that qualification by her kind heartedness. For the first time ever, it gave her the deepest feeling of pain to see people glaring at her in the cell. She thought of how to explain these to Ali who she could now see walking along the corridor towards her cell, accompanied by the police officer. She lowered her face and wished the floor under her feet would open up and swallow her.

"I did not do it," she told Ali Jaiye, weeping profusely like a freshly cut banana tree stem. "I set out to go and help Victor. A note from Ben called me to help him. I burgled no one, and nowhere," she continued, following and sobbing behind Ali to the small space allowed Ali to talk with her privately. There, Ali made her take one chair while he took the other.

"Did you do this because you were still determined to go back to Ila?" Ali asked her.

"No, sir," she managed to answer. "You know, sir, that no shame is more than that of stealing," she added, inferring the age-old culture of Ila she knew Ali was aware of. "I would rather die than return with such shame. When I return, I want it to be with honours."

"Good. In that case, you will have to do more than crying. You can use the short time we have left to relate the whole story to me.

"So, where is this note from Ben?"

"The police have it."

"Did Ben personally speak with you?"

"No, he didn't and has not. I have not set my eyes on him."

"And Victor?"

"He too didn't, and hasn't either."

"Why didn't you seek Uggi's opinion, and go with him in the first place?"

"He wasn't in the college. I thought it was a chance I could take to please Ben and reduce his hostility to me. I am sorry I was so foolish." She was forcing herself to be calmer now.

"Then to the note again: if it had invited you to go and help Victor – or Ben – why didn't you wait outside Ben's studio for one of them to arrive before you went inside? Don't you know the type of person that usually forces himself into people's dwellings?"

"The doors were open. I thought they were already inside waiting for me."

Time wouldn't allow Ali Jaiye to go on. He felt satisfied with the few answers he had cruelly obtained from Jacq, her glaring mistakes notwithstanding. "Okay, you listen. Tomorrow, you are appearing before the magistrate. Meanwhile, the police have refused to allow your bail before the appearance. By luck, this could change if I am able to get a solicitor to come here before the end of the day. I will also see if Ben can be of help. Everything is blurred and crowded, but stay calm, speak with no one again, and expect me or the lawyer back very soon."

Immediately Ali Jaiye was out of the police station, he wanted to see Ben first before any other person. Twice, he stopped by the roadside phone booths and made calls to Ben's house and office. On each occasion, the phone rang endlessly at the other end with no one picking up the receiver. Then, Ali shifted from his eagerness to speak to Ben to that of listening to Uggi's version of the event. He diverted to Uggi at the college.

Uggi knew nothing about the incident, and was equally shocked. Over the weekend and up to that morning, he had been too busy to pass by his dad's. He believed Victor also knew nothing, as Victor had told him nothing. But about half an hour back, both he and Victor had seen Ben within the college premises going towards the administrative block. It was likely he was still around, because his car was. Uggi was correct, as just at that moment Ben appeared, walking to his car. Ali paced across to meet him while Uggi searched for Victor.

Profoundly, Ben made it plain to Ali that he was not interested in discussing the issue. If anything about it was worth discussing, it had better be how he would be compensated for his loss. Unless someone discussed that with him now, he would sue Jacq again on completion of her first jail term. He however feared his loss was total as Jacq was only a poor robber with no means to pay him. But he wouldn't mind seeing Jacq paying for her crime with a jail term, deportation, or whatever. He, Ben, of all people, an indirect mentor of Jacq, should not have been robbed by Jacq.

"But if you are not interested in discussing it with anyone, why have you with the college?" Ali, sceptical of his friend's claim, asked. "I suppose that's why you are here. Or, is the college going to compensate you for the loss?"

"That's a different matter altogether, Ali. I only came to warn the college not to let my art prizes go to rogue students. My current form can take no more 'slaps'." At that, Ben closed the discussion, leaving Ali with the only likely friend he would ever get in this matter – the lawyer.

At the police station, it took the solicitor a little but tough time to convince the sergeant and win police bail for Jacq. At first, the sergeant had held on to his fears over the character of Jacq, that someone who he would not reveal had informed him of Jacq's recent conviction for treason and felony. Jacq's solicitor had technically convinced him of the lack of *locus standi* of such whisperer or his allegation, because the circumstances surrounding the case were unknown. Besides, it didn't happen in Scotland, and the law culture of where it did was notorious enough. The solicitor warned how the magistrate's declaring such an allegation *null and void* could openly ridicule the sergeant; and he, the lawyer saw no need for all that. Finally, the lawyer had given a personal undertaking to produce Jacq in court anytime she was required until the case was disposed of.

So, within an hour of his arrival at Charles Street, the lawyer had signed for and collected Jacq like a registered parcel from the post office, and was out of the station. He left Jacq with Uggi who had accompanied him on Ali Jaiye's instruction. Uggi was to look after Jacq at home until Ali would return home from work. However, this particular arrangement and expectation endured only for a short, regrettable time.

It was Uggi who phoned his father shortly after the lawyer had dropped both him and Jacq at home. He alleged Jacq had suddenly assaulted him in the house, and he could no longer stay with her. He would return later to relate the story. Jacq was also too distressed on the phone to talk with Ali about the quarrel. Ali had to abandon his office at the cathedral to run home.

* * *

Jacq, the lone occupier of the house was miserable, sobbing and red-eyed. With her state of mind, Ali could not readily find an easy point from where to start with her.

"You have been a father to me," she finally broke the ice, "and Uggi, a brother. But now sir, you will find it difficult to know that the same Uggi was the man behind all the problems I have encountered since arriving in Glasgow. He was also behind this, which could send me to jail. Really, he was."

Ali knew Jacq was already agitated mentally and physically especially by the latest happenings, but he never believed she could be so troubled in her mind to the point of being unable to recognise all the goodness Uggi had meant and done for her. Tears on her face apart, Ali wanted to recognise her utterances as a joke.

"He wrote the invitation note to Ben's studio?" Ali asked the only logical question he could think of.

"No, sir," Jacq answered.

"He burgled Ben's studio and told the police it was you?"

"No, sir."

"Okay then, let me drop my briefcase and return to hear the 'yeses' parts of the problem."

He entered his bedroom, dropped his briefcase, hung up his coat, and returned to Jacq. He was ready to listen.

"Sir, Uggi is a royal cultist; or better still, a devil cultist. He is an *Eagle*."

Ali listened. He could not think of a remote source for Jacq's branding. He eagerly awaited more of her sentences, in the form of expansion or substantiation of what she just alleged. His eyes oscillated between Jacq's eyes and mouth.

"In Glasgow here," she resumed, "he is a loyal representative and servant of King Jap. Like the king himself, he is a member of Ila's *Order of The Eagle* cult. By accident I saw his pendant. I picked it up from the kitchen floor it fell on and gave it to him. He did not deny it wasn't his. He planned my arrest, and could not swear he knew nothing about how my other problems here were instigated. He is secretly but actively working for King Jap."

Still Ali was mute. He glued his face at hers, listening to her statements that were now to him, the type that befitted the mouth of someone in need of the favours of a mental institution.

"You need to stop there," he intercepted Jacq at last. "What is this *Eagle*; and how does it make Uggi a representative of Jap? You need to explain clearly. Up to now, I cannot make sense of what you have been saying."

It was true Ali couldn't, even though he tried to, as Jacq's nonsense grew longer to him. He did not have to tax his memory much in order to know that none of his past education on religious cultism mentioned a name like *Eagle*. His knowledge of Ila's prominence with *Orò* and *Ifá* cults also assured him that both were synonymous with justice and wisdom. And of course, he remembered the ordinary flying eagles, the type that he knew could be booby-trapped for meat, using dead rats, chicks and ducklings as baits. Could it be one of these that Jacq was stammering about?

"What *Order of The Eagle*?"

"It is the secret cult headed by King Jap. Each member enjoys unlimited powers to plunder and embezzle as much as he wishes from the sudden found wealth of the kingdom. The cult was behind the arrest of every member of my family when it saw us as a danger to its operations. The membership was five – King Jap, the leader, as the *Head Eagle*; then the *Eye Eagle,* the *Claw Eagle,* the *Beak Eagle* and the *Wing Eagle.* With Uggi's membership now, probably the office of the *Nose Eagle* had been additionally created to sniff out more citizens to be murdered.

"The *Eye Eagle* pried on me and made the allegation against my family. The *Claw Eagle* was sent to prevent our escape, while the *Beak Eagle* headed the gang that softened us up for interrogation. Nek, my husband, was the first *Wing Eagle*, responsible for shielding the members, while Sese Abram was the *Beak Eagle*. Quite often my husband used to clash with the *Claw Eagle* over the bizarre conditions in which the *Claw Eagle* loved to hold the suspects. The *Eagle* controlled our arrest, trial and conviction, as well as the abrogation of our chiefdom."

"How then do you think Uggi has joined such a dreadful group? How?"

"Well, sir, I wouldn't know how he joined. But I saw his pendant. It is rare – and only awarded to the rarest and most loyal inductee after a special initiation."

"Special initiation?"

"Yes, sir. It was usually done secretly inside one of the shrines, in the middle of the night, under the cover of the darkness. The one being initiated undergoes tests of extreme endurance, loyalty and brotherhood. Among the tests is using the real claw of an eagle to draw out some blood, 'blood of brotherhood', from the member's left arm for other members to suck. Towards the end of the initiation, the inductee takes a strong oath of allegiance to King Jap first, and to other members next. He will then be awarded the pendant to aid his interpersonal identification and communication. From then on, the loyalty of the newly initiated member was to other members only – not even to his father!

"Please, sir, believe me. I saw Uggi's pendant; and he denied neither the membership nor what the membership has made him to do to me. For that, I do not want to see him or ever have anything to do with him again. Never!"

Without admitting them to a distraught and sobbing Jacq, Ali was aware of the on-going gang culture in Ila. The painful inflictions were being made in the name of true culture; and were fast sinking the traditional good name of the kingdom. Ali was further aware of this behaviour compelling right thinking Glaswegians to boycott Ila. But realistically, he was too far away to see the root of the degeneration. More than before from around the kingdom, he now came across people who related how they preferably jumped at the opportunity of self enslavement to the buyer-masters of Glasgow. These people talked about how they peacefully socialised with other slaves, ex-slaves and emigrants to Glasgow, Liverpool, London and Virginia who they came across in Glasgow. The Glaswegians knew of Ali's ties with Ila and he lived with the shame it occasionally produced. He had sent Uggi to Ila to see firsthand, analyse and think of a way to cleanse the culture – not to embed Uggi in its present form or to encourage Uggi to import it into Glasgow.

He wondered truly what kind of woman Jacq was – how she knew so much, and how much more of herself she was yet to confess to him. He was convinced that though Jacq's story about Uggi and the initiation might have been emotionally exaggerated, they were weirdly sweet, strange and serous enough. He must summon Uggi to return to him at once.

"This is the cause of the matter, dad," Uggi told his father, laying the *Eagle* pendant Jacq had seen with him on the dining table he sat by with his father.

It was a beautifully crafted, three-inch full span eagle holding tenaciously to a sword with its beak. Ali looked between it and his son – awed! "Are you a member of the *Order of The Eagle*?" he asked Uggi, dreading the answer that would come out of his son's mouth.

"Well…Well…" Uggi found answering too heavy and difficult for his mouth.

Ali was slowly becoming angry, devastated and terrified of his son. So, Uggi had gone out of his way in Ila to join the devils and the devilish among the people of his roots! "In that case," continued Ali, "you – and not the pendant – are the cause of the matter. You have no basis to blame a lifeless piece of silver. I find it sad, Uggi, to discover you caused all this."

"No, dad, both Jacq and Victor were the causes of the matter, Uggi finally responded. "Those were what I was searching for words to express. Both of them, Jacq and Victor in that order, were responsible."

"Then you must explain that."

"Were it not for Jacq and the state in which we met her, we wouldn't have had a cause to be initiated in the first instance. Jap's first given condition for sparing her was that we got initiated and then carried the masks. Dad, are you saying we should have done nothing?"

"But then you shouldn't have carried the support for Jap to Glasgow. And you shouldn't have cut yourselves and shared in the blood drinking in the name of an initiation. That was a wilful somersault into pure cannibalistic criminality!"

"First dad, I carried no support of Jap to anywhere. In fact, I never had any for him. It would have shown if I did or do. And secondly, I, personally, did no initiation, and saw no blood sucking."

"But you had the pendant. How did you get it? Jacq said it was never, ever granted for nothing."

Quite reluctantly, and strictly within the bounds of modesty, Uggi related the whole story of the initiation to his angry father. Ali weighed it with what he heard from Jacq, and opted for the plausibility of Jacq's. He was thoroughly appalled by his son's activities, and his son inescapably knew it.

"If I have brought you up to taste the holy wine as the blood of Jesus, how could you drink other peoples' blood in Ila? If I have guided you to show your allegiance to God, Jesus, and this kingdom you now live, why have you sworn to worship the inhuman mortal called Jap with his bunch of embezzlers?

"Why, for God's sake, my son, have you gone to commit a crime, the type that was more serious than the one you claimed to have saved Jacq from? Why, Uggi?"

"Okay, dad," Uggi sighed after a long silence. He was ready to cast away a modesty that had bedevilled him before Jacq and his father primarily, and before God and Jesus spiritually. "I swore no oath and drank no blood. It was Victor who did those. It was him who was duly initiated."

Uggi sounded yet unbelievable to Ali. "Were you on a siesta, or was it during your night sleep when Victor was being initiated?"

"Actually, I passed out due to the cruelty on the two volunteers doing it on our behalf.　I passed out when the shrine's cobra sank its fangs in one of them, and would not unlock the fangs. Victor thereafter voluntarily replaced the two men and continued with the induction. He took the oath of allegiance after he completed the prescribed tasks. Then, he was given two pendants – one for himself and one for me. That was what happened. It was all because of Jacq. Dad, she was the cause of the matter.

"I am sorry, dad. Because Jacq won't believe me, will you please explain this to her for me?"

"Now that I know, I will," Ali promised his son as he watched him run out of the house in remorseful tears. Ali knew he had to explain it to Jacq alright, but it wasn't the moment for that yet. Speaking again to an uncooperative Ben was to him, more urgent now than ever.

"I am sorry, Ben," Ali started with Ben who he had toiled without cessation to track down on the phone. "In the light of the new developments you cannot abscond. It is in your own interest that you don't even dream of doing so. You are a part of it – its planning and execution." He was crisp and purposefully blackmailing. He could no longer dillydally over the time to call Ben's bluff and compel him to be reasonable. Jacq's court appearance was only hours away!

286

At first Ben sounded angry on the phone. Then he went incoherent, and ended up being wisely quiet. Ali took that to mean he had pierced Ben and successfully implicated him. He wished he could see Ben's actual temperament at the other end of the line. Perhaps, he imagined, Ben initially sat down in anger answering the call. Perhaps, Ben grew angrier at the mention of his criminal complicity. Perhaps the reality pulled Ben up his seat and paced him up and down to the maximum distance the phone's receiver cable could extend uncoiled. Perhaps Ben quickly reasoned straight, unsure of how next he would be whacked by the problem. Perhaps Ben finally sat down, sweating in shivers! What Ali was sure of however, was Ben's readiness to clear up things with him – and Jacq. That readiness must have pushed Ben to asking him, Ali, just a short time to arrive at his house for an important discussion.

"Be frank Ben, what do you have against Jacq?" Ali renewed the pressure on Ben as soon as Ben arrived in his house.

"Me? Against Jacq?" Ben disguised the shock. "What could I have against her? Nothing. Did she...?"

"Look, she knows you hated her from the moment you first saw her. People don't have to utter hatred; it glitters before it's ever mentioned or shown."

"She is arrogant, Ali; but that doesn't bother me a bit. How will it, Ali?"

"You influenced and pressurised Victor to send her out of your house. You influenced Victor's decision not to return to Venice with her. You planned the current problem in which she finds herself. That is how.

"I believe her because I now have the proof. It is concrete, and being reserved till who knows – tomorrow at the court, or any other time."

"Look, don't be silly, Ali," Ben spewed out with the last of the tactical strength left in him. "How could you believe that nonsense? Because I hated her burgling me, what's wrong with that? For the charges for compensation I intend to press for in the future, what's unfair about that? What's wrong in expecting a foreigner to behave decently and legally on a land that accommodates her? You don't find yourself at Loch Ness and think you know the lake more than Nessie!"

"Well, Ben, you want to know that is wrong – and unfair? It is this, in this envelope." With measured violence, Ali shook the pendant out onto the table before them.

"You know this, don't you? They say it represented the membership of *Order of The Eagle*. You must have sponsored Victor for this apparatus of fear, intimidation and illegality. And as a friend, I am disappointed." He went on without giving Ben a chance to respond.

"You and your son must have been working with the spirit of the evil *Eagle* to persecute Jacq," Ali summed up. "This is wrong and unfair. It needs your urgent attention – tonight, Ben – before Jacq's court appearance.

"It is our joint headache – yours, Victor's, mine, Uggi's and even, Jacq's. For now, you have to lead it to a just solution."

That just solution was before the lady magistrate. Before the judge, Ben forced himself to tactically withdraw all cooperation with the prosecuting sergeant.

Jacq did not immediately understand the "you may go" pronouncement of the lady magistrate. In fact, she hardly heard the pronouncement. Her mind was out of the courtroom viewing imaginatively the inner walls of a British prison and the inside of an aeroplane that she would be put on, on deportation to Ila in Africa.

"You are absolutely discharged," the magistrate explained. "You are free to go about your business," she clarified to Jacq. Jacq found no word to speak, but instead wept on the shoulders of Ali who moved in and got her out of the dock.

It left as the only guilty person in the case, the supposed-to-be-experienced police sergeant who had brought a case not fully investigated before the judge. The judge saw the case as one of

288

those time and taxpayers money wasting ones, and she warned the sergeant against ever repeating such in her court.

Calmly, the sergeant took the tongue-lashing, preferring it to any form of the force's internal disciplinary action. He prayed that everything about the case, as it involved himself and Ben, died at that. He vowed never to allow the masked behaviour of a big man or any masked amount of money to influence his professional behaviour again. Never.

CHAPTER NINE
The Atonements I

The court case was over, but certainly not the bother among its *dramatis personae*.

From the moment of Jacq's acquittal the previous day, through the night, Ben Mackinnon had worried about what could be the spill-over from the case. Would the police officer, who illegally favoured him and soiled his professional reputation before the law for the favour, return to have his own back on him? How about the security man and the receptionist he planted when luring Jacq into the trap at Commercial House: when they learnt how he had made a u-turn in the saga, would they think he had selfishly used them? Would Ali and Jacq continue to see him as a devil? Ben knew the answer to each of these questions would be a yes – and a shame on himself.

"But everything is about business, and for business," Ben consoled himself. "In business he who accords shame any importance is *a nobody* who will profit nothing but zero from business." His father, when alive, had handed down to him several stories to back up this belief – stories of immoral invasions, expeditions and conquests that were shamefully and premeditatedly ordered by different sovereigns. If then any sort of respect had been accorded 'shame', the national wealth captured and brought in to build and sustain the cities would never had been there. Neither

290

Victor nor Uggi would have been in Ila to save Jacq and bring her over to Glasgow of established wealth. Ali Jaiye would not have had the chance to come, learn and settle in Glasgow either. Certainly, Ali would not have had the chance he deftly used to save an idiot like Jacq who was threatening his family business!

He believed he was right with his occult reading of Jacq when he first met her; and for this wizardry, he thanked Davey, his late father, for passing the special knowledge to him. He saw Jacq as being more devilish than himself, as being dangerously intractable and indefinable. He believed that the only person Jacq would respect – and, as the mad man would a burning fire – was Ali. On his way to work that morning, he must visit Ali and make Ali impress on Jacq the need to let sleeping dog lie now that he had cooperated with Ali to set Jacq free. Tactically shying away from the intended reason for his coming, he obtained Ali's permission on the phone to pass by.

Ben wished that someone else had come to answer Ali's door bell. Jacq had derived no joy from answering the bell. She had been unfortunate to be vacuuming the carpet around the door when the bell rang and Ali asked her for the favour.

"Good morning, Miss," Ben greeted Jacq at the door. He wore a confident smile as if nothing had happened between the two of them; or as if whatever had was a special blessing from him to Jacq.

"Morn-ing," Jacq reluctantly responded, her eyes shut halfway, her mouth gathered and lips sprouted short of a hiss. She led him to a sofa and remorselessly abandoned him for his host to come and meet him. The case had denied her the previous day's college attendance, and neither her morning chores nor the presence of Ben would deny her that morning's.

"Thank you for your efforts yesterday," Ali met Ben with, with a warm, triumphal handshake. "It worked out very well. Now we can put it behind us."

"Yes," agreed Ben. "That's why I decided to see you – to exchange views on how to truly put it behind us."

"Well, it has naturally relegated itself into oblivion, hasn't it? And we shall keep it there? Or, do you see it differently, Ben?"

"Honestly, I do – until I know how Jacq sees it. She is sullen and still shaky. Does she appreciate my efforts, feel satisfied that I backed down from the court case? If she doesn't, I can foresee more problems arising before long."

"Why do you talk like this, Ben? You mean she won't be happy with her new-gained freedom? Have you got a reason for such a notion?"

"I have never told you this, Ali," Ben confessed. "I once looked into her face and was able to read it using my special knowledge. What I read from the look was scary: hard-heartedness, unforgiving resentment, irrationality in thinking and deeds. These were what I saw. Very scary."

Ali kept his composure hearing Ben's weird talks. "Looked into her? With your special knowledge of what, and saw what?" Ali asked him.

"Simple. Her face: its straight sides and angled chin meaning arrogance, its flatness to the forehead confirming her strong-headedness and unaccommodating personality. Her eyes: their short, straight eyebrows meaning her unfriendliness to people, their lower white sclera depicting temper, aggression and rebellion. Her *mooth*: its many lines of untrustworthiness on the lips, its raised angle of vanity and again, arrogance. Even her nose has the roundness of an abrasive person, and her ears the thickness of one who's too obstinate to hear or take an advice. She *gied* me lots of *doots*."

Ali feared what was actually going on inside Ben's brains. He was however sure Ben wasn't drunk. He had never seen Ben drunk. "Are you clairvoyant now, Ben? I can't call you a juju priest because as far as I know, you can't point a compass at the direction of Ila, and so can't be one of their wizards.

"But Ben, did you not read her palms as well?" he teased.

"I would have, or her soles; but there was no way she would show them to me. But I noted her fingers when she briefly rested them on her door handle. The abnormal length of her ring finger confirmed she must be a wild and reckless *besom*," he belittled her.

"Ben, you sound strange, quite strange. But whatever your reading was, Jacq has none of those in her character."

Ben made no further fuss. "Anyway," he resigned, "the more important thing is that you stop her from remaining in any of them. She should move on now and make the best use of what life has to offer her. Please impress it on her to let everything about the court case – and about Ila – die with her recent acquittal."

"On that I agree with you. The same way you must talk to Victor; and I to Uggi. I agree that any further reference to the case, or to her conduct in Ila, is likely to equally disgrace you and me, in and outside the church.

"As for Jacq, she is a wonderful lady. We must all appreciate how she uses her strength to suppress the immense pressure she is constantly under. She deserves all the help she can get from us."

Just then, Jacq left her room and shut her door. She was walking past the living room where Ben and Ali sat, aiming for the main door. She was on her way to the college.

"Please give us a minute of your time before you go out," Ali called her attention. Jacq stopped and made the small diversion to the two men.

"Ben and I have been talking," Ali said when she was near enough. "We have been discussing the unfortunate incident that led to the court case – that vindicated you.

"Now that the case is over, Ben wants you to let it die forever."

"Is that why he is here then?" Jacq asked Ali.

"Yes, principally. I have told him I will talk to you."

That Jacq slowly removed her big, long-strapped college bag from her shoulder was to Ali and Ben an indication of Jacq's willing readiness to listen and go with the wish of both men. She remained on her feet, silent.

"Won't you say something, Jacq?" Ali asked her.

"Must I really say something, sir?" she responded.

"Yes, Jacq, it's better you do," insisted Ali. "Better you say your mind and we put this behind us as Ben had suggested."

"Well, sir," she broke her silence. "Here is it, if you insist that I speak. Ben's wish is the typical wish of a sadist. The sadist tortures his victim and still wishes the victim to pretend no pain, to pretend all his sensory organs are dead. Where the victim is barely alive enough to do so, the sadist wants him to beg for more of the torture.

"Frankly, sir, Ben and his son, Victor the *Eagle*, deserve permanent residence inside the satanic premises of King Jap and Sese Abram.

"I don't want to be late for lectures, sir; so I must leave. Now I am ready for them, ready for the next evil they may have for me in their plans."

As Jacq flew out of the door, Ben wished he had cut her short when she was pouring the insults on him. He wished he had prevented his ears from absorbing the terrible ridiculing from Jacq. He regretted he had no chance to counter Jacq before she ran out. He wished he could get off the sofa and run after her on the streets, grab her from behind and tongue-lash her reciprocally. He felt the immense pain of being unable to do any of these.

"I have never before been insulted like this in my life," he said soberly to Ali, after an agonising while. "I told you the type of person she is, didn't I – that you need to put the *hems* on her? I hope you now believe me. Now I must go, with the belief that the war still continues."

Ali said nothing. He let Ben out of the door, pretending not to see the fiery fire in Ben's eyeballs.

* * *

The day's lecture, as if doing Jacq a special favour, started on a soothing note for her. First, before its commencement, none of her fellow students had appeared to note she did not attend lectures the previous two days. If any of them had, he did not ask her any question.

Secondly, the topic was about Christian saints of African origin. Bob Watson, the theology lecturer, was a soft-speaking and patient Scot. A fortnight before, when teaching about the 'greats' of Christianity, he had listed not a single African among them. The omission, one, had appeared funny to Jacq who wasted no time in faulting Bob Watson over the content of the lecture. She told him how she had read that all major religions, paganism including, had their roots in Africa, and questioned how no African saint had been mentioned in Bob Watson's list. However, instead of getting angry with Jacq, Bob had promised her he would soon devote a full lecture time to treating Jacq's question. This day, he had refined the treatment expansively by grouping the African Christian saints according to the regions they served.

Bob Watson started with African North – Mediterranean to Red Sea zone. It was a good mix of good and bad. It was the zone her people, the Ilas now behaving badly with their notorious masquerading, migrated from, and was the bad of the mix. She was however proud as Bob Watson also listed the kindness and miracles of Anthony, the Father of all monks; Pachomius, his student; Shenouda, the introducer of crafts, trade and writing to the monasteries; Maurice of the Thelban Army; Alexandra, the Pope of Alexandria; Mark, the eye-witness-writer of the oldest of the four canonical gospels; and Catherine, the rebuker of the maxim ruler, Emperor Maximinus. She was feeling pleased with the later part of the lecture – that all wasn't bad after all, with her roots.

Yeoman Smith took an excuse and came in at the tail end of the lecture. In addition to being Jacq's course tutor, Yeoman was her group's painting and sculpture teacher who Jacq least respected. Jacq had always wondered why arrogance had denied Yeoman, a black teacher, the wisdom of listening to black students and learning about their true culture from them. Without a feeling of loss, Yeoman also felt the same about the black students from Africa, and about Jacq especially. And as soon as Jacq saw him heading towards her, she guessed that the day's peace which started that morning with the abandonment of Ben in her home was about to end. The principal wanted to speak with her in his office, Yeoman told her.

Going to meet the principal in his office bothered Jacq the least. With how she had managed to cope with all the problems besieging her so far, the principal's, if one, she would also cope with. She believed her ability to absorb problems had now got to the stage where problems should wisely stay off her path or else they were devoured. She knocked on the door of the principal's office at the end of the long corridor on the first floor of the Administrative Building.

The voice of his secretary invited Jacq in. She was a fellow chorister in the cathedral; and for a moment, meeting her calmed Jacq's inner mind. "Do you work here?" Jacq, excited, asked her.

"Yes. I am the secretary, a month old here today. What brought you?"

"To see the principal; he sent for me."

"Okay; let's see." She connected the line to her boss to inform and confirm. Yes, Jacq was being expected. The secretary should let her come in forthwith.

It was Jacq's first time of entering the principal's office, and the moment she entered she knew she had another 'bother' to confront. That within that short moment Yeoman Smith was already with the principal, seated cross-legged intimidatingly beside an empty chair, suggested she was in for a rough meeting.

"You are Jacqensica?" the principal asked her. No greetings.

"Yes, sir."

"Take that seat." Casually. Unfriendly. The only empty chair was placed about a yard apart from Yeoman's, both facing the principal's on the opposite side of his large wooden table.

Jacq obeyed. She could see that a lone blue wallet file in the middle of the table before the principal had her name boldly printed on its back.

"Would you like a cup of tea – coffee?" she heard the principal ask her, casually.

"No; thank you, sir," Jacq replied. True, one half of the office was lavished to the standard of a chef's own kitchenette, but which man will accept the hospitality of a likely foe without ending in a hospital for an antidote for poisoning!

"Now we must come down to the point," the principal started. "The college needs to obtain answers to certain issues about you. Would you mind providing honest answers about them?"

"That won't be a problem, sir."

"Now, Jacquensica, the first question is this: Have you ever been involved with the other side of the law?"

"No, sir."

"Why we must know you may wonder. This is a highly respected institution, one that renders a big service to this city and beyond. Our graduates spread all over the country and to all corners of the globe, proudly rendering various development services. That is why we are concerned with the behaviour and integrity of our staff and students. That is why we must know. Do you understand?"

"Yes, sir."

"Did you burgle Ben Mackinnon's art studio last Friday; and were you caught trying to escape?"

"That was never the case, sir," she reacted to a question she least expected, though one that did not baffle her. "If anything, the studio was already broken into before I got there. Ben Mackinnon sent me a note, begging me to come and meet Victor Mackinnon, his son, and give him a hand to do some shelving. He sent the note

297

through Sam Mahoney, a student in this college's Department of Geography. Victor is also a student here."

"Is that so; and are you sure?" the principal asked, somewhat impressed by her detailed answer.

"Yes, sir."

Of course, both the principal and Yeoman Smith knew Victor so well, as the son of one of the most important college mentors. His father, Ben, was the donor of annual prizes for 'Overall Best Art Student' and 'Female Student Best Costume'. The principal turned on his computer to search for Sam Mahoney. The search was negatively going on when Yeoman asked Jacq the next question: "You don't seem to remember me, how you first met me, do you?"

"Yes, I do," replied Jacq. "You welcomed us and introduced yourself on the day of our enrolment. Then you conducted us round the college."

"That wasn't the first time we met, Jacq," Yeoman said. "We first met outside the college, you can't remember?"

Jacq couldn't, truly.

"You were with two of your friends at the Black Culture Week exhibition inside the cathedral museum. I was the person you chided on how we knew nothing about African culture, gods and the like when we sought your opinion – as we did of all our visitors – about the exhibition. I headed the group of three at the inner reception desk. Remember now?"

Jacq slowly remembered the day, the venue, the moment, and her candid opinion to three of the organisers. She remembered one of the faces she confronted uprightly, without any concealment – Yeoman's, a foe she was unaware of, but who had already spotted her! Her grudging course tutor! "Now, I can remember. It's a long time."

"I remember Victor Mackinnon was with you that day. Was the other man Sam Mahoney from Department of Geography?"

"No, that was Uggi Jaiye, another student here."

"Well Jacq" the principal interrupted without any prejudice to the conversation between Yeoman and Jacq, "I have listened to what you had said so far. I have searched for Sam Mahoney on our enrolment list and could not find that name. We would have called him to confirm he gave you a letter from Mr Mackinnon. But have you got the letter here with you – or, at home?"

"No, sir."

"Okay, I will call Ben Mackinnon to talk about this note he sent to you."

"Ben!" Jacq screamed agonisingly. "Please, sir, don't talk about me or about the note to Ben. Please."

Both the principal and Yeoman noted the intensity in Jacq's objection and pleading. They exchanged a 'we guessed as much' look.

"The principal is only trying to help you," Yeoman came in. "He wants to establish what you said happened to you, but you are not helping the situation. Sam Mahoney is not on the enrolment register; yet, you don't want Ben Mackinnon contacted. Okay can the principal contact your other friends here, Victor Mackinnon and Uggi Jaiye, to attest to your character?"

Jacq was fed up, and she remained silent. She thought of Victor and Uggi being devoted members of the *Order of The Eagle* and loyal representatives in Glasgow of evil King Jap! She breathed out the obvious answer: "No, sir."

The two interrogators were thoroughly astonished. They felt Jacq's past that someone had already whispered into their ears had truthfully caught up with her, leaving her with not a single soul to vouch for her. The principal turned the pages of Jacq's file before him. Then he dropped the next bombshell in two questions:

"You are from Ila in Africa, yes?"

"Yes, sir."

"Were you ever convicted of high treason over there?"

Again, Jacq was silent. A 'yes' would present her as a dangerous criminal long before a 'no' would prove the off-

299

handedness of her conviction. She remained silent. The principal was impatient.

"Well, Jacq, neither your silence, answers nor objections have been useful to us – and to you," the principal said. "But unfortunately, we have to discover the true answers before you will be allowed to continue in the college.

"I have checked through your file. The application form you completed for your admission said nothing about what we want to know. But I can see you are being sponsored by the St Mungo Cathedral Foundation and that Rev Ali Jaiye signed for that body. We shall contact him and the cathedral for references and discussion. What we obtain from him will determine your status in the college. For now, Jacq, you are suspended."

* * *

The principal's voice on the phone to Rev Ali Jaiye was gentle enough. Most voices to him were, to the man many residents of the city respectively associated with the great St Mungo Cathedral.

"I am the principal of Glasgow College, calling about Jacquensica Nek."

"Yes, principal," answered Ali. He was attentive at once, eager that the principal continued. "What about her? Is she alright?"

"We noticed that the cathedral is being responsible for her bursary, and that you signed her form on behalf of the cathedral."

"That is correct, principal."

"The college has got some serious reports about her; and I must discuss them with you on behalf of the college. She has already been suspended until the issues involved are resolved. That means until we can have some words with you."

Again, negative reports – about Jacq? A suspension? Ali's heart raced frightfully. "So, when was she suspended; where is she now?"

"She was here, in the last hour. She has already left the college premises."

"Ok, principal, can we talk about them now, on the phone?" Ali asked, perceiving the seriousness of the new problems with Jacq. "Or can I come over, right now?"

"No, make it Friday morning. Ten o'clock?"

The telephone conversation was on a Wednesday afternoon, making the agreed Friday hopelessly three days away for Ali. He called his house, expecting Jacq to be there; no one picked up the phone. He called Jacq's number – she had just joined the mobile phone generation – her phone was dead, switched off. She was frightened that Ben's mystic reading of Jacq some hours ago could be correct after all: arrogant, stubborn, unadvisable, strong-willed – coupled with being troubled, persecuted, lonely, and now suspended! The next she would consider for herself could be a suicide, if she had not done that to herself already. Once more Ali packed up and headed for home.

Ali met his house quiet – dead. Not even the wind was moving. He called out Jacq's name repeatedly but received no response. He paced through the lounge, living room and kitchen, to Jacq's room door. He turned the handle of the never-locked door in order to enter and search for clues. Strangely, the door was chained from inside. Now, he became thoroughly frightened for the worst. "Jacq, are you there," he shouted, banging the door repeatedly. Nothing.

"Will you please open this door, Jacq?" Ali pleaded. "I know you are there. Please, open."

A momentary movement – which stopped. He feared she was wriggling in the pains of an unfinished hara-kiri.

"Please open now, Jacq, before I break the door. Do you hear me?"

She heard him. She unchained and ran back to her bed, knelt on the floor beside it and buried her face in it, sobbing. She was already a pitiful shadow of herself.

301

"Don't worry," Ali cheered her up. "All will be well. God is in control," he repeated severally. The consolation sat her up and reduced her tears.

"Someone had already taken my past to the college," she told Ali. "Someone most wicked."

"Was that what the principal told you? He only called me that you are under suspension; and, that I must come to the college to talk it over with him on behalf of the cathedral."

"Yes; he asked me about my conviction in Ila, and about the burglary at Ben's studio."

"Don't worry," Ali cheered her up again. "The miracle that saved you from the jaws of Jap and the teeth of Ben Mackinnon will save you from any other tongue of persecution. Leave it to me, and don't worry. We shall get a favourable resolution on Friday."

The same night, about three o'clock in the morning, Ali experienced the first glimpse of how Jacq had been coping and how she would continue to cope till Friday. A murmuring noise coming from her room caught the attention of his ears. He got into his dressing gown and walked to Jacq's room door.

"Stop it; go back; stop pursuing me; leave me alone," he heard the noise clearer now. He debated with himself if an intruder, perhaps a rapist, had climbed down from the roof into Jacq's room. He gently opened to confront whoever it could be.

"Get back; leave me alone," he heard Jacq utter, this time, as her body thrashed about in her bed. The intruder was no other person but herself. She was having a nightmare!

"Wake up, Jacq," Ali patted her lightly. "You are in a bad dream. Wake up."

Jacq opened her eyes startled but grateful that she had been freed from the relentless bombardment some evil spirit had placed on her in her sleep. She was panting, like one who had just abandoned a marathon.

"Nobody was pursuing you. You were having a bad dream. And you are perfectly safe in the name of Christ. Turn your side now and go back to sleep."

Instead, Jacq sat up, scared, after Ali had gone out. She would not return to bed again that night. Her dawn had arrived – to the worries of Ali when he discovered that.

"I am sorry that I have to come back this morning," Ali told the principal on the phone that Thursday morning. "I know we fixed it for tomorrow, Friday, but can we please do it now? The whole thing is causing serious degeneration of Jacq's health. She stays with me, do you know?"

"I didn't know that, Reverend. But as you have that reason to insist, then it shall be about 4 p.m. That is the earliest I can do. Will that be okay with you?"

"Yes, thank you, principal."

* * *

Finding one of his choristers was the secretary to the principal of Glasgow College gladdened the heart of Rev Ali Jaiye – just as the secretary was proud to welcome her cleric to see her boss.

The secretary expected Ali to arrive the time he did; and her boss, the principal, very soon after Ali. The principal was taking an unscheduled tutorial class which he should be ending about the time Ali arrived. The secretary was to assure Ali he wouldn't have to wait for long before he would return to see him.

"He called me about Jacq," Ali told the secretary. "Do you know what it's all about?" he asked her, curious.

"No," she lied. Quite true that initially, she knew neither the anatomy nor the skeleton of Jacq's offence. Later however, after the principal had pronounced his interim judgement on Jacq, she was directed to write and despatch Jacq's letter of suspension. Additionally, about two hours before Ali's arrival, the principal had instructed her to get Jacq's file ready on his table. Then, the principal had been especially derogatory about the file, referring to

303

it as 'the file of that devil, Jacquensica Nek'. How could she ever tell her pastor that her boss had labelled one of his choristers a devil? Lying to her pastor would make a holier alternative. "He has not discussed it with me," she extended her lies.

When the principal returned, he was accompanied by Yeoman Smith. Rev Ali Jaiye promptly followed the two men into the principal's inner office.

The office setting was unchanged from the previous day's when Jacq was there. As Ali was slowly sinking into the chair Jacq used, his eyes caught the file bearing Jacq's name sitting on the desk, before the principal.

"Rev Jaiye, meet Yeoman Smith," the principal introduced the third man with them. "He is Jacquensica's art and course tutor, and I believe he will aid our discussions."

A short exchange of pleasantries followed. Rev Ali Jaiye believed he was meeting Yeoman Smith for the first time. But Yeoman told Rev Jaiye they had met once before: he came to the reverend at the cathedral to collect the church's donation to the last Black Culture Week. It pleased Ali, even though he could not remember Yeoman's face.

"Now, since she stays with you, did she tell you why she has been suspended?" the principal addressed Ali.

"She said nothing – ate nothing, drank nothing. She is very distressed and is crying a lot."

"She said nothing and answered no question here too," added Yeoman, "despite the principal's gentle efforts."

"And that evasion solved nothing," resumed the principal. "We have to know the facts to be able to consider fairly and protect rightly the good name of the college. Unfortunately, she was not helping; and that's why we called you as a last resort, because you signed her papers on behalf of the cathedral."

"Alright, gentlemen," Ali responded, "tell me what you want to know, and let me see how much I can be of help."

The principal rolled out the alleged sins of Jacq, as he was aware of: the strong-headedness, waywardness and rebelliousness in her traits; her felonious conviction in Ila and her lucky escape from being consequently executed; her unwarranted burglary of Ben Mackinnon's studio, the chase through the streets of Glasgow before she could be apprehended, her being charged to the court, and the inescapable long jail terms that awaited her.

Yeoman Smith could not miss the opportunity of adding his own first ever encounter with Jacq at the Black Culture Week arts exhibition, and the later clashes she had with other lecturers and her fellow course-mates.

Ali listened intensely. When both men had stopped, he felt sad that they mistook Jacq's silence for guilt and pronounced wrong judgement on her. Much as he now suspected the single origin of these allegations, he preferred to calmly wait and ask the principal and her course tutor some questions.

"These are serious allegations, gentlemen," Rev Ali Jaiye responded, "and I am very surprised to hear them. But first, can I ask who the sources were?"

"Well," retorted the principal, "asking for the sources won't help; the single source was doubly credible. At this stage, and as the representative of her sponsors, it is important that you volunteer any information which would enable the college to resolve it."

"There is a reason why I asked," Rev Ali Jaiye was adamant, "and I will gladly volunteer all what I know. The only source I can think of is my friend, Ben Mackinnon; and if I am right, he has intentionally lied to you."

"Yes, it was him," the principal boldly admitted. "You know his contributions in prizes and other support to the college. They make it impossible for him to see something harmful to the college and remain quiet. Besides, he remains the poor victim of the robbery. Lastly, if the police had already charged Jacquensica to

305

court, what other authenticity do we need – except to pretend and wait till when Jacquensica is marched into the prison?"

"When did Ben report this to the college?"

"Why is that important?" asked the principal.

"Because if they were long reported, Ben and his actions could be excused. If they were as recent as Monday, then, Ben is being mischievous."

"Again, why?" the principal wanted to know.

"Because since Monday, Ben has known the allegations were not true. We actually discussed them together again yesterday in the morning. We both know Jacq was innocent of what happened to her in Ila and in Commercial House."

"Well, Reverend," came in Yeoman, "you need to throw some light on why the allegations were not true. Just as the principal has said, we knew Mr Mackinnon was a victim. And if you disbelieve this, what about my actual experience with her? She generously but wrongly bared a rude dressing down on me and my team. She cursed us that we were ignorant of masks, masquerades and African gods, and were disrespectful to the gods. She failed to realise that it was her people who had falsely usurped the dictates of these idols. Her mind was totally closed to the progressive interpretation of what they represented, quite unlike how an aspiring theologian's mind should reason.

"In the lecture rooms, she never listens or wants to learn from anyone. I suspect she sees herself as one of her kingdom's goddesses who we must kneel before to appease. She has that delusion that she is bigger than the college!"

To throw just some light? Rev Ali Jaiye realised he must shine their rays in bundles to both men for him to successfully defend Jacq. "Gentlemen, I am happy you invited me here," he started with. "You see, the young lady is a fine, upright person. If she was ever guilty of anything, it would be of having strong will, made even stronger by the hell she went through.

"Starting with Ila, it was true she was condemned to be executed. It was because she took on the masquerades for oppressing the people, especially the women – single-handedly! She called for a change.

"Of course, she respects the local gods and masks, but abhors the terrible way the group of King Jap was using them. She accused the group of developing the masks to cheat, steal and rob.

"In a 'world of men only', this was an affront to the new con men led by the king – a taboo that had to be cleansed once and for all. For that, the king sentenced her to death, revoked her family's chiefdom, castrated her husband, and put her only child, a small girl of five, into slavery. She was spared the guillotine on the condition that she accepted an everlasting banishment to Glasgow. This is the genesis of her behaviour since she arrived here.

"Men, masks, masquerades, gods and ancestors, she loves and respects them for what they are, but as long as one does not impose a way of life on the other. She respects the statue of The Holy Virgin Mary in the church and admired Christ on the Cross. She loves St Mungo at the museum and reveres James Watt at George Square. She has allowed none of them to overrule her life. She wants other people to adopt that way. She hopes to preach it through theology and Christianity."

"But she broke into Ben Mackinnon's studio; and it has got nothing to do with such beliefs and respects you just mentioned," Yeoman reminded the Reverend. "She did what no one must preach."

"She didn't do it."

"Really?" asked the principal, unbelievably.

"She didn't. If at all it was broken into, it was before she got there."

"But she was arrested and charged to court," Yeoman again reminded Rev Jaiye. "How would that be so if she didn't?"

"Because Ben was mischievous! The magistrate realised that and acquitted Jacq immediately, and at the same time he rebuked the police. Ben should have shown you a copy of this judgement paper which I have here. He had a copy since that Tuesday morning. Ben behaved badly."

Rev Ali Jaiye opened his briefcase, removed the copy of Jacq's letter of discharge and acquittal, and handed it over to the principal. The principal examined it and passed it to Yeoman Smith whose scrutiny too, failed to dent its genuineness. The three men were silent for a moment.

"Now, on a very serious note," the principal broke the silence, "why would Ben Mackinnon have so behaved to Jacquensica? What must have been the reasons?"

"I don't know for sure," answered Ali. "That was also why Jacq was too dazed to speak when she was before you.

"Ben is a good friend of mine," Ali went on. "But he seemed to have a grudge against Jacq ever since the day he knew that Jacq successfully partook in the Venice carnival. Jacq however believed the hatred started the day she arrived in Glasgow from Ila."

"This is getting more serious and interesting," the principal could not hide his feelings. "Did Jacqensica actually take part in that carnival? And if she did, how did that offend him? How would that offend anybody?"

"Well, something to do with his art trade. In Venice, Jacq was commended by all the newspapers for her acts and her unprecedented charity; and was co-opted into the Carnival Arts Committee. Because this Committee has influence on arts in Europe, Ben, as an art dealer, feared this could affect him and his family trade negatively. Without success, I have twice tried to convince him these could never be so."

Rev Ali Jaiye's story was one of the most fascinating both the principal and Jacq's course tutor had ever heard. It was totally unexpected, extraordinary. "Reverend, are you sure this is the true story?" the principal asked.

"Yes, it is. The young lady is sound and strong. She loves arts, loves tradition, loves her ancestors, and loves Jesus Christ; but has neither pity nor patience for anything or anyone creating a collision course among any of those. What she needs most now is our encouragement, not persecution. We should know she is not our perfect Jesus Christ."

The principal, now won over by Rev Ali Jaiye's talks, sighed with relief. "Seeing you here has been timely and useful," he said. "Or what is your opinion, Yeoman?"

"Yes, sir," agreed Yeoman Smith. "You could forgive her and give her another chance, now that we know what really happened."

"You heard that, Reverend?" the principal asked Ali. "That chance we shall give her; and she shall get a letter to that effect. She should be able to return as early as tomorrow.

"But you shall do us all a favour," the principal continued. "Teach her the art of talking and preaching into people's ears – even if that would mean stepping down a ladder or stooping down a length to get to the level of the target's eardrums. She should stop becoming angry at people who could not know what she has been through; everyone has gone or will go through one tragedy or the other, one way or the other.

"She should stop concealing her experience. An experience concealed is as useless as it is dangerously explosive.

"You shall have to advise her on these – please."

"Well, Reverend, I am not ashamed to confess," came in Yeoman, "that you have to forgive me.

"Initially I was of the opinion that you were trying to protect the bad deeds of another black person. Actually at a point, I almost interrupted you to say 'look, I am black too'. I am happy I was patient.

"My first encounter with Jacq gave me that terrible impression of her. She too would have to forgive my judgement. Anyway, I will speak to her when she returns."

"Reverend," the principal cuts in again, "I can see that Jacquensica has got a lot to offer. Luckily, I have Yeoman here with

309

me. Together with Bob Watson, her theology lecturer, we will help her to explore and develop her talents fully. From now on, she must present her thoughts more appropriately and promptly."

"Thank you both," Rev Jaiye expressed his appreciation. "I shall do my best; but only you will have to forgive me as I can never be better at teaching than the great teachers of this illustrious college."

The two college staff welcomed Ali's compliment with laughter. In the laughter the principal left his chair and went out to the secretary. She was to prepare Jacq's letter of recall immediately for Rev Ali Jaiye to take along with him.

"Actually, she is in my car," Ali told the men as the principal returned from his secretary. "Should I call her here to apologise?"

"Oh no," objected the principal. "There is neither a need nor a reason for that. In fact, we owe her an apology and I tender it. She must however find time to see Mr Smith. He will be happy to direct her."

* * *

Jacquensica felt happy with her vindication, now by her college, after the court's. She was pleased that it would be bad news for Ben Mackinnon when, probably through his son, Victor, he learnt that she was still a student of Glasgow College. She wondered triumphantly which direction Ben would turn his face should she accidentally bump into him.

"But wait a minute," she suddenly told herself, realising that it was exactly one week since Ben's burglary plot would have landed her inside Glasgow's 'Bar-L' and wrecked her hopes of ever securing herself and her family.

"What is so special about this man Ben Mackinnon?" she queried herself. "Why must he be allowed to get away each time he perpetrates his acts of evil on people? Why can't someone just deflate him? Why can't that someone be me, Jacquensica Nek, his biggest victim? Why...?"

She did not forget that not long ago such a confrontation, then against Jap, dearly cost her, her family, her natural habitat, and almost her life. But with the current exposure of Ben and his son, now would be a safer time to confront Ben with Victor. In a free and lawful society like Glasgow's, she would not allow her being a stranger to deter her. Surely, if Glasgow had put indigenes above the law and above its immigrants, would she not have already completed a week in jail? Oh yes, she would confront Ben now, call his bluff, and get him off her back once and for all. What's better than showing the same eye the dirty pore it had oozed out? She would, that day, Friday – inside the same Commercial House. Inside the same studio!

The sight of Ben's car hardened Jacq's heart. It stood innocently inside its port beside the Commercial House. "The vehicle of the wicked waiting for the wicked," she thought to herself. A wish inside her wanted both the car and its owner destroyed. Another pushed her inside the building through its main entrance door, to the immediate lobby that was its main reception. "Good day," she extended jointly to the two familiar occupiers of that zone of the ground floor.

The surfacing of Jacq inside Commercial House brought the two people at the reception to a reluctant attention. Just exactly one week ago a major drama had happened between them and this returning caller. Only that now, they were in the earlier hours of the day.

"What-do-you-want?" the huge lady at the reception asked. She had recovered ahead of her colleague from the shock of seeing Jacq.

"You mean you are surprised at my resurrection from the depths of prison? Well, I am here to see Ben, Mr Ben Mackinnon."

"You cannot see him," the security man said firmly and unapologetically. "He left no word that he is expecting you."

311

The Masquerade

"That is unbelievable," Jacq countered him. "You both work with him and still forget that he is a busy man, one who is sometimes too busy to remember everyone on his appointment list. This time, I expect you to call him and confirm. That won't be too much to do I suppose."

"He is expecting no one now – and certainly, not you," the security man was adamant. "You must leave now. If you don't, I will call the police."

"Call the Highland Regiment and the Fire Brigade if you like," Jacq cared the least. "That won't be strange to me – not anymore. But if you do that, this time Ben Mackinnon will blame you for not notifying him that I was here for him. Can you tell him Jacquensica Nek is here for him, waiting?"

Jacq's deadly radiating confidence succeeded in subduing the bravado and diligence of the two people manning the ground floor reception, killing outright their threatening intention to call the police. The security guard urged the receptionist to inform Ben of Jacq's presence.

As Jacq listened to the conversation from the receptionist's end of the line, she was able to guess what was going on at the other end. The worry, she could correctly guess, was on Ben's unseen face: Yes, Jacq...yes, Nek...yes, the lady...yes, alone...yes, that she must see you...yes, that you are expecting her...yes, he already told her he would call the police...

"Look, my dear lady," Jacq interrupted the receptionist, "The conversation is unnecessarily long." She intentionally raised her voice appropriately loud and clear to the point that Ben would understand her at his end, and would not accuse the receptionist of distortion or fabrication. "Tell him that if he is not ready to see me and talk now, that I will leave before the police are here. But I will also leave my message with the two of you here, along the streets I was chased, and with the policemen. It will make it easy for the police to know who they want when they arrive – whether me, or

312

him together with Victor, his son. Ask him again if he still doesn't want to talk before I leave!"

The receptionist kept the handset held firmly, unable to replace it due to Jacq's fear-inducing words, and to how Ben might take cutting him off from hearing Jacq's threatening intentions. She feared being in the middle of two shouting antagonists who have made her the medium through which they exchanged unpleasant messages. She was relieved when she heard Ben, from his end of the line, breathe out his next instructions. "Allow her to come in," he said. "Send her up."

* * *

Jacq did not have to wait at the second floor reception before she could see Ben, for Ben was already out there waiting for her before she could complete her steps to it. He wasted no time in adding his deceitful smile to his physical presence. "Good to see you," his receptionist unbelievably heard her boss say to Jacq. To Jacq, of all people! "Please come in," she heard the wonder continue in rapid succession that gave Jacq no chance to talk.

With played calmness Jacq followed Ben into the studio, through the two doors she could still remember, into the more inner chamber she had no idea existed. She was amused at Ben's holy comportment. She could not predict her expectations – and she didn't care. Now with a different frame of mind, and for having the good luck of walking behind Ben, the shutters of her eyes captured many images of rare artefacts they both passed by. They couldn't miss them – with their incredibly high selling price tags displayed in boxes, shelves, stands and hangings. No appreciative eye would!

"So, Ben is such a rich man," she said to herself, "a man with a whole museum to himself! Perhaps, one day, she or someone she knew would be able to ask Ben how he acquired the huge collection. Perhaps, he would voluntarily talk about it today – to her! Perhaps none of her thoughts was realistic she thought, as she took her seat inside the unique art room that was Ben's office.

"So, why are you here this time, Jacq?" Ben asked her.

"It can't be for an ulterior motive, Ben. We are now together, aren't we?" She was apparently relaxed on the chair Ben gave her.

"Were you threatening me at the ground floor reception? I heard you clearly. I want to know what brings you here."

Jacq restrained herself from laughing at Ben's response which indicated his fearful uncertainties.

"Seriously, Ben, I come as a friend. And, if you have already formed your group of friends, I wish you would squeeze me into it."

"You didn't sound like a friend," Ben doubted, staring her in the face, perhaps doing his mystical reading of it again. "I heard you on the ground floor; your threats were not those of a potential friend, Jacq."

"Excuse me for that, Ben. Having left the college to be here, only to be refused entry, was frustrating enough. Frustration can elicit venomous actions – including such words that you heard. Thanks for changing your mind; I am happy to see this side of you."

"Meaning?" He was still cautious, studying the guest he could not trust.

"Meaning your humility! You must have spent a fortune to have this museum. I have never thought someone having as much as this could ever be so humble and simple, like you are."

"Well, thank you, Jacq." He was beginning to feel at ease. "I take that as a genuine compliment from someone who knows the real arts, masked and unmasked."

"You must have seen all the lands, seas, and forests for you to actually assemble the best from them. As I followed you, I could also see that some parts of my kingdom as well as parts of my Egyptian ancestry are well represented in your collection." Jacq rose from her chair, heading to one attractive artefact shelved higher to the right of Ben's chair. "You don't mind that I look round the artefacts, Ben?"

"Thank you for all the compliments, Jacq. Today I wasn't expecting you; and it is time for me to go. We shall find another time for that."

Already, Jacq had moved close to the object. It was in a clear glass cube measuring about six inches on all sides. The object, a shining brass cobra, sculptured with an aggressive head, rose, was ready to bite.

Under her friendly stance, Jacq brushed aside any substance in her host's explanation. She craned her neck excitedly toward the box – to the embossed platting screwed on to it: *Order of The Cobra*! Another cult!

"Please return to your seat, Jacq" Ben instructed, half showing the extent of his displeasure at Jacq's wayward interest in the object. "Leave viewing till another day when there will be time, and when I shall be able to take you around."

"Okay then, Ben, if you promise a next time," she accepted, occupying her chair. "And that next time too, I promise to tell you another reason why I am here."

"Another reason – what other reason?" Ben asked, startled. "You didn't say that before?"

"I didn't," Jacq admitted. "But there is another; and no time for anything else now, according to you."

"But you can give a hint, mention what it is all about, can't you? Then, we can leave discussing it till that other time."

She adjusted herself on the chair. "It is about an apology," she said, firmly.

"An apology? What apology?" He laughed, misreading Jacq's intentional vagueness. "I don't need one, if that is another reason for your coming. I have long forgiven you. I wouldn't have worked for your freedom before the magistrate if I hadn't. Is that clear to you now?"

Jacq held back her laughter. Instead, she gave a small, victorious smile in the realisation of the depth of ignorance Ben's wealth of artefacts had plunged him in – it had prevented him from identifying to whom the apology was owed.

"I mean you owe me an apology, Ben – for what you and Victor put me through. You need to apologise for both of you. That would prove to me that you have truly changed, and repented. I want your apology."

At once the time to go, which Ben said had arrived for him, fled – banished from his mind by Jacq's demand. A most unscrupulous demand! Biggest insult and disrespect! Again, from Jacq – the same Jacq! He managed a sarcastic smile and the shaking of his crossed legs. The unexpectedness of the demand had rendered him bereft of an appropriate response.

Jacq was unruffled. She seized on the shock and confusion in Ben's reaction to stand up and resume another round of viewing the decorated walls of Ben's office. She ended again at the boxed cobra, this time, stretching out to it. She wanted to hold it, to be certain she read the inscription right. *Order of The Cobra – Mackinnon I*! Her move ignited Ben's bottled composure:

"Stop it Jacq, and get back to your seat!" he barked. "Or better, get out of my studio.

"You deserve no apology – not from me, and not from my son. I regret knowing an ingrate like you. So, leave this place now!" He was foaming, spitting.

"That won't be a problem for me, Ben; so, stop shouting," Jacq responded coolly as she returned to her chair. "I know you won't offer an apology. Have I not just read the *Order of The Cobra* and your name on the box? I know what the *Cobra* was all about: the first cult in the kingdom of Ila to aid, abet and practise exploitation of the people; the group that invented the immoral, dishonest use of masks and masquerades in Ila. The earlier gang of sellers, buyers and sponsors wound together by tentacles of cheating, bribery, corruption and thievery!

"So, Ben, you are a deadly *Cobra*; and your son, a murderous *Eagle*. Your gangs believed they could do no wrong –

until you were overruled by a magistrate who feared neither a deity nor a devil.

"It is now my turn to challenge you and your son. And I will do so on the streets, in the college, in the church, in this building, and if need be, before the magistrates. I have nothing to lose from any revelation by you and Victor. Keep your belated apology, Ben. Good night."

Jacq stood up and walked out, opening and shutting the two doors behind herself one after the other on her way out. After the second that brought her before Ben's reception, she came face-to-face with Victor just passing by his father from the college. She moved to the side of the receptionist to let him pass. "Hello, *Senior Eagle*," she mockingly greeted him with. "And how is Uggi, the junior one? Do you realise the holy choir is not supposed to be for people like you? Both of you need a thorough repentance to remain a part of it."

More from embarrassment than unpreparedness, Victor was dumbfounded. He felt the shame of Jacq's pronouncement as he watched her vanish down the stairwell. His eyes and those of his father's receptionist met; and he wondered if the receptionist understood all that Jacq had just said. She might not yet know what the *Eagle* was in the occult; but she wouldn't be so daft as not to know what a choir – the holy choir – was. He walked in to his father's office, dumbfounded by Jacq's insulting attack.

* * *

After Jacq had stormed out of Ben's studio, seen off with relief by Ben, Ben was still outside his inner office pacing and blaming himself for allowing Jacq in, in the first place. That was when Victor entered; he met his father red-eyed and angry.

"You just missed that evil woman. She harassed me for close to an hour."

"I saw her; we met by the reception," Victor responded.

"Did she say anything to you?"

"She derided me before the receptionist. She called me *Senior Eagle* and referred to Uggi as *Junior Eagle*. She asked why both of us were still in the church choir."

"What a mad woman?" Ben remarked. "I went my *dinger* and almost *banjo* her *mooth*," he admitted his near readiness to hit Jacq's mouth. "Can you imagine the devil seeking to reform the church? So, she is that mad, that she has extended this to the choir and to the son of her only remaining mentor. Her indecency knows no bounds! What a pity! I must reveal this to Ali on Sunday at the church."

"It doesn't matter, dad. Since returning from Ila, it has been my intention to leave the choir anyway. And with this pricking from her, I believe I have left, leaving Uggi there to do what suits him. That will be his problem."

"But nothing – and no one – should push you out of the choir just like that, Victor," Ben objected strongly. "You have been a member, possibly before she knew what a church is, and before she knew the grammatical difference between the words right and wrong."

"Still dad," Victor insisted, "I am not going back. I don't want to commit murder – which any further embarrassment from her could force me to do to her."

"The decision is yours, but I strongly object. She did the worse to me, and I am not letting that make me mad.

"She taunted me as a *Cobra*, and one of the initiators, aiders and abetters of bribery, corruption, exploitation, you name it, in Ila. Can you imagine that level of insult? Can you, Victor?"

"That won't put me off what I have to plan for her next," Ben continued. "I won't allow that."

Victor was speechless as he followed him into his office where both men took their seats.

"You see what I meant, what I foresaw of her the first time," Ben resumed his anger, now to his son. "Did I not say that everything about her was evil? Did I not say you shouldn't have brought her to Glasgow? How more right could I be?

"I was right from the first time I set my eyes on her. She was talking and behaving rudely, that I was at her door too early in the morning. In those days if I were her master, would she have had *mooth* to talk even if I have jumped into her bed in the middle of the night? Within this short time of being here she has mislabelled you, insulted me, and had the wrecking of my family name and business within her grasp. Victor, I wish you never brought her here. I really wish you hadn't. It's as if she'd cast her devilish *cantrips* on us."

This same song of blame again, Victor thought inescapably. The thought evaporated any pity he had felt for his father since joining him in the studio. "When will this stop, dad?" he asked him. "You have blamed me almost daily for this. I believe it should stop."

"It may stop, Victor; but I don't see its repercussion on us stopping."

"Then, you shouldn't have sent me to Ila. You should have gone yourself – with Uggi or his father. I reject the blame totally. I have never for once seen Uggi's father blaming him, or seen Uggi apologising to his father over Jacq's coming. His father is your friend; have you ever seen him blaming Uggi on the same issue?"

"Well, I still feel strongly about it. And I am not happy about the recent discovery: you shouldn't have become an *Eagle*. It has given these fools something to gossip about."

"Has it really, dad?" Victor asked him. He could not believe that his father had even doubled the grounds for blaming him.

"Yes, it has."

"But if granddad's membership of the *Cobra* did not persecute his life, and you accepting him for what he was gave nobody something to gossip about, why should my being an *Eagle* be different? Why should there be a case at all, dad? You seem to be fanning it, dad.

"Besides, you told me to make powerful friends in Ila for future contacts – like granddad did. What friendship can be stronger than being in the king's inner circle? It has achieved what you want and saved a condemned woman. Why should that embarrass you?"

"I just don't know Victor. Sometimes I regret not being an initiated *Cobra* myself. I would have blinded that evil woman with my venom and watch her die in agony. That is all she deserves; and I leave that to you. It is the next thing, the next stage." He was pitifully depressed.

"The next stage, dad – what next stage?"

"Are you still asking me, son?"

"Yes, I am."

"Now, you are an *Eagle*, aren't you? As an *Eagle*, Jacq is an enemy to you, to King Jap, and to me. You are supposed to know your enemy and turn them into your meat. You are supposed to claw them down on the streets, in the classrooms, on the fields, in the markets, and in their sleeps. Then, you are supposed to peck them to death. Jacq is our enemy!"

Mystically, Victor knew his father was correct. Legally, however, he knew both he and his father must step carefully.

* * *

Later at home that Friday, Ben was frightfully mindful of Jacq's two ferocious attacks on him in the last three days. He was desperate for time and the tact he needed to douse Jacq's infernal fieriness and wash away the ashes before it would engulf him, his son and his family business. Next Sunday at the church would be that appropriate day and place to flag off his counter-attack. Before then, he would avoid Jacq the way a mollusc, irrespective of the hardness of its shell, must avoid salt. As for the methodology he would use, he discovered it to have presented itself in Jacq's recent unguarded utterances.

Came Sunday, Ben waited patiently up until a few minutes to the start of the morning service. He made a quick reconnaissance of the choristers in the vestry to confirm the absence of Victor and Uggi. From there he went over to Ali.

"Victor and Uggi are not here, do you know that?" he asked Ali. "I have been to the vestry to see if they were with their colleagues getting ready but they were not there."

Ali attached no importance to Ben's reported observation. The service still had ten minutes to start – a whole ten minutes for the noted absenters to join the choristers. Besides, there had been some previous occasions when Victor and Uggi were late, and a rare few when both of them were actually absent from the church. "What is the big deal in that?" Ali responded. "Ben, you have plenty of time in your hand – plenty enough to spy on two big choir boys!"

"No, Ali," Ben subtly disagreed. "What I want to tell you is that they are not coming – they have stopped coming to the church."

Now Ali was lost.

"Well, I don't know how else I can tell you. They have both decided not to have anything to do with the cathedral again – now that they have been excommunicated by no other person but Jacq."

Still, Ben's words offered no additional clarity to Ali's puzzled mind; they worsened it. Ben must say more.

"On Friday, Jacq told both boys that for being members of the *Order of The Eagle*, the sacred cathedral is too holy for them, meaning they should find an appropriate place of worship for themselves."

"Jacq or Uggi told me nothing; how did you learn of this?" Ali asked.

"Oh, I expected them to have told you. It all happened in my studio on Friday. She came in, called me a devil, and demanded an apology from me and Victor for injustices she alleged we did to her. Then, she said the church was not a place for Victor and Uggi, for being members of the *Eagle*. Next, she threatened to fight and expose me on the streets and in the law courts. Hasn't she told you this?"

"No, she hasn't." replied Ali, surprised.

"Later that day Victor told me he has convinced Uggi, and that they are staying away from the church."

"This is serious; I would have done something about it. You should have called me on Friday, or yesterday. It is too serious for both of us to ignore. Too, too serious, Ben!"

The patience Ali imposed on himself to the end of the service was made even longer by the non-appearance of Victor and Uggi within the church premises that morning. He was anxious, and felt he could not wait to get home before finding out from Jacq what had actually happened when she was in Commercial House. At the end of the service, he called her into his office.

"Why were Victor and Uggi not in the church today; do you know?" he asked her. He was cool outside, fuming inside.

"I wouldn't know, sir," she answered.

"Ben just told me you excommunicated them, that I should not expect them in the choir anymore. He said you were at his studio on Friday to do that."

"No, sir. That is not true. Ben had again selected the part of the story that suited him."

"What does that mean – that you didn't return to Commercial House, see him, attack him, and tell Victor and Uggi something?"

"It is true I met Ben in his studio at Commercial House. I went because I decided it was time someone confronted him over his evil deeds. I was determined to be that person. When I met him, I demanded an apology for his and his son's sins on me. Uggi was not there; and I only met Victor on my way out of the studio."

Worry and disappointment began to engulf Ali, over Jacq's confessed return to Commercial House. "So, you went for his apology – and did you get one?"

"No, sir, I didn't. He wouldn't give one. When I eventually discovered why he wouldn't, I wasn't surprised he refused to."

"Which was what?"

"You want me to say it, sir?"

"Yes; if you are sure you have it."

"Yes, sir; I have it. There I discovered that Ben was also an occultist, an active member of the *Order of The Cobra*. Believe me, sir. I saw his brass insignia beautifully boxed with his name engraved on it. I saw it and reached it before he could stop me. He must have passed the cultism to his son so that they could continue to work with Ila monarchs to corner resources meant for the whole kingdom. And back in Ila, we were told how, like the *Eagles*, the *Cobras* were above the law, bigger than any offence, and how they must not give an apology for whatever bad deed."

Ali least expected such another mammoth discovery by Jacq. He was lost for immediate words over the discovered Satanism of Ben. In fairness, Ali believed he had no reason to doubt Jacq.

"What other strange materials did you believe you saw inside the studio?"

"I did not know for sure, sir. Quite a lot of carvings and statues resembling works from Ila area. Many of them were among those displayed at the Black Culture Week exhibition."

"Did you say Victor and Uggi were not there with you two?"

"No, sir. I was with him alone in his office. It was after he refused to apologise and I was going out that I met Victor at his father's reception, outside the main studio door. It was there I asked him to share with me, my honest opinion of his father and of his friend: they all needed a special, cleansing prayer to remain holy enough for the Cathedral. I just wanted them to be good Christians."

"And your threat of attack on Ben, what was it all about?"

"Actually it was a challenge: that until he adopts good Christian mannerisms, I will always expose him openly in the church, on the streets, in the courts, and at all the places he had himself attacked me unjustly. He can do me no more damage."

On a scale Ali never dreamt, he saw the extreme finality in Jacq's vent. He agreed Jacq had unquestionable reasons to be that

323

hard, but was quietly angry that Jacq could, as a Christian, not forgive Ben and Victor – and could not forgive his son who had apologised in person to her as well as sent him to apologise on his behalf. What steel Jacq's mind must have been made of! He must find a way of settling her mind before she would attack Ben – or possibly Victor or Uggi – in any of the public places she had listed!

"I am surprised Jacq, that you did not consider the damage this feud could cost the church. Or did you?" Ali asked Jacq.

"I did, sir," she promptly replied. "I also considered how a cost is inevitable – and how whatever it is would be cheaper now than later. The more Ben gets away with his wicked ways the more he will continue, until he inflicts irremediable damage on someone. This is the right time to stop him."

Ali couldn't believe the visible, ionic charge and change being exhibited by Jacq as she spoke. She didn't look the same girl whose moods he could boast to know. He watched her talk determinately of confronting such a noble of Glasgow! "Did you ever meet Ben or come across him before you came to Glasgow?" he asked her.

"No, sir. And thank God, I didn't. If I had, he would have long laughed over my dead body. But now I have got enough to confront him with.

"Sese Abram was like him. Neither I nor my husband confronted Sese in time. See where that landed us today. Once, Sese was disgraced and demoted with his masquerade. That time, we, as it turned out to be, fought for and obtained his restoration to our peril. This is the right time to…"

"J-a-c-q, enough of this" Ali interrupted her. "I have called you here so you might listen. I disagree totally with your intention; and you should drop it forthwith. I will not be a party to it."

"I don't expect you to be, sir. That was why I didn't inform you before I met him inside his studio."

"Listen to me, Jacq, I say again," Ali exploded angrily at Jacq. "You don't know what you are talking about. Certainly you don't know its implications. And if you think you do, then, list them before me now."

Jacq refused to utter a word, talk less of making a list. For once since the conversation began, she was forcefully quiet.

"Jacq, so you see," Ali seized on her silence, "it is impossible for you to just come from Ila to Glasgow and know Glasgow more than Ben – or more than me. Ben is a powerful man here. His ancestors have always been. And to be fair to him, until you arrived, no one had ever associated him with any wicked arbitrariness."

"Sir, that wouldn't be due to him being a good person, but more, due to the unawareness of the people. The big spots on a leopard take time to attain their sizes."

"So, retaliatory confrontation is all that you can think of now? How can selfish thinking, the type you are alleging Ben possesses, cause you not to mind how it will affect me, Uggi, and possibly, you too? When you pull a runner, it pulls all other things along its path. You are studying the Bible and arts, aren't you? Where in your studies have you come across any goodness in confrontation and retaliation?"

"Sir, I am not speaking of retaliation. That's unnecessary now that I have survived their plots. But confronting Ben especially is necessary; otherwise instead of being remorseful and repentant, he'll go on persecuting and destroying.

"You have been all goodness to me; and I fear that you and all that you have worked hard for in Glasgow would be Ben's next targets. Honestly, sir, this is how I feel."

Ali said nothing in the following minutes. He rose and walked to a set of scriptural bibliographies and pulled through them as if searching for a particular reference. He returned empty handed to his chair. "Well. Jacq," he heaved heavily, "let's go home. We shall talk about this later."

That "later" time for Rev Ali Jaiye came that evening. In fact, Ali presented it before both of them at after-dinner. "Jacq, I have thought over the discussion we had in the church," he called Jacq's attention as they were both finishing their dinner.

Jacq pushed her plate to aside and rested her back on her chair, her eyes penetrating Ali's. She was eager to hear Ali's thoughts.

"Yes, I have thought over it," he repeated.

"Yes, sir," Jacq responded, disappointedly. She wished Ali would just go straight to the point.

"You would be surprised that I have bought your idea of confrontation, but disappointed that it is someone else that I believe we must confront."

"Someone else? Victor? Uggi?" She was anxious.

"No, Jacq. Someone stronger, but connected with Ben and the other two people you mentioned."

"King Jap?" She could not wait to know.

"No, Jacq. We have to confront Mr Devil – Satan. The three of them were always good until he went into them and influenced their behaviours. It is him in each of them – whatever his degree of influence – who we shall have to face and conquer."

Jacq felt amused at Ali's utterances. Now, Ali was talking of Satan and separating the Mackinnons and Victor from him. She saw in it, a deliberate indecisiveness that lacks a true solution. "But, sir, how are you going to face and conquer this, Mr Devil?" she asked.

"How? We shall see. And I expect you to suggest something. Think about it; and tell me in the morning, or anytime tomorrow. It is already time for bed."

"Well, sir, my suggestion is ready with me right now, if you want one from me. It is the same whether I say it now or tomorrow. Just the same."

"In that case, tell me now. That will give me something to throw my brains at, in my bed."

"I learnt of the reality from Ila," she started with. "That was when Sese was the real Mr Devil, masquerading in the Fire

Spirit. He grew into the law which even King Jap could not break. It took my husband's initial subtleness followed by his hidden physical and verbal assaults to subdue him. After that the kingdom was able to tie Sese up until he was tamed. Therefore sir, one needs some savagery to conquer a beast. Even, water will never tame a fire until it confronts it with superior fierceness. Whichever way, nothing gets tamed until it's met with a wild confrontation. Even Bob Smith taught us that in the class. And he teaches only from the Bible."

"Eh, Jacq," interceded Ali, feeling he had heard enough. "For God's sake, go no further on that. He must have taught you from something else. No line of the Bible prescribes violence for violence in that sense. And only a Bible-thumper will teach the contrary. And I'm confident you don't have a teacher like that in the college."

"Oh no, sir," Jacq disagreed promptly. "He lectured us about exorcism which is about violence against the same type of devil we've been talking about. He lectured on how a greater violence must be used to counter the devil. Was he not correct then? And how about the *Law of Moses*?"

"Oh Jacq," he said unbelievably, "you are definitely more than what I see. Much more!

"To an extent, your teacher was correct. But it is a different case now. He must have been discussing a more serious case, the violent type fit only for higher clergy to handle. And more important: how on earth does one face Ben to inform him that he and his son need to be exorcised of the devil? How do you tell a pillar of the church he needs atonement?"

"Unless Ben is more foolish than wicked, he must have known that from the hint I already gave him. As his friend you can follow it up, or tell any of the senior clergy to tell him. After all, the Bible respects no evil. And if you permit me this time, I can return to him and deliver the message."

"Oh, Jacq!" Ali screamed delightfully. "We'll talk tomorrow. Just go to bed!"

CHAPTER TEN

The Atonements II

Throughout the night, Rev Ali Jaiye was haunted by the reality of him having to take Jacq seriously. Normally, for both of them being of the same Ila cultural ancestry, the reverse should have been the case. In Ila, whatever was its quality, the age mattered. He knew he was Jacq's senior by at least two decades; and that consequently Jacq should have listened to him and obeyed his instructions. After all, age was age, naturally God-given, not purchasable from the market!

Ali was grateful to his Lord for enabling him to mature adequately with his age. His maturity had guided him to recognising that Jacq, though younger in age than him, was in fact 'older' due to her dramatic experiences of life. He saw Jacq's pendulum of life as having experienced a heavier weight and pull that had swung it across an arc of local affluence, destruction, near destruction and near death. In coping with these positions along the arc, these events had made her shorter life more aged. They had also hardened her, to the point of ignoring his advice. They had made her most determined to challenge Ben Mackinnon irrespective of how he, Ali, felt about her making such challenges. Overall, Ali conceded, Jacq earned it all – his respect and the right to be respected.

About Jacq's allegation of cult membership against Ben? Wild, wild; surprise, surprise. How would Ben have been initiated?

How would he have collected an insignia when he had never been to Ila? Through the emissary of the Devil's nightly flights? But then, her earlier allegation about Victor and Uggi being in the cult was incredibly correct. And this against Ben could also be.

"Have I, Ali, ever noticed any cultish behaviour in Ben?" he asked himself. His answer wobbled through a probability to a yes: Aha, no wonder why Ben would dabble uncontrollably into clerical decisions he was least knowledgeable about, dwell persistently in anger, and not tolerate what he could not control. No wonder why Ben maliciously interpreted the physical physiology of Jacq, why he ran people down. No wonder why Ben quietly guided his fortune but noisily donated peanuts. No wonder why Ben was vengeful. Now, he, Ali, has discovered why Ben had not a close friend outside the dubiousness of his art trade. Aha, no wonder...! What a wonder! As early as possible on Sunday, he, Ali, would need to bring it to the knowledge of Rev James Scot, his senior in the parish episcopacy.

* * *

"Rev Scot, I need your help," Ali opened up as soon as they both sat in Rev Scot's office. "There is a serious war going on between Ben Mackinnon and my Jacq. I have intervened and got nowhere. The quarrel has extended to Victor, and may be, to my son, Kazuggi. I fear it would go further – up to me and the church."

"You live with your son and Jacq," responded Rev Scot. "And you see your friend Ben from time to time. Why haven't you spoken to them?"

"I have, time and again. Who wouldn't like to be a peace maker and remain blessed as the son of God? Ben and Jacq had been intransigent. Very intransigent."

"How, and why?"

"Initially it was Ben who persecuted Jacq relentlessly. He forced her out of his house which she shared with Victor and Kazuggi; had her in the dock for a phantom burglary she knew nothing about; and got her suspended from the college. He believes Jacq is a bad character and openly declares war on her. Jacq was just fortunate to withstand his bombardments."

"Ali, you don't mean these stories."

"Yes, I do. They are not stories; they're facts.

"Jacq, on the other hand, had unearthed Ben and his son's active memberships of illegal cults in Ila where both of them had sworn allegiance to its king. This was where my son was involved before, but he has repented. Now, Jacq wanted to get revenge by exposing Ben and his son. I pleaded with her to forgive so that she too would be forgiven by the Lord. But Jacq insisted the only way she would forgive Ben was if he stopped his wickedness and submit himself for exorcism. She wanted his son, and possibly, my Kazuggi, to submit themselves too."

"Ben, stop, stop, stop. It's getting complicated now. What does Jacq know about exorcism? What does she know?"

"She learnt about it from the college. She reckoned Ben, with his son, was so devilishly wicked that he needed to be cleansed with a powerful ritual like exorcism. And one more thing, Rev Scot: Because of this quarrel Victor and Kazuggi have not been to the church or sang with the choir for two consecutive services. Last week and today, they stayed away. Or did you see either of them?"

"Well, well, well, this must be serious then. I least expected something so grave. We need God's intervention to avert the parish experiencing its first upheaval in over a decade.

"But come to think of it, and leaving the young men out of this now, there's no way Ben could be a cultist. He identifies actively with the church. He has never failed the church. Unless you, his friend, know more than this about him."

"To an extent, I agree with you," Ali said, reserving his new thought on Ben. "But let me show you what I have with me here." He opened his drawer and brought out a brown quarto envelope. Slowly he shook out its content on his table. "This is the insignia of the *Order of The Eagle*, the cult Victor and Kazuggi joined. This one was Kazuggi's. He repented and gave it to me to burn. Victor still holds his dearest to himself.

"For Ben," he went on, "Jacq saw his inside his studio office. It was the *Order of The Cobra*, with his name, Mackinnon I, printed on its box. She saw it!"

"Ok, ok; now I see," Rev Scot sighed. "I believe God is now showing us where to start. Mackinnon I, did she say?"

"Yes, that it was expensively engraved on it."

"That's not Ben. That's his grandfather, Thorburn Mackinnon. He used to sign that arrogant name. He did not want any part of Scotland to mix him up with other Mackinnons, that he was Mackinnon number one – *esclusivo, numero uno, primus inter pares*!" He derided Thorburn's vanity.

"He was reputed to be well travelled. The cathedral's Mackinnon Charity was actually started by him; even though he gave very little to it and much to the already rich and powerful who he deemed could protect his business.

"No one knew he was involved in the devil like this. Who would ever imagine someone as new as Jacq would be the one to discover that unholy aspect of his life? Can he still be feeling satisfied he had successfully carried and hidden it with him inside the Nacropolis?"

"That is our marvellous Lord in action," responded Ali, thoroughly amused. "Did He not make Laban to overtake Jacob and reveal Jacob's secrets to Laban? You can't keep anything away forever from His people; and certainly, never from Him.

"You could well be right about Ben and his grandfather. But so am I sure about Victor. Ben himself, and Kazuggi, had since confirmed the story after Jacq exposed it."

"So what do we do next?" asked James Scot.

"That's why I called you."

"Rev Jaiye, this issue before us is a delicate one. We have to be swift in dousing this Satan's inferno that is already creeping into the church.

"Whichever way it's considered, I think your Jacq is a clever lady – clever at discovering things, and to know about exorcism. Probably she also knows about jinn, the great Yajna, and the great 10 Kabbalistic Sephiroth.

"I also believe it's the devil trying to take control of God's flock; and that a powerful prayer is necessary to destroy him.

"But such prayer cannot exclude Jacq herself. All of them need the deliverance."

"All the four – why?"

"Absolutely; all the four of them. Quite absolutely." Rev Scot was emphatic, unapologetic. "You see, this Evil Spirit, he infects different souls with different severity, gaining full control in some and just a foothold in others. Of an initiated but living victim like Victor, he could have already gained full control. On a sympathiser like Ben, or a repenter like your son, the devil could maintain a strong foothold. We mustn't take chances. You don't gamble with the devil."

"But why should Jacq still be included? She discovered all these, didn't she?"

"Yes, she did. That is what the devil does best – deceives any soul he wants you to leave alone so he can return later at his pleasure to devour that soul.

"We should remember how in 2 Corinthian 11:14, the devil transformed himself into an angel of light!

"Yes, she did; but that she grew up in the masked devils' den of Ila warns us not to take chances. That she was unable to forgive outright is another warning. The four of them have to be delivered back to Jesus Christ."

Ali wasn't totally convinced, but he chose to save time by going along with Rev Scot. He knew his son, Kazuggi, had not only helped Jacq to conquer the masks in Venice, he had also repented openly and had submitted for burning, the evil insignia he did not actually swear to in Ila. And for Jacq, Ali knew she had fought evils and devils all her life – from Ila to Glasgow. She had exposed the unexposable and taken on the untouchables so much so that she should need no further delivery of any kind. One important source of contentment however: Rev Scot did not use his being the father of Kazuggi to include him, Ali, with the four to be exorcised. "Who will deliver them?" he asked instead. "I believe this to be the next important question."

"In the name of Jesus I will," Rev Scot readily volunteered. "And you can assist me, for the experience," he added. He had done exorcism before, and knew Ali hadn't been trained for it. "Jesus Christ who cast out the devil that held the worshipper inside the synagogue of Capernaum will lead us.

"But we shall have to obtain the permission of the Diocesan Bishop. His agents will have to assess the physical and psychiatric state of each of them. Then the bishop will tell us the extent of the devil's involvement with each of them, and how the delivery shall proceed."

Ali still had another question for Rev Scot. "Who will invite the four people?" he asked him.

"Ben can invite his son; and you, yours and Jacq."

"Fine. There wouldn't be much problem with that. But with Ben, how do you inform him he has a devil in him, and that he needs to be exorcised? Who will tell him that? Who?"

Instead of Rev Scot, two hard knocks on the door answered Ali's questions. The person knocking, a female church member, waited for no authority. She barged in, creating fright in the two clerics. "Ben Mackinnon! Please!" she shouted.

"Oh Lord Jesus," Rev Scot exclaimed with a worrisome look. His mind told him the intruder must have been listening, and must have collected vital information from what was meant to be shared only between the two men. He wondered if she had entered to carry Ben's invitation. "Did you answer Ben Mackinnon?" he asked the lady, most anxious to know if she overheard the discussion, the question!

"Yes. He is outside."

"Tell him to come in," Ali told her, taking it as an opportunity for a joint invitation from himself and Rev Scot.

"He can't. There's a big *collieshangie* out there now; and he's right in the middle of the fight. Come out and speak with him." Her stressful command prompted them out to the churchyard.

There, two clusters of people stood twenty yards apart. The first was smaller, and it stood entirely inside the churchyard. The second was about three times as large as the first, having been swollen by inquisitive passers-by in its position on the street pavement next to the lawn end of the churchyard. The two clerics tarried at the first cluster.

"You must put your witch on a tight rein, Rev Jaiye," a voice, Ben's, meant for Ali bleated at the two men. He was highly distressed and sweating. The creases on the arms of his jacket indicated he was earlier tightly restrained by the arms, by some of the church attendees who surrounded him.

"That Jacq, your jungle witch won't get away with this, this time," Ben foamed on. "She's yet to understand what it costs to defame or to assault. The courts will descend on her, and the warders will finish her off. Those I will ensure." He had turned the generous grass under his feet into a mortar he was angrily pounding with his feet.

"Why don't you calm down, Mr Mackinnon," Rev Scot urged him. He was grateful Ali maintained his cool in the face of Ben's insults. "You need to see what state you have put yourself in the church premises, Ben."

One man in the group managed to tell the clerics that the problem centred on Ben Mackinnon and Jacq trading insults after the church service.

"And where is Jacq now?" Ali asked the explainer.

"Over there," he replied, pointing to the larger group occupying the part of the church lawn that merged into the street pavement.

"Can someone please call her here for me?" Ali asked.

"Not that way," objected Rev Scot. "We must go back with them to my office so as to prevent the devil re-resurrecting.

"Go for her yourself please. Then meet me and Ben with her in my office."

"This witch, she called me a cultist," Ben resumed angrily as Ali with Jacq followed behind Ben and Scot towards Scot's office. "She called me a devil, and a liar. And I am dragging her before the magistrates."

"You called me a witch repeatedly," Jacq shouted her response at him. "And you too will have to prove that before the magistrates. You have tried that before, haven't you? And you failed, didn't you?"

"Enough of that," Ali ordered, furious. "I have told you, warned you before, that I must hear nothing like that from any of you."

There was a short silence.

"Now, I want you to go straight home, please," Ali ordered Jacq again, before Jacq would enter Scot's with them. "We want to talk with Mr Mackinnon. I shall talk with you when I return."

Jacq obeyed, leaving Ben to lay out his grievances without further brawling arguments.

"All those names, she called me. She said the church doesn't need me or my donations – that my donations are too filthy for the church. She said all the insults publicly. I won't have problems finding witnesses for the hearings!"

"Please calm down, Ben," appealed Ali. "You are an elder in this church. I have talked this with you many times; but like Jacq, you didn't listen to me. I must make a nice cup of tea for you to prove I wasn't offended by your insults on me."

"Rev Jaiye is right that you should calm yourself," Rev Sot seconded. "You should forget about court – or witnesses. Jacq would probably have her ideas and witnesses too. So, how would your armies of witnesses fit into a tiny courtroom?

336

"I want you to picture the whole problem," Rev Scot continued, "and determine if for Jacq it has been all points or all pointless, some courage or all stupidity, some truth or all false. Start with Genesis, and Revelation will come with the solution!"

"Jacq will not drive me to further argument," Ben said, still adamant. "No one here will as well."

"Jacq is not here, and no one is driving you," Rev Scot disagreed. "We are only two clerics and one elder here before God, within His premises. Therefore we must seek the truth only.

"You have your points, but sometimes a point could be so difficult to prove that the exercise would be worthless. Any court case would negatively impact on you. It could also, on your son, us and on the church.

"And by the way, did you analyse the crowds that gathered round you out there?"

"What about them?" Ben, still angry, asked Rev Scot.

"Most likely they started as one, before splitting into two. You had the small one, and she the much larger. In means that in any public brawl between the eminent and the commoner, it is easier for the commoner to attract more sympathy over the eminent. Please think about that. Your tea must have gone cold. Do you want Ali to make you another?"

Ben reached for his tea without uttering a word. From then on, he was quiet, seeking composure. He heard incredibly how it was the quarrel that both Jaiye and Scot were discussing inside the church office of the former when he and Jacq were actually fighting over it outside on the church lawn. He listened to how the two clerics claimed they identified the strong arms of the devil in the matter, how a strong prayer would be required to expel the devil, how he and others affected must surrender themselves to the prayers, and how the approval of the diocesan bishop would be obtained for the prayer.

Ben Mackinnon raised not a single objection.

The Masquerade

* * *

It was 6 o'clock on Friday, the morning of the last day of Rev James Scot's three days fast. He was inside St Saviour, the smallest of the cathedral's three chapels, confident he had enough time on his hands before others he expected would arrive. He expected two separate parties. One was of Ali, Uggi and Jacq, to arrive in an hour's time; and the other, of Ben and Victor in two hours. If the parties could arrive on time, the task he had before him would be over in time. His mind told him the event wouldn't be a long, complicated prayer, nothing beyond a basic deliverance.

He solemnly knelt himself besides the lone desk in the chapel. He was starting the final preparation; or, just throwing a first punch at the Evil Spirit – with a special prayer for Ali Jaiye whom he had chosen to assist him. Ali would need the prayer, he convinced himself, allowing his conviction to override Ali's ecclesiological status. He had no doubt that Ali was deeply dedicated to, and advancing in priesthood. But one thing no one could obliterate about Ali was his ancestral tie with Ila, the citadel of masks – ugly masks carried in satanic masquerading. Even though Ali, like himself, had been preparing and fasting for the past three days, an extra prayer for Ali now would doubly guarantee that the evils from the ancestry would have no power over Ali in the course of the prayer for delivery.

"Oh Lord Jesus," Rev Scot went on, "please, for me and in this day, support Ali as he supports me. Help him as he helps me. Strengthen him as he strengths me. Raise him above the current behaviour in Ila and let Ila have no influence on him as we pray today…"

The prayer was over, followed by a cheerful hymnal song, as he walked towards the grey metallic cupboard that secured the sacraments. As he was unlocking it, he continued with the hymn:

Lala, lala, laala! (Holy, holy, holy!)
Laala lala laala…! ((Lord God Almighty…!)

338

The voice of Ali complimentarily joined his singing from behind as he opened the cupboard. Ali had just left Jacq inside his own office, and arrived to join Rev Scot for the preparation, as planned.

"May the Lord bless you, my good Reverend," a pleased Rev Scot promptly interrupted Ali's humming to welcome him. "You brought them with you?

"Uggi and Jacq, yes?"

"No."

"No?" Rev Scot was surprised. He had already prayed his heart out for this day, that God totally disabled Satan of his powers of intervention and prevalence.

"Well, I have brought only Jacq down with me. Uggi opted to come with Victor – with Ben. Jacq's in my office."

"Thank the Lord for that," Rev Scot sighed. "This day shall never be one for Lucifer."

They both said 'amen' simultaneously.

"Put your Bible down and join me," Rev Scot instructed. Like a good student privileged to participate in a scientific experiment, Ali obeyed.

Rev Scot lifted out two folded, fringe-ended stoles and gently shook them out. One was wholly purple; the other, purple on one side and white on the other. As he shook them out he personified them in the name of the Lord, beseeching them to bind to suffocation, any Evil Spirit that would dare to venture into that chapel, or venture into anyone ever setting his foot into the chapel that day. Then he shared them between his neck and Ali's. As each man wore his, he felt in him the powers of the Cross and Shield of St Benedict that were embossed on at both ends. He felt the powers outshining the lustre of the silk the entire stole was woven of.

The next Rev Scot took out were two identical medals. Though only the size of a florin, but going by the reverend delicacy with which he personally pinned them on both stoles, one might thing that they were priceless gems from Mars. "This is for St

Dominic," he told Ali as he decorated him. "He was the Saint who expelled 1500 demons out of one heretic! We are coming to bless both together – together with the next I would take now." That next one was the Scapular of St Michael; and Rev Scot monopolised it, slipping it over his head through its two white and back strings.

Lastly Rev Scot carefully opened a communion set and passed on to the table some of its contents: two coloured glass cruets, one silver pyx, two silver candlesticks, one silver spoon and two silver Crosses. At the table, while Ali lit the candles, Rev Scot filled one of the cruets with holy vinegar and the other with holy water mixed with salt.

The blessing of the sacramental that followed was partly generic and partly specific. It started with the generic, with *Per Deus omnipotens...* to which Ali was made to read out simultaneously *Almighty God...* in its English translation. It moved to the blessing of all the medals with *Exorcizo vos, numismata...,* Ali also reading *I exorcise you medal...* from the prayer card. *Sancte Micheal Archangele, defende nos in proelio...* was the last. Now Rev Scot was confident he and his assistant inside the sacred walls of the chapel were fortified with all the powers and prayers required to reconcile the four people he was expecting as the congregation. Quite timely, Ben Mackinnon, his son Victor and Uggi had arrived, their party being led in by no other person but Victor!

At first, the group headed towards the west end of the front pew, the end nearest to where the table of the sacraments was set. By the time they reached that end, Victor suggested a detour to the eastern end of the same pew.

"Could you come over now?" Ali summoned Jacq over the phone. "We are all waiting for you."

Any of them in the chapel who cared – and all of them did – to watch Jacq enter could see the sternness and unfriendliness that glossed her face. She stared at the men on the pew, avoided them, and continued to the centre of the third pew behind the men.

"I welcome you all to this chapel of our Lord," Rev Scott started to sermonise.

"And Jacq," he next called, "can you come forward and sit closer so that we can make a greater congregation?"

Jacq complied, rising slowly, with great doubts as to the correctness of Rev Scot's assertion. If the might of Jesus has no problem covering those large Sunday congregations – nave, stall and crossing – inside the cathedral, why would it in a small chapel of only six people? She continued to the pew next to her, the one between hers and the men's. Still aloof, but less so, and to the partial satisfaction of what Rev Scot took as constituting greatness in a congregation, Jacq settled alone on its west end. Ben, aiming at lessening the tension moved near her and sat, giving her no further room to move elsewhere.

"Good God, deliver me from this evil man," she murmured as she sat upright and allowed her hands to feel the small crucifixion chain she wore round her neck.

* * *

Bishop Scot directed Ali to share out the hymn books among his special invitees. When this was fully accomplished, he was ready for the prayer.

"Hymn number 300," Rev Scot called out. "Holy – Holy – Holy, Lord – God – Almighty", he added more than its title. It was a hymn with which he loved to celebrate God's strength, as well as assure victims of adversaries of the temporariness of their misfortune. It was one which kept the memory of the song writer, Reginald Heber, in him – and which he believed should do the same in every true faithful:

> *Holy, holy, holy! Lord God Almighty!*
> *Early in the morning our song shall rise to Thee;*
> *Holy, holy, holy, merciful and mighty!*
> *God in three Persons, blessed Trinity...!*

"I am going to talk briefly about 'Love – with forgiveness and faith'", Rev Scot told his guests.

"Love," he went on, "is very prominent in the Commandments.

"It's beyond 'I love you', beyond 'I love you to pieces'.

"It's what 1 Corinthians 16:14 tell you to conduct all your affairs with others with. In Leviticus 19:18 God calls it forgiving and making your fellow as yourself. John 4:8 testifies that love is God; and therefore the greatest of faith and hope. It's the greatest thing you must all start to show to each other now.

"Stop jealousy; it is not love. Stop swindling; it is not love. Stop glooming; it is not love. Stop being aloof; it is not love. Stop bragging; it is not love. Stop false preaching; it is not love. Stop mistrusting; it is not love. Stop being forgetful; it is not love.

"Stop being un-Godly; it is not love. Stop being un-loving; it is not Godly!"

He paused to observe the face of each member of his congregation. He saw nothing unusual.

"Therefore, as we congregate together we are going to pray together. We shall beseech the Lord to restore that spirit of love and forgiveness in us – with that of faith in Him. I believe each of you here has your faith in His powers and in those of His son, Lord Jesus Christ. You believe, don't you, individually?"

Everyone in the chapel answered in the affirmative.

"Good. Then let us pray." He was quite pleased with their unflinching faith in God and Christ. The voluntary, abiding expression he saw on their faces was one that could expel – and had expelled – any form of evil in any of them. Now he could thank God and Jesus for their faith.

"God of earth and all that abide on it, in Your holy name!"

"Hear us, our Father," Ali chorused.

"God of the planets, known and obscure, in Your holy name!"

"Hear us, our Father."

"God of heaven and the day of judgement, in Your holy name!"

"Have mercy on us, Jesus."

"God – Holy, Gracious, Majesty – in Your holy name!"

"Let our supplication come to Thee, our Father!"

"That Your children, Jacq, Ben, Victor and Uggi are able to renew their faith in you today, we thank You. We thank You that the faith has restored love and forgiveness in them. We beg You to let these values be everlasting in them. Let no powers shatter the faith in them. Forever, let the faith guide them in their dealings with themselves, with Your church, and in their everyday life. Let this be, in the name of our Redeemer – Your son, Jesus Christ. Amen."

"Amen," all responded.

"The Lord's Prayer."

"Our Father who art in heaven...," they all intoned the ancient chant, "...Amen".

Rev Scot felt thoroughly satisfied that the prayer was successful: no satanic python had reared its head while it lasted. He acknowledged the wisdom of the devil to leave his people alone instead of pulling punches with Jesus. It was time – just – to end the prayer, and for everyone to return home.

"Now, 'The Grace', all of you," he issued the last order. "All of you will please come out here and link your arms as we recite it."

Bravely, Ben held Jacq by her hand and led her out to the space between Rev Scot and the first pew, to where Victor also led Uggi. There they formed a small anti-clockwise circle of Ben, Jacq, Victor and Uggi, with Victor's back nearest to Rev Scot. As the formation progressed, Ali shook his burning incense vigorously, rapidly jetting and coiling its fragrance round the small congregation.

"'*The Grace*', all of you," Rev Scot announced again to his special quartet, now tightly inter-linked and ready. "May the Grace of our Lord…" he led the citation. He was not to finish it. Neither he nor anyone in inside St Saviour would! Victor wouldn't let anyone!

"Leave me alone!" Victor screamed and broke loose from Jacq's hold, and then from Uggi's. He turned to Jacq and gazed with hatred at the small crucifix she had round her neck and which had made an unbearable impact on him. "Leave me alone!" he yelled again and ripped the chain off Jacq's neck. Rev Scot surged forward instantaneously to intervene but was violently pushed down by Victor. "Leave me alone; you don't touch me!" he would not stop yelling the phrase. He returned to where he sat before the link, hot, sweaty and obsessed with the instructional protest.

"We won't leave you alone!" Ali bravely shouted to Victor. "Jesus Christ has touched you," he added as Jacq and Uggi ran to assist Rev Scot back to his bottom, dragging him backwards to safety while Ben watched in shock.

"Jesus Christ orders you to say who you are," Ali went on. "You can't hide yourself – not anymore." He moved towards Victor, his stole ends blowing, his emblems shinning, and the incense he carried burning even more.

"I ask you with the power of Jesus, who are you? And where are you from?"

"Stop there; and come no further," Victor bleated. "You must be ashamed of not knowing where I came from. I have not disturbed you. You must leave me alone!"

"Don't leave him," Rev Scot, slowly rising onto his feet instructed Ali. "Vinegar and holy water – the cruets!"

Jacq raced to the table of the sacraments. She rushed a sign of crucifixion on her forehead and chest, threw a crucifix over her head onto her neck to replace the one Victor tore from her, and raced back to the clerics with the cruets.

"Stand here firmly with your faith in Lord Jesus," Rev Scot told Jacq on her reaching where he was. "You are safe in the name of Lord Jesus," he added as he took only the vessel of the holy water from her. With the water in one hand and his big crucifix in the other, he joined Ali and took over the battle against the Evil Spirit.

"Now that we know who you are, in the name of Jesus Christ Our Lord, bestowed to the world by God through holy Virgin Mary, I command you to leave Victor now! Leave Victor! Leave us! Leave this holy chapel! Get out now and destroy yourself!"

"Who are you to command me? You are not King Japeedoe!"

"I am the faithful follower of Lord Jesus Christ. And in His holy name, and those of blessed St Michael and all the Apostles and Saints, I command you serpent to leave Victor now and destroy yourself. Leave, and drink your own poison!"

"Lord Jesus, have mercy; Lord Jesus, have mercy," Ali complemented Rev Scot's commands.

"Leave me alone," Victor resumed again. "Leave me. I disturb no one." Now his voice was softer.

"No. You must leave. You are defeated by the all-conquering, heavenly Armies of blessed St Michael. You must know that. Your time is up, Lucifer!"

Rev Scot took a single step forward, towards Victor, cruet of holy water in his hand. He opened the vessel; and with the generosity that the narrowness of the vessel's neck could permit, splashed the holy water over Victor. Like a fire incendiary, the splash exploded the devil inside his agent.

"I told you to stop!" Victor yelled with anger – and in the great agony Rev Scot meant to inflict. He charged at the bottle, now smartly passed to Ali, then back to Scot in a wild, baton-changing, relay manner. His Satanic frustration grew as he chased the bottle of holy water. It peaked when he grabbed Rev Scot and threw him against Ali with a force that again sent both men to the ground. Then he faced Jacq.

Jacq was now alone, ready to be devoured by the devil that had just floored two male clerics. She felt the force of her faith and courage standing with her. She wasn't bare after all! Victor's past

345

reaction to her crucifix and Rev Scot's holy liquid came to her mind. She still had them with her! Victor was staring at them on her more than at her! The forces of the relics were restraining the beast!

Her left hand found the crucifix on her neck. She raised it like a show-off to Victor while at the same time held her bottle of vinegar forward in her right hand. "Get out of Victor in the name of Jesus," she said, inching forward. "I am not scared by you! Get out of here!"

"Drop the silly thing round your neck and that in the bottle!" Victor counter-commanded. "Drop them or I destroy you!

"Okay, the bottle; or I destroy you now! Give it to me!" He inched forward, both hands stretched out, ready to receive Jacq and the bottle. "Give it to me!" He was ready to pounce.

"Never – *èèwọ òrìshà*," Jacq called his bluff and continued:
Never; in the name of Jesus Christ.
Never; èèwọ òrìshà;
Never; in the name of the Most High.
Never; èèwọ òrìshà!

Suddenly Jacq's prayer beat Victor to a standstill, followed by a slow, backward retreat – just as Rev Scot was back on his feet, and in time to see Victor exhibiting his fear of the oil, the Cross and the chant.

"Thank you Jacq; hand the cruet over," requested Rev Scot, relieving her.

"Now Satan, get out, I command you!" Rev Scot shouted with a warning throw of vinegar at Victor. Successfully, Victor ducked and evaded it. He was however unable to duck Rev Scot's second throw that hit him before he could regain his balance from the first dive. Victor advanced his backward retreat into a slow run, pursued by Rev Scot – up to a corner of the chapel which both men could not go beyond.

"In the name of Jesus the Lord, I command you Satan to leave!" he ordered again, now emptying the holy content of his bottle on Victor.

"Oh Jesus Christ!" bellowed Victor loudly and agonizingly. For a moment he stood still, thinking of launching a counter attack. Then he wobbled and dropped full length on the floor of St Saviour! As he rolled on his side his mouth split some thick green liquid. He passed out, still vomiting.

"Don't touch him!" Rev Scot forbade Ali and Jacq. "Now is the time for prayers, time to deliver him to Jesus the Lord."

"I suggest we chain him down now," Ali said, "before he can spring up again and interrupt the prayer."

"No sir, we can't do that," Jacq sharply objected before Rev Scot could speak. She was astonished at her mentor's suggestion. She wondered whether Ali was thinking Ila, showing his ignorance of the pains of being physically manacled. "He is already helpless, down and out. Chains won't help him – or us."

"Jacq is correct," Rev Scot agreed. "Victor needs no further chaining beyond what Satan had done to him. Besides, both of you must remember we are doing this as a cure, and not as a punishment. We must pursue the door of the unchaining which prayers have opened to him."

With Victor lying unconscious on the floor, Rev Scot had all the time to invoke the most appropriate prayers, using the sacraments that were most effective, and the help of his two assistants who were most faithful to Jesus Christ.

The round of prayers continued for about half an hour when Victor, now semi-conscious, muttered to his deliverers that he had his insignia with him there in his pocket; and that he had actually taken control of the soul of his granddad's insignia that was in the Commercial House studio. Within another half hour both insignias were set on fire outside St Saviour, the burning rekindling some strength in Victor. He shared the strength between rolling over severally and repeating the name of Jesus Christ.

The burning also set off a strong whirlwind inside St Saviour. After about two minutes, before every eye then inside St

Saviour, the storm spiralled itself forcefully out through the window of the chapel.

"Now, let's join hands and move him," Rev Scot requested of his assistants. "It's safe to do that now."

As they moved Victor about a yard away, Jacq wiped as much of the vomit as she could from him. Then, they covered him with a piece of white linen, with Ali's Medal of St Dominic put over him to prevent the Evil Spirit ever returning to him.

Rev Scot invited nearer to them other members of his congregation who were still in fright. "It's all well with him now," he announced. "This time we shall truly link over him and say The Grace."

Ben Mackinnon broke down in tears – of joy and gratitude – looking at his son sleeping in peace. "Thank you very much," he repeated to Ali and Scot as he sobbed and embraced each of them. He was timid towards Jacq, but never Jacq to him. She moved forward and cuddled him with all her heart, causing him to sob even more. "Promise you will visit my studio again. Please tomorrow; promise?" he begged of her.

"Certainly," she nodded.

* * *

Again, Jacq was unsure of what to expect from Ben Mackinnon. Ben had met her at his reception and was leading her into his studio office. The last time, most acrimonious, also almost ended in a police affair; and she expected the day's visit to contrast favourably. This time, she had nothing ulterior planned in her mind. And Ben too, she could see was all smiles, smiles that were more enthusiastic than treacherous!

"Other than 'thank you very much'," Ben opened his mind after seating his guest, "Jacq, I don't know what else to say, what else I should tell you – where to start. You believe me, don't you, Jacq?"

348

"Thank you too, Ben," Jacq replied with a cautious smile, balancing herself on her seat. "I believe you, Ben. I have no reason not to – not anymore."

Ben was pleased for his turn to savour the good from Jacq. He prepared tea for both of them, and resumed his chat. "It was a good opportunity I had in the church," he went on. "I was able to see your true heart – clean heart. I was able to see your brilliance shining to everyone, beyond what anyone could ever imagine! Jacq, can you picture me missing such an opportunity?" For a moment the smile on his face disappeared, overrun by earnestness.

"Thank you Ben. But…"

"There is no 'but', Jacq. Missing it would have meant missing this one with you now. It would have meant me missing the opportunity to atone for my sins to you. And, that would have killed me. Jacq, I am truly ashamed and sorry for how I have behaved to you."

"Ben, let's put that behind us and move forward. You are forgiven, Ben. Forgiven!"

"No Jacq, it doesn't come just like that. Certainly, you know about this thing, atonement, more than anyone else. I need to make the confession before you first, don't I? Is confession not in the sequence, Jacq?"

"Sequence?"

"Yes, Jacq. And, don't make me feel too big to follow it. You need to hear my confession, why I did certain things, before you can know how to accept my apology. It won't take long. And where you suspect I am being evasive or unclear, stop me and ask for an instant replay. I want to be totally relieved – like my son is now. I know I can't be unless I follow the full sequence."

Jacq watched the determination and pain on Ben Mackinnon's face. She reckoned they must have been so needling that they pushed his mouth to talk so fast. At that speed and flow she knew she had less than a half chance of explaining her own version of atonement to Ben. She could only try.

"I am not God – not Yahweh, Ben," she reminded him.

"I know you are not, Jacq," Ben agreed. "But I sinned against you. That I also know."

"Ben, I repeat that whatever you did to wrong me, you are forgiven. It requires no blood sacrifices nowadays."

"No, Jacq, I insist – please," Ben imposed. "I must make my confessions to you first, and make them with necessary sacrifices. If after that you still forgive me, then I will be happy, and be grateful to you."

Jacq dropped her resistance. She settled to listening to Ben Mackinnon:

His great-great-great-grandfather, Collin Mackinnon, was the first ever Glaswegian, and white man, to set his foot on Ila. He was an industrious general merchant sponsored by the King of Great Britain to explore the possibilities of trade ventures in that region of the world. Also sponsored with him was Rev Jamie Macdonald who became the first person to introduce Jesus Christ to Ila. Collin later became prominent in the slave trade which suddenly became the 'trade of the moment'. It created immense wealth among the chiefs of Ila, the farmers of the Americas, and the merchants of Scotland.

Kelan, Collin's grandson and the first art dealer in Glasgow, was also inspired through discovering the pricelessness of Ila arts and artefacts. This further encouraged him to explore the trade, up to Egypt where the Ilas claimed they came from. Carvings, statues, paintings – all subjectively represented on every street and corner of Scotland – were either born or developed through Kelan. Kelan was them; they were him.

Kelan's grandson was Davey, his own father, and the only one he, Ben, grew to know with what had remained of the family business. Before Victor's visit with Uggi, Davey was the last in the family to visit Ila.

As he, Ben, grew, he saw his father narrow down the art trade to 'collections' only, which was equally very lucrative. Ben was soon to discover that the huge profits were due to the unconventional nature of the 'exchanges'. His father was using underhand payments and gifts to sponsor local looters of artefacts in Ila and throughout the kingdom! Davey was encouraging stealing and maintaining clandestine contacts with looters!

At one time, he, Ben, withdrew his support from his father, and persuaded his mother to do the same. The withdrawal softened his father. He pleaded with him, and with his mother through him. He wished he and his mother had refused his father and stayed adamantly away from the business. Exactly one week after the reconciliation, his mother, driving home after collecting an artefact, was caught up in a heavy storm. The wind tore a big branch off a sessile oak and it crashed through the windscreen of her car, fatally crushing her skull. The memory of this catastrophe, regarded as a sort of 'repayment', eventually killed his father and stopped him, Ben, from ever visiting Ila when he had the chances to do so.

One positive thing he could remember about his father was that he maintained the charities set up by his father and grandfather, and affiliated to the Cathedral. One of them paid for Ali Jaiye's father to come from Ila to Glasgow for pastoral studies – tuition, feeding, and extras. It enabled himself and Ali to interact at certain similar levels, and hence the friendship between them. Another of the charities got actively involved with students' welfare programmes in Glasgow College; and yet another in arts prizes awards in the metropolis.

His, Ben Mackinnon's, sending Victor to Ila was, among other things, done to widen Victor's horizon in the business atmosphere that was already traditionally familiar with his family – and in the company of his friend, Uggi, who was already genetically rooted to that area of the world. Ben trusted the visit would give Victor the opportunity to make, develop and maintain contacts that would help the family business in the future. Never was Victor sent there to betray Britain, Scotland or Glasgow, or to spit on our Queen and bow to King Japeedoe. Never was he sent to turn against the

351

church and embrace the *Eagle*, to become an *Eagle* instead of being a young director in William Alexandra Smith's Boys Brigade!

"Now, see how the *Eagle* had affected him negatively, and equally infected me through him and through my father's *Cobra*.

"From the first mention of your name I hated you as much as King Japeedoe did – perhaps much more. I planned your exit from my house. I stopped Victor from returning to Venice with you. I bribed the police and my staff to nail you. I planned your expulsion from Glasgow College. I was just about turning against Ali for constantly rescuing you. I hated you so much that I blamed Victor for joining the fight to secure your freedom in Ila. You see what I did to you, how I masked badly against you?" Ben was shaking with shame, the wells of his eyes becoming filled with tears of remorse.

"You see now, all the atrocities I committed against you? I should have known that you are a fine *smeddum* and not a thug." He was wiping away the tears. "Now that you know, can you still accept my apologies and forgive me?"

"Yes, Ben, I can; and I have. So, stop crying."

"Thank you, Jacq – for your true love to me and my son. Thank you so much.

"But Jacq, I still have one more question. Which is: What do you want me to offer as a sacrifice to your big heart?"

"Oh Ben!" said Jacq unbelievably. "Talking of sacrifice again? We have long passed that."

"Okay then. What I mean is that what do you advise I do to improve in the areas where I have behaved badly? This is a serious question, Jacq."

"Well, Ben, if you mean about Victor as it affected you and me, Jesus had solved that by evicting the cause. If it is about the college as it affected you and me, Jesus had also solved that by returning us to the good books of the college. Both had taught you and me some lessons in righteousness.

"The same lessons," she continued, "should apply to the third area, your family business, which I knew nothing about because I am not a member of your family."

"How can you say that?" Ben disagreed sharply. "You are more than a member! You saved us more than any member had ever done!

"You know what Jacq? I think I haven't done what I should have done first. I should have shown you the business first. You already knew Victor and the college, and it helped your decisions. Now I will take you round the studios to see what the business looks like. After that I will again tender my request. How about that?"

"Well, Ben," Jacq responded, unsure of which way to answer Ben.

"Let us just get up and walk round. I even remember promising you that last time you were here."

Jacq realised she had no way of wriggling out of her host's invitation. She rose, to Ben's pleasure.

"It would make sense to start from here," Ben said, pointing to a large, framed mirror that doubled as a paternity family tree. "That is the history of Mackinnon Arts – the founders and the runners – up to this day."

Jacq took an enthusiastic look at the framed black scripts. Under the topmost, capitalised name of the organization were seven doubly spaced names of seven family members, and the period each member lived. She read the script:

MACKINNON MERCHANTS
Collin Mackinnon   1730 – 1800
Dugal Mackinnon   1765 – 1845
Kelan Mackinnon   1800 – 1880
MACKINNON ARTS
Thorburn Mackinnon   1850 – 1935
Davey Mackinnon   1895 – 1991
Benjamin Mackinnon   1951 –
Victor Mackinnon   1975 –

"Quite interesting," Jacq could only remark. She wasn't thinking of the agelessness of the organization or the artistry of the mount. Her interest was in the oddity she has found in the display. "Why has a woman never been shown in the organization?" she asked Ben. "Has there never been a female in your family line?"

Ben felt uncomfortable as he sought the answers to Jacq's questions. "Well, I believe the men thought of the rigours required to maintain the best in African arts and so, excused the women."

"Did you reason in the same way to choose Victor?"

It looked as if Ben's answer would never come. "One thing I have not told you," Ben started soberly, "is that I was divorced fifteen years ago. The terms allowed me to keep Victor, while my wife had Victor's sister. Her mother was able to poison her mind against me. Up to now my daughter has refused to see me."

"I am sorry to hear that. But Victor's sister is not the first female in your family tree, or is she? Did you not just say your mother died for the organization?"

"Well, Jacq, you've asked the right questions. But you know what? I have no moral courage to answer them." He held the door open for Jacq to go into the studio he numbered 1, a room she was now familiar with – she was trapped in it once, and she had passed into Ben's office through it twice. Disinterest generally showed all over her face as she struggled to shut her memory from the ugliness of her first encounter with that particular space. Following Ben reluctantly, she walked to the door on the immediate right of the one they just entered through. "Where does this door lead to?" she asked, pretending not to see 'Visual Room' above it.

"The Visual Room," Ben answered, opening the door and exposing the stark darkness of the room. Then he switched on its lights. There were eight chairs in two rows, with enough space for another eight. A library of films was piled on an antique stool by the side of its large screen.

Both of them returned into Studio 1 and continued into Studio 3.

For Jacq, Studio 3 passed for a 'General Assembly' of metallic arts and paintings, as well as for an expensive bazaar in price tagging.

On its floor were wide, yard high, chocolate coloured chests of drawers that went round. Arranged sitting atop them were assortments of artefacts. A clear height above the assortments were two rows of adjustable shelves, also loaded with more artefacts. Jacq, now excited, asked no questions – until they were both before the biggest statue in that room. Jacq stopped and studied it with curiosity. The horse rider: his heavy helmet strapped to his thick chin, his eyeballs pupil-less, his short-sleeve shirt tucked into his shorts, his firearm more like a walking stick than a pistol, his leggings extending from the shorts into the boots. The horse: its mouth ajar like that of a barking dog. The overall wooden colossus: a carving of indefinable disproportion of the body parts.

"What are you thinking, Jacq?" Ben interrupted her. Want to say something?"

"This, like, like… *Elémpe*," she stammered. "Could this be *Elémpe*?" She had only seen its pictures in Ila. She had heard stories of how the statue magically guarded the palace of Ila. She had heard many narratives of the story of its disappearance from Ila.

"You guessed right, Jacq. That's *Elémpe*, from Ila."

"Oh good Lord; and what a statue! It's the whole world you have gathered here, Ben. Not just Africa that I have always heard Glaswegians associate you with!"

"Well, it's their opinion. You will have yours by the time we have finished with the viewing.

"Actually your people carved two originally; and both ended inside this studio. Grandfather arranged for them to be stolen from your palace. He took as insulting, the sight of a depiction of a Scottish horseman doing a sentry inside the palace of Ila. The second is now in the city museum. And of course, finer replicas abound all over the city."

"He stole them? So that was the true story!" She moved closer and saw herself pitifully dwarfed beside it. "How come it was easy to steal an object as massive as this – and from the palace?" she asked Ben.

"Grandad arranged it all; and he said he found the arrangement easy. He realised that an Ila is 'umbilically corded' to bribery – that with the right price anyone in your kingdom would steal for you a woman from under the brood of a honeymoon. He relied on Ilas' excelled sense of stealing before feeling."

"That, really, is a shame, Ben."

"Indeed. Another, which would surprise you, is that the then king planned it with a small group of men around him. The king – head of the kingdom!"

"Lord Jesus! And how did they cope with the weight?"

"Well, they did – and delivered. Now all weight related problems have disappeared." He invited Jacq to push the statue herself while he stretched his hand under it and adjusted something, away from Jacq's sight.

Jacq proceeded to its back and pushed the statue away from the wall towards the centre of the studio. With ease it obeyed her command. She stopped and looked at Ben.

"Hollowed and wheeled," Ben met her surprise look with. "Leave it like that and return to the wall itself."

She obeyed, and could see that the statue was actually positioned in front of a hidden door.

"Turn that handle before you and open the door – to Studio 4."

"So it is a door you have hidden away with *Elémpe*!"

"Yes, granddad believed *Elémpe* would mount a better security sentry here than in Ila. And it has worked ever since!"

Apprehensive, she twisted the brass handle and pushed the door open. Instantly she was taken over by dazzles of artefacts and unsure which way to drift first.

To her left, constituting a third of the studio space was a congregation of African gods with their paraphernalia of authority. They were mostly frightening, angry about their powerlessness. With price tags hung on them, Jacq was witnessing the first ever market of enslaved gods! *Sàngó* and *Èsù* which she had seen at the Black Culture Week were among them. Anyone able to offer the sale prices on them could have them under his roof, and possibly order a fighting match between them! The scene rendered her short of words. She turned and approached her right – the bigger, raised, two-thirds space that was separated by a fenced gate which was also a part of that phenomenon.

Both the fence and the gate were of gold – or so they looked with the glitter they beamed. To Jacq the knee-height of the fence and the man-height of the gate rendered them more of pure anaesthetic than of a physical deterrence. As Ben commenced unlocking the gate, Jacq, in her thought, gave kudos to the honest instincts of modern Glaswegians. She knew that had it been in her kingdom, elite thieves would have scaled the valuable fence and made away with the masks that it segregated. The masks – the best of Ila Kingdom and other African masks and headdresses! According to Ben Mackinnon, they were the exact contemporaries of artefacts that inspired Pablo Picasso, Max Pechstein, Amedeo Modigliani and Athanasius Kircher.

The rare collections from different parts of Ila Kingdom included full face masks, full head covers and head-dresses in wood, terracotta, ivory, bronze, brass, fibres, leather and careful mixtures of any of them.

From the west of Ila were masks of golden Asante, Akan, Baule, Dogon, Senufo, Bambara and Yaka.

From the east they were of Kongo, Punu, Chokwe, Makonde, Ahmara, Luo, Lega, Oromo and Luba.

From the north were those from Egypt, Somalia, Berbers and Tuaregs.

357

From the south were those of the Zulu, Ndebele, Shona and Herero.

The collection emphasised why Ben Mackinnon was more Ila than an Ila person and more African than Africa. It showed why he stood to protect his family business by whatever means he could find.

"Why have you chosen to amass this huge number of special masks and headdresses?" Jacq asked Ben.

"Because relatively they are easy to steal; that's the honest truth," he answered after a pause. "They are easy to ferry, to store, to re-decorate, to replicate, to sell! African masks have both the quietest as well as the most disguised values!"

The end to the inspection in that section brought both of them to another door, opposite the side having the golden fence. The door was of African mahogany, smaller than standard, and crafted all over in relief with scores of African zoological life. Ben informed Jacq that the crafting job was by a renowned family of Ila carvers. Ben pulled it and led Jacq through – astonishingly for Jacq, into Ben's office where they both started from. A full, rectangular tour of Ben's institution had been completed.

On the way to her chair, Jacq paused again and gazed at the mirror of Ben's family tree. Its crafted names echoed back at her as those names of Glaswegians who were so wise that they explored the land of a people ignorant of their own earthly position. They were of Glaswegians who were smart enough to value a people too thick to recognise their own value. They were of Glaswegians who were so enterprising that they underpaid the thoughtless elites of Ila for the products they, the elites, looted to sell. More importantly, they were names of Glaswegians who were primarily and deeply patriotic that they left within the nation of Scotland the proceeds from their expeditions, lootings and business deals!

Ben made two more cups of tea and carried one over to his guest. Then standing by his desk, he directed his eyes to pierce Jacq's. "Now that you have seen all," he prompted Jacq, "you can make your pronouncement about my request, and I shall believe you."

"Ben," Jacq responded, "all I have to say now – or to add – is that you and your line on that family tree have done well. From your collection, your achievement has been great."

"It can't be great, Jacq. How can it ever be? Or are we talking of greatness in stealing – eminence in sinning?" He was getting agitated and frantic by Jacq's seeming untruth.

"Believe me, Ben, it is. You have cleared your line and yourself of the sinful part. It is only my Ila elites who are still awash with such sins. You have atoned and your sins are gone, Ben."

"Gone? To where? And who despatched them? Until that is done!" He marched to the mirror of the family tree, snatched it off the wall and smashed it on the floor. The glass shattered into pieces, flowing in all directions as Jacq watched Ben in awe.

"What my family did could never have been great. Every part of it has been sinful. So sinful that it was demonic. So demonic that Victor had to undergo exorcism, and I am still searching for a true atonement. Is that not the case?" Ben was hysterical.

"It is not, Ben. I have seen all you have here. You don't have to destroy anything!"

"Everything – everything in the studio – I believe I must destroy, for the sake of true peace and salvation."

Jacq calmed him down and objected to his intentions.

"Alright then," Ben agreed partially, "can I have the artefacts returned to where they came from; or sell them and return the money realised from the sale?"

"No. The monetary values that you and Ila placed on them caused them to be stolen in the first place.

"Then if you would repatriate, how do you move those of them already being enjoyed in public places in Glasgow? Who do you hand them over to – the same thieves?

"The same questions will again arise if you sell. To who do you hand over the proceeds – the same elite thieves who will kill any of their kinsmen for daring to ask how the money would be spent?

"Consider a physical or monetary repatriation only when the Ilas have successfully risen against their treasure-looters. Repatriate when they have restored the true worth of masks, masquerades and masquerading. Do you understand me, Ben?"

Ben, in momentary quietness, considered Jacq's counselling. "How soon do you envisage such a time to come – if ever it would?" he asked pessimistically.

"The sooner you can join me."

"But I have joined you, soul and body. Can't you see that? Ask me to prove it anyway you want. Ask me now."

"Can you follow me back to Ila?" she challenged Ben.

"Yes, Jacq, I will come, if that's what you want. I've always wanted to – to regain a part of the opportunity I once lost. And if you are thinking of bringing more people, I will help."

"More people?"

"Probably you want Rev Scot and Ali to come. Probably you are thinking of getting King Japeedoe and his group exorcised during the visit. If that's so, my family charity and the church will be made to help towards the cost."

"That would have been nice because there's no hell Jesus cannot redeem. But my thought is not in that direction, Ben. It is towards getting my daughter and husband released by Japeedoe – if he has not killed them. Your presence can help."

"Your faith in Jesus will even help more. We shall continue to pray they are unharmed. I am ready. Or you want Victor to come along as well?"

Victor? The man Japeedoe still believed to belong to his cult? "That will be excellent," Jacq readily agreed. "Victor and Uggi actually promised Japeedoe to return!"

"What are we waiting for then? Halleluyah!"

"Halleluyah, Ben."

CHAPTER ELEVEN

World of Masquerades

Jacq saw the events of two months ago in replay – perfectly: In the middle of Mr Bob Watson's bible lectures with her group, Yeoman's face making a purposeful intrusion, his mouth seizing an excuse from the teacher, his steps heading towards her on her seat, the same mouth again delivering to her an invitation to nowhere but the office of the College Principal!

The class over, she was on her way to see the Principal, her heart throbbing with intrigue: Did the college or any of its satellites still have an axe to grind with her? Had someone in Glasgow not forgiven her, when she had herself forgiven everyone that had wronged her? Was she living in a fool's paradise? A summons to the Principal's office, again? Again!

Both the Principal and Yeoman were already on their seats when she arrived – the same seats as previously. The conspicuous empty one beside Yeoman but facing the Principal, Jacq knew was for her; it was, like last time. She wanted to break the omen, by remaining on her feet instead of taking seat. The resistance the lasted only to the moment of the Principal's insistence.

"Now Jacq, what do you say to them?" the Principal asked her.

"To what, sir?" she responded, frightened and unsure. "I am sorry I don't understand."

"Yeoman," the Principal called, "haven't you shown them to her? Has she not seen them?" Jacq diagnosed the dissatisfaction in the Principal's questions.

"I am sorry; she hasn't seen them," Yeoman apologised. Bob asked to see them briefly and pass them on to her, to return them to you when she has finished with them." As the explanation lengthened it thickened the Principal's displeasure, turning it into anger.

"I asked you to see them and pass them to Jacq. You took them and asked Bob to see them and pass them to Jacq. Strange, it is, Yeoman. It looks like asking, agreeing and inaction that will never end. A bit of disappointment. When will the relay end?"

Regret showed all over Yeoman. He rose to redress the situation, sliding out to retrieve whatever they were, that were kept away from Jacq.

"Sorry about that, Jacq," the Principal saw Yeoman off with. "Let's hope Bob has not given them to someone else to see before passing them to you." With that hope, he diverted to the file before him on his desk, pulling it nearer and opening it in rapid noisy ruffles. He must be looking for something inside it – something he couldn't find, something that could be invisibly attached to the outer back of the file! "Secretary!" he called out, replacing his bell with his voice. "Secretary!

"Secretary, can you tell me what's going on here today?" He directed the fury at his officer now before him. "I called for the file of Jacquensica Nek; not for Jackie North's. What's wrong with all of you today? Can I have Jacquensica's please?"

The secretary apologised, took the wrong and returned with the right file – just in time to beat Yeoman's return to the Principal's.

362

"To Jacquensica, please," the Principal directed Yeoman with what he was clutching, before Yeoman could take his seat. Two newspapers, from Italy.

Jacq rushed through the first from the front to the back, and just looked intensely at the second. She could identify two things: the college library stamp each carried front and back to deter any in-college newspaper thief, and her group's pictures at the Venice Carnival.

"Have you seen them before?" the Principal anxiously asked Jacq.

"No, sir. But I know they exist. The secretary to the *Comitato* told me about them."

"And what's your opinion – about them?"

"No opinion, sir," Jacq replied after a short pondering. "I shouldn't give one for myself, sir."

"Really?" the Principal asked with amazement. "But don't be surprised that we have our opinions already. Of you and the presentation, mine are very good while Yeoman's are excellent; not to talk of Ben Mackinnon who was so proud of you that he obtained the newspapers for the college, from his trading colleagues in Venice. We all congratulate you.

"You are thinking that it's just for only you, but no. It's also very much about Ila you came from, and about Glasgow College you proudly indicated to the Venetians as your college. We all congratulate you and wish you a successful completion of your course."

Humbly, Jacq thanked him.

"And now, Jacq," the Principal went on, "here is my next question to you: Are you staying or returning to Ila at the end of your course?"

"Neither, sir," she responded.

"Why?"

"The church, my sponsor, will decide where I go; but certainly, not Ila."

"I can understand the church's basic involvement, but not the non-returning to Ila?"

"I am banished from the kingdom by the king," she volunteered. She realised she was in a situation where she did not know what Ben had said about her. "I'd love to return to Ila, but I am banished."

"I am sorry," the Principal said, repeating the same at the end of Jacq's summary of the reasons for the banishment.

"But not to worry," he continued. "You don't appear like someone whose talents can be killed. It is their loss. A kingdom that kills and expels talents can never rise from the termite-invested grave it is burying itself in.

"The church will surely be happy to keep you, and so will the college. It is because we spot, develop and keep talents like you that we have a great pool. From the pool we export. And of course, Yeoman will be happy to have you as his assistant when you have finished; isn't it, Yeoman?"

They all laughed.

"Now you can go back," he resumed. "But don't be shy to knock on my door at any time. Congratulations again."

Both Jacq and Yeoman rose to walk out from the Principal's Office.

"Oh, Jacq, I forgot to mention," the Principal halted their exit. "Ben Mackinnon has ordered more copies of the newspapers – for you and your sponsor. I will let you have them as soon as they arrive."

* * *

The principal got the newspapers one week after he commended Jacq. This time, Yeoman Smith volunteered to deliver them more efficiently; he was eager to seize another opportunity to chat with Jacq.

"What pushed you to do it?" Yeoman asked Jacq when he had sat her in his office.

"Desperation."

"Desperation?"

"Yes. I was desperate to prove myself to Rev Ali Jaiye."

"Why?" Yeoman was puzzled. "He has always believed you, always pleaded your cause."

"At a point," Jacq started to explain, "he was the only person in Glasgow who believed me. To reinforce his confidence in me, he sent me to Venice Carnival last year. At Venice I flopped and disappointed him badly. It cast some doubts over me in his heart. While others mocked me for the failure, he pitied me, got me the college with the sponsorship, and then challenged me again."

"Does that mean you were at two carnivals, sponsored by him?"

"Yes. Last year February he sent me, to demystify the masks and masquerades before my mind. Before then, they were troubling me in my dreams. He said it was because I did not love Christianity the way I told him I did. 'If there is one thing that can't be shared equally it is love,' he said to me. 'What you have shared with Christianity is the least love, one your heart does not extend to Christ himself. It is too little and so, too weak to reinforce the arteries of your heart and the walls of your brain. Following the masquerade of your husband ensured that. King Japeedoe and his masks knew that about you and used it against you.'

"Then he gave me another chance to purify my soul and live in peace. He was the only man who could do that. I saw the chance as the last, and was determined not to squander it."

"Is he your uncle-uncle?"

"What do you mean by that, uncle-uncle?"

"Don't tell me you don't know, Jacq." They were both amused. "We, African- Americans and African-Caribbeans, got that from you Africans. With you everyone is everyone's brother, sister, father, mother, auntie and uncle; but the blood ones are brother-brother, sister-sister, father-father, mother-mother, auntie-auntie and uncle-uncle. Is that not so?"

Jacq could not help laughing, marvelling at her course tutor's knowledge of the people of her kingdom. "Okay, my uncle – and father – then," she said. "I met him here through his son, Uggi – my brother!" She hoped his answer had complimented his good knowledge. "His help and understanding surpassed that of a blood relative."

"Ben Mackinnon said he was like that to everyone, especially in the church. He said he always challenged himself for the chances the church gave him."

"I believe that is correct, from what I have been able to see of him."

"But then there was one thing I didn't understand. If Rev Jaiye thought you were insincere with your faith, what did he think of you being a masquerade in Venice?"

"Proud. Elated."

"What – a pastor? Strange!"

"Well, if that's how you see it. But then, that affiliation – of a river to its source! Can anything be more important to the river? He is an Ila, don't forget." They both laughed.

"But seriously, sir, he wanted me to see firsthand, how masking and masquerading are supposed to be. He wanted me to see them as objects of fun, not of fear; of recreation, not victimisation. He wanted me to influence Ila with what I would learn in Venice."

"And how does he expect you to do that?"

"I am going back, aren't I?"

"You told us you were banished, didn't you?"

"Yes, by King Japeedoe – not by the gods, not by Jesus Christ. Japeedoe merely employed his masquerades to carry out his will."

"Anyway, it's even good that some of you African-Africans are now thinking right about your mask culture. Do you know that on many occasions we other Africans feel ashamed not of the masks and masquerades, but of what the African-Africans made, and still make, out of them?

366

"That's why we have our own and do them in open and civilised manner. That's why Europe and the Americas copied our way – how Venice was there for you to learn from."

Jacq could only smile to hide the shame imposed on her by the sting from Yeoman's utterances. She remembered she had a near-similar experience in Venice when some Venetians claimed to have the *primo e il megliore* of the culture – the first and the best. Then she was just able to disprove their claim. But with her now was a brother whose line of ancestors was brutalised by his brothers' ancestral masks and masquerades. Here was a brother who had moulted off the yoke from his brothers, and was now beside a sister who herself was groaning under the yoke from a brother-brother! She knew she wouldn't win the argument with Yeoman.

"Yes, you are right to evolve your own," Jacq responded. "I believe my kingdom owes you for that.

"Is yours like Venice's then? I bet it is better."

"I can't say if it is. But I can say Venice's evolved from ours. And based on what I learnt about yours I can say it's better than yours.

"In and out of our Carnival," Yeoman went on proudly, "no one stays behind the mask to steal money or valuables, or rob communities of diaries and poultries. We don't mask up and sell, flog or torture our people. It is never – nothing like that."

Again Jacq returned to her grin of internal chagrin. She could see Yeoman's expression as being beyond a claim of cultural superiority. She could see in it a vent of anger and pains from the injustices the men under the African masks had meted out on his ancestors. Her heart cursed the king, the powerful, and the not-so-powerful people of her kingdom – those whose brains were so malnourished that they could not think beyond hiding behind the masks and looting the kingdom. The embarrassment kept her silent.

"I have a good video of our Carnival in New Orleans, if you don't mind," Yeoman resumed, breaking the silence.

"Could you let me watch it, please?" Jacq begged.

"Oh, yes. Apart from my town's, the College also has videos of other places, including those of Port of Spain, Rio de Janeiro and London. We can both sit and watch them in the college's film studio. But it won't be today, Jacq. Another time. Tomorrow afternoon?"

"That will be great, sir!"

* * *

Port of Spain Carnival:

An intensive shuffling by Jacq preceded the choice of this video for the starter. Her main attraction was that out of the four video cassettes that Yeoman Smith collected from the library, it was the only one that had pictures with the title on its jacket. The other three had just the titles. The pictures – of an Indian with a massive feathery head-dress and of a half-masked stilt walker in a white suit of no trend – had attracted her curiosity.

The film commenced with a huge street jamboree that was different in space and sound from Venice's, and in orderliness and composition from Ila's. Black adults constituted the majority in and along the parade; but then, active participation of white adults, native Indians and Asians rendered the street at that moment a world's melting pot.

The masked depicted themselves in singles as birds, beasts, insects, tools, history and colonial administrators. Jacq believed many of the depictions actually deposed hers in Venice. She marvelled at how successfully joint efforts had hilariously advanced the art of masquerading in Port of Spain.

Jacq refused to buy the running commentary at the start of the film. She found it funny hearing the carnival in Trinidad and Tobago was the brainchild of French aristocrats. It was never, and could never had been, she contested. The former freed black slaves that made up the majority of the population were born with their mas and music culture; the native Indians had plumes in their feather costumes long before the first French man ever set his foot on Port of Spain!

Jacq would not miss some mas characters which, though were less flamboyant, hilariously depicted the daily lives of Trinbagonians. There was the aristocracy of the white settlers in Dame Lorraine comparing with the pauperisms in the white face-painted minstrels. She saw knowledge in the up-to-date colloquialism of Pierrot Grenade, and the pride of profession in the Cow mas. In Moko Jumbie mas however, was the satire of Gnu Ko, similar with Ila's Igunu Koko, the tallest masquerade who used to intimidate spectators into giving but was daft enough to leave the collection and pocketing of the money to his dwarfish guide. Jab Molassie projected Ila's Alagbo, the thuggish mas often restricted by strong men pulling the long, strong chains he had round his waist. The long pitch-forked Jap-Jap, and the crafty, *robber-talking* Midnight Robber were like her home junior masquerades, the cheap trouble makers who would raid women households and morning markets, on errands. In Bat mas she saw the Ila societal 'yes' man – neither a bird nor an animal – always chameleonic.

Jacq saw a marvellous invention in the pans and steel bands. What an ingenuity that had guided the black settlers into inventing the instruments from steel, pans and pots! She saw how the fear-orientated deprivation imposed on the African slaves had been their pivot towards the invention of a set of unique musical instruments for both the carnival and the wider world.

That all the parades shown proceeded and ended without intimidation or exploitation won Jacq's heart. At Queen's Park West where they efficiently terminated, she admired how titles and prizes were openly bestowed on individuals and groups for outstanding performances. She believed that had it been in a civilised and straight Ila, she would have got her own all-female float, and won the crown of Calypso Queen. More important she would have done so without exposing any of the honourable parts of her body, like some ladies had costumed so skimpily. She also believed her husband would have won the Soca Monarch; and her chiefdom's Dancemaster group would have flatly beaten Jemba Couple to the double titles of Panorama and Road March Champions! Overall, she found the film homely and relevant but reserved speaking out her opinions.

* * *

Mardi Gras of New Orleans:

"When Iberville, a French explorer coming from Biloxi, landed by the Mississippi River at a point sixty miles south of New Orleans on the March 3, 1699," the commentary commenced, "the first thing he unpacked was the carnival of Mardi Gras. Because it was the day Mardi Gras was being celebrated in France he named that fort Point di Mardi Gra.

"As in the other parts of the Gulf, carnival was subjected to several bans and re-bans by the French and other subsequent rulers of the area. They feared the African slaves, with their drums, dances and ancestral worships, would conspire with the native Indians to take over Mardi Gras. The birth of the mystic Cowbellion de Rakin Society in co-provincial Mobile changed all that. From then, not only were peaceful parades organised, other peaceful mystic societies sprang up locally. Among these, in 1857, was Comus, a six-man Orleans organization that was a direct off-shoot of the Cowbellian. Comus named itself the first *krewe*...

"Now, New Orleans has more than a hundred krewes – and that is a count after some had ceased to be active. Krewes of Rex, Zulu, Bacchus and Mardi Gras Indians are among the existing ones that have attained the status of super-krewes through special contributions. Doubloons and the carnival colours of gold, green and purple were introduced by the Krewe of Rex. Krewe of Zulu is synonymous with coconut throws, while its constant lateness enables members' friends to join its floats along their routes and upon the payment of a small fee. The Krewe of Bacchus is popular for ensuring a large assemblage of national and international celebrities. For Krewe Mardi Gras Indians, spectators would line up to see their spectacular, sequined feather costumes, as well as to catch glimpses of Big Chief to Big Chief threats of 'You *humba*;' 'Me no humba, you humba!' One expects the other to humble himself and bow for him!

"Other distinctions, these krewes do show through their names:

Politics and conquest from Napoleon to Caesar krewes,

Communal and territorial identifications from Jefferson to Shangri-La,

Knowledge and wisdom from Thoth to Muses,

Sexist from all-male Centurion to all-female Mysterieuses,

Greek gods and mythologies from Orpheus to Pegasus,

Goddesses from Ọṣun to Rhea,

Tribal from Mas Gras Indians to Zulu,

Oddities from Chaos to Nemesis...

Such are the grace and craze of New Orleans Mardi Gras Carnival ..."

Next, Jacq was confronted with what she believed was a most crazy aspect of the film. It was called 'boobing', on a crowded revellers' street posted Bourbon Street.

From a crowded first floor balcony, and in a quick but haphazard succession, three young women leapt unto the street below them, landing on a pre-positioned soft pad. All that each of them had on was a topless bikini.

As they landed they were greeted by the cheers of the waiting spectators and the sound from a stationed soca band. Baring every bit of their chests at first, they rapidly cupped their breasts with their hands and started to dance.

Three other women, in feathered tiaras and positioned with the band, rushed to the three dancers. Within seconds they were able to replace the cupped hands with enough long beads and necklaces. Jacq found the craze the dirtiest ever; and that the improved covering should have been extended to cover their bikinis   . That

371

would have won them the decent , gorgeous look of the maidens of Ọṣun in Ila.

"Appalling, appalling," Jacq muttered at the screen. "Public nakedness was not an option for women in Ila."

"Wait for more; wait for more," the voice over the screen assured her – before Yeoman could finish carrying out her instruction to stop the film.

"What exactly is Mardi Gras about?" she asked in protest. "This is pathetic – graceless. Can we change to another film?"

Yeoman smiled, concealing his disagreement. If there was a carnival he admired most, and could defend, it was the Mardi Gras – his New Orleans Mardi Gras! He was born and reared in New Orleans and he knew how it worked. What Jacq needed from him was that explanatory defence!

"What you saw was only part of the fun of Mardi Gras," he told her. "It represented neither a parade nor a krewe."

"But what a fun gone too far!"

"Well, tourists and spectators love it. That's why whenever they take a break from the parades they flock into that street, and in fact, to every corner of the French Quarters of the city. The fun has to continue."

"What's there to continue – or to start – in that? Breast flashing for fun?"

"Well, yes, and many others: night balls, day balls, gay parties, lesbian parties, singles parties, all those sorts. What we saw is 'B for B' or 'boobs for beads'. It is the fastest for any bead hungry woman to fill her appetite – all free, plus extras.

"Plus extras? What extras?"

"Smiles, cheers, from the givers!

"There is also 'B for C', boobs for coconuts! No carnival is a carnival without some fun. But at the real parades you don't flash before you are showered with Orleans gifts.

"And you may like to know, Jacq: that's the street I first met the principal five years ago. Both he and his wife on Easter break, came to Mardi Gras."

"Jesus Christ!" Jacq exploded. "The principal and his wife? Was she flashing too?"

"No. Both of them had just been disappointed with the accommodation they pre-booked. By luck they stopped me to ask where they could get a decent alternative. We discovered each other's professions during the exchanges. Then he invited me to join Glasgow College's Department of Arts."

"Really amazing, that was," Jacq responded.

"It was, Jacq. So let us continue with the film. You want to know more about the carnivals, don't you?"

Jacq sighed and agreed. "The grace, the craze," she murmured and prepared herself for whatever next. Incidentally it was another 'craze'!

A bar along Bourbon Street was packed full of merrymakers. Behind the serving counter were the male head-server and two female assistants. On the table before them was a long line of twenty-four wine glasses divided into two shorter lines of twelve glasses each. The shorter lines were carded A and B.

From two large tin jugs, each sweating of cold, the head-server filled all the glasses with a specially prepared cocktail the commentator called *sazerac*, a rye-based whiskey. Then, two men dressed for the occasion came forward, each to a row of the wicked-looking concoction. Then the barman's whistle and the spectators' cheers signalled the two men off to a race to being the first to down his twelve glasses. The more glasses each man guzzled the louder the cheers and the applause.

The competitor at A crawled to the eighth glass and stopped, his eyes watery red and his throat a choking incendiary. He could advance no further.

That at B raised the spectators' enthusiasm by speeding to his fifth glass and reverted to a disappointingly slower but steady speed. At the eleventh the strength of the whiskey was set to remove the tracks before him when the deafening cheers of the spectators came to his rescue. "Mardi Gras! Mardi Gras!" they hailed to hoarseness, pounding and applauding – until they pushed him to down the twelfth glass, to finish his line.

Amid a thunderous ovation, the barman relieved the drinker of the last empty glass while the first assistant replaced it with a garland of beads and flowers. Then he put on the table before the winner, a round, colourful, roped, twelve-inch cake prize.

The crown and crowning were to follow. The barman collected the green, purple and gold diadem from his assistant, raised it and turned a circle with it. He satisfied himself that the crowd had witnessed its inscription: Mardi Gras *Sazerac* Monarch! Then he turned again and stretched out to the champion. But the winner was incapable of seeing either the crowner or the crown in his hands – incapable of seeing the reward for his hard drink! The powerful alky molecules of *sazerac* had displaced the cerebellum and the occipital lobes of his brain. He collapsed flat out – amidst even more merciless cheers!

"In and around carnivals of the masks why do people get so intoxicated?" Jacq asked herself. The ugliness at the *sazerac* show had just reminded her of similar witnessing with *òguròò, bùrùkùtù, umqombothi* . . . and *ganja*! "But wait a minute," she halted her breath, "I saw nothing like this in Venice," she said and braced up for more of the ugliness, gracelessness, and craze. Surprisingly the next scenes gave her none of these.

It was a sales outlet, an off-road garden market of beads. The commentary emphasised how, in the past, the beads used to be made of rare metals, ionised iron and glasses. Now, in order to produce them cheaper and safer, they came mostly in plastics. The market garden did not have the scenic beauty of the foot bridge market on the Rialto but its spaciousness and neat surrounding put it in a class incomparably higher than any of Ila markets.

374

Tons and tons of beads hung on the strong, standing hangers and pegs. Yet, more sat, packed inside the cartons, about on the ground.

Their sizes and circumferences varied so much that no faith clergy, spiritualist, occultist or jester, would encounter a problem making his appropriate choices. Some of those on the pegs were so long that they would need to be doubly twined around the wearers' necks. Some shone, some glowed and some sparkled – permanently or intermittently, wholly or partially – along their circumferences. Some also had attachments which varied in types: medallions, hearts, skulls, weapons, animals, insects, jesters, games, and sovereign flags.

The sales scene shifted to a shop thrice as big as Jacq's favourite Shop 42 in Venice. It stored a large number of plastic masks which were sequined, feathered, or both. Jacq was not surprised to see Venetian masks among them, but she was that they were more expensive than other masks in the shop. A good mix of other items: capes, wigs, tiaras, crowns, combs, shirts, vests, bow-ties, gloves, socks, music albums, video CDs, musical instruments and tableware, made it a complete shop for visitors to Mardi Gras.

The video rolled to the parade scenes – three principally, on different routes. One was of Krewe of Zulu on Lundi Gras, and the other of Krewe of Bacchus on the preceding Sunday night. Each krewe was a sea of heads that paced and stopped, drifted and dithered, opened out and closed up, and marched along its route like a large colony of ants returning with their catches carried aloft.

In Zulu, Jacq counted up to fifteen floats before she lost count – forced to in her struggle to cope with their exceptionalness. Its parade was led by three marching musical bands, each in a colour of Mardi Gras. Behind them, on the first motorised float, a huge rubber work of Chaka the Zulu boldly charged his spear with one hand and defended himself with a leather shield with the other hand. Other bloated images on the other floats included the gorilla, tiger, eagle, chicken and dignitaries. They were mechanically and robotically enabled into performing live activities.

From their 'golden thrones' the King and Queen of the parade flaunted their wealth and majesty through generous 'throws' of the longest beads, the biggest stuffed toys, expensive doubloons, and the most beautiful cups. The dancers below them on the same float gave out cheaper versions of the gift items – together with the unique-to-Zulu 'golden nuggets' painted silver, gold, green, purple or white, all crested 'Z' for Zulu.

The Krewe of Bacchus was equally dashing, artistic and giving. Its night time parade, and the presence of America's celebrities on its float particularly, gave it the twinkle of cosmic stars.

The last of the parade scenes was of Mardi Gras Indians. More head dressed than masked, they hooted along a street on foot. From the Spy Boy to the Flag Boy, and Chief to Big Chief, the masquerades had the most flamboyant of feathers and beads Jacq had ever seen. Their communication networking was intricate, executed by dancing, hooting, hand signals and the rhythmic drumming. She loved the threats they exhibited, threats made empty by their preoccupation with protecting their highly flammable costumes rather than making inter-tribal or inter-krewe attacks.

* * *

Rio de Janeiro Carnival:

"Rio lives for carnival – soccer forgiving – and both the statue of Christ the Redeemer and the twin-mountains of Corcovado and Sugarloaf stand firmly, confirming that." That was the commentator, at the start of the film of Rio de Janeiro Carnival.

"This film," it continued, "though summarised the Rio Carnival in only thirty minutes, the spectacularity of the carnival and the magic of the *Escola de Samba* it showed lasted for over an hour, while the preparation was an entire year's hard work by the school.

"Rio Carnival was born out of the merger of early Christian processions with the modes of black African dances and worship in Bahia. It is intensely staged in the last four days before every Ash Wednesday.

"Since 1945 it had been spearheaded by the neighbouring and suburban groups, the *bloco* and *monoblocos* that evolved into Samba Schools. Deixa Folar at Praca Onze formed in 1926 was the first school. Because the formations embraced the paganish African dances, early Porto-Catholic led governments grudged their successes and stirred up riots at the carnivals in order to justify banning them. Peace reigned to this day when carnival was accepted as a national expression of Brazilian cultures. Today, Rio de Janeiro has more than a hundred *blocos* which formed into over seventy Samba Schools that design and produce costumes, masquerades, floats and dances for the carnival.

"Each year a School picks its colour and theme, and these are coordinated by the School's Carnival Designer. Such a theme is usually a piece of story, history, event or high imagination brought to modernity deeply, vigorously and completely.

"During the carnival, parade competition among Schools of Samba is fiery and fierce. A school in the Special Group wants to be judged the best. Those in Groups A, B and C aspire to move to the Special Group. Those in D to F want to move up the league so that they could parade inside the Sambadrome, the 80,000 people, half mile long, concrete stadium, designed by Oscar Niemeyer and built in 1984. The Samba Dome...! Welcome to the Sambadrome...!"

The 'flagging-in' of the School's parade from Sector 1 of the Sambadrome burst the fusion that had, up to that time, held together the determination of the paraders with the expectation of the spectators.

At the forward surge from the starting point onto the dome's 'runway', pyrotechnics rocketed toward the sky in intensive lavishness that not even Hunan in China could dare. They boomed, shrieked and crackled in illuminations that mushroomed, crowned,

377

tabled, poled and crisscrossed into delightful disappearances over the spectators in the stadium's Sectors 1, 3 and 2 east. They were joined by more hooting, whistling and flag waving of the teeming *espectadores*. Swiftly, these joiners were drowned by the heavy percussions and songs of the entering Samba School parade.

Jacq had never seen anything like this. She saw it much bigger than, and different from, the Mardi Gras. She least anticipated a spectacle that would surpass the New Orleans'. She watched on the extravagance in disbelief:

The lady flag bearer, *porta-bandiera*, semi-plumaged, half-naked and protected by the male *mestre-sala*, spun to the front in careful acrobatics. Swarming the invasion behind them were the drummers and the bum-, waist- and chest-swinging *passistas*. Now the revelry was in full force, served along by the numerous stewards of the flow.

The membership of the parade was unbelievably massive. Jacq wished she could count it, that she would have counted up to four thousand. It was split into colourfully distinct wings that managed their own dances within the allocated bounds of 'Economy of Life', the theme of that parade.

At a point along the runway, every member became calculatedly drunk with his act. The membership drummed louder, sang louder, danced more, and regrouped with high precisions from break-ups. They were at the point where stationed the first set of *julgadores*! From their long box these judges watched intensely, pens and papers firmly in hand. The commentary said there were four of such positions spread along the danceway. Each position had ten judges individually scoring a school on ten categories.

For this theme there were six floats, all lavishly designed to look parcels of natural jungles. The forest of the leading float had fruiting trees with birds and animals feeding on the fruits. The second float depicted flowering trees, bushes and shrubs. Bees, birds and butterflies hovered above them causing them to drop their pollens on a flowing river. The third float had a number of trees just cut and starting to fall. As they fell, toco-toucan birds, a giant anteater, a banded armadillo, butterflies, bees, pollens and leaves were seen diving. "Stop felling our lives!" screamed the script.

A low tree with a large umbrella was prominent on the last float. Rain, sun and rainbow were depicted above it. Under it sat the King of the Parade on his lavish throne. He was happy to sit with his queen and a number of rare pets, contented to occupy imaginatively the throne of his 'Garden of Eden'!

Most of the *destaques* were near-nakedly costumed, and were unruffled by their braless-ness. It was easy to see how their bones and nerves contoured as they danced to the samba *batucada* rythm of the bands put in place before and after each float.

The mandatory timing of a parade on the runway – the commentary pegged it at a maximum of eighty minutes – terminated the parade scenes at the Apotheoses Square of the Sambadrome. From there the floats and the dancers took different routes out of the stadium. The timed exit was to allow the judges to meet and collate their marks at the Square, ready for the announcement of the winners on the morning of Ash Wednesday. It also allowed a School to prepare for its galas.

If she hadn't seen this film on Rio, she concluded, there was no way she could ever imagine what she saw, her perception of the previous films, participation in Venice's carnival, and bitter experience in Ila, notwithstanding.

* * *

London Notting Hill Carnival

As Jacq would learn from the commentary of this film, the composition of the major elements that constituted the London Notting Hill Carnival, LNHC – history, administration, time, programme – were different from those of Port of Spain, New Orleans or Rio de Janeiro.

In its history, two sources meandered and finally 'confluenced' to it.

The Masquerade

Source number one was that of Claudia Jones, the assumed 'mother' of the event. Claudia, a Trinidadian communist of African-Caribbean descent, lived in Harlem from where she was deported to London in 1955. In the UK she discovered herself inside the type of racialism and 'MyCarthyism' she had fled from – in the middle of both the fascist British Union and the anti-black Boys Brigade wrecking havoc on African-Caribbeans of the Windrush generation, their off-springs, friends, and other black people.

Through writing, publishing and open activism, Claudia toiled to encourage strong solidarity and self-awareness among the African-Caribbean communities in London. Her efforts produced a series of indoor carnivals that started with London St Pancreas Hall's of January 30, 1959. In the same year, Caribbean style, she launched the Mardi Gras.

Claudia died in December 1964, but her memory among the black communities still lived on through several commemorations, the annual Claudia Jones Lecture being one of them.

Source number two was that of Rhaune Laslett, a white lady who, by staging the first street party in 1964, gave birth to the urban carnival in Notting Hill. Before then she was unaware of Claudia's in-hall carnival parties.

Rhaune's party started as an outdoor one, but it instantly flamed into a street party, the first ever! There, the steel band from the local Coleherne Pub in Earls Court played to the procession of local businessmen, Gas Board and Fire Brigade in floats drawn by horses and carts that were supplied free by the local stall holders of Portobello Market. The unexpected huge success of the party-turned-carnival encouraged Rhaune to re-schedule it to August 1965.

Rhaune ran the carnival till 1970 by which time the annual event had become more African-Caribbean in attendance and patronage. She retired, handing over its administration to Leslie Palmer, a Trinidadian. Since the time of the rescheduled parade of

380

1965, LNHC had grown from a much criticised event to one where the peace-keeping policemen partake in the dancing. It had grown, from being African-Caribbean to becoming London communal, and from a gathering of about a thousand dancers to the biggest street party in Europe.

"Four things stand the carnival out," the commentary went on:

"One: It is staged during every last Monday in August. Other carnivals are pre-Lenten, taking place between Epiphany and Ash Wednesday.

"Two: Its biggest musical competition is free. This is the Panorama National Champion of Steel Competition of the Saturday preceding the Carnival Monday. Usually, more than fifty steel bands take part.

"Three: There is a separate children's parade. This comes up on the Children's Day, the Sunday before the Carnival Monday.

"Four: The parade route is single and long. It's over three miles long, covering six streets – Great Western Road, Western Park Road, Chepstow Road, Westbourne Grove, Kensington Park Road and Ladbroke Grove – of west London…"

Jacq loved the scene of the Children's Day parade. It was the first clip of children's multi-floats she had seen. Though the participants sharply varied in age, they were uniformly beautiful in their fanciful masks, flamboyant costumes and light mini-props. In dancing groups, they spread over a long distance, sandwiched between heavy bands whose wattage emissions recognised no childhood in the young revellers' eardrums. The floats were judged at an early point on the Great Western Road.

The members of one special children group were individually costumed in their wheel chairs, yet they danced and spun with greatest incredibility, one that moved Jacq close to tears. She closed her eyes and searched for her own daughter, Sariya. Was she also ill and in a wheel chair? The thought worsened when two of the wheelchairs collided as they spun, and another parader in the group was fast enough to intervene and save the situation ahead of any of the parade stewards. In a similar accident in Ila, she imagined Sariya would have got no access to a similar helpful intervention – not one from another child, a palace steward, or her mother! "Why has the world been so wickedly discriminatory?" she asked herself.

The main adult parade scenes were a blend of Port of Spain's without being dominated sound-wise by the steel bands, New Orleans' without 'throws', and Rio's without the *wings* on the runway. Jacq was truly thrilled that such a cultural dynamism existed in 'nearby' London; and that London could be the biggest centre of positive cultural diversification in the universe she knew.

Sounds were mounted on huge trucks from where the heavy sounds of steel pans, reggae, soul, hip-hop, soca and calypso blared. Each band had its own revellers dancing at the front and back of its truck. More than in other carnivals, the bands and their floats represented more nations and nationalities. She could count floats from Jamaica, Trinidad and Tobago, Haiti, Cuba, Mexico, Puerto Rico, Bolivia, Barbados, Venezuela, Brazil, India, Malaysia, Japan, Poland, France, The Netherlands, and Russia.

One reggae band hilariously summed up the internationalist projection of London Notting Hill Carnival at the front of its parade. Leading it, a carnival queen – more 'worker' than queen – dragged behind her a large blow-up of an Atlas globe. Between the globe and the reggae truck were about a hundred dancers, followed by about another hundred behind the truck. They were lightly masked and costumed to depict different tribes of the world!

Ila costumes? There was none of them. Costumes from Ila's neighbouring kingdoms? Jacq could see none. Instead, Jacq saw an open world of masks and masquerades without Ila, a world that had left Ila behind to wallow in the miseries from Japeedoe and his inner-circle of masquerade thieves!

"We should go and reflect first and then come back to exchange our questions and answers", Yeoman told Jacq at the end of the film. Jacq agreed; the following Monday would be ideal.

* * *

Rev Ali Jaiye waited calmly for Jacq to return from the college, from watching the carnival films she told him Yeoman would show her. Ali was sure seeing the films would have packed Jacq full of stories. He was right.

"The films sent my original lines of thinking off-course," Jacq related to Ali, "– to the realities that I could never have imagined correctly."

"Did you like them?"

"I did. They were a great experience. We watched four magnificent carnival films – of Port of Spain's, New Orleans', Rio de Janeiro's and London's. My only regret was that I was not taking part in any of them. I wished they were not just films."

"Well, you have your future to visit any of them and take part," Ali consoled. "But if you were to visit those events which of them would you go to first?"

"Port of Spain's," she was certain.

"Why is that?"

"Their masks and masquerades were the simplest. They most meaningfully related to masks, masquerades and life in Ila. It also lacked a masquerade which I would have loved to design, depict, and seek to add."

"That sounds interesting," Ali said. He wasn't surprised of Jacq's artistic inventiveness. "And what would the new addition have been?"

"Well, if without mercy they depicted the French aristocrats who first lorded them, they ought to have also the kingdoms that sold them into trouble. And, who should have represented those more than a Japeedoe? They should have depicted him clawed and fanged, the blood of his people he had murdered dripping from his mouth."

"That's where I disagree," Ali responded. "People need to outgrow the nasty parts of history, learn from them and move on.

The Masquerade

Good leaders and historians must encourage this among their people. That was what they did right in the carnival zones you saw. That is what is yet to happen in Ila and its neighbouring kingdoms. Ila is yet to have those leaders and historians at the helm of affairs.

"Now, let's leave that to a side. Tell me what you found interesting about the films."

"Actually, sir, they were all exciting," Jacq admitted. "They were the greatest cultural evolution ever.

"But then," she offered her only negative, "there was too much nudity among the women in the parades. That was an invitation to prostitution; and the Bible spoke strongly against this."

"I disagree with some aspects of what you said, Jacq. There is nowhere in the scriptures where nudity *per se* is pronounced sinful, otherwise the innocent newborn will be a bundle of sins. What is sinful is to attach indecent thinking to nudity. Do you know there are hundreds of tribes who live without sinning in the stark nudity of new babies?

"Think about the bad effects of Ila's fully clothed masks and masquerades on us, and you will award higher marks to the nudities and exposures you saw in those films.

"Of course morals and rules should apply, but they must not apply to just the women. They must also apply to men, if not principally. Don't you agree?"

"Well, sir, I agree more than disagree, if I may put it that way."

"That's good enough, Jacq; and it encourages my next question: Now that you have acquired some knowledge of the carnivals have you thought of how to use the knowledge?"

"Yes, sir," Jacq didn't hesitate. "Before today, I have always thought of sneaking into Ila, save my husband and daughter, and sneak out with them. Since seeing the films I have broadened my intentions to teaching Ilas about the evolution of masks and masquerades – about how not to carnival!" She was damn serious; and Ali could see that.

"But they will kill you; they don't want you. They will kill you on your first night – kill you and whatever remains of your family in Ila. Have you considered that?"

"Yes. First, I will ensure 'they' is restricted to Japeedoe and Sese Abram only. Next, I will complete whatever I have to do before any of them know of my first night."

"Are you sure you want to do that, Jacq?"

"Yes, sir."

Jacq sounded unbelievable, most impressive to Ali.

"Okay then," Ali said, "something further to help you as you make up your mind: Just give me one second to fetch it for you."

Ali disappeared into his bedroom and returned instantly with two pictures, each the size of A3, both rolled into one. Old age had stiffened them and turned them from 'black and white' to 'brown and grey', but the prints were still clear enough to the eyes. Jacq struggled to unroll them into singles to see. Her eyes were all tension as she looked at them repeatedly.

"What are these?" she, in cool shock finally asked Ali. "Crocodiles – eating what?" She was horrified, doubting if she had seen right.

"It's the same crocodile being fed with different limbs of the same man, inside the palace of Ila. It happened many years ago; and it could still be happening now. Ben Mackinnon handed them over to me, for a reason. They had a tragic story behind them – really a tragic story. I believe now is the right time for me to tell you the story.

"You see, since you told me a bit about yourself on the day you moved in, I have found out more about you in Ila. Ever since I completed the findings, I knew you deserved the story and that I will tell you."

Jacq could not imagine the extent of the tragedy Ali had for her from his research. Most frightening to her was to know that Rev Ali Jaiye had successfully pried into her life in Ila. She feared Ali

385

had discovered some disturbing 'local facts' that had tragically or incredibly linked her with Ben Mackinnon. Inescapably she resigned to hearing Ali.

"First, have you ever heard of Tantalo?" Ali asked her.

"Yes, sir. Tantalo, the Tiger, who the stories told us successfully defied all the male gods of Ila and after that challenged the goddess of Ọ̀ṣun River , belittling her for being a female. That the goddess led other gods to attack him one night of the festival. That they overpowered him, killed him, and ate him. Was it not that one?"

"Exactly that one, Jacq. There were many versions of his story. But the version you just gave was the palace's. Unfortunately it was the only one the palace released; and it was untrue. Tantalo defied human injustices, not the spirits. He wrestled with no one, but was overpowered. He committed no sin but was executed. He was devoured by no spirits but had his body shared between the then Japeedoe and his pet crocodile. What you just saw in the jaws of the crocodile were sections of Tantalo's limbs."

Jacq remained puzzled, more so as Ali had confirmed the incident happened many years ago, long before Ben Mackinnon himself was born! How could Ben had got, or taken, the pictures? She didn't know whether to believe in re-incarnation. But, re-incarnation of the wicked? "Excuse me, sir, I don't understand," she admitted again. "And I am frightened."

"You will understand now, Jacq. And as you do, you need to be braver, not frightened.

"Tantalo was my great-great-grandfather.

"He was a very strong man who achieved more than his ancestors to become the first High Chief of Ila. By his title he, among his duties, pronounced judgements on the most important cases. A case was where the reigning king instructed Tantalo to pronounce a death sentence on his own brother who he had framed within the palace. The prince's sin before his brother was his growing popularity with the rarely visiting Scot, Kelan Mackinnon,

Ben's great-grandfather. The reigning Japeedoe feared such a growing popularity may encourage his brother to successfully challenge his crown.

"A week before the start of the annual festival, which was also one Tantalo was expected to deliver the capital punishment, he, Tantalo saw the spirit of his dead father. The spirit warned him, Tantalo, against any injustice. If the king wanted his brother's blood split unjustly the king should make the pronouncement directly. So, Tantalo hesitated and attempted to convince the king to spare his brother. Tantalo's pleading turned the king against him, with the king branding Tantalo as being pro his brother, and more of an advocate than the most senior judge of the kingdom of Ila.

"The king reacted badly when Tantalo finally refused to pass the judgement. The king declared a night curfew and summoned the dreaded *Orò*, led by the reigning Fire Spirit to seize Tantalo in the middle of the night. My great-grandfather and her small sister were the only ones who saw Tantalo lured out forever into the darkness. Then the palace issued the strange and untrue bulletin it wanted the people of the kingdom to believe about the high chief.

The next problem for the palace was how to complement the bulletin with ensuring the body of Tantalo disappeared without a trace. The palace proposed to 'weight' it and throw it into the local River Òşin for the fishes , crabs, rhinoceros, crocodiles and the legendary rainbows to feed on. The palace abandoned that plan when it feared the goddess of the river might become angry that the corpse of her high chief son was clandestinely dumped in her water. She could send it back to the embankment for the people to see!

Next the palace considered treating the body the same way for the bigger River Òşun a few miles away . Again it changed its mind: Òşun, known for blessing the barren with the fertility of the womb, would not only refuse to be so associated with taking innocent life, she could impose divine punishment on the killers and their children.

387

Dumping the body in the ocean would solve the problem, the then Fire Spirit finally suggested to the royal committee of death. The ocean was mighty and it had trillions of inhabitants who would devour Tantalo's body, bone and flesh, long before *Olókun,* the King of the Oceans himself, would ever be aware of the dumping! He, Fire Spirit, would prepare some special slaves to take the body on the two hundred miles journey to the coast.

"That will be a respect too much and undeserving for a rebel," the king overruled. "It will be a problem for simplification turned into one of complication." Bravely, he volunteered to eat Tantalo's heart, brain and sensory organs in order to add Tantalo's to his own strength and wisdom. Had it been now that hydrochloric acid abounds, the king would have ordered a drum full, dumped Tantalo in it and watched him disintegrate, hair and marrow.

"But the soul of my great-great-grandfather refused to sleep. Two days after the abduction, Kelan arrived in Ila. On his direct way to the palace, he, as usual stopped to call on High Chief Tantalo. He met the household in a state of despair and confusion caused by being unable to know where *Orò* had taken the head of their estate. He left them and continued to the palace where by chance, during his escorted tour of the palace, he saw and recorded the gory story. In those days cameras and pictures never lied.

"The royal – executive – murderers still had another problem: they must quieten the two family witnesses to the abduction. The king offered as a bribe to my great-grandfather the title of his murdered father, but my great-grandfather refused it. Correctly anticipating royal persecution from his refusal, he quickly married his small sister away to a suitor in the nearby kingdom. Since then her family had remarried into and blossomed in Ila. Thanks to the family's maintained links with the Mackinnons and Christianity which started during the life and time of High Chief Tantalo. You, Jacquensica Nek, are a direct descendant of that sister of my great-grandfather. You are of High Chief Tantalo!"

Jacq was still, trying to adjust to the strangeness she found with Ali's story. "Sir, do you mean it, that we are of the same blood?"

"Yes, Jacq, that is it – the same blood. That's why I pleaded with you when I had to, and insisted when I had to. If in doubt don't you see the striking similarity in our life patterns? Blood is not only thicker, it is stronger than water."

"Oh my God, now I can see," Jacq accepted, bursting into hot tears. "I can see clearly the similarities – in our denials, persecution, victimisation... oh, my God!"

"Also in our fights for societal justice, in our search for communal openness, for understanding among those we offended, and above all, for our common quest for true spiritual guidance from Christ and our ancestors."

Jacq returned to another moment of serious reflection, which she eventually broke. "Now I feel thoroughly ashamed," she told Ali.

"Ashamed? Why?"

"That Yeoman Smith was right," she accepted. "He was right that our masks and masquerades and culture have always been awful and sinful, that those of his people are the only correct advancement.

"Now that I have heard you, my will feels too weak to throw my questions at him. This will be the first time I will ever be caught in such inadequacy. I have to agree to his interpretations of the films he showed me. I can't ask him questions."

"Oh no, Jacq," Ali objected. "You ask Yeoman questions if you must. I never said our masks, masquerades and carnivals were born awful and sinful. Those that existed before the historical hijackings were designed for the physical and spiritual well being of Ila.

"Their origin and existence were nothing but beneficial. Our earlier ancestors masked up as reindeer to catch the reindeer for the community to eat. They masked as a monkey to catch the true

389

monkey to rear. They masked the crops to produce better yields and masked as guards to keep the pests and thieves from the yield. They masked as the spirits of our grandfathers to promote the spirits of peace and love in the living generations. They masked as the spirits of justice to discipline the bad boys of the community, as well as to reward handsomely the community's good boys. Tell Yeoman all this if need be; and answer his questions, Jacq. Do you understand?"

"Yes, sir, I do."

"And remember to tell him what they used to mask with: woods, barks, leaves, fruits, seeds, soil, water, leathers, fibres, feathers, stones, jewelleries, metals and colours! They masked with any item usable for the purpose of benefiting not only the compounds but the kingdom at large. They used nothing and did nothing to benefit only the private or family pockets, never the kings' or the high chiefs'.

"That was how it started and lived in Ila. That was before 'evolution' would even give its own births. Tell your teacher these, with all the confidence of your experience, and of your ancestry with High Chief Tantalo, the human Tiger of Ila.

"Ask him your questions and let him ask all his. You will discover you are not as far apart as you think, or as he believes."

With full attention Jacq heard and absorbed the most serious talk ever to her from Rev Ali Jaiye, her mentor and newly discovered blood. All the same she still had two burning questions to ask Ali. Her first was: "What if Yeoman's questions are – as I guess they will be – based on the minuses of masks and masquerades of Ila?"

"That would be honest of him, to the innocent depth of his knowledge. Having now known and seen much, you should be able to balance the equation.

"Yes there were minuses; but they have always remained permanently outnumbered by the pluses, leaving the equation balanced at pretty pluses. Agreed?"

Jacq's genuine smiles indicated she did.

"Your second question?"

"What then became of my great-great-great-uncle, your great-grandfather, after he married away his sister? "

"The palace arranged for him poisoned. He was on his death bed when he begged the Scottish clergy who had always been a sympathiser to the family of Tantalo, to take my dad, his grandson, away to Glasgow to become an evangelist."

"Then, it means we have always be a family of runners and escapees, isn't it, sir?"

"No, not that way, Jacq. Rather, a family of lucky ones who are able to escape from the jaws of the unjust. There's no shame in that. We never quit, never get frightened."

Jacq was unsure of that last bit. Never quit? Never frightened? How would anyone define her and Ali's sojourns in Glasgow? How would anyone judge her great-great-great-uncle hastily marrying away his sister to somewhere outside Ila? What about her own surrender in coming with Victor and Uggi to Glasgow? How can anyone define this as appropriate to a direct descendant of High Chief Tantalo? She took a deep breath.

"Never quit, never frightened, and we are in Glasgow?" she asked Ali.

"Yes, Jacq, under the love and direction of Jesus Christ.

"You would even love to know," Ali continued, "that this week the love and direction had overwhelmed Uggi, our only family member who was timid. He came over to me in the church after the worship, still in the choir rope, and apologised for ever insulting me for sending him to Ila. He used to believe I had merely sent him to witness a most cruel crudity of a people. Only once – and with reluctance – he had looked at the prints I made from the film he used at the Kings Square. The look made him hateful of anything of Japeedoe or his town masquerades.

"On Sunday he was even more hateful. He wished I could send him back to Ila and Japeedoe. He would set ablaze the palace, the Square and any of Japeedoe's drunken masquerades he could find."

"But, sir, do you see Uggi fulfilling such a wish?" she asked Ali. "He had missed those chances, hadn't he?"

"I don't know Jacq. But it is fair to say Uggi has never failed in his determinations." Jacq only listened; she gave no verbal response.

"There are more things you need to know of," Ali continued, "– more things before you ask me." He turned to a set of drawers and took out another roll of photo prints he purposely had there that day. "Take a good look and remain strong," he added as he handed it to Jacq. "The black and white is the last of the Ben Mackinnon's you saw. The coloured three were shots from Kazuggi. Both Ben and Kazuggi now want them used as soon as possible, as strong exhibits against the leadership in Ila."

The pictures were self-evident enough. One, the black and white, was a further highlight of Tantalo's tragedy with his skull, intact, resting beside the now sleeping crocodile. In the second, Jacq saw herself being dragged to the stakes. In the third, she and her husband were deposited by the stakes. In the fourth Japeedoe, his queen, Azzanaite, and her children were in a jubilant mood as Fire Spirit stood over her and her husband as prisoners of the kingdom.

"These pictures will come with me," Jacq eventually cried out. "They will, to the palace of Ila. Someone in Japeedoe's ancestry will have to be made answerable."

Jacq's ranting put a smile on Ali's face. He wondered if Jacq understood what she just talked about, if she had learnt enough to change the kind of behaviours that had persistently blocked her from making right judgements.

"How and when?" he asked her. "Have you considered? I am disappointed that these are not the questions already uppermost in your mind.

"In the past Jacq, you neither planned nor timed right; and it made your life a hell on earth. Which actions triumph without them? None."

* * *

Jacq had all her questions about the films ready for Yeoman Smith. In less than an hour she would confront Yeoman with them right inside his office.

With intent, the questions were as negative of the Caribbean Carnivals as she could make them. She meant to overwhelm Yeoman with them so that she would escape Yeoman's barrage about her kingdom's carnival. She would avoid the type of intelligent shaming she suffered in the hands of Yeoman at the Black Culture Week exhibition where she roped herself into Yeoman's virulent tongue-lashing. She took to a lonely lawn and sat down to study the questions on her list. They would silence Yeoman to her design, she believed, as she went over them one by one:

One: Like in Venice, why was the history of carnival turned upside down in Caribbean and North America cities?

Two: Why did most parade groups choose to name themselves after European gods and goddesses instead of those of Ila and Africa?

Three: Why were only the French aristocrats and Roman generals mocked, and people like Japeedoe, the evil post-graduate of looting and slavery, spared?

Four: Why were 'boobing' and near-nakedness allowed so shamelessly among women carnivalists?

Five: Where were the talking drums? Had no one ever heard of them in these parts of the world?

Six: Why are lesbo-gay parties allowed? Why were the different-sex parties not merged, even if forcefully, to compel the revellers to interact in true Biblical friendship?

The questions were satisfying to Jacq up to that point, the point she rose and started to walk slowly to Yeoman's office. She

393

made a few steps, stopped and sat quietly for another while, meditating in tergiversation:

One – History: She, Jacq, should have no business bothering herself about any carnivalist turning the history on its head. After all, who dictates how stories and events are turned into history but the winner? Japeedoe of old turned history against Tantalo while the reigning Japeedoe turned it against her, Jacq. The Caesars, Cleopatra, all turned history against their conquests in the same way the winners of the World Wars were not exceptions. If future Ilas worked hard, they too could change the cultural history of Ila to what they would want it to be.

Two – Parade naming: Where is the sin in a group or a person naming itself or himself what it or he was most comfortable with? Did the group aliases of 'Duiker Women Beauty Society' and the men's 'Cat Backline Wrestlers' not exist in Ila? Did one of her ancestors not proudly answer to 'Tiger'? Was Ben's ancestral nobility in Glasgow not represented by among other things, two stark lions struggling to wear a human crown?

Three – Mocking: If due to a cross between stupidity and foolishness Ilas could not mock their brutally stealing leaders, why on earth should she expect the carnivalists of the Caribbean islands and the Gulf of Mexico to do that for Ila?

Four – Near nakedness: Jacq concluded she was just being jealous of the total freedom she found with the women revellers. Back home in her kingdom, carnivals or no carnivals, women must wrap up like Egyptian mummies, with the eyes hardly being seen. Over there, the near-nakedness – or total nakedness – could only be 'certified' by the same cheaters, men who ensured the women were never heard. Why now should she, Jacq, see the women as being too emancipated? In Venice, was it not such an extension of freedom and openness that enabled her to parade in St Mark Square and win prizes? Was she now saying the freedom was too much?

Five – Talking drums: Most likely that the carnivalists had considered the bad aspects of the talking drums – their ability to turn two friends into two opposing warriors through what they sounded out. Or probably, they had identified the vanity and arrogance that usually engulfed the people who the drums chose to praise for money.

Six – Lesbo-gayness: Though she believed this was terribly immoral of the members, she only hoped God would raise someone to preach to the groups, the words of Leviticus 18:22.

Surely now, she agreed the problem before her was beyond questions of antagonism. She looked at the sheet again, squeezed it into a ball and flung it away on the grass. Ali's urge that she should plan and act now had gripped her, and she knew she required help to make the right plans. She advanced to her 'litter', picked it up and finally walked towards Yeoman's office smoothing out the 'ball' as she went along.

"Now, your questions, Jacq?" Yeoman was the first to ask as soon as Jacq walked in. He was eager, and had been waiting. "And let me see where I can help. Where I can't, we may have to replay the relevant tape. I still have them here."

"Questions? What questions, sir?" Jacq was emphatic.

"Yesterday you asked me some, which I could not answer. You promised to bring the full list today, didn't you?"

"What I have with me today is more important than questions. The films you showed me actually provided more answers than my questions. Today I need your help, sir. That is what I have here."

"My help? How?" Yeoman was unable to hide his surprise.

"If only I could impart on Ilas a bit of what I have experienced about carnivals here, that would have been very useful. I need to plan this out. Can you help me?"

For a moment Yeoman gave no response. He engaged his thoughts in searching for the complexities of the dangers and costs that must be involved. Was Jacq expecting him to plan with her the formation of krewes, the setting up of Schools of Samba, or the teaching of carnival lyrics in French and Portuguese to the population of her kingdom, Ila? "But you are banned from Ila, aren't you?" he asked her at last.

"Japeedoe and Sese: may it be those two that God will ban," she swore. "With your help especially, I can overcome the banishment. That I know."

"Why me? You are from Ila; and you won prizes in Venice!"

"Why you? I hope you will forgive my words. By ancestry you suffered from the actions of the masks and masquerades of Ila. You grew in the Caribbean to witness and cherish the development of carnivals into the existing modernism. You are an art teacher who had taken part in the Mardi Gras and has assisted curious visitors to carnivals. Were you not at the head of that masterly planning in the College, there would have been nothing like the Black Culture Week.

"As for my success in Venice, it was all down to luck. Now is a different circumstance where I need your help, where I must not fail."

"But Jacq…"

"There's no 'but', sir. Please say you will help me. Now is the time for me to plan how and when I will enter Ila. I must not fail. My worry is that Rev Ali Jaiye and Ben Mackinnon had promised to assist. But they want me to show them the plan first – to get serious with it. Now is the time you can help me with it. I am not ashamed to beg you to help me." Jacq remained pitifully persistent.

"You must have been quite pleased – to be so honoured by the two big men."

Yes, it's looking like that. They promised to make Uggi and Victor available if I need them. But then, you are in a more central position than any of them."

"What then do you expect me to do – to assist in planning 'schools' and 'krewes'?"

"Not necessarily. To enter Ila I will need the logistics, the materials, masks, masquerades, all the things we have both seen."

"You mean just some of them, Jacq. Some will do for your case. We are talking of a mammoth project to be executed in dangerous circumstances, under the machetes of your King Japeedoe. Mammoth projects require mammoth planning, Jacq!"

"Yes, sir. Rev Ali Jaiye made me to realise that – that it is way beyond just asking questions."

CHAPTER TWELVE

Return Preparation – Glasgow

The principal's smiling face beamed inside the main hall of Glasgow College. He was pleased that a theme as presumably ordinary as 'Modern Face and Body Masking' could be so successfully developed into a project of great dimensions by his staff and students. He was glad Yeoman Smith, his senior arts teacher, successfully convinced him into supporting it. He was pleased the funding and time he approved for the students of arts and fashion departments who undertook the project had not been a waste.

The satisfaction followed him as he mixed with a few special visitors who were in the hall to see the students' works before they would be taken down from the assessment stands. The visitors were that early so that after the viewing, they would still arrive at the college's graduation ceremony following later at the Peoples Palace.

Ben Mackinnon and Rev Ali Jaiye were among those distinguished visitors. They were the men Yeoman and Jacq used to gain the principal's approval for the project. The principal was happy to meet them, and happier to conduct them round personally.

For their own reasons, all unknown to their host, Ben and Ali were equally excited. At every mask and costume the students displayed, the men stopped, commended it, and asked relevant questions. The interaction indicated to the principal that the two men were not disappointed – Ben over his increased art students sponsorship and prizes, Ali over his making the Cathedral to increase its annual donation to Glasgow College.

Inside the Peoples Palace, Yeoman was the first to reap the dividend from the students' project. In his welcoming speech, the principal praised the hard work and excellent vision of Yeoman Smith as a lecturer. He described Yeoman as a clever man who had acquired a wealth of professional experience from people, countries and continents. Fortunately for Glasgow College, the principal identified further, Yeoman had used the experience to beautify the ugliness, widen the narrowness, and develop the underdevelopments in the Arts Department. He announced how, due to Yeoman's suggestion, the institution's Black Culture Week was being expanded to end on a weekend with a fully costumed children carnival. Approval and support had been received from both the Cathedral and the *City*, and a committee was already mapping out the carnival's final route – likely to be from Peoples Palace to Royal Exchange Square, George Square, the great Clyde River on the Bridge Street, and back to Peoples Palace. After thunderous applause, he announced Yeoman Smith as the new Head of the Department of Arts, resulting in more thunderous applause.

It was Yeoman's moment and he knew it. He stood up and waved proudly in acknowledgement of the ovation. As he waved, he wished one of the fellow lecturers he was sitting in-between was Jacqensica Nek. He would have made her rise with him, wave with him, and share with him in the success and glory that shouldn't be his alone.

"She was the architect of this, its real architect," Yeoman echoed soberly to himself as he sat back on his seat. Yes, he remembered the day after he watched the carnival films with Jacq. That day he expected some rude questions from her but got some humble requests instead. That day, just four months ago, he had seen the wiser side of Jacqensica Nek:

"You can get some masks for me, can't you, please?" Jacq had asked her teacher after he had agreed to help with the planning. "I would want everyone to welcome me wearing one on that day."

"You can't be serious," he remembered himself telling Jacq. "Where do you expect me to get them from – New Orleans or Port of Spain? Where will the money come from to mask a whole town?"

"You can have them made here, right in the college," she was sure.

"How?" he had asked, totally unaware of where she was going.

"You will soon give the students their end of year projects to do, isn't it? Let each of us, the arts students, produce and submit a mask as a project. It will produce enough to choose from, and to modify if necessary."

Jacq's suggestion had taken Yeoman by surprise, disabling him from giving an immediate response. The suggestion he knew to be wise, but it did have two problems. One, the wisest of the students must have already had in his mind what projects he wanted to do, and must have been gathering materials for them in preparation. Two, if the college must impose additional projects, then it must provide the materials for them. Two serious problems he believed Jacq could not envisage.

"So you want everyone in Ila to mask up for your return?" he had asked her, smiling. "And you want the masks made by your course mates?" he had ended, laughing loudly, to Jacq's uneasiness.

"I wish I could think of something better," she had remarked.

"Yes Jacq, you are smart; accept that from me. It isn't that I am dismissing or mocking your wishes and suggestions," he had complimented and assured her. "But have you imagined a return where every face is masked? Can you still remember the aspect of Venice you criticised?"

He remembered how the questions had humbled her and sunk her self-confidence – which actually, he had enjoyed.

"Like I said, I wish I can suggest something better."

"And I said your suggestions are okay." He was still laughing. "But it's great fun when some faces are masked with unusual masks; and greater fun when other parts of the body besides the faces are also masked for a carnival. Now you can see why we, at Mardi Gras, are steps ahead of Africa and Europe," he had teased again, the lightness of the taunting causing Jacq a smile of amusement.

"You know what, Jacq?" he had continued. "We are going to include other facial decorations, as well as costumes."

Jacq had remained silent, beaming at Yeoman's mouth.

"I will convince the School of Fashion to do the costumes," he had hardly ended when Jacq had leapt on her feet and gave him a warm 'thank you' hug.

On freeing from Yeoman, her hug had become a crazy impromptu dance. Then, all of a sudden, she had stopped, looking dejected. "But how can I be of any help to you in the planning? It looks like I can only pretend, and submit my own project."

"Quite the opposite, Jacq," he had countered. "You will have initial roles to play; and should remember that the whole project ends with you because it's about you – about your re-entry into Ila society."

"Initial roles? I can't wait for you or anyone to tell me what they are!"

"You said Ben Mackinnon and Rev Jaiye promised to help you, didn't you?"

"Yes, I did. They did."

"Now we should exploit that promise, coupled with their recent warmth to me. We must seek their financial support for the college and for the project. We have to confide in both men what our targets are. With more of Ben's donations and sponsorships, and Rev Jaiye's bearing on the church for the same, our problems will be minimal. With leverage from the two men, I will be able to convince the School of Fashion and the principal."

"I will pray it turns out that way with the principal, sir. But can it be that easy with him?"

"With finances being available, the first major hurdles would have been scaled anyway. I know the principal will authorise the funds for the required materials, and allow the hours and space. He will do that – for his soft spot for the arts."

"That sounds quite heart-lifting," Jacq had noted, to Yeoman's nod. "But can I extend the optimism with another suggestion?"

He had not understood her, but given her a go-ahead all the same.

"Since you are sure the students will produce the masks and costumes – many of them – can we select some for a Children's Carnival here in Glasgow? The principal and the city would admire you for that.

"You again!" he had screamed at Jacq. "Your brains never stop thinking of carnivals, and your heart ever pulsates for masks. The City hasn't even got an adult carnival and you are talking of masked children's. We are not sure yet of how many masks or costumes the college project would produce yet you are talking of an excess for the children's. Jacq, aren't you counting the chickens…"

"Well, sir, you led with the first optimism for a reason; it won't be a sin to join you. There was no Cultural Week before you had it established. It won't be out of place if you should upgrade it to ending with a children's carnival.

"It doesn't have to be rigorous – just a short procession of fun for the children. It could be from the Palace to St George Square, or any of mother Clyde's bridges and back. Just a happy procession that will make the children sing and dance to 'Let Glasgow Flourish' under the banner of *Lion Rampant*."

He had seen Jacq's input as a sort of social and intellectual incitement. It had given him courage that had driven him to approach the principal with the suggestion as his own. The principal had accepted it, and had been emboldened by it to approach, seek and obtain support from old sponsors like Ben Mackinnon and the Cathedral; and new ones like the City Merchants and City Council! Bravo, that the student project had been successfully concluded, with increased numbers of student awards. Bravo that the children's carnival would happen. He wished Jacq was actually sharing the glory with him on that setting!

Only the principal and himself, Yeoman, had so far been the acclaimed public winners in the whole show. Very soon he was certain, before the graduation ceremony would end that day, Jacq's fellow students and college staff would also applaud her when the principal announced her as the winner of the prize for The Best Arts Student. It would be a good consolation for him to have the chance of showing his indebtness to her, to compliment her warmly. That chance came within the hour – and Yeoman promptly seized it.

"Congratulations, Jacq," Yeoman tapped Jacq on the shoulder, after he found her at a photo session in the beautiful Palace garden. Uggi was beside her laughing and watching as Jacq was about to take a group photograph of Ali, Ben and Victor. "Am I interrupting a happy moment?"

"Oh, Mr Smith, thank you!" Jacq responded. "And congratulations too, for your promotion." She stopped the camera, turned and hugged him. "You have interrupted nothing. If you have, it's a good one!"

"Congratulations and thanks to both of you too," Yeoman said as he swiftly walked to Ali and Ben, and shook their hands warmly. "Without you, none of us would be here now."

"Yeoman, you are a sound teacher," Ben complimented. "I am happy for you that the principal recognised your great worth today. Each time we discussed your department, he would bring you up as a good pillar of that department. Actually, I am surprised the announcement didn't come earlier.

"You must join me now in the photos. Uggi will take the first shots. We are all one big family, aren't we, everybody?"

"Of course, we are," Ali answered on behalf of 'everybody' now happy and laughing. "Or, where can you ever find such a big family – of artists, intellectuals and clergies?"

Jacq insisted on her clicking the shutter first. She was followed in turn by Yeoman, Uggi, Victor, Ben and Ali. Another guest at the graduation was humbly waylaid by Yeoman to finish the session by taking the pictures for the grand group, the 'big family'. Then they all set to disperse and go home.

"Jacq, and my other big students," Yeoman's voice rang out, in-grouping Victor and Uggi with Jacq. "I am inviting you for a dinner. When can we fix it to, to make it easier for you?"

"Ah, really?" Ben spoke before Yeoman could have an answer. "You will fix it to no time, Mr Head of Department, because I am inviting everybody here now instead. Sunday evening after the church service, in my humble home!"

* * *

Yeoman was the last to arrive at Ben Mackinnon's house for the dinner. Because he wasn't a Cathedral goer he couldn't directly join Ben, Ali, Jacq and Victor from the church to Ben's house after the church service. By the time he arrived the table was ready, lavishly set.

Rev Ali Jaiye rose to formally get the party going. "Can someone – Mr Smith or Jacq – please bless this table?" he asked. In such a gathering dominated by senior clergy, it would be doctrinally abnormal not to show appreciation to the host for providing the dinner, and to Jesus Christ for giving that host the means to make the provision.

Yeoman's eyes met that of Jacq with each asking the other if its carrier would do the prayer. Yeoman felt he couldn't do it. He felt too shy and amateurish. "Jacq, please do the prayers for us," he smartly passed it on; and Jacq took it.

It surprised Rev Ali Jaiye that ten minutes into the dinner no one had spoken about the graduation day or any of the events that were closely linked with it. Perhaps everybody wanted another day for it. Perhaps everyone was waiting till after the end of the dinner. Perhaps each person was expecting the other to start it. Perhaps, perhaps he, Ali, should table it, start what was most memorable in his mind. "Why has nobody mentioned the graduation day?" he threw the question at everybody, jointly. "Or was it too good to be remembered?"

"Nothing could ever better it," Ben answered, for others too. "It's the fallout that has assembled us here now, isn't it? It's why I am hosting the new Head of Department of Arts before his principal would!

"The masks and costumes of your students were great. They were finer for purpose than I ever dreamt. They were as artistically scary as they were inviting – as they should be!

"Mr Smith, you are brilliant – brilliant!" he concluded cheerfully.

"Thank you, Mr Mackinnon – and Rev Jaiye," Yeoman responded. "Thanks to you both. Your support perfected the successes that were achieved."

"And that reminds me of a serious omission that needs correcting," Ali raised a point. "Our young men here, Victor and Uggi, deserve the accolade too. Neither Ila nor Jacq would have come this far without them, our great tourists!"

"That's correct, sir," Jacq readily agreed. "Without them my body would have rotted to the bones wherever it would have been thrown. May be my daughter's and husband's have rotted already. I dreamt they..." She was crying.

"Oh, not again, Jacq," Rev Jaiye interrupted and stopped Jacq. "This is a gathering for joy, prayer and hope."

"Reverend is right," Ben agreed. "I suggest we suspend further talk about this until after dinner." None of them questioned the suggestion.

"Is it possible for you to spare more time, Mr Smith?" Ali asked at the end of the dinner.

"Yes. Is everything still okay?"

"All is okay. Quite okay. Just to use this opportunity to discuss the next steps, about Jacq's trip back to Ila."

"Sure, Rev Jaiye. I have the time for that. Actually I expected it."

It appeared Ali and Yeoman had spoken for everyone at the table with the topic they had raised. Ben moved them to the chairs of his living room.

"Have you made further plans with your students' products?" Ali asked Yeoman as soon as everyone was seated. "The principal told us some of them would serve for the kids' carnival as well."

"That's true," admitted Yeoman. "But that won't affect us negatively. The children's carnival was actually thought of and used as a selling point to the principal.

"And it reminds me of something else, a disclosure you all don't know. It's also a positive one; and I feel this is the ideal forum to make it."

"Yes? Go on then," Ben challenged Yeoman.

"It's about the children carnival the principal mentioned to you," Yeoman began. "Actually, it was Jacq who suggested it. She guessed the principal would love it because Glasgow would attribute its origin to Glasgow College. For that he would support the arts and costumes project. Even the idea of the masks' project was Jacq's."

Yeoman's revelation had everyone gagging for more. For a few seconds after he had stopped speaking, the room still remained quiet.

"But, sir, it's unnecessary to disclose this," Jacq, unprepared, told her teacher and broke the silence. She was certainly embarrassed. "There's no need for the revelation, sir."

"There is; there is now, Jacq," Yeoman maintained unapologetically.

"You didn't mean all you have said, Mr Smith, did you?" Ben Mackinnon asked.

"Yes, that's the truth," Yeoman confirmed. "I only expanded her suggestion to include the costumes."

"That's most incredible," Ali said. "Now I won't be surprised if the suggestion to approach me and Mr Mackinnon for our support and approval came from Jacq. Did it, Mr Smith?"

"No. She said you had already given your support and encouragement, that you have urged her to present a plan she would be happy with. She said the same of Mr Mackinnon.

"Only the principal she was still scared of then – of what he could do. Fortunately with your joint input, we got round it."

"That should be enough about me, sir," Jacq leaned towards Yeoman and sought silence from him.

"No, not yet. Not after I have got the joint applause you deserve...

"For Jacq, everybody, please!"

In the standing ovation of the 'family', Jacq sat, her head lowered onto her hands, in tears of joy. She was too shy to look into any of the faces that focused on her.

"Good, really good that everything has been moving remarkably well," Ben commenced when the applause had died down. "This is a credit to everyone here. Now we must talk of what we have to do to achieve the final goal. May be we should first listen to what Jacq has to suggest. I am sure she's full of ideas."

"Oh Jesus," remarked Jacq, frightful and unprepared. "Please, sir, I would decline. I just want to listen and go with whatever you all put forward.

"What can I say when my uncle is here. He has more experience of Ila and Glasgow than I will ever have.

"What's my experience of masks and artefacts compared with Mr Mackinnon's?

"My arts teacher is also here in our midst. He knows all about masks, masquerades and carnivals.

"And so are Victor and Uggi. They participated and knew how it really felt and should feel in Ila.

"Or at best, if I have something to add as you go on, I will not hesitate to add it."

"But still, we must start from you," Victor came in. "When do you have in mind to return to Ila?"

Jacq replied she wanted to be in Ila for the next festival, six months away, just before Christmas.

"Well then," said Victor, "it might require me and Uggi to be there before her, before the carnival. Though we are supposed to be there for the festival but it might not be easy for Jacq if we don't go first."

Yeoman asked Victor for more light on what he had just said.

"That next festival is when Uggi and I are to be there. Jacq is now telling us she wants to be there, at the same time. There could be trouble for her over there unless we find time to go before her to find out the true situation of things. We must prepare the way first."

"Victor is right," Yeoman agreed. "He makes a point that is worth serious consideration."

"Yes, I think so too," Ben also agreed. "This means we don't have the time basically. Jacq might have to delay going back. Besides, we are not sure if the masks Mr Smith has in the college are enough. Are they, Mr Smith?"

"No, they might not be," Yeoman rooted the pessimism. "Worse is that the College Calendar poses an obstacle: with the long vacation just starting, we can't get the students to do more in the next two months, and it will mean we have just three months after the vacation."

Yeoman also reminded them that the principal might not allow all the masks to be shipped to Ila because he was not aware of the real reason behind the project in the first place. He would want most of them preserved for the children's carnival.

"In that case, we can take those I have in the studio and join them. It may ease the pressure. I have told Jacq she could come for them."

"And I have said no. I still say so. Those in the studio are too priceless for a thing like this. I am sure there are other ways to go round this."

"Well, unless we can supplement by buying some pieces from Venice," Ben suggested.

"Alright then, can I suggest something?" Jacq asked.

"Oh yes, Jacq," answered Ben Mackinnon.

"Supposing Mr Smith tells the principal how the college, through the Department of Arts, could earn extra cash from the sale of masks and costumes, starting with what we want now. The church would opt to be the college's first customer, and give the principal a tight delivery time." She paused, pricked by the discomfortingly dead silence by everyone in the room with her.

"E em...," she dragged, "I am sorry; it's only a suggestion."

Yeoman could not help leading the others in a big smile, and another round of applause for Jacq. "That's my student," he claimed, "– more of a pragmatic businesswoman than a student!"

"And our friend," Victor joined in, "– more of two women ..."

"Than a woman!" Uggi completed Victor's extension of Yeoman's complimentary joke.

"And my great niece," Ali took his turn, "– definitely more of a good priest!"

"I believe that will work with the principal, to give us more time and space," Yeoman said. "Only for variety could we need some pieces from Venice – and Port of Spain – if necessary.

"With this anticipation what should be next is to consider how soon the two of them could go. It has to be soon. We would need their report to finalise the project."

Ben agreed with Yeoman. Victor and Uggi should go now that the college was on vacation. Going now to assess the actual need would reduce the cost of preparation in Glasgow. Though King Japeedoe was not expecting them before the next festival but they could tell him they were there to know his needs for the carnival.

"Actually, I suggest only one of them should go – and this week," Ali said. "I am also of the opinion that it should be Victor." His secondary reason was that sending just one person then would save them some money which would be better used towards speeding up the project. Primarily, King Japeedoe and his chiefs, from all indications, would be happier dealing with Victor. Now that voice communication between Glasgow and some areas of the kingdom are possible, they from Glasgow would be able to keep in touch with Victor about what he had to do, as well as watch over him.

"Victor, what's your opinion?" Yeoman asked. Yeoman was the only one there who didn't understand why King Japeedoe and his chiefs would be happier with Victor.

"I will go – happy to go," Victor agreed. He knew Ali was right for many reasons: First, from when he was there last time, he realised that an Ila person would show more love – and blind obedience where necessary and unnecessary – to a guest or a visitor of a skin different in colour from his own black. Such a different skin could be white, yellow or toned, and it would not change his attitude. He remembered how all eyes were on his pair with Uggi while they were in Ila, and how Glawanu had attributed their success with King Jap to their colour and foreignness.

Secondly, for being the only one in his group to complete the harrowing initiation into the *Order of The Eagle*, he had won the respect of the priest, Sese and King Jap.

Thirdly, he realised how ruthlessly he was made to perform as the female of the Jemba Couple masquerades before the king and Sese.

"Are there specific things of need you want to go with?" Yeoman asked Victor.

"Of course, yes," Ali answered before Victor would. "You don't go to Ila without being basically self-sufficient in your needs. It isn't that the kingdom doesn't have enough of their own to satisfy its people. It is that the ruling gang continuously steals what are for the people, leaving the people to beg for every item from their guests and visitors. Oh yes, Victor will go with whatever he would need, and watch over them."

"Apart from personal needs, would he not go with some gifts?" Yeoman asked again.

"All will be taken care of. The personal needs are the most important; and he should go for them now. Gifts would not be a problem; he might not need to buy one."

"I don't understand," said Yeoman.

"I don't either, Ali followed. "Which community is ever so easily swayed by gifts more than Ila? Gifts are important among what control the souls of the people of my kingdom.

"We were once told of an old belief that still exists about my Ila: If an Ila man is your host, he asks you what 'gift' you have brought for him; if he is your guest he asks what 'gift' you have left for him!" Everybody laughed.

"I don't dispute that," said Ben. "But unless their appetite has changed the only gift they understand is money. From what I know they have equated that money with kola, equating their age-old traditional fruit of communion to monetary extortions."

Ben Mackinnon went on to give two reasons why he was suggesting monetary gifts. "Have all of you forgotten that one

411

Scottish pound has a hundred pence in it, and a hundred pounds ten thousand pence?" he asked the sitting. "Even if Victor has to go with the number of pence that would go round the whole Ila population of about 250,000 people, that's just 2,500 pounds! It's what a single person can singly and easily tuck in his pocket. I am not saying this is the exact amount he should carry. It could be more, or less. But certainly, whatever cash would go round better.

"My second problem has to do with how to select who should deserve a gift. Should the gifts stop at the king and his households, at the high chiefs', chiefs' or the elders'? I know that Ila currently has eight high chiefs excluding the disgraced Dancemaster, nearly two hundred chiefs, and over two thousand elders. How do we ferry gifts across for such numbers – including their households, concubines and the like," Ben rounded up jovially, sending everybody into peals of laughter.

"Oh God, Ben, you are exaggerating things!" Ali cut in. "How did you get those numbers? Come on, Ben!"

"I am not exaggerating," Ben insisted. "Just give me one minute to show you I am not." Ben went to his study and fetched a large sheet of paper. Before he sat down he handed it over to Ali. "See the situation for yourself," he said to Ali as Ali took it and Ben turned to go to his chair. "That's how it is in Ila now," he added.

Ali browsed over the sheet with amazement. It was a hierarchical structure of Ila, dated less than a year ago. It detailed the whole of the kingdom, from the king to the number and distribution of the high chiefs, chiefs, elders and ordinary citizens who statistically totalled the over a quarter of a million population.

It also showed the kingdom's demographic set-up: two special quarters, one for the king the other for the high priest; seven general quarters, each headed by a high chief; twenty five compounds per quarter, each compound headed by a chief; a hundred and fifty houses per compound, each house headed by an elder; and an estimated ten persons per house, given Ila a population of about 260,000 people.

"How on earth did you get this, Ben?" Ali queried.

"Well, trade secret, I suppose…of my family business. We have always kept it as up-to-date as possible."

"Good document though, I must acknowledge," Ali said as he set off the paper on a round journey for others with him to see.

"So you see why I would have preferred that Victor goes mainly with money.

"Ask them to do something and they will demand for monetary gift first. Ask them not to do something and they will equally demand for a monetary gift. Give them a non-monetary gift which they can't sell for money and they will destroy it wilfully.

"So, Victor only needs to take some extra cash with him. Unless their appetite has changed – which I doubt very much."

"Are you talking of brown envelops?" Yeoman asked, joking.

"Yes, seriously," Ben answered. "It doesn't matter to them: brown, red, blue, orange, whatever. The receiver can always share what he wants and pocket what he wants. You just see their bulging eyeballs following it for its contents, from your pocket into theirs."

With the all round smile and laughter that followed Ben's analysis based on his father's experience of Ilas, everyone appeared to have agreed with him – until Victor spoke. "Daddy," he called, "that's only correct to some extent. Some of them will still want some gifts other than money. Do you know that last time we didn't leave with any of our things – watches, alarm clock, slippers, shower gels, soaps and shavers? It was either they begged for them or we gave them out voluntarily."

"Victor is right," Uggi backed his friend. "Special gifts to the king, queen, Sese and the palace servants will help him win their favours."

"Okay then," Ben went along. "We shall also see to that. Any other thing about the gifts?"

"Yes, for the shrines," Jacq added.

"The shrines?" Ali asked, unsure.

"Yes, sir, gifts for the shrines – at least the Main Shrine. They are in there all the year round. It is the kingdom's institute where they are happy to gather and advance their knowledge of evil. It could be helpful to keep them together there as much as possible until everything is over. A gift of money could be given to keep their bar inexhaustible. They are easily manoeuvred when they are drunk." Collectively they agreed with Jacq, in order to make things easier for Victor.

Jacq's next request for material gifts was for the members of the *Eagle*. They are clandestinely nearest to the king; they were the most effective tools he used for stealing and sharing. She believed that a gift from Victor who they still took as their member would not only endear Victor to them, but would as well put him above any suspicion.

"And the last I can think of," she was concluding, "is equally important: a Cross pendant for Victor's neck, and a mini Bible he will carry in his pocket." She was pleased no one raised an objection.

Two weeks after the dinner, Victor was prepared, ready and on his way to the kingdom of Ila.

* * *

When Victor's jeep stopped at Bilitie Inn, he found himself before a different building. It was neater, freshly painted, and extended into adjoining sides and back plots. He was pleased Bilitie had attained such an improved look just within the nineteen months he and Uggi last left the hotel.

Victor's name, more than his colour, rang a strong bell with the male receptionist. With modest discreetness, the receptionist excused himself to speak with his boss first about the new arrival.

"Victor, from Glasgow, aren't you?" the manager came out of his office and asked Victor directly, to be sure.

"Yes, that's correct," Victor answered. "Are you expecting me?" he queried, believing that no one connected with this project had told any native he would be coming.

"No, I'm not. But most important is to thank you for remembering our hotel. I am Latief. I was here last time – as assistant manager then.

"What happened to your friend, Uggi? You came with him last time."

"Uggi is well but busy.

"I can see a lot improvement has gone into this hotel."

"Thank you, Victor," the manager responded. "Actually there have been changes all over Ila, though they don't all mean improvements. Later when you have settled down you will see some of them."

That 'later' came so fast, just as the manager was returning to his office and two of his staff were getting Victor's things from the jeep:

A young man crashed in through the main entrance, shoving aside the manager and knocking down himself and one of the case-carrying hotel staff in the ensuing collision. The crasher recovered first; and with no time for explanation or apology, he fled past Victor with the barest breath remaining in him.

Through the first flip door, he ran into the inner part of the hotel. His apparent pursuers, two junior masquerades, the type Victor had seen at the Royal Market last time he visited, saw him disappear; and they continued the hot chase – and search.

Victor, quite unprepared, was shaken. "What is going on here?" he angrily asked the manager. "Isn't your masquerade carnival another five months?"

"I am sorry, Victor," the manager apologised for the offence he neither committed nor could stop. "That's one of the changes too. Nowadays, Fire Spirit deploys the junior masquerades anywhere and in anytime. He and the king said it's for the security

415

of the kingdom. But before you go back you shall see that it is for their grip over the kingdom, for the security of their pockets."

Faster still was the capture of the man the masquerades searched for inside the hotel. Within minutes, they captured him and dragged him out by his shirt and trousers. He was bleeding heavily from the nose, having been knocked down and dealt some blows.

"What has he done?" Victor asked the masquerades as they pulled their victim past him without any notice of him. Victor, infuriated, ran and overtook them, stopping them by the reception.

"What has he done that you want to kill him?" he asked boldly. He wondered his luck to ask this sort of question at every entry he would make into Ila. "His nose is bleeding; what have you done to him?" he queried the spirits firmly.

"You ask him what he has done to himself," one of the masquerades answered Victor.

"He was fleeing from the tax he has to pay," the second masquerade boldly told Victor the man's offence. "He thought we masquerades couldn't run, that he's the only one with the limbs and leaps of the cheetah. Or that Bilitie is a sanctuary no one must enter." The masquerade was scornful of their detainee, and of the place he sought for his refuge.

"What tax?" Victor asked the second masquerade.

"The little tax that was demanded from him," the first masquerade replied. "'He who profits from the Royal Market must pay the crown'; or is that not what they say?"

"But I paid," the arrested man swore protestingly before Victor and the hotel manager. "I had just paid to two spirits when these two came. They saw me make the payment and the spirits who took it confirmed to them they took it. These two waited for the first two to disappear; then they turned to me and demanded the same tax again."

"The huge profit you made must have turned you insane," the first masquerade insulted the captive. "Good, you confessed you made the payment to neither of us."

To Victor, the man's story sounded weird, and the masquerades' behaviour brazenly unfair. He was not aware of what the taxation system in Ila was, or what changes it had experienced. He wasn't aware that everything in Ila nowadays, from the ordinary tree leaf to the God-given air, attracted a Royal-Sese tax. The amount imposed is impromptu, undefined and indefinable. It was usually pronounced by the junior masquerades, who were also its collectors.

The collection was always violent; the masquerade-collectors must compete to bring the highest amount to Sese Abram, their de facto boss. Maintaining the highest collections was a self-recommendation before Sese and Jap for promotion to carrying a senior mask. A junior masquerade thus had a special reward each time he was able to force a trader who had already paid his tax to pay another to him directly. Like the trader, the masquerade knew no one fights a spirit – you could only pay him or appease him in some other way!

"But I..." the man started to explain himself again.

"To whom, did you hear him?" the second masquerade angrily stopped the captive talking.

"So what is going to happen now?" Victor asked.

"Two things, the second masquerade snapped. "First, my friend, the manager, you will always look after your door because of silly men like this one.

"Secondly, he will have to pay. We may have to follow him to his house to fetch us his tax."

"How much is the tax?" Victor asked. Seeing another hostage case so soon on entry was becoming too much for him.

"Equivalent to three pounds or five dollars only," the same second masquerade said. "Do you want to pay for him?"

Victor was shocked to hear such an intelligent and calculating mouth from behind the mask. How had the masquerade managed to narrow down correctly the zone he came from and know the currency they spent there? What plaque has so devastated the

417

local currency so much that their spirits had to make transactions in foreign currencies? Another of the changes? Victor was puzzled. He would pay for the hostage.

The masquerades trailed their eyes intensely after Victor's hand as it searched his pockets for the amount they demanded. To them it was a search taking too long. It came out with two pound coins and tendered them. "Here, the only coins I could find. I have only notes."

"Not to worry," one of them said, after swiftly securing the coins from Victor, "bring a note of five pounds sterling. We shall give you your change."

Victor's empty hand returned to his pocket. When it re-surfaced it was with some sterling notes in which was squashed a chained pendant. Victor put the chain out of his way by throwing it over his head, round his neck, to leave the pendant dangling before resting on his chest. It gave him the chance to sort out a fiver. "Keep it; no change," he said, tendering the note to the masquerade holding the coins.

"Hold it; don't take it!" the other masquerade restrained his fellow spirit, holding his wrist. "Return the money he gave you," he further ordered.

"We will allow him to go," he turned to Victor and said. "I swear we will."

"Swearing means nothing here. You would release him only to re-arrest him. Take the fiver, keep what you already have from me, and let him go now."

"Alright, go now," the last spoken masquerade ordered the bleeding detainee. Readily, the detainee thanked his luck and Victor, and jumped out of Bilitie, painfully but almost with the same speed he got inside it.

The masquerades glued their eyes to Victor's chest – at the *Eagle* pendant – and were frightened that Victor would not take the coins back. In panic, the holder of the coins placed them on one of Victor's luggage and the two masquerades ran out.

"So, you are now a special friend of the king," Latief addressed Victor.

"I don't know about that," Victor replied.

"You know why they fled in disgrace? They saw your pendant, and feared Sese and His Highness would punish them for failing to recognise it earlier before they disrespected you.

"Do they know you are here – in our hotel?"

"No, not yet."

"Soon they will know. Those ones will tell them a VIP is in town, here."

"They won't," the staff said, "because they would be in trouble for their demands."

"But they would be in bigger trouble if they should fail to report the sighting of an important visitor," the manager believed. "Are they no more the royal policemen?"

"Thieves serving thieves – all thieves incorporated," murmured the staff.

"Anyway, Victor," said Latief, the manager, "that's Ila for me – and you. Welcome to Ila – again.

CHAPTER THIRTEEN

Return Preparation – Ila

"Did you say Glawanu – from the palace?" Victor asked the hotel staff standing outside his room door, notifying him of Glawanu's request.

"Yes, sir. He is with the white horse, and another *ẹmẹṣẹ̀*, male slave. His Highness already knew you are here."

Victor saw it as another of those changes – snooping and fast paced passing of information. He had barely checked in an hour ago! Perhaps Ila had madly caught up with the walkie-talkie and mobile phone technologies as Glasgow. Or how else could the king have known he was in town and sent the servants to fetch him?

"Did you say two of them?"

"Yes, sir, two of them with their horses. The white horse had no rider."

The white horse? It sounded nothing but pure insignificance to Victor. What was significant to him was that last time, when the same king sent two similar emissaries led by Glawanu to himself and Victor at the same hotel, there was no joy derived from them. Their coming this time too could mean trouble.

"Okay, lead only Glawanu to me," he told the staff, assuming that the sealed friendship between Glawanu and himself with Uggi was still intact. "The other man should wait behind."

"You again, Glawanu!" Victor shouted his happy greeting as soon as Glawanu was let into his room. They hugged and shook hands. "You are looking good. I can see the change."

"Thank you. You too."

"How did you know I am here?" he asked, seriously.

"Two masquerades saw you, didn't' they? We could doubt one, but not two. They ran to the palace."

"That's fast. The same way they ran into this hotel – those thieves!"

"Thieves? Those masquerades that saw you?"

Victor narrated what they had done.

"Then, did they see this insignia you wore on your neck? By the way it is different and beautiful."

"They saw it – in my hand and when I wore it. That's when they ran away."

"That's very serious – and strange," responded Glawanu in disbelief. "But let us leave that for now.

"Where's your friend?"

"I came alone; and I hope there's no problem with your coming this time."

"Oh no, Victor. The king always speaks highly of both of you, and more highly of you in particular. That's why he sent the white horse for you."

"'White Horse' whiskey?"

Glawanu explained. It was the horse meant only for those King Jap held dearest to himself. All the palace horses were brown, but a horse automatically became 'white horse' once fully tacked white: saddle, saddle-cloth embroidered with royal emblem girthed with leather, reins, wide nose band and a long leather shin boot on each of the four limbs between the hoof and the hock, all white.

"Brilliant, but I won't need the horse," Victor said after Glawanu's explanation. "I will be following you in my jeep. I have got some stuff for your king.

"But Glawanu, tell me what has changed, what I need to know before I meet the king."

"A lot has; but none of it threatens you. We don't have the time now because they are all waiting. But the good thing is that I now live outside the palace – with my young family. There will be plenty of time to talk. Besides, you will know exactly what you want from me after His Highness has spoken with you."

"Now, if I may ask you, Glawanu," said Victor, "Are you an *Eagle*? You know what that means, don't you?"

"I am not. Why do you ask?"

"Because King Jap seems to make you lead important errands."

"I am not. Once I wished I was. But the king wants me to himself and the palace only. I don't mind."

Victor opened one of his cases, took out a box of 'His and Hers' watches and handed it to Glawanu for him and his wife.

"Thank you," Glawanu said, jumping with joy as he opened it and its gold plate shone at his face. "Thank you. Now I am becoming a controller of watches from you!"

"And of money maybe!" Victor complemented, passing two crisp ten pound notes to him.

Glawanu expressed his gratitude and assurance of indebtedness. He was ready for the happiest ever return ride to King Japeedoe's palace, to end His Royal Highness' expectation.

Barely had Victor taken his seat when King Japeedoe walked into the Lion Hall. "Nice to see you, Victor; and what a surprise!" he welcomed him warmly. He was accompanied by Sese Abram, and each of them gave Victor a handshake. "And your jeep is elegant too," he added.

"So is this *Eagle* you have round your neck!" added Sese. "It's one that will best fit my Almighty! Great that you still respect the *Eagle*!"

"Thank you, Your Highness – and Sese. But how did you manage to see my jeep? I know you could see the pendant on me."

"Never mind," the king said, laughing loudly. "Yes, we can see it; and we are proud of you. My spirits first told us about the jeep. And I saw it as you drove behind the white horse into the Eagle Square."

"Eagle Square? Victor confused, asked.

"Yes," Sese intervened. "The old Kings Square now re-named and re-beautified."

"The spirits reported nothing about the insignia?"

"No," affirmed the king. "Probably they didn't see it. It's the first thing they must look for and report about our important visitors. But one of them said he knew you, *Eagle* or no *Eagle*."

When Victor had taken his seat, he fetched two envelopes from his backpack. One was fuller of Scotland pound notes than the other. He gave the fatter to King Jap and the other to Sese. They were his gifts for them, all the way from Glasgow. Both recipients were elated as they opened and peeped at the contents. "Please call me one of the women," King Jap told Sese, the order briefly sending Sese out of the hall.

"Thank you again, Victor," the king repeated, "and how long are you staying?"

"One week."

"Good. I have got a lot to discuss with you," the king said as Sese returned, accompanied by a beautiful woman in her thirties. Her dressing was beaded, simple but classy.

"This is my queen, Musli," he formally introduced her to Victor. "She's second to Azzanaite who you and Uggi met many times last time." Then he turned to Musli and introduced his guest, "Victor, the same Victor you've heard me speaking about."

Victor pondered over the introduction and wondered what had become of Queen Azzanaite. In the end he rested in the belief that it was neither the time nor his business to doubt King Japeedoe. His preparation from Glasgow would still take care of whoever was the queen, or were the queens of King Japeedoe.

423

"Please arrange dinner for three," Jap added after Musli had said her welcome and turned to go.

"Please, excuse me, Your Majesty," Victor called her, halting her slow steps. He handed her an envelope of the same bulkiness as the one he gave to Sese. Thanks flew out to Victor from her heart and mouth before she went out of the door, under Sese's look of envy.

"How about your friend?" the king resumed with Victor. Why hasn't he come?"

"He is very busy now; but he is coming as promised for the main festival."

"We won't miss him anyway if he doesn't come," Sese snapped.

"Yes, we won't," the king agreed and narrated why: After Victor and Uggi had gone with Jacq, the kingdom historians dug deeper into the Ologbonjaiye's family line that Uggi claimed. They discovered it was the line of a notorious traitor who lived generations ago. Then, the traitor betrayed the kingdom and the gods duly made him to pay for his sins. It must have been the same family trait in Uggi that caused him to faint before the rites of initiation, and prevented him this time from finding favour with time and return with Victor.

"And you know what?" he rounded up. "Our historians have now connected the blood of Jacq to that of Ologbonjaiye. See how evils swim in the blood!"

"Uggi is a good person, Your Highness," Victor defended his absent friend. "He's already preparing for the next festival; and he sent some presents for the shrine. They are all in the hotel."

"That's good then," the king brightened up. "Good for him redeeming the sins of his great-great-grandfather. Tell him I, the supreme custodian of the shrines, also need gifts from him." There was seriousness in his laughter.

"Now how is Jacq?" Sese threw the question that was uppermost in his and Jap's minds.

"Jacq, have you forgiven her? Or intend to do so?" Victor asked, unsure but not minding a miracle.

"What?" retorted Sese. "Have our ears heard you well?" He couldn't hide his hostility. "Would anyone ever contemplate doing that?"

"Sese, I only wanted to know," Victor calmed Sese's outburst and King Jap's noticeable uneasiness. "Even if anyone should contemplate that, there's no Jacq in existence to receive the gesture. She died six months ago."

"You don't mean that Victor, or do you?" Sese asked, in disbelief.

"On that Sunday morning her friends in the church thought she was at home. We at home thought she was in the church. Later we found her body in her room, already rigor-mortised."

King Jap was startled, Sese happier than shocked.

"Are you sure of that?" King Jap asked. "Her friends still believe nothing, nobody, death included, could ever touch her! They have that conviction that she is a powerful woman who will voluntarily climb a ladder and ascend into the heavens when she's tired of this world. It's urgent that you show us she is really dead."

"Jacq died, Your Highness, Victor emphasised. "Who would she have imitated with immortality? I have the proof in Bilitie."

"That calls for a big celebration," King Jap said, smiling gleefully, "isn't it, Sese?"

"It does, my Almighty," Sese agreed. "Remember the premonition I told you I had that time, about six months ago – that Jacq was dead? Yes, I saw her collapse inside one funny place of worship. She was not revivable; and her body wrapped in the black of the devil was tossed out of the window into a strong whirlwind that carried it away. My Almighty, if you had believed me the celebration would have started since then!"

For Victor, the dinner actually shattered some myths that had long surrounded the monarch. He witnessed Jap eat and drink normally, like any other person. He chewed rapidly and noisily with his small jaws, but talked least when eating. He told them talking when eating was the shortest route to getting choked and pissing out the food through the nostrils. He regularly broke the rapidity of his morselling to have some drinks, lecturing on how one must soften the block at the mixing stage, and not after it has settled in the mould.

Victor found the disproportion in the volume and assortment of the provision senseless and strange. The three diners were like three domestic cats gnawing at a dead elephant, like three cats licking the water of a large lake. It was delightful for Victor to discover that Sese's Almighty, the chief spirit cum custodian of the shrines, and the owner of Ila Kingdom, was a human after all!

"Thank you for the dinner, Your Highness," Victor appreciated. "It has been a long day and I must go and rest." It was 7 p.m. and both the king and Sese agreed with Victor.

"But before I go, Your Highness, I have a gift for you from my father."

"A gift from your father?"

"Yes, Your Highness." Victor carefully took out a six inch clear cube. The edges of the cube were trimmed golden. He gave it to the king, together with the stunning brass cobra it boxed: 'Order of the Cobra – From The Mackinnons to King Japeedoe'!

King Jap could not stop turning it round and round excitedly, finding the side from which to have a better view of the gem of a gift. Instantly, he connected the present to a re-occurrence of history.

"Mackinnon of Glasgow is your father?" Jap asked, completely astonished.

"Yes, Your Highness."

The king passed the gift to Sese. He rushed to Victor and clasped him in a hug that, in all whole-heartedness, combined royalty with a lost but newly found brotherhood. "Why did you not tell me this last time?" he asked as he let go Victor.

"You gave us no chance. At a time you wanted to, but Sese, I am sorry, intentionally blocked you. We could not talk. No one would listen..."

"I am not being made a scapegoat, am I?" Sese asked, quite displeased with Victor's claims.

"No, Sese," Victor replied. "Uggi and I knew you didn't mean to offend us with it. We know what patriotism is all about." Sese appeared calmed.

"It means your father has told you how well the Mackinnons are connected to the royalty of this great kingdom. I have never met your father, but my father and grandfather met him and shared the table with him here as I have just done with you. Just imagine the wonders of history!"

"No, that wasn't my father. That must be his father, Davey, or his grandfather, Thorburn Mackinnon.

"My father, Benjamin, shortened Ben, is the only Mackinnon who has never been here, due to his poor health. But he cherishes this kingdom, sent me then, and sends me now. It took him all his regards to make the *Cobra*. He believes the real members of the *Cobra* could be dead, but their offspring in the *Eagle* must still be alive, destined to prey with more precision and invincibility."

Victor's words set the excitement in King Japeedoe higher. He laughed with Victor, unable to fault Victor's presentation. Suddenly he saw Victor as he would any of his sons – well placed above any of his two queens!

"Look, Victor," the king called him. "You are sleeping in the palace today. The palace is your palace; and I am sure we can make it more comfortable for you.

"Sese," he turned, "go home now and come back the usual time tomorrow. Victor will be my guest tonight. And nothing will change that."

Sese however tried his luck at changing it. He was already having funny thoughts from when he saw Musli given the envelope of the same thickness as his. He was sad that King Jap shared the

427

table with Victor. He was frightened of the freshly backdated bond between King Japeedoe and the Mackinnons represented by Victor. He was cold and jealous that Victor would stay the night with his Almighty. "My Almighty," he said, "Victor seems to want to stay in Bilitie. I can escort him back and go home from there."

King Jap wouldn't have that. He wished Sese an instant good night.

* * *

The best Victor could get out of Jap after Sese had gone home was a permission to go to Bilitie Inn so as to take what he would need for his night stay in the palace. Easier and faster than he ever dreamt, he was pleased the project was being propelled fastest forward by bribery, the institutional masquerading of the kingdom. On his way to Bilitie he wondered continuously what the kingdom with its people really was: If Ilas were such big slave traders in those days, how now have they managed to become slaves and servants to money? Now he was sure that more gifts will definitely knock their senses dead enough to enable him achieve all he was there for. Appropriately, he had all the gifts for them ready in the hotel!

He was pleased that Jap had acceded to his request and allowed Glawanu to accompany him in the jeep to Bilitie. He used the opportunity to know where to always find Glawanu, where Glawanu lived with his wife and year old daughter.

Victor's 'innocent' response to him notwithstanding, Glawanu believed Victor had pulled a magic on King Jap. It was the only explanation he could think of as to how King Jap had invited Victor to be his guest for the night. It was a feat he had never seen anyone performed. Anyone, himself including.

"I have not seen Nek and Sariya," Victor opened a most important topic in his mind to his escort. "Where are they, and how are they? It is important I know what is happening to them."

Glawanu didn't know where they were presently. He learnt Sariya was ill somewhere. Before that she was being cared for by Bambo who Victor should still remember. This changed when the notorious Sam, the head of the palace guards, caught Bambo colluding with Nek and both of them were arrested. Since then Bambo has been 'removed from circulation' entirely. Glawanu prayed Nek's punishment wasn't even worse – that he had not already been 'stopped from circulation'. He, Glawanu would trace them as soon and as careful as possible.

"Please trace them; trace everything for me. I have something for you to make the tracing easy." He gave Gwalanu a small camera he had already loaded. "You can keep it after I have gone.

"In secrecy you will take the photographs of all you think I should know of, and I will exchange the film and take it with me."

"Thank you," Gwalanu, delighted, said. "I will do my best. But don't waste time before you ask His Highness about their condition. It's urgent."

And ask did Victor do as soon as he returned to the king, before he would be shown his guest room. He was bold without being rude. After all, both Nek and Sariya were core parts of the initial agreement with the king, a part of the problem at hand.

"Your Highness, what about Nek and Sariya?"

The king told him they were well, doing well.

"Can I see them?" Victor requested, the requisition visibly startling the king. "They are a part of the deal, aren't they?"

"They are. But first things first, Victor. You remember your friend's story of last year – of the tortoise who went to borrow a garment from his friend?" He broke into a hilarity guarded enough to conceal his fears. "My own priority comes first – the proof that she is dead. The proof was one of what you went for at Bilitie, wasn't it?"

"Alright, Your Highness, can we have a stool?"

"Will that be okay?" the king responded, pointing to one at the end of the hall, opposite to where they sat.

Victor replied it would be; and King Jap waited for no servant or for Victor to bring it. He walked to it and lifted it back to Victor. "Thank you, Your Highness," Victor remembered to compliment him. "Can I suggest you come and sit by me?"

"Oh good," the Almighty of Ila readily obeyed the command of a poor Glaswegian. He would have no fear seeing Victor's hand returning into the backpack again. The past dips had been thoroughly rewarding to him.

Victor's hand came out with three enlarged photo prints which, like in a game of poker, he carefully spread on the stool. The spread invited King Jap to stare at and then pick up the pictures. One by one, he turned both sides of each picture and looked. Then he waited for Victor's explanation.

"The pictures were taken the day after she died," Victor started, "which was the day she was buried. The photographs were of her coffin, lying-in-state, and her grave."

The explanation over, Victor paused for King Jap's reaction, expecting it to be a happy one.

"Didn't you say she died six months ago?" the king asked after a deep sigh.

"Yes."

"Why are the pictures so new?"

"They were taken six months ago; the printing was just last week for you to see. We didn't print them then because we felt they were of no importance to us."

"Why was the body so honoured?" He could see the gorgeous bridal dress intricately laced and embroidered, the arm-length gloves resting folded on her chest in a well cushioned open coffin. He could see the beautifully crafted white wood coffin on its own, and the stone grave in which both the body and the coffin were rested. "How did a criminal merit all that in Glasgow? Or was she made a queen before she died?"

"We did all that for her so that her death wouldn't put us in trouble – to escape suspicion."

"What suspicion? You said she died in her sleep, didn't you?"

"Yes, but you haven't asked how. Just sleep doesn't kill."

"Meaning?"

"We did it – I and Uggi. If we had not so cared for her body we could have been suspected of the murder. We induced her everlasting sleep."

"Did you?"

"Yes, Your Highness, we cleared her from the way forever. All the pictures are for your keep; I have the negatives to do mine."

King Jap turned on his seat and hugged Victor powerfully for a long time, his eyes wet. "Thank you," he started. "May she sleep forever and decay in the sleep like a felled log.

"May you and your friend live forever like the sky.

"As no one ever knows the source of the ocean, may no human know and block the source of your happiness.

"Today, Victor, you become the tortoise – you will age in health.

Today, you become the fly whisk – you will ever disperse your enemies like the whisk disperses the flies.

"Today, you become the baobab – no bad human hand may ever be long enough to chain you in.

"You become the new moon – you will ever be welcome and admired by both the young and the old.

"From now I trust you as mine, more than I have ever trusted any man, woman, or spirit in this kingdom."

Victor was satisfied he was on course. He took out the last picture he had with him and gave it to King Jap.

Intensely, the king looked at it and identified the object it contained.

Had it been customarily ethical he would have branded Victor a spirit of spirits. But he, as king, must accept no one as

431

being more 'spirit' than King Jap. And where there was a definite one, he, King Jap, must not be the one to recognise him. "How did you know *Elémpe*? He asked. "Where did you find it?"

"My father has it in his custody," Victor replied. He wanted to send it back to you – to where it came from."

"So you know all about *Elémpe* then."

"Yes, quite fairly. My grandfather handed it over to Glasgow for the general use of the people. It is now enhanced with beautiful wheels to make it easily transportable for viewing around Glasgow. My father successfully requested it must come back to resume guarding the Kingdom of Ila." He felt proud of his father, prouder of the decision.

"How generous and thoughtful – typical of all Mackinnons!" the king praised. "But tell your father he should keep it. As you can see, Ila has already got enough replacements to continue the guarding.

"Besides, my father and his father had already had their shares of that *Elémpe*. Therefore, let your father and Glasgow keep it as their shares."

"Most thoughtful of you, Your Highness," responded Victor after a measured silence. "Had it not been for lack of time to complete the freighting formalities, I would have brought it down with me without a formal consultation. Or what is the essence of having an allegiance to the *Eagle*?

"I swore to my father that you would love it, if only for its history, quality and value – all superior. Honestly, Your Highness, I would wish you have it for the kingdom, and for you – and me!"

The next short silence was Jap's. He really wished he could see what was deepest in Victor's mind was. Could it be as simple as Victor was saying? Did Victor really mean what he had just said? He wished he could read Victor right.

"Why would you wish that we have it?"

"To tell you the truth, Your Highness, I take that *Elémpe* as the greatest valuable constant. Ila and Glasgow had had their shares of it. So had your royal fathers and my fathers. Shouldn't you and I have ours? Rightly, we should, Your Highness."

It sounded clear, just. King Jap wanted Victor to make it clearer.

"Let me bring it back here now that Glasgow is ready to release it. After a short while in Ila we can take it out exactly the way it was taken out before, to anywhere it would be more profitably sold. What we will realise will mean big wealth for me and you. It is a last chance, Your Highness."

King Jap stood, pondered and took a brief exit out of the hall. Outside, he wished he was an oracle, or a witch doctor, instead of an assumed spirit. He would have been able to predict what were to come, the aftermath of the proposed recovery, re-looting and the re-sale of the *Elémpe*. Very unfortunately, the operation was such that one could not risk involving a third party – soothsayer or witch doctor. All the same, he must give a response. He returned, ready for one.

"Okay, Victor, I agree. But both of us being of the *Eagle*, must do nothing like a betrayal, promise?"

"Yes, Your Highness, I cherish my oath."

"When are you bringing it?"

"The best time would be the time of the carnival, this carnival," Victor replied. "I understand it disappeared after a carnival; it will be remarkable to reappear at another. The people will welcome it generously. They will revere you and it."

"When should it disappear again?"

"Whenever Your Highness is ready."

"Where would it go?"

"Anywhere the highest bidder is waiting – Venice, London, America – as long as it is somewhere far away from Glasgow and Ila. Anyway, I will take care of that."

"Deal then, Victor. You are a brother. Let me say good night now."

"But Your Highness, you still haven't said anything about Nek and Sariya."

"Make that your first, priority question tomorrow," the king said, amused. "For now someone will take you to your guest apartment, for a relaxation you thoroughly deserve."

And so disappeared Jap.

* * *

The carers were two – a male servant to carry Victor's backpack into the guest apartment, and Queen Musli herself to supervise the carrier. On seeing the two, Victor reasoned Glawanu must have finished work and returned to his young family down town.

Victor viewed the queen's presence as unwarranted, however high the esteem the king must have held him. The lavish en suit was ready, perhaps ever made ready, before they got there. Therefore, within five minutes of leading Victor in, Musli dismissed the servant to return to his living quarter.

"Is there anything we missed out that you will need, Victor?" Musli asked as soon as the door closed behind the servant.

"Thank you, Your Highness. More than enough is here as I can see. You have both been kind. So, you can go."

"Yes, I will Victor. But let me ask you one thing: Why does His Majesty like you so much?" She slowly moved close to Victor for an answer.

"Well, I don't know for sure. But thank him for me, for that. He is a great king, his kingdom a great one."

"Do you like him the same?"

"Yes, of course," he answered a question he deemed unnecessary.

"Do you like him and all that belong to him?"

"Yes, Your Highness," Victor replied dismissively, knowing that it was impossible for anyone to know or like all that Jap ever possessed, that the question made no sense.

"Are you sure of that, Victor?"

"Yes – all that belong to His Majesty," he lied, wanting to be left alone. "Or how would the tenant not like the pets of his landlord – if he is not ready to move?"

"That's a nice one Victor," Musli broke into a giggle. "The king is truthful, that your sense of humour is great. Would you accept me as one of his belongings, his pets, then?"

"Your Majesty, you are his queen – more than just his belonging."

"Good, and right." She moved closer and gripped his hands, forcing eye contact. "Then show me now you like me equally like, if not more than, his belonging. She drew Victor to her body, her mouth at the centre of a most disarming smile, aiming at his.

"No, Your Majesty, we can't do this. We mustn't." He was struggling to free himself from Musli's amorous advances. He remembered the episode that played between the Glaswegian Queen Langeoreth and the palace soldier. "Please go, Your Majesty, before I get into serious trouble."

"We can't, and we won't get into trouble," Musli assured Victor. "For your information, he knows I am here with you. He takes you as himself. Because you are him, that's why I am with him – with you. He wants me to be here for you. Take me, Victor. Or, are you refusing me because I am the junior queen?"

Victor felt the arrival of a new problem, either in accepting, rejecting or protesting Queen Musli's moves. "Please let's leave this idea till another time, I am begging you," Victor seriously pleaded.

Musli gave up, with deeply touching kisses to Victor's cheek and neck. As she left the room, she programmed her memory to hold that phrase, another time, in a handy periphery for easy retrieval. That retrieval time was just three hours later, precisely 2 a.m.

When Victor woke from the first round of sleep, he thought he was in the middle of a dream – albeit a good one. It was the lights that came on which terminated the sleep. He saw the five feet and ten inches slim figure of Musli walking towards him from the direction of the bathroom. She was totally nude.

In colour, her body was a young bronze, made even younger by her dwelling under the roof of royalty. Some shining black patched areas – of hairs on the head, the eyes, the new-moon-like eye brows, the pair of nipple dots, and the triangularly trimmed pubic hairs – amorously punctuated the pigmented brownness of her body. When Victor jumped out of bed – to a no place of escape – he cursed his natural height for being shorter than Musli's: it forced a direct, levelled focus of his eyes on the blackness of her nipples and the space between her vulva and her pelvis.

She strolled to a frozen Victor, seized him and pressed the raw warmth of her body against his. "Till another time' you promised; 'another time' is here now," she told Victor who was breathing heavily in her arms.

"Please, leave me, Your Majesty," Victor pleaded. "It will be a betrayal of the king."

"No, Victor. The betrayal will be if you should reject me now that he wants you to have me. That will be his and my betrayal, his disappointment and mine.

"How do I go back unable to fulfil his wish? He might even believe you don't like him as much as you promised him you did." She collapsed on to the bed sobbing atop Victor whom she had eventually pulled down with her. "He will conclude neither me nor you he really loves trusts him..."

"Stop crying please," Victor appealed to Musli, wiping her face with a part of the bed linen. "And by the way, when did you become the queen, and what has become of Azzanaite?"

"Azzanaite is still the senior queen and she is fine. I moved in six months ago, and which man wouldn't prefer a younger woman?"

"You can still tell him his wishes really happened between us, can't you? What I want from you first is trust and good friendship; and 'another time' will really come before we know it. I will actually need your friendship." He buttressed his appeal with another envelope to her and convinced her to return to her bed.

"Thank you, Victor; and I promise you my trust and friendship. I want you to follow me to the bathroom to see how I got in here so that you don't think I am a ghost of my great grandmother."

In the bathroom, Victor waited, looking on as Musli put on the nightie she downed as soon as she entered the suite. Then she went out through the biggest mirror, a revolving piece that doubled as an escape door, into whatever was her part of the palace.

* * *

When, at 8 a.m. the following morning, King Jap knocked on the door of Victor's suite, Victor assumed his second day in Ila had just started with the trouble he had anticipated. He braced up and opened for the king.

"Did you have a pleasant night?" King Jap asked him.

"Thank you, Your Highness; I did," he said, wearing a brave face.

"I am happy you did. I knew you would. Did you see my queen?"

Victor was silent.

"It's nothing to be embarrassed about. Every river, however great, has its sediments. On occasions, things totally un-royal are secretly done to keep the royalty – but with the indispensable support of trust. So, now you know how much I trust you."

"Thank you, Your Highness."

"You see, Victor, I have come here this early because I want us to talk and finish the talking before Sese would be here. Yesterday I could read suspicion in Sese. He was unhappy you stayed here with me. It had never happened to him; and he had never seen any white man so treated. Therefore I guess he would be here much earlier today than his usual noon time."

Victor was attentive.

"Throughout the night," King Jap continued, "I thought over the goodness you've done for this kingdom and to me especially. Nobody has been so kind, loyal and precise."

"Thank you, Your Highness."

"Do you remember the chiefdom of Dancemaster – of Jacquensica and Nek – I announced I was scrapping last time when you were here?"

Victor did.

"We scrapped it; but now I want to restore it and make you the chief of Dancemaster. What do you think of that?"

"Thank you, Your Highness, for the honour – and kindness," Victor replied. He was flabbergasted. "But going by what you told us about Dancemaster, I can see some problems."

"Problems? What problems?" the king asked eagerly.

"We have the Jemba Couple to do our outing in, don't we?

"Or are we bringing Jemba Couple to Dancemaster chiefdom to replace the Dancemaster masquerade?"

"No, no, no. I shall promote two junior masquerades to carry the Couple. You shall use your wisdom to manage Dancemaster totally.

"Now, your next problem?"

"As I am a native of Glasgow will your chiefs accept me?" he asked, his scepticism sending King Jap to a loud laughter.

"Who are they when I am what I am, and they know who and what I am?" he crowed. "Who would lead the question and risk his rank? Which of them would volunteer his skull to crack the sweet coconut? You see what I mean?

"Anyway, not to take chances," he suddenly made a u-turn. "Give the gifts you have for them to me now. They will speak to them before they would meet you, and so keep the biggest mouths shut. Do you have something for them?"

"Yes, but in the hotel."

"That's still good. You can go for them while I am still ironing these out with Sese."

"Then you said you have razed the compound," Victor reminded King Jap of the third problem.

"Yes, but when the hands raze, it won't be the legs that would raise; it will still be the hands. The whole kingdom will join hands. This is the birthplace of cooperatives."

Victor made more of his pretences, until King Jap ruled he must accept the chieftaincy. Deep down, Victor loved it. It was an honour that went beyond the dreams of his project organizers in Glasgow.

"Supposing I finance re-building it, Your Highness?" Victor asked.

"You? The building?" Jap couldn't believe his ears.

"Yes, Your Highness. Finance it. If acceptable I will put down what I have now. From Glasgow my father will surely help. So would Uggi and his father. I will import the wonders and generosity of Glasgow to the chiefdom of Dancemaster and the entire kingdom of Ila."

For King Japeedoe, Victor's determination and pledge sealed it perfectly. As soon as Sese arrived, he, King Jap, would hand him the necessary royal directive. It would be mainly in the form of an events time-table which Sese must sell to and follow up with Ila chiefs and members of the *Eagle* fraternity. Sese would be mandated to use that day to intimate fellow chiefs and summon them for a meeting at the palace the following day. Sese would then start the meeting with them, with giving them the gifts that Victor had for them. Then he, the king, would take Victor along and join them. There, he would royally announce to them that Victor would be a chief.

The morning after the chiefs' meeting, both the installation of Victor as the new chief and the start of rebuilding the Dancemaster Compound would take place simultaneously. After the installation, and up to the end of the following day, Victor would make a quick tour of Ila. The next day he would meet fellow members of the *Eagle*. Then he would go to bed early to keep fresh for his return journey the following day.

Victor made a last suggestion to the king. "Why can't my meeting with fellow *Eagles* be scheduled for the day after that with the chiefs? It could be better to meet them before my installation."

"That won't be necessary," the king said. "Your titling is about the kingdom, just as all the chiefs are. The *Eagle* is about personal business. Even without a meeting you can identify a brother-member of the *Eagle* where and when you meet him.

"Besides, which meeting of the *Eagle* would ever be more important now than any between me and you? You know the answer will be 'none'."

* * *

Victor was in the main hall of the Palace when, as usual, Sese Abram reported. Before he could settle with Victor, King Jap called him alone to another chamber of the palace.

"Sese," King Jap called without wasting time, "the news is that I am making Victor a chief," he said point blank. "What's your opinion?"

In the simplest of circumstances, Sese would have barked an angry 'no' at his Almighty; but protocol forbade him. He was quietened by shock, expecting his Almighty to throw more light on the announcement. Jap didn't.

"Chief...of which masquerade...quarter...Jemba?" He was totterring.

"Of Dancemaster Quarters. It is still vacant. You know that, don't you?"

Again, Sese was quiet, struggling to prevent a lapse to the shock he was just recovering from. He could not believe the scale of his Almighty's sudden insanity.

"But you have cancelled that title forever."

"Cancelled, yes. But forever, no. It has all got to do with our interests: mine, yours, the kingdom's. During the night, I was able to convince myself that it has to be done."

The phrase 'during the night' resounded repeatedly with the speed of lighting in Sese's brain. During the night? That was the period the stupid Victor shared with his Almighty inside the palace. Victor must have given his Almighty more 'envelopes', more gifts, all convincingly fat. That must have been it. Victor must have stolen the favour from his Almighty with a 'kola'!

"But the compound was long destroyed and the ground levelled, as you commanded."

"Yes, Sese. Or do you think I forgot? But it can be rebuilt. We can do it, still with our same hands."

Sweat visibly gathered on Sese's forehead. He wished King Jap was another chief of the same rank as himself. He would have most impolitely ordered him out of his sight. Or a junior chief of the kingdom; he would have despatched him to the mad men's dungeon of Ila.

How, Sese thought furiously, could Victor have suddenly deserved a title, talk less of a most senior one, in Ila? How could his Almighty forget so soon the wars the cancelled chiefdom of Dancemaster waged on the kingdom? How could the king expect him, Sese to support the resurrection of a chiefdom that had once defeated him in a fight, causing him to be demoted?

"In my opinion, my Almighty, it would be better and safer to leave him comfortably with the *Order of The Eagle*.

"At best, allow him to carry Jemba or any other mask he prefers; and allow him to visit the kingdom as much as he wishes – with good presents. My humble opinion, my Almighty."

"Thank you for it," Jap acknowledged the opinion. He knew that at that stage and in that state, he didn't need it. "You are against it, and I can understand why. I was too, at first. I considered the cons and I hated it. Next I considered the pros and I loved it.

441

Finally, I considered both the pros and cons and I snatched it – for the sake of the kingdom."

Sese Abram was not going to concede. "My Almighty, it's the security aspect that I fear," he lied. "He will know too much about us, and dangerously expose us to Glasgow. It will not help my job as the chief security officer of the kingdom. Besides, we have seen how these people from Glasgow can be so unstable."

"Well, Sese, I see it differently," the king responded. "But whichever way I see it, you can rest assure that your Almighty will never compromise or endanger you, your duty or the kingdom. My premise is this: If for our sake he killed the formidable enemy we couldn't kill, what other proof would we require to know he would join you to boost our security? I actually learnt he and Uggi narrowly escaped paying with their lives for killing Jacq.

"And you know what, Sese?" he continued. "He suggested we make incursions into the neighbouring kingdoms to further boost our security. He promised he would get us all the support."

"We are already doing that, aren't we?" responded Sese, unimpressed.

"Not that way, Sese. Not just raiding and running. He means we should conquer the kingdoms, impose our rules, and control their masks, masquers and masquerades. As a chief of our kingdom, he will back us with enough arms from Scotland."

Just like his Almighty was adamant, Sese was hardened against the whole idea. "But my Almighty, how can we even be sure Jacq was truly dead? Victor could be playing a game to impress us. I know it, that it's only here in Ila that people don't joke with 'the man died'." He was full of suspicion.

"Okay then, Sese, give me one minute," Jap asked Sese with confidence. He disappeared to fetch his copies of the photographs about Jacq.

"Here, the photographs, the evidence," he handed them over to Sese. "She wasn't powerful forever as we all believed she was."

"Now I agree; she is dead," Sese declared after some minutes of serious scrutiny of the pictures. "But I fear she's not gone yet – I mean her spirit. If she wasn't buried with the full ritual her spirit will still be dangerous. Did he say how she was buried?"

"He didn't. We should ask. Even if he says yes, it would still be wiser to do our own burial for her. We should tell him to bring along three of her clothes when next he is coming. Then we can do it at the start of the festival week – for everybody to witness."

Sese agreed.

"And one more thing, Sese. Victor has volunteered to bear the cost of building the Dancemaster Compound. There's bound to be something in it for me and you."

For the first time since being with the king, Sese gave a true smile. He unhesitatingly asked how his Almighty would want the installation plan to be drawn.

"Intimate all the chiefs today," Jap ordered Sese. "Call them here tomorrow for a meeting so that Victor can meet them and receive their blessing. I will advise Victor how he should play his part and card to gain their unanimous nod.

"The following morning we shall do the installation and start the re-building.

"As there's no Dancemaster court yet, the rites will be here at the palace. After it, you will all go and support him at the building site."

"Is he also bearing the cost of the installation?"

"Of course, yes. Or you expect me – or you – to bear it? Have you forgotten that the days of pauper chiefs and pauper installations are gone? Sese, your Almighty recognises no pauperism!

"Now you can go and sort out further details with Victor."

* * *

443

The Masquerade

Sese Abram, after his meeting with King Jap, deliberately took a longer route back to Victor. He needed the time to ponder over his own approval of the chieftaincy.

Yes, he was convinced Jacq was dead. But more convinced he was that Jacq's ghost still lived on earth, and would soon start to ravage Ila with vengeance. It must have been it that was behind the approval of a new Dancemaster in a bid to dethrone him and his Fire Spirit chiefdom, as it had happened before. Or to pitch a new Dancemaster against Fire Spirit so that King Jap could corner more of the common loot without challenge!

He realised that now that he had consented before King Jap, he could not dissent behind him. He reserved himself to believing in the king's assurances of gifts from Victor. He, just like King Jap, also had a mouth for 'kola', and pockets for any excess 'kola' his mouth could not manage!

"Congratulations, and all hail, Victor. You are aware, aren't you?" Suddenly Sese was cheerful. He shook Victor's hand.

"Aware of?"

"You are the next Chief Dancemaster. My Almighty has approved it. He was waiting for me to approve as well; and that's what I have just done.

"What do you think of the honour?"

Of course, it was something he loved, a project prayer heard, the feeling of which he needed not to show Sese. He knew Sese's glorification was with neither merit nor sincerity, but he wasn't going to tell him so. "I haven't thought anything about it. But thank you both for the honour," he said.

"My Almighty wants me to forge ahead with the plan, with you. He wants everything – installation and all – completed three days from today."

"How would you do that?"

"Hard work, and hard cost. Luckily it's nothing like the pains at the *Eagle* initiation.

444

"My Almighty also wants me to explain to you the difference between the celebrity you are now and the controller of Dancemaster chiefdom and spirit you will become once you are installed.

"As a chief you will become a celebrity of the highest order, someone who everyone knows but who cannot know everyone. But as the controller of the chiefdom's spirit you become a spirit yourself, an extraordinary being that knows everybody – and everything. My Almighty wants you to be aware of all this."

"How will it possible that I will know everything and everybody?"

"Victor, that won't be your problem, but everybody's. What's most important is that they all believe you know them and know everything, as the spirit's controller. In that capacity you don't argue with your subjects. Instead, order and question them for their answers. And know when to talk to them as a celebrity, when as a chief and when as a spirit through the Dancemaster."

"Am I to carry the mask of Dancemaster myself then?"

"No. To approve someone to carry it. Yours is to collect and spend what Dancemaster collects, after you have given my Almighty his due from it. I will look for someone from your chiefdom to carry it for you."

"And would the person be initiated into the *Eagle* first?"

"No. *Eagles* are essential for Jemba Couple because they are royal masks whose carriers are supposed to perform other rituals which only the king's confidants can perform.

"Then as you are aware," Sese went on, "the kingdom you are taking was scrapped when Nek, misguided by his wife, Jacq, was its chief. Do you know why that happened? So that it would guide your behaviour, my Almighty wants me to tell you if you don't know. Do you?"

"The scrapping or the mis-guidance?"

"Both."

"I don't know," he safely said. He had listened to versions from Jacq and his father, Ben. Each presentation was scarcely above vagueness.

Sese was ready to present his own version – for his own safety – to Victor:

Nek and Jacq fell into the trap of greed, arrogance and overreaching, the type neither King Jap nor Sese would wish Victor on ascension.

Trado-culturally, Dancemaster was a powerful spirit of all women. He performed for them the combined duties of Bastet, Isis and Hather.

Because beautiful women used to dance round Dancemaster, Nek, the mask's controller, bragged that it was because he was such a beautifully handsome man. He believed he was more beautiful than all women – and than the parents from whose eggs those women were formed. Assisted by Jacq, he turned all women into his tool – until they pushed him, raised him and crashed him. That was the bitter pill of arrogance!

There was another thing Victor must learn from. It was that when Jacq pushed Nek to confront him, Sese, and his Almighty, neither Jacq nor Nek knew that the Fire Spirit was already being oiled by Sango and Hephaestus, and that his Almighty Japeedoe truly descended from the lines of Amum, Ptah and Ra. So, the trouble-couple ended up being abandoned by Seth and apprehended by Maat and Themis. That was the history Victor must learn from – that no one but the fool thinks he's forever smarter than others!

"My Almighty is ready," Sese went on, "to restore all the powers and privileges of Dancemaster to you, but you must not attempt to use them against him or me.

"Among the spirits, your Dancemaster comes third – only after any of my Almighty's and my Fire Spirit. You understand – third, third?"

446

"Yes I do. Meaning that my masquerade will dance at the carnivals before the big three – before Worshipper, Aroso and, Kaka..."

"No, Victor. You will dance last, after them, like Jemba couple did last time. You shall have the advantage of incorporating the best steps of the preceding masquerades. Since last year, such has been the dancing line-up for the biggest masquerades."

"I told His Highness I will bear the cost of the installation."

"He told me; and that is good. You are a truly good jobber – he ties down no job that doesn't tie him down! That you are not waiting for the women's contribution for it will speed up the arrangement. But you will reap it in multiple folds from the women in no time."

"About how much will it cost?"

"Oh yes, I have done the calculation. Everything will cost you a hundred pounds sterling. You give me the money, and I will do the arrangements."

"A hundred pounds?"

"Yes. A hundred," Sese confirmed, fearing Victor had acquired the Ila's local art of haggling and was going to ask for a lesser price. "Only a hundred."

Victor looked into his backpack and selected a hundred and thirty pounds in notes. He put a hundred inside an envelope and handed over to Sese who was already smiling, watching triangularly between Victor's face, hands and backpack.

"That is it, thirty pounds, for you," he added. "Or would you want the thirty in an envelope?" Victor added further even though he knew what Sese's answer would be. Sese grabbed both with thanks and secured them inside his pocket.

"That's good of you, Chief Dancemaster, if you don't mind me being the first to call you so. Now I shall despatch the notice for the meeting to the chiefs, and report back to my Almighty."

"And after that will you take me round the town?" Victor asked. He claimed he was eager to familiarise himself with the town of his chiefdom, the chiefdom of his compound, and the would-be-compound of his masquerade. "It will make further planning easier," he added.

"A very good idea," Sese agreed readily. "I don't see my Almighty objecting to that." Normally, and only from a close watch from 'behind the window curtain' was a visitor permitted to see the impermissible in Ila. But it would be different with Victor, an approved chief with installation just hours away, a loyal *Eagle*, grandson of *Cobra*, one who could betray nothing of what he would see.

The outing was concluded to later in the day. Sese would have attended to his prioritized assignments, and Victor would have returned from Bilitie he had to go. It suited Victor, gave him more time to call his sponsors on his special phone.

* * *

Victor drove along, directed by Sese, towards Dancemaster Quarters where Victor would have his compound, court and shrine. Three miles of roads passing by the Main Market connected the palace in the old city to Dancemaster Quarters at the west end of the town. It was an opportunity with which he began to see Ila in a different light, one better than how he alone, or he with Uggi, saw it previously. He could see a potentially bigger city that was cruelly dwarfed, a naturally progressive kingdom where the naturalism had been denaturalised by the thieves at the helm of its affairs.

"I never, in my wildest, dreamt it could be this uniquely urban here in Ila," he spoke with Sese.

"Well, I could see why you didn't. But it could be. It is, as you can see." He was lost in the negativity of Victor's words, mistaking them as high praise.

Most roads, wide or narrow, were clean and tarred, whatever was the quality and current situation of the tarring. So were the houses clean and visibly bustling with their commercial and residential occupants, all mixed in their activities. Strangely but

448

extravagantly in that broad daylight, the street lights were left turned on, without any reasonable visual effect on the streets or the houses. It was, to Victor, a funny contrast to the initiation night at the shrine when the required street lights were turned off for the sake of culture. Perhaps another of the changes; but a stupid one that had replaced normal night-time lighting with lighting under the sun!

"Turn in at that road on your right," Sese pointed at the next road ahead as they were driving beside the market.

"Park, and let us use our legs for the rest," Sese directed again when they had barely gone ten yards after the turn-in. He had something important to show Victor. It would be difficult to see it when later the market was full, too full to access what Sese must now show to Victor.

They arrived at a conical pile of specially cut rocks circum-fenced by a wall one foot high and ten feet in diameter.

"Look well between those rocks, and you will see some chain lengths."

Victor complied; saw the big links made from about half an inch diameter rods.

"You are now at the Security Centre Point of your new kingdom.

"That chain, the first king, Ajagunla, long after he died, descended back to earth using that chain. Then he came to assist Ila to resist, repel and win a joint attack from the neighbouring kingdoms.

"After helping to win that war, the descended king tied the two ends of the chain round his waist and descended into the earth below him. His soothing instruction was that any reigning Japeedoe should pull the chains to bring him back to fight whenever there was a difficult war. The chain was the everlasting link to him, the ever ready saviour of Ila. Since then, the neighbouring kingdoms had remained under our wilful trampling.

The Masquerade

"Once, a king pulled the chain for a test. Within a twinkle of the eye, thousands of armed dwarfs swarmed out from under the stones humming 'Where's the war? Where's the war?'

"They discovered the call was a hoax, which was strictly forbidden. They turned onto the violating king and clubbed him to death before they returned to the earth they came from.

When they had gone, the next king ordered more rocks deposited onto this spot to discourage more of such a deadly prank.

"In other words we, Ilas, have always been immune to defeats at war and subjugations," Sese rounded up boastfully. "Instead, we waged wars, captured men, women and materials, kept who and what we wanted from them and sold away who and what we didn't. That's how you have some of our citizens and materials in Glasgow."

Victor felt amused by Sese's story. He thought it was all nonsense. First, he thought Sese was attempting to equate the chain-sensitive Ila king with Kentigern in Glasgow. Even though both allegedly performed feats towards securing their cities, it makes more sense that Kentigern was normally born, and that he died normally, without a resurrection. Who has ever imitated, or would ever imitate, Jesus Christ!

Secondly, Kentigern established a church on the spot he secured Glasgow. Why hadn't any of the past Japeedoes organised a church in the same manner, instead of organising some market stones and chains? In fact, there was no single church Victor could see in the vicinity. The only place of worship he could nearby was a mosque. And apart from his observation that this mosque was taller, larger and of bigger capacity compared with Glasgow's at Gorbals, Sese could not relate it to the past king whose assumed chains and rocks they were standing by. Victor suggested they resumed their journey to Dancemaster Quarters.

At the quarters they went down three streets insignificantly, and ended at a large space at the centre of the quarters.

450

Considering the temperate climate of Ila, the small and weakly scattered weeds on the massive parcel of land suggested it was well kept – to ensure no evil ever again grew or was grown on it.

"So, Victor," Sese called, "this is where the compound was, and will be – where you will build it. Do you like it?"

"It's beautiful – from where my Dancemaster Spirit will be commanded!" he laughed with excitement.

"Of course, yes. Mine is in my compound and directed from there, isn't it?"

"I suppose so, Sese. That's why I would love to visit your compound too."

"Don't worry, Victor. You will know the compound of your Fire Spirit. I would have said now, but my Almighty wants me to visit some compounds unfailingly today – for your sake. So you are likely to know some others' before mine, because I shall take you round to see them first."

"Which ones'?"

"Those of the three biggest chiefs and masquerades. I mean Aroso, Kaka and Worshipper.

"I have got your gifts for them; and my Almighty wants me to wet their appetites with them today, before tomorrow's meeting of the chiefs." This explanation satisfied Victor.

"This piece of land is quite sizeable and level," Victor resumed with a compliment. "In Glasgow it would have since gone for a neighbourhood park for young mothers and their toddlers. Why haven't you done that?"

"And if we had, what would you have met to build on?"

"That's interesting," Victor mocked indirectly. "What happened with the contents of the compound? They were removed before razing, weren't they?" Jacq had mandated him to find out what King Jap and Sese did to her family belongings before they destroyed the compound.

451

"Better to burn down a major evil together with the lesser evils it created round it. That's my Almighty's belief and instruction. Everything was burnt – except anything the junior masquerades who carried out the assignment found to be useful to them. But that wasn't directed."

Next Victor told Sese he would need all the help to manage the anticipated huge building when he finally moved in. "I would need personal assistants to run the rooms, the courts, the shrine... Can I have those working here before to assist me?" Silently, he wished Sese would agree.

"As a chief, Victor, you won't have any problem running the compound. Adequate servants will be provided for you. So will be plenty of women to choose from. They will all be fresh and trained. But the women, you will have to train and adapt to your taste."

"But Sese, having some of the old hands would make things easier for me, isn't it?"

"Sorry, you can't have them. Because they connived with Jacq and Nek they had all been removed and given other jobs."

"So, what other jobs?"

"Actually, nothing. They were banished; some *zoo-ed*."

"*Zoo-ed*?"

"Yes, caged. They were lucky that none of them was sent to be *abattoir-ed*, slaughtered. That is what happened to all aiders and abettors. You will soon see some of them." For Sese, that closed that line of inquiry of Victor's.

* * *

Sitting inside the palace hall for the meeting were High Chiefs Sese, Worshipper, Kaka and Chief Priest, together with one each of their senior chiefs.

Sese's announcement to them was straight. "Our Almighty has decided to install Victor Mackinnon as a chief – tomorrow morning," he stated. "What do you think about this, my dear chiefs?"

Sese knew he was not to ask for their opinion, but to sell the one he had reluctantly agreed with King Jap to them. But since he still saw an unhealthy rivalry brewing between himself and a titled Victor in the future, he would, before the king arrived, seek an indirect way of moving the chiefs against the installation.

"What grade of chief; and for which chiefdom?" the senior chief to High Chief Kaka asked Sese.

"High Chief; for the chiefdom of Dancemaster," Sese answered.

"Strange and unheard of," the first questioner remarked, to Sese's undeclared satisfaction. "Who is this Victor Mackinnon? The same man who helped Jacq and Nek to escape punishments to their sins against the kingdom?"

"Well, yes," Sese was happy to confirm.

"From where did he start as an elder, promoted to a junior chief, and a senior chief, before he would become a high chief?" the same man vented more anger. "Is the hierarchy being turned upside down? Would that not create chaos for him and the kingdom? He won't even know from where to start!"

"Okay, and thank you," Sese remarked with contentment. "Now, let's hear from fellow high chiefs if they feel the same way." Sese wanted an all inclusive discussion, and was sure his titular colleagues would think the same way as the senior chief who spoke.

"Before their opinion," the same man came in, "I will like to say that I speak for myself as well as for the senior chiefs here. So, whatever are the opinions of the high chiefs, we feel promoting someone above us just like that is not fair. And that we were so ignored and cheapened in the process was even worse. We don't mind saying this anywhere, including before our Almighty, and face the consequence. How we are being overlooked is not fair."

"What is not fair, and how are you overlooked?" King Jap shocked the assembly to ask the protestor. He had arrived and

453

entered earlier than he told Sese he would; and had heard a part of the protestation. He was accompanied by Victor.

Overwhelmed by the jolt from the unanticipated intrusion, every face in the room looked away, upstanding in silence.

"I heard what he said – all the rudeness against me and my high chiefs," he said, still calm.

"We were just about to explain the situation to him when you entered, my Almighty," Sese responded.

"Just about? Why should he have to say that much before you would think of explaining, and solving his problem? Why must you wait till the blister festers before you treat it?

"Now that I am here," he turned to the senior chief whose outburst he had just caught, "tell me what you have in mind, while everybody sits."

"He is sorry, my Almighty," Sese blocked the senior chief from talking. "So are we all. You can proceed with the important thing you called us here for."

"To nothing and to nowhere, nobody is proceeding, Sese," the king said firmly. "He said he would speak his mind. Now let him, if that would help him and other senior chiefs to the right things."

"I am sorry, our Almighty," the senior chief now rose, determined. "I mean no disrespect to you or your high chiefs – and certainly not to Victor too. Our protest is against another incident of the high chiefs denying us our rightful dues.

"We discovered that Victor sent some presents to us and that only Chief Priest and High Chief Worshipper passed a bit of it to their senior chiefs. All the other high chiefs buried everything in their pockets. Why after this, was High Chief Sese still asking for our opinion about the installation?" The allegation stiffened Sese, Aroso and Kaka on their seats.

"Now I see," the king acknowledged. "Kaka, Aroso – and Sese, was that true?"

"Truly, our Almighty, not quite," Kaka volunteered an answer. "But Sese gave us only..."

"Okay Kaka, enough there," the king stopped him. "Stop and get back to your chiefdoms before you would publicly launder your dirty linen. Truly, I am disappointed in all of you. You must all put it behind you now. Personally, I will redress it for you all."

King Jap was being tactfully even-handed by not blaming or vindicating any of his chiefs. He knew the problem started due to how the system was overplayed by everyone, including himself, but excluding Victor. It started when he, King Jap, handed to Sese for the high chiefs downwards, only half of the money gift he collected from Victor for them. Sese also did something similar – took his own greedy cut before passing over what he could to fellow high chiefs. Sese was only protecting the secret when, the previous day, he made Victor remain outside in his jeep while he went into the houses of the high chiefs to deliver what he could to them. Only Chief Priest and Worshipper who met Victor by chance then passed something on to their senior chiefs. And by innocent misfortune, the benefited senior chiefs had spilled the beans to their colleagues shortly before the meeting got underway. Jap believed if anything was to be blamed it had to be the kingdom's thieving culture of unfair proportionality, which they all still regarded as normal.

"I shall compensate you all, and you shall be happy," he said, repeating the promise, when Victor rose to back him.

"Don't allow this to spoil your day," Victor said. "I have still a few things for you – some here, some in my hotel." He watched his utterances diffuse the tension on the faces of the chiefs and their Almighty.

"You hear that?" King Jap, elated, asked his chiefs. "He's here for us; and we should be here – and everywhere – for him. It's what makes the honey go round – this sort of cooperation."

"Long live our Almighty," greedy High Chief Kaka leapt up and applauded. "Owner..."

455

"Owner of all..." other chiefs joined Kaka, singing heartily, and for the meeting to proceed party-like among the attendees.

* * *

Victor's installation started at 7 a.m. on Tuesday. Already, Sese Abram and Chief Priest were in Dancemaster Quarters, and had assembled its seven traditional elders to witness the chieftaincy cock fight. The gruesome fight-to-the-death must produce a winner who, within the following couple of hours, tradition would upturn to be equally a loser.

The fight was meant to wish a new chief victory over foes seen and unseen, human or object. So, after the fight, the priest would take the victorious cock with him to the venue of the installation and kill it for a special libation by the king. In the end it must be the new chief's first meal after he had taken the title. He must consume it totally – beak, claws, blood, heart and flesh!

A king's installation was different, and more elaborate. Two rams were always used, making the new king's first meal last long according to the largeness and voraciousness of his appetite. The current Japeedoe was rumoured to have used two humans for the ritual fight; and that he devoured the winner all alone. The undertones were once loud, that he matched what his great-grandfather did to High Chief Tantalo the Tiger!

By 10 a.m. the stage at Eagle Square was set for Victor. A chief must be installed before noon, that the gods would grant him a longer reign.

The gathering was large. On one side sat the chiefs of Ila. Next to them was another group, seated, and comprising of the queens, princes, princesses and those on the king's special invitation.

Separated away on the opposite side by a twenty yard space was a much larger group of men, women, children and friends of the Dancemaster chiefdom. Everyone was gaily dressed. The trumpet announced King Jap's imminence to appear, while his stool carrier customarily confirmed the same.

Within minutes the king arrived; and everybody rose to greet him in the usual song. When he had taken his seat, the chiefs filed out to give him the longest and last in the series of the greeting.

Set beside the king was a very old, small, crafted wooden table, the Installation Stool. Sese supervised three boys loading its top with a covered brass dish, a long thumb-thick red bead, a tiara of green leaves and feathers, a sword and a cow-tail lash. Then he bowed to the king and announced why they were all there that morning. He called out the chief priest to take over the proceedings.

After he too had greeted King Jap, the priest proceeded carefully across to the group from the Dancemaster chiefdom. Arbitrarily he told one of the men sitting there to stand up for the crowd to see. "Is this him?" he turned to the crowd and bellowed the question.

"No!" the people answered.

The priest selected another man and ordered him up. "Chiefs, is this him?"

"No, not him!"

The priest's next selection was a man who sat purposely hidden away in the third row. He was Victor Mackinnon.

"Is this him?!"

"Yes!" they roared, prompting the priest to bring Victor out.

Slowly, the priest removed Victor's shirt and replaced it with a white shawl over his shoulder. Then he hauled him to the king where he was ordered to kneel like a captured enemy combatant dragged before a no-nonsense commander.

"Who do you say he is?" King Jap formally asked the priest.

"Your subject, Victor Mackinnon."

"Why have you brought him before the crown?"

"The people of Dancemaster chiefdom said I should bring him. They want him as their high chief."

"Now I understand," the king said, adjusting himself, relaxed. He then turned to the chiefs and addressed them: "My dear chiefs, do you want Victor Mackinnon to join your council of wisdom, guidance and devotion?"

"Yes Your Highness!"

"To represent the interests of Dancemaster Chiefdom among you?"

"Yes, our Almighty, Owner of all…"

"Then the crown shall carry out your joint wish," he responded, his response drawing the priest nearer to the loaded wooden stool beside him.

"Open the silver dish and let him tongue the cockerel," he ordered the priest.

The priest complied. Victor tasted from a barbecued drumstick of the victorious-but-yet-slaughtered chicken that was left dipped in its blood.

Next, King Jap touched Victor's chest thrice with the bead and gave it to the priest to wear round Victor's neck. Next he instructed the priest to put the tiara on Victor after touching his head with it thrice. Lastly, Victor rose, and the priest belted the sword and the whip round his waist.

At every step, the king chanted some prayers. However, those he said after Victor had received the belt of sword and lash were the most significant for the event. "Now you have the sword to defend your Chiefdom," the chant went, "and the lash to deal with anyone in any way you wish. The crown hereby pronounces you the High Chief Dancemaster of Ila Kingdom, and wishes you a long, peaceful and prosperous reign."

To the king's last pronouncement the crowd responded "amen" and Sese signalled the music to start. Victor had the traditional sequence of dances to do – alone before the king, with the priest before the king, with fellow chiefs, and with the people of his chiefdom.

Before the last two dances, Sese held up the gathering and made a short speech. The dancers should show their support for the new chief by giving him cash gifts as they danced with him. He announced he, Sese, would lead his fellow chiefs in dancing and giving. He was however, forever, silent on the two maidens he had ready to collect the cash on behalf of Victor, for his Almighty – and himself!

The only other speech was from the king before the last dance. He reminded his subjects of how no Chief Dancemaster would be complete without his compound and the chiefdom's masquerade. By the next festival, coming in five months time, the compound would have been built and the Dancemaster spirit would have returned there from the heavens. Rebuilding of the compound would therefore start immediately after the on-going ceremony. It would be on the same spot the previous one stood. He, their Almighty, was mandating them to dance in the streets with the new chief to the building site and watch the workmen in action.

And who among the crowd could dare disobey an instruction of Japeedoe? Who, except someone with two heads, or one who's tired of living in the kingdom of Ila?

Because none of them could, they all joined in the musical procession of the new chief, Victor, to the spot earmarked for the building of Dancemaster Compound.

At the site, Victor occupied the quarter's traditional stool and received several honours and homage from his subjects. For once, he saw a positive efficiency in Sese Abram – and King Jap. He could hardly believe that they had already set the physical building work in motion since the crack of dawn! About a dozen men spread out digging along its marked lines of foundation, while another dozen mixed some cement, moulding some of the blocks required. All the workmen were being served by some select women of the chiefdom who fetched water and prepared food for them in

459

the open. Victor was told that as soon as he departed with his fellow chiefs some of the musicians would be shifted nearer to the workmen to boost their morale.

"Give it four weeks," Sese boastfully told Victor, "and it's your completed compound that would sit there. It is not beyond our cooperatives."

"Yes, Sese," Victor replied, intentionally not asking Sese whether in Ila's world, such cooperatives were bribery inspired or were freely volunteered.

* * *

At 12 midnight exactly, King Jap and Victor walked backwards into the purposely dim-lit hall of the *Eagles* meeting inside the shrine building. The king had mandated Victor to lead while he followed closely behind him.

More for witnessing the first ever attendance of Victor into the temple, with how nicely fitting they perceived the cult's clothing on Victor, the members welcome the duo with intoxicating applause. The ovation continued until the new arrivals turned round to their brothers in cultism for Victor to take his place among them, and Jap to occupy the chair reserved for the head of the cultists, the *Grand Eagle*.

Like other fellows, Victor was in a hip-length, raw skin tabard. His tabard, unlike the other members' had no portfolio printed on its lower front. Above the tabard, round his neck, he hung his *Eagle* pendant; while round his head he had his six-inch wide membership leather band. All bands were brown, except those of Sese and the chief priest which were red. For Jap's head, it was a small diadem, bands free.

That the cultists were at the shrine an hour before Jap and Victor gave them time to perfect their preparation before the duo would arrive. Benches and chairs in mixed arrangement were decorated at armrests in cloths of eagle prints. So decorated was the chair for King Jap which the fellows had positioned to face theirs. It wore in addition, on its narrow back, a cloth apron of the group's symbol. In its front was also placed a tripod holding a six-foot fully beaded rod, the Staff of Authority, with artwork of an eagle at its top. When the members had got everything in place they shared the rest of the time between the gifts from Victor, savouring kola with alcohol and puffing tobacco or marijuana.

"Long live *Grand Eagle*," they all hailed Jap as each *Eagle* gave the next a 'hi-five' and then raised his clenched fists. "Forever may you fly; forever may you peck," they ended the traditional prayer. The prayer assured King Jap that though the earlier applause was meant for the generous Victor, the members still respected him as their leader.

"Long live my fellow *Eagles*," the king beamed back. "Forever may you fly; forever may you peck. Please, sit down."

Next, King Jap told the fellows what his original plan for the meeting was: that each *Eagle* would meet Victor at Bilitie and discuss his area of duty directly with Victor. But he had abandoned that plan because it could compromise the secrecy of the cult. Moreover, with the short time in the hands of Victor, individual meetings would create a never-ending affair.

"This, in no way, does not imply that Victor is a novice to the cult," he warned them. "He isn't, having become an *Eagle* before becoming a high chief, and having become the first ever direct high chief in Ila.

"Not just this, within two years he succeeded in solving the major problem the kingdom was unable to solve in four. Therefore, every fellow also needs to learn from him today how to fly in turbulent skies."

Kaka rose ebulliently. He thanked *Grand Eagle* and demanded on behalf of fellow *Eagles* to know what great problem Victor had solved. "We are not sure if it's what we've heard on the grapevine," he said. "If it was, for how long can a palm cover the flames effectively? It's about Jacq's demise, isn't it?" Other *Eagles* were quite amused.

461

The Masquerade

"Yes, about Jacq," the king admitted. "Like the great *Eagle,* he and Uggi seized her alive and preyed on her alive until she was dead. If you have all heard it let all of us applaud Victor once again!" Heartily, all cultists obeyed the order.

As Victor looked round the happy faces of the clappers, he was surprised to note that even though every high chief was an *Eagle* not every chief was. Instead, there were a few chiefs, some elders and a number of Ilas he had never met, a number who projected more ordinariness than substance. It reminded him of the main criterion for membership which both Sese and Chief Priest had once told him and Uggi: determination to pass a test of endurance, and then, to serve the king, self and fellow *Eagles*.

Victor was particularly shocked to see Silas in the meeting of the cultists. Silas, the trouble-evading husband of Bambo, who wouldn't allow his wife to speak against the king's open judgement on Jacq!

"Thank you fellows," the *Grand Eagle* said to tamp down the applause. "Before we go on we need to introduce ourselves, this being the first meeting Victor would attend, and the first after our expansion. The introduction will exclude a senior member, High Priest, who can't be here for this meeting.

"I would start with myself: King Japeedoe, the *Grand Eagle* and Worship Master of the skies. Thank you. Now, Sese."

"High Chief Sese Abram, *Master Eagle*, Chief of Staff to the *Grand Eagle*, and Link-Wing between the *Eagles* and Grand Master."

Victor wished that Sese had expanded more, but he didn't. He gave the nod to Kaka to introduce himself.

"High Chief Kaka, the *Lift Eagle*."

"What is *Lift Eagle*?" Victor interrupted him to ask, before his lack of understanding of the titles would develop into a complication inside him.

"I do the lifting, after the substance has been spotted and confirmed. They could be *leaves*, *dust*, *horns* or *faces*."

462

"I am sorry, Kaka," Victor stopped him again. "I understand nothing of those words. What do you lift? What do you mean by 'lifting'?"

"Okay let's make it this way," King Jap intervened. "Aroso and Kaka should take Victor to the 'warehouse' now and let him see what we have been and shall be talking about. Just for about fifteen minutes."

Disappointingly for Victor, the 'warehouse' was nothing more than a massive room with no goods stocked in, in the professional sense. At best it was an ugly showroom for what the *Eagles* stole and held for sale.

Immediately on entry, the site of stuffed animals caught Victor's attention. They were a middle-aged elephant, a calf, a crocodile, an ostrich and a parrot. Aroso explained that the animals were displayed for their tusks which the *Eagles*, for security reasons, called *horns*, and their skins they called *covers*; and both the ostrich and the parrot for the feathers they called *lightweights*. Next, Victor was shown two pots of marijuana, masks, statuettes and jewellery – which the *Eagles* referred to as *leaves*, *faces*, *tripods* and *dust* respectively.

"Once the position of an object we want is confirmed, it is my duty to arrange its disappearance from that position, and then its reappearance inside Aroso's care," Kaka boasted.

"Oh yes," Aroso complemented. "Then, I handle the storage, valuation, sales and shipment."

Victor listened, hiding his revulsion at the two colleagues he was supposed to share an evil gangsterism with. His patience and cooperation eventually deserted him at two fish tanks, one of assorted surgeon fish and the other of cichlids. The water in both tanks was cloudy and foamy, every fish dead!

"We should stop it here and return to the meeting," Victor said angrily.

"You need to rename your *warehouse* the morgue. You kill your mammals, reptiles, fishes, plants and trees, so where do you

463

hope to find the replacements? In the near future where would you find more of them to lift – and to sell and have money to share? Surely the *Eagles*' way can't be like this." He turned to go, ignoring Sese's putting the blame on the *Steward Eagles* posted to look after the storage.

Back at the meeting, Victor hardly expected Aroso to add anything more about himself. He had been able to confirm Aroso as one who 'warehoused' murders and thefts, valued them and sold them for profits for the *Eagles*. He was the *Eagle*'s criminal intelligentsia!

Worshipper talked about himself next: the third *Master Eagle* whose responsibility it was to spot a job to be done, or create one. He was respected as patient and quiet; and for these, people freely told him of possible jobs. He knew best how to set the savannah on fire in a way that the *Eagles* would profit from the helter-skeltering of the animals that would try to escape such fire! He claimed the people sometimes mislabelled him as being unintelligently lavish; but he preferred that to being seen as selfish.

Silas claimed to be another *Master Eagle*, in charge of internal security, and for which they called him *Peck Eagle*. He had in his team, many *Steward Eagles* including those who checked in the members into the shrine. He claimed to be an excellent eavesdropper, an efficient pre-emptor on the enemies of the members.

Next, the *Grand Eagle* directed they went straight to the day's – the night's – business now that Victor had learnt some of the terminology, seen a number of sales objects, and understood the portfolios of the key *Eagles*. He wanted the deliberations to be short so that Victor would have a few hours rest before starting his return journey to Glasgow.

The *Treasurer Eagle* rendered the periodic account. Usually, it was the first thing at every gathering; and it dictated how subsequent topics were treated. The account was healthy, due mainly to Victor's donation. Without it, it wasn't. Incomes from *leaves* and *horns* had stood the same as the last period. There was nothing from *faces* and *covers*; and less from *dusts*.

Also there was hardly any money coming from the kingdom's shrines made up of the *Òrìshà* temple, the mosque and the church. What every *Deacon Eagle* in charge of each of the three branches realised from his unit was just enough for the basic sustenance of the unit – or so each *Deacon Eagle* rendered!

Aroso, quick to realise Victor's enormous potential was however optimistic about the first part of the treasurer's report. "Now with Victor's tentacles spread beyond Glasgow and Ila, the sales could improve significantly if he could sit with me for a joint look. That would be a help to the *Eagles* of his new kingdom. Am I not right, Victor?"

"Of course you are," Victor affirmed. "After here you and I shall sit together and work out everything. If I have to delay my departure by a day, so be it."

"Up, up *Eagles*," they all chanted for Victor's willing sacrifice. "Forever may we fly. Forever may we peck!"

"Then," Aroso continued, still standing, "I will leave the second part of the treasurer's report to you all," he concluded, pleased that he had successfully opened an avenue for a direct rapport with Victor.

The temple arrived at two solutions for the second part of the account. The first was to engage the strong power of false prophecy. In simultaneous unison, all the three units must falsely predict an impending doom on the women and children of the kingdom. Prayers of all devotees backed by sacrifices of money and materials must be prescribed for its avoidance or curb. The presentation and management must be pessimistic and frightful.

The second was to use show donors at devotional gatherings. Each unit must carefully select two to four trusted worshippers at a time. The selected persons would be given handsome money to donate publicly before other devotees. At the point of donation each 'donor' would announce how he had been

465

blessed due to a particular previous donation he made. He must then call on every devotee to do the same, to invest in God and the gods.

The *Grand Eagle* wanted to know from Kaka if the planned poaching of elephants in the neighbouring kingdoms was having problems.

"It isn't," Kaka replied confidently. "Aroso's stock will be higher within a fortnight," he boasted. He was also upbeat about the new species of marijuana he had been able to steal from the farms of a neighbouring kingdom. "Their cultivation in different farms of Ila is progressing. Our gods-endowed soil is even better for them. Soon *Eagles* would compete better in yield, grade and revenue," he assured them.

Silas tabled the case of three of Kaka's chiefs. They had been using their compounds to plant seeds of discord around by withdrawing their people from standard communal works.

To this case, Sese summarised the *Eagles*' acceptable answer: Kaka would arrange for arson on the farms and barns of both the lesser and the least rebellious of the three chiefs. Kaka would then implicate the rebel leader as the arsonist and bring him up for justice of dethronement before their Almighty and his chiefs, for others to learn from.

The next topic, well timed, was introduced by the king. Two mornings earlier, he had expected Victor to raise it with him in the palace. "Have Silas and Sese resolved the case of Nek, Bambo and the little girl?" the king asked.

Suddenly, Victor's head was clearer. Was it because the king preferred to discuss it first with the *Eagles* that the king waived him from the question three nights ago, he wondered? His face jotted between Sese's and Silas', trying to catch which of them would be the first to respond.

"It is almost solved," Silas replied. "Nek had confessed; but Bambo hasn't enough. So, yesterday I sent Nek to the Lower Dungeon to 'waste'. We still have to extract more from Bambo before her final punishment would be pronounced.

"As for the girl, she is now well enough to return to her servitude in the palace," he concluded. A short silence followed her speech. Kaka ended it.

"Why should it take that long to break a woman and obtain her confession?" Kaka asked. "Or, have you got a Jacq incarnated in your hands? I guess you were lenient with her because she was your wife."

Silas's face turned red. "What you just said was a load of rubbish," he snarled at Kaka. "Rubbish and nothing more!

"Was it not me who nabbed and nailed her in the first place? Then you never said she was my wife.

"When she was handed her first punishment I made the wardens enforce it mercilessly. That time too, you didn't see her as my wife.

"When she connived with Nek over the girl, I was the one who exposed it; and no one talked of her being my wife.

"But now that I am in the middle of a breakthrough with her you are alleging falsely, foolishly..."

"Peace, *Eagle*! Peace, *Eagle*!" *Grand Eagle* shouted at the fighting cultists. As he did he held high and pointedly the Staff of Authority he had before him. Then he addressed Kaka directly:

"An *Eagle* must see clearly and peck right," he cautioned Kaka. "Silas was right and you were wrong. Silas is a fine *Master Eagle*, and I lead you to apologise to him.

"Other *Eagles* can still make their contributions, please."

Victor seized the chance. "But the *Grand Eagle* did promise to let Nek and the girl go free by the next festival," he reminded the king. "I don't know about Bambo though; but that was the promise eighteen months ago."

"Yes," the *Grand Eagle* agreed. "That time I wasn't the *Grand Eagle*, and wasn't talking as him. Sese then wasn't a *Master Eagle*, and wasn't talking as one. You two were more of tourists than *Eagles* and so, were talking like tourists. Now, you are a strong *Eagle* and should therefore talk and think like one.

467

"Remember you proved it, that forgiveness is never a word in the dictionary of the *Eagles* – that every *Eagle* must equally remember that forgiveness allows the forgiven person time to garner the strength and re-offend the forgiver."

"But this is a different case," Victor asserted. "Nothing would be fairer than to suspend actions on Nek and the two females till Uggi is here for the carnival. We both hold our pendants in the highest esteem, and project them as such in Glasgow. We should meet them alive and well when we return with our guests."

At that point Silas rose to make a grim suggestion. "Let Victor return with her to Glasgow later today, and there deal with her the way Jacq was dealt with. That will make my stand clearer."

"I don't have the time or the space for that now," Victor promptly replied. "But keep her and the others till the carnival time, and that will be considered then."

"Is there going to be a new spirit by the next carnival?" one *Eagle* asked.

"No," Sese replied, "except Dancemaster."

Kaka still had more to say before the meeting would end. "*Grand Eagle* and fellow *Eagles*," he bowed and greeted. "I have a proposition that I think you will not regard as being weird. It is about Victor.

"We heard of how he was initiated as a courageous *Eagle*. Up till now he has done great jobs for the *Eagles*, and promises to do more. But we can also see him here as the only high chief with a rank at par with *Steward Eagle*. May I propose that he is elevated to a *Master Eagle*."

The support for Kaka's suggestion was spontaneous, and apparently total. Sese, the only one who hated it, was not courageous enough to display open dissent. Sese had his worst moment when on approval, the *Grand Eagle* customarily called on him to decorate Victor with the red leather head band and lead Victor to him. Then, with the king leading, he joined the traditional

468

chorus: "Long lives *Master Eagle*! Forever may you fly! Forever may you peck!"

"Before we disperse," the *Grand Eagle* said next, "let Sese and Aroso summarise our expectations and the new *Master Eagle* to summarise his. Then we can exchange them for both sides to work on."

"I will leave that for Sese to do," Aroso said. "I still have a session with Victor later." The withdrawal pulled Sese up to speak, stammering and stumbling on the expectations that were more personal than *Eagles*'. 'Loyalty, cooperation and secrecy', he repeated times without number.

But he was also clear enough, that one of the most unpardonable sins an *Eagle* could commit was to promise and not to deliver on the promise.

Victor expressed his confidence to deliver. He would usher in an era of increased wealth and comfort among the *Eagles* and the chiefs. In particular he would work to expand the businesses of the *Eagles* once he knew the problems firsthand from Aroso.

He also wanted all *Eagles* to influence a speedy completion of his compound. It would be from there that the race for the kingdom's increased wealth would be flagged off at the next festival of the masquerades. It was in there he would assemble the dignitaries from all parts of the world. They would dance with the Dancemaster spirit and with Ilas, splash wealth on the compound's spirit and on the people of the kingdom to which the spirit belonged. Certainly, he expected the *Eagles*, chiefs and citizens to welcome his guests with open arms.

* * *

Victor not only failed to have time to rest before he would leave that morning, he also did not find time that day to leave.

By dawn on his way back to the hotel, he stopped by Glawanu's, woke him and gave him a guarded report of what happened in the meeting.

469

"Almost what you heard and saw was true," Glawanu told him. "There, they always bare all with passion and ruthlessness."

"And was Silas true about his wife?"

"Yes. He traded her in to gain the king's favours, to share in the privileges of the *Eagles*. And Azzanaite, her queen sister, couldn't give a damn.

"Every one of them betrayed something to join the group, and will betray more to remain in it.

"Only Nek refused to betray something, his wife. Consequently it landed his family in this calamity."

"So, how is he doing – Nek, with Bambo and the girl? Like Silas said?"

"Largely so. The child's health has improved; I have been detailed to return her to the palace sometime today.

"Bambo is in her cell at Sese's. Nek, can I say, is inside a special one, also at Sese's. He will be starved to death there."

"Okay, listen, Glawanu. Since midnight a few things have changed for the better, as you will discover. But now is when I need your support to improve things even more. Can you promise me?"

"Yes. I swear, on the life of my little daughter."

"Now, I will hand over something most important to you." Victor brought out a mobile handset from his bag.

"This is a Nokia, and it is perfectly safe," he introduced it to Glawanu, handing it over to him. "No one must see it on you. Not even your wife so that she doesn't run into trouble like the other women did.

"Now you've got two gadgets. Be extra careful with them."

Glawanu took it trustingly and admired the phone whose name sounded like a local dog's. He was still wondering...

"Between now and when I come back, myself and Uggi will be able to talk to you on it," he said, starting a half hour lesson with him on how to use it.

When, later, Glawanu called secretly at Bilitie to deliver some materials Victor wanted to return with, a couple of hours more were spent perfecting Glawanu's handling of the mobile phone. The perfection included trial calls from Glawanu's set to Uggi and Jacq, and separate return calls from Uggi and Jacq to Gwalanu's set.

He intended to give one to Latief, the manager, who had then agreed to their friendship, but his sponsors in Glasgow objected to a proliferation. So, instead, he gave the manager a nice radio for his reception desk with some cash for himself. Then he told him Glawanu would brief him about his future needs including the mobilisation of townswomen, and the accommodation his large team from Glasgow would require, for the next carnival.

The extra hours, among other things, caused Victor a day's delay in leaving Ila. But his sponsors back home didn't mind. It had all worked out well, well beyond their expectations.

CHAPTER FOURTEEN

The Return

The morning meeting inside Ben's studio took place two weeks after Victor had returned from Ila. Victor had arrived earlier for the meeting and arranged on a large table, all the exhibits he returned with from Ila. These were the photographic prints of the palace, Eagle Square, Bilitie Inn, the markets, Dancemaster Quarters with the position of the proposed new compound building, the Main Shrine, the mosque, the church, and Sese's compound complete with its horses, dairy and prison. There were also those of King Jap and his queens, as well as those of Glawanu and his wife.

Physically were specimens of a Dane gun, a machete, a set of bow and arrow with two arrowheads, a leather shield and Victor's *Eagle* tabard.

The heaviest single object Victor brought back however was the main mask of the Dancemaster masquerade which he wanted to renovate for his official outing. He was allowed some small artefacts which he was expected to sell and direct the proceeds to the renovation.

To each participant arriving, Victor offered a preliminary explanation of what each item he returned with actually stood for in Ila. His explanation about Queen Musli was largely found unconvincing, causing him some moments of light embarrassment.

When everyone was seated, he started his full report. He was grateful for the opportunity and support. Particularly he thanked Jacq for her understanding, for not reading an offence to his inability to see Nek and Sariya while he was in Ila. He was grateful she understood the tough, impossible circumstances that had prevented him from doing so.

"You did your best within that situation," Jacq had said. "At least it's nice to know they are still alive, and in whatever condition. Let us just get there, and I will sort that out first." She broke into tears.

"What is this, Jacq – again?" Ali, disgusted, asked. "Sobbing again? How can you convince us you are brave when you can't control your emotions? You continue like this and you will lead us into trouble in Ila. Tears and rational thinking are never on the same side of the brain."

Ali wasn't finished yet with Jacq. He wanted to stop Jacq's incessant weeping once and for all. He tongue-lashed her heavily, lecturing her on how everyone at the meeting had his reasons to be emotional, yet it had to be only Jacq who couldn't control hers.

"Do you think that I, and my son, Uggi, are happy to be uprooted from the land of my birth? You think Yeoman is pleased about the culture of criminal masquerading that sold off his forefathers as slaves? That Ben can't be emotional about how he had to give up the business of his forefathers? Where is the post of the Quartermaster of Crying in our current logistics?" The comical nature of his last question lowered the tension in his serious rebuke.

"Rev is right," Ben joined in. "What is important is to plan how the scheme will not go *agley*."

"I am sorry, very sorry, sir," Jacq felt the guilt and apologised.

"Jacq and gentlemen," Yeoman subsequently called, "what next, now that we have heard Victor? We have only three months. Where are we starting from?"

473

The Masquerade

"I suggest from masks and costumes," Ben suggested. "Going by Jacq's desire we shall need plenty of them.

"Or, Victor, from your experience, could you tell us what you think of that?"

Victor agreed with Jacq's aspiration. He was hopeful of the promises Glawanu, his wife and Queen Musli gave him, that they would mobilise women and children for the finale.

"That puts pressure on Mr Smith then," Ali said. "He might have to break up the Glasgow College into many Samba Schools." Everyone laughed at the light hearted suggestion.

"Possibly, yes," Yeoman Smith concurred. "Could mean Jacq returning to Shop 42!"

"I won't mind that," Jacq said, chuckling. "Actually I called Shop 42 the day after Victor travelled. I told the manager to get the catalogue ready for me."

Jacq went further to revealing other contacts she had renewed in anticipation on that day. One was with Alfredo Dotti, the secretary of the Comitato – and his wife. Both of them were willing to visit Glasgow and possibly join the group on the histo-cultural journey to Ila.

Another was with Mark and Patrizia Ceriani in New York; and the couple volunteered similar offers. They wanted the Peacock Group show of Venice repeated inside Ila's Eagle Square – with the exact costumes the quartet used modified with some rare glasses that would come from their New York foundry.

"In that case," Ben reasoned, "the problem is about solved. I should remind us that I still have many artefacts in this studio reserved for the project.

"Is there any other thing about the masks – and costumes?"

"Yes, the theme," Yeoman reminded them. "It is necessary, to guide us. Should I work on one satanic, or one idolatrous – like the kingdom has always been?"

"No, Yeoman, never so in the ages past," Ben disagreed authoritatively. "What's happening is of relatively modern trend. My records can testify to that."

They all agreed instead to a theme that would pray for the kingdom. Using various small masks as a backup, they would express the theme with five principal floats.

One float would be that of a dove, the great religions' bird of peace and deliverance, noted for symbolising the renewal of life, for being untouchable by witches and wizards...noted for Noah's connection...for carrying the olive branch!

Another float would be that of a butterfly, to wish Ila leadership a completely metamorphic rebirth from their sins to proper humanity. In addition it would give the ordinary citizen a sense of grace, beauty and freedom.

The third float would be that of an elephant. It would pray for Ila's wealth, strength and majesty, for the kingdom's patience, wisdom and intelligence.

The fourth float would be of the sheep and the Shepherd. May the Lord watch over and direct the people of Ila, and prevent them from getting lost forever!

Without regret, they had earlier jettisoned the choice of either the lion or the tiger, two animals which though strong, were noted for using the strength negatively for anger and terrorism, for tearing and destroying other souls!

Similarly, a rejection also had gone to the bat, a double-faced creature that was neither a bird nor an animal, a hypocritical creature ever thinking with its world in its head turned upside down.

The fifth float would be that of Dancemaster spirit and the people of Dancemaster Quarters. Victor, their chief, would stay with that.

"Which of the floats am I going into?" came the next question from Jacq.

"That's the question, Jacq," Ben answered with all seriousness. "My personal answer would be, none.

"I think the next question ought to be about how you are going to appear to your people – not in which float. The other could be about how we can successfully counter Ila's violent reaction when its people discover that we've come with you they hate, dead or alive."

Ben's contribution moved the next phase of the meeting to discussing the inevitable war. Straight back they all returned to the specimens from Ila, starting with re-examining the applicable weaponry:

Machete and sword – every guard and junior masquerade carried one while ordinary citizens are banned from carrying them. They were deadly and could severe limbs and heads, or rip bowels open with single cuts.

Longbow, arrow and arrowhead – every guard and junior masquerade underwent archery lessons and tests with the type Victor brought back. It was a deadly type, feather-fletched for precision, metal-tipped for deeper piercing, and poisoned tip for quick kill.

The Dane gun – the deadliest of Ila weapons. It was rare, and legally restricted to a handful of chiefs only, which was a relief to the Glaswegians. Besides, loading was slow and for one shot at a time, curtailing its usefulness in the type of the siege being anticipated.

"Would they really use any of these on anyone?" Yeoman asked.

"But, sir, what type of question is that?" Jacq snapped in her first open doubt of her teacher's intelligence outside arts and artworks. She wondered if he hadn't heard enough of a people that currently basked in torturing people and engineering human disappearances. A people who had prepared her for the guillotine; a people who in the past had fed her own people to the crocodiles and sold away her own children for bottles of Scottish rums and packets of Virginia cigars! What a question from a teacher who must have got a short memory of history! It all shone in her eyes, on her face.

476

"You don't believe they can do that, do you?" she asked Yeoman.

"Well," Ben intervened, "what is important is to plan our defence. We are not just anyone. We are going to be combatants, wrestlers against the status quo, enemies!"

Uggi had a suggestion based on his experiences of Ila and Victor's weaponry collection. "Why can't we use the armour?" he asked them.

"Armour?" Ali asked his son, praying he wasn't going nuts. "To level the people, the palace, or the Eagle Square? You can't be serious!"

But Uggi was deadly serious, as shown by his explanation. He meant armoured wear like stab vests and bullet-proof ones which should also be consequentially spear and arrow proof.

Uggi's pointer was accepted and developed. Every one of them would have one in one form or the other. Victor and Jacq would visit Glasgow's Municipal Textile Mills to make necessary inquiries. They knew that the mill, established more than a century ago as a cloth weaving outfit, had lately expanded into knitting and garments, specialising in ballistic and Kevlar products. It had become the first port of call for Glasgow police, soldiers, paramedics and those in danger of getting shot or stabbed in the course of their duties.

They also considered how they would carry their deadly revolvers without letting the Ilas know. One or two, once fired at any unreasonable senior masquerade would smarten the junior ones to be quiet and peaceful.

The end of the meeting saw Ben conduct the participants round the studio. He wanted to show them those artefacts he had suggested should come to Ila.

At the masks, Jacq still insisted on her objection. "If fighting is that inevitable why should we go with them, or wear them to fight?" she asked Ben directly. "How can we guarantee the extent of damage they would suffer?" Her insistence forced Ben to back down, agreeing to re-open the topic after the coming carnival was over.

"But this one will have to come," Victor said as they were all by the *Elémpe*. "I promised Jap it would. You don't object, Jacq, do you?"

Jacq didn't. She, instead, gently pushed the statue forward and backward on its wheels before turning it round on its axis. She felt it move smoother with lesser effort than it did the first time she saw and pushed it. "Can you please open its back again, Ben?" she pleaded.

Ben unlocked and opened it, allowing Jacq to admire its massive hollow which she suddenly jumped into. As she did, her weight and instability rolled it on, in time for Ali to catch it.

"Ah, Jack," Yeoman remarked. "Don't tell us it should be turned into an armoured vehicle for you to hide and ride in!"

"I am sorry she apologised in the midst of the laughter generated by Yeoman's joke. This time she believed the joke was intelligent enough to confirm she wasn't too way out in her hidden thoughts about the statue, relevant to the inevitable war.

* * *

The date and time of arrival of the group from Glasgow to Ila Carnival was specially directed by Glawanu. Actually, King Jap had expected the group two days earlier than the Tuesday it arrived. But the visitors had chosen to raise the king's anxiety by being late, and to play safe by their hour of entry. By 6 a.m. when they were incoming, all the junior masquerades on sentry at the borders had vacated their posts with whatever loot they could muscle from some innocent citizens on behalf of the king and his gang.

"I never expected this day," Ben said with positive pensiveness as Victor drove deeper into town, the 14-seater van leading the batch of eleven of them in four vans. He had however stopped short of telling the kind of day, whether one he would visit Ila by himself, or one his son would ironically lead him into the legendary business place his own father had failed to lead him. Others in the van met Ben's comment with total silence, indicating that they were full of their own expectations too – or lack of them.

"The roads and their modest planning, the houses and their numerousness, the humble but tasteful decorations," Ben had resumed the praise, "it is all incredible!" He spoke with a praising mood that was obviously guarded by the chromosomes he must have genetically inherited from Collin Mackinnon. This time others agreed with him – that the hours might be early, but nothing on the streets of Ila appeared to be slumbering.

Bilitie Inn was their first point of call before they proceeded to the palace. There, the manager, Latief, waited, eager to show them their reservations as placed by Glawanu, and to assist them in any necessary unloading of their vehicle.

By design Mark and Patrizia Ceriani, disguised as ordinary tourists, were already there. They had been, two days earlier, to spy on the events. Jacq, heavily disguised and totally unrecognisable to anyone outside the Glasgow group, joined the Cerianis.

When the group arrived at the palace, Queen Musli, just on her way out, was the first to recognise Victor alighting from the leading van. She halted her outing and retreated into the palace in speed.

"He's here, Victor from Glasgow!" she screamed through the door separating her and the king in his bedroom.

"Thank heavens! With Uggi?"

"I don't know, my Almighty. But there are a lot of them, in four vehicles...just parking."

Musli's ignorance about not knowing Uggi, the king could excuse. When Uggi and Victor met her Almighty at the last carnival, she was neither a queen nor was she among any of the Ilas who welcomed the duo. All the same, the news spurred up the king to don his diadem, grab his whisk and proceed to where he could peep at the visitors.

A pair of the gateman and a junior masquerade running inside met him. "I know, I know," he pre-empted them. "How many are they?"

"Eleven, including High Chief Dancemaster and Uggi." Now he was sure it was the Glaswegians, and that his two days of waiting were finally over.

"Good. Lead them at once to the Lion to sit. Then bring Victor and Uggi to me at the rear hall. Now, now, please!"

"Hello, brothers," the king met them, hugging them one by one – much to Uggi's amazement. "Are you well?"

"Thank you, Your Highness, we are," Victor gave the response.

"And greetings for the season, the festival season," Uggi added. "May you see many more."

"Amen, now I know I will. You nearly killed me, coming two days late. I was watching all directions for you. Sese has given up. He advised me to do the same."

"Well," said Victor, "Sese has always been the starkest doubting Thomas to my person and anything progressive. We are sorry the preparation took longer than we expected."

"But now we are ready, Your Highness," Uggi took over. "We are here for the kingdom, to give the biggest of all carnivals."

"How many people came with you?"

"Fourteen came to help us," Uggi said, to Jap's excitement. "Nine are here with us, three in Bilitie to look after our reservations. We thought we might need the reservations for the women."

"Apart from that," Victor added, "we projected the carnival all over Glasgow and Venice. We expect many tourists to arrive before Saturday."

"That, is the combination of chieftaincy and the *Eagle* working well in the two of you," Jap commended. "The junior spirits have already confirmed an increase in the number of Europeans arriving in the inns. Fortunately, the Dancemaster

Compound is ready. It has enough secluded areas for your women too. We got it ready as you wanted us to do!"

"That is great," Victor said. "Now, do you want to meet our friends?"

"Oh, Victor, you want me to call that an unnecessary question, but I won't!" King Jap joked.

"But before we go to them, about Jacq's clothes, do you bring them?"

"Oh yes, Your Highness," Uggi replied, "first thing we packed." He took a big wrapped plastic bag out of his backpack and handed it over to the king.

"Are these surely hers?" King Jap wanted reassurance as one by one, he took out the items: a blouse, a skirt, a head scarf – and a pair of big dark glasses! "So, the gods blinded her before she died?"

"Not totally," Victor said. "But they were all hers, what she used to feel most comfortable in." Then he suddenly paused as if he had remembered something, reopened his backpack and brought out a smaller paper pack. "More of her clothes, Your Highness," he said and gave it to the king. "Her undies."

"Undies?" Jap asked, ignorant of the word, opting to shake out the pack's contents to find out. A matching set of tricot pants and brassiere fell on his hand; with them, a wild fit of excitement.

"Aha, undies – black as well!" he shouted with astonishment. "How else can one prove she was ever dark inside, however bright she appeared on the outside?"

Suddenly he had one more thing to be jubilant about – the extraordinary brilliance in the thinking capacity of Victor and Uggi. He offered to share with them how he arrived at his judgement:

Just after Victor had departed Ila, Chief Priest discovered that he, the king, and Sese, had forgotten to include two other important things in the list of items that would be required for the rite of passage ritual; and that they were Jacq's head and private hairs. How the thoughtfulness of Victor and Uggi had solved that

481

problem! There're bound to be strands of Jacq's head hairs on her scarf, of armpits' on her bra, and of her lower private parts' on her pants. It was all a testimony that the gods wanted her dead, dead with her black and evil mind! It would make the job of our Chief Priest easier to during the night.

"I am happy we brought everything," Victor said with pride. He looked across to Uggi and both men in their minds wondered how the king and his chiefs would have felt or done should they know that the true source of all the clothing items was a charity shop in the Barras area of Glasgow. "We pray it all goes well for the Chief Priest tonight."

* * *

The first night's sleep of the Glaswegians at the Dancemaster Compound of Ila was interrupted by the midnight sound of the gong. It was coming from outside, by the main door of the compound. The secretary, Alfredo, and his wife were the first it awoke, and the first among the visitors to be at the window to peep.

There were three men outside the door, all masked and wrapped up in pieces of white cloth. One wore the largest mask – of a dreadful crocodile head above his massive necklace of feathers and beads. He cruelly clasped a black chicken upside-down by the legs, in his right hand. He displayed leadership of the pack.

The second man's mask was light, and of a human depiction. He had a set of big metal gong and beater in his hands, and hung a small bag containing 'Jacq's clothes' across his shoulders.

The third man, similarly lightly masked as the second, had a strapped drum hanging down his front from his neck.

"Ritual – a burial ritual," Victor who had now joined the swollen company of peeping tourists said. "The man in the big mask is the chief priest, the other two, his aides. The masks they wear are for protection against the death that strikes whoever they are trying to bury."

"And who is he?" Alfredo asked.

Victor was quiet, not willing to give the secretary an answer. He could not rationalise it to him how the burial was for the Jacq who was with them in the group. He believed an attempt at answering was bound to attract endless questions. Understandingly, Uggi and Ben also added nothing to the earlier explanation Victor had given.

There was another short burst of the instruments, and a stop. Then the Chief Priest started his incantations which, inescapably, revealed to the peepers who the ritualists were supposed to be burying – Jacquensica Nek!

The end of the first round of incantations saw the instruments re-started, this time continuously and in unison. The Chief Priest moved between the players and commenced plucking the feathers of the live chicken, freely throwing them on the ground around them. Next, the trio formed a file and turned away from the main door of the compound. From there, led by the Chief Priest, and making alternate sideway turns at every other steps, they embarked on a long drumming and plucking trek to the bank of River Qin.

"You know what, boys?" Ali addressed Uggi and Victor as soon as the file disappeared. "Call Jacq now and warn her. Though no one knows she is here, she still needs to be careful tonight that they are gunning for her soul and spirit."

Uggi complied straightaway, but got no response – Jacq's phone was dead!

"Try Patrizia then," Ali hurriedly suggested. "Don't mind the hour of the night."

Victor called Patrizia, and had to wait anxiously for a reply. That reply came in another three minutes, three minutes that felt like three times ten minutes! "She's out of the room she shares with her friend. We can't find her. The hotel receptionist just discovered someone or some people used the backdoor to the hotel!" Suddenly the Glaswegians group saw an indication of a big trouble starting so soon. They feared Jacq had been exposed and arrested at Bilitie she was hidden, or had been killed by Sese's men.

"It means we are in trouble already. The priority will be to rescue her now, before it's too late."

"Until tomorrow morning the junior masquerades are all over the places," Victor reminded them. "The only thing we can do now is to intimate Glawanu."

Glawanu was distressfully brief in answering Victor. "She's safe now," he said. "She ventured out but I have recovered her. Talk to you later." He cut off with no time to explain where Jacq was recovered from or taken to on this dangerous night of the rituals.

By the time the Chief Priest reached the river bank, the hen was completely de-feathered. His assistants started an arranged fire while the Chief Priest said more incantations. The priest killed the hen by slashing its neck, collected Jacq's purported clothing, and dropped all in the fire.

Within minutes, the assistants carefully collected the ashes, meant to be Jacq's soul and spirit, into a special calabash and handed it over to the Chief Priest. They were to be scattered over the running water of the legendary River Òşin.

The Chief Priest sprinkled the ashes in measured bits. He was delighted to watch the flow spread them out into reduced thinness until total oblivion. So the spirit of the dead Jacq had gone, washed away forever. Or so would it finally be, once the return journey to where they started from, the old Dancemaster Compound of Jacq, was completed.

The personal feeling of success lived with the priest for the next three minutes. It stopped when, about two hundred yards after the file left the bank, Glawanu suddenly appeared and stopped them. The Chief Priest knew it was a bad omen.

"My Almighty wants you urgently," Glawanu told the priest. "He wants you now." The message was firm.

The Chief Priest feared the likely implication of the unprecedented interruption and attempted to say so, but Glawanu was quicker at reading him. "There's trouble in the palace; you have to terminate this here," Glawanu said, bluntly.

The problem the Chief Priest met at the palace was just tapering, still far from starting a descent to solution. It was happening inside the bedroom of Queen Azzanaite to the senior queen herself. King Jap swiftly led his senior-most priest in, to her.

"She's being troubled," the king lamented to the priest. "She just came round from a long faint."

The Chief Priest moved nearer to the queen lying on her bed. He could see her panting and gasping. He put his hand on her forehead and gauged her temperature. He was after all also the chief native doctor of the kingdom, one whose wisdom in healing transcended those of the emerging western physicians in Ila. He felt the dampness, and the enormous body heat that stopped the dampness from forming bigger rivulets of sweats. "What has been troubling her?" he asked the king.

"Jacquensica, Jacquensica – Jacquensica!" Azzanaite cried out. "I saw her. Her ghost appeared to me. It is true. She was at my window, staring at me! Half her face: pure white!"

"That's her problem, the problem," the king told the priest. "That's her claim since she came round. Glawanu and the guards searched round but saw nothing."

"Was it anything to do with the on-going ritual for Jacq?"

"I don't think so. Actually, the ritual went on well. The fire devoured her bird and her clothes quite fast; and the river freely went away with the ashes. We were just returning to the compound to complete it when Glawanu met us."

"Or, could it be for the detour ahead of the completion?"

"Well, no. Otherwise all this would have only started about the time of the detour." He offered to go home and fetch appropriate concoctions to calm Azzanaite. He was yet to get out of the palace when Sese rushed into the palace, a junior masquerade on night sentry in his compound running behind him.

"What are you doing here?" Sese managed to stop and address the Chief Priest, rudely. "Do you know you haven't banned the soul of Jacq? It appeared you have actually strengthened it. That is why I am here to see our Almighty!" It was a serious indictment, serious enough for the priest to turn back and follow Sese to King Jap.

"It is beyond my understanding," Sese cried as the three entrants were before the king. "Let this masquerade who saw her say it in his own words."

The masquerade unveiled to highlight the frightful experience of what he saw: It happened just about an hour ago. He saw a lady walking regally along inside Sese's court. He saw her from the back. Her regalia were similar with Queen Azzanaite's, and he believed it was her at first, at that strange hour and place. Then he approached her only for her to turn, and her face became that of late Jacquensica. Then she gave a ghostly shriek and asked him if he was ready to follow her to the heavens. He was speechlessly glued in deepest fear when the ghost disappeared. Just over an hour ago!

"That's what happened, my Almighty," Sese summed up. "You may have to ask Chief Priest if Jacq is stronger in death or the Chief Priest had preformed the wrong rites," he challenged.

"I can see where you are going, Sese," the priest, full of anger, responded. "Why couldn't you be brave enough to ask if the queen is in league with Jacq? Did the masquerade not just say the spirit she saw was Queen Azzanaite turned into Jacq?

"We all know, don't we, that when two spirits collide, the winner vanishes while the loser is left weak and sick – like the queen is?

"And lastly, Sese, to your question when you met me by the gate: Were you patient and civil enough for me to answer why you met me here at 4 a.m.? No." He asked the king's permission and stormed out – to see what he could do regardless of Sese's silly deductions.

Sese, on the other hand, remained unrepentant after Chief Priest had departed. He was, even after the king had related to him the coincidence in the sighting of Jacq's ghosts. "All the same," Sese still insisted, "it's absurd of him to say the queen had a devilish linkage with Jacq. If two people could simultaneously sight a woman's ghost he claimed to have banished, then it would be foolish for any person not to identify his inefficiency as a priest. Chief Priest needs to upgrade his knowledge of dealing with supernatural beings."

"Supposing Chief Priest is right?" King Jap asked Sese on reflection.

"Pray he isn't, my Almighty."

"If he is, then the kingdom is in trouble of being haunted by that witch. It means we would still need to encourage and not dismiss Chief Priest, isn't it?"

"Well," Sese agreed partially. "Actually, I would like to think that more of Silas is what we need most now."

"Why? How?"

"Fighting a ghost cannot be entrusted to the spiritualism of a single person. We have to put the physical and the intelligence on standby as well. We will not allow the festival we expect to be the best to be turned the worst."

"That's good thinking, Sese," the king said. "And do you know what that means?"

Sese didn't.

"Meaning you don't divide over a common danger and fight to win it. Meaning me, you, we, must show solidarity with Chief Priest. Meaning you should apologise to him for insulting his efforts. Can you do that when he returns?"

Sese agreed to; and he did.

But Sese also went beyond that. For the remaining days before the finale, he strategized more vigilance around the kingdom, using Silas with his junior masquerades. Keeping it from King Jap, he mounted a serious vigil on Uggi who he didn't trust; and on Victor, the formidable rival he suspected of playing certain games with the death of Jacq. Jacq, and not just her ghost, could still be alive!

* * *

For the team from Glasgow, the final preparation for the finale of Saturday started the Thursday before when suddenly, at the palace, the team had two boosters to its strategy.

First, at the palace Sese Abram told the team the order in which the masquerades would dance. It was one he had convinced King Jap to endorse and one different to what he had told Victor six months ago. Kaka, Aroso and Worshipper would take to the floor first and deliver all the donations they received before the king. Then they would dance back to the Main Shrine which was nearer to the palace than to their respective quarters, and there disrobe. Their followers would then dance back to Eagle Square to honour Dancemaster's group and the king's Jemba Couple. His own, the Fire Spirit, would be too busy arranging the dances. The arrangement suited the Glaswegians who saw in it, a great blessing that the powerful masquerades would not be in the Square to start an attack or resistance when Jacq showed up in the Square.

Victor rushed to complement the arrangement. "On behalf of my team, I am providing two vans with loudspeakers to go round the town and remind the people to be present on Saturday."

"Excellent, excellent!" the king responded.

"I will go round in one and Uggi in the other."

"No, you won't," Sese cut in harshly, unmindful of the good feelings the offer had given his Almighty. "You are a chief who should send others on errands, understand? We shall get some other clever people to send."

"Glawanu and someone from my quarters?" Victor asked, trying to influence Sese's choice.

"No, not necessarily. I shall sort that out myself."

"We can do it this way and avoid an argument," the king tried to prevail. "Uggi, you go with Glawanu in one van; and Silas, with any clever one in the other. You, Sese, can choose that clever one."

Sese wished he had the power and audacity to disagree with his Almighty. More for his own position, he felt the king was again wrong and being careless.

The second of the moment's boosters was borne out of the first. As Glawanu led Uggi round to invite the people, he became more of an *Eagle* to Uggi than to either King Jap or Sese. Well above caution, he poured answers out to Uggi's questions on the strategic who is who and where is where in Ila relative to what the Glaswegians minds wanted to discover. With the guidance of Glawanu, now spoilt with gifts and promises of more from Uggi, Uggi was able to extend a selective invitation to some people as Gwalanu followed him round. Such people would report to Dancemaster's Quarters from the following day, Friday, to become trained as a follower of Dancemaster's masquerades.

The duo's tour ended at Dancemaster's Quarters where they met the same elders who Sese had gathered on the morning of Victor's chieftaincy installation. This time it wasn't a chicken fight they were gathered to arrange. Instead, they had the Glaswegian gifts to share with fellow citizens of the chiefdom, the people who would follow Chief Dancemaster and his float on Saturday.

For the first time, the elders let it be known to Uggi that they were unhappy at the abrogation of their quarters' title and masquerade in the first place. They assured Uggi that now that both had been restored they would rally everyone round with wholesome support in any way Victor and Uggi might wish.

They were about to disperse when four junior masquerades barged into the gathering. Their apparent insulting behaviour forced the tongue of Uggi. "Why are you people so disrespectful?" he asked them.

The Masquerade

"People?" one masquerade asked. "We are spirits, can't you see?" Now they were giggling.

"Who gave you the authority to come here?" one of the elders asked.

"High Chief Silas gave us the authority," one of the masquerades answered.

Silas did, instructed to, by Sese Abrams. Sese had given the instruction without informing the king who he suspected would not support the action. Sese, believing that the round-the-town-tour was taking Uggi and Glawanu too long to complete, had told Silas to send the junior spirits not only to join and watch the entourage but also to remain permanently stationed in and around Dancemaster's Quarters.

"We shall report you to High Chief Sese," another elder bleated out at the masquerades. "Now that we've got our own chief, end why can't we breathe peacefully?"

"Personally I will take this to Chief Dancemaster and the king," Uggi joined the last elder. As he did, the mention of the king, more than that of Chief Dancemaster, withdrew the masquerades to other selected parts of the Quarters they were instructed to watch, for the entire duration of the period.

* * *

The finale of the finale had finally arrived, ushered in by King Japeedoe's most extravagant entry into the Eagle Square. His accompanying crowd was big, and it included his two queens and their children.

Instead of riding in on a horse as usual, he arrived hoisted up on a leather pad shoulder-hoisted by four men, like an old pope.

This time he didn't dance round the square to win the people's hearts for donations. He knew that the presence of the Glaswegians in full force would compel the gifts to dance to him.

Fire Spirit hopped menacingly up and down the Eagle Square, partly entertaining the people and partly warning any

490

potential trouble makers in the environment. He eventually steadied and stopped before King Jap, paid homage and started his announcement.

"The magic and superiority of Ila," Fire Spirit blared over the microphone he took from the set-up before the king, "the nationality and internationality of the kingdom, and the guiding efficiency of the spirits of our ancestors, have all combined, to disallow anyone, from spiriting away, any of our gods and spirits!

"They have enabled our Almighty, to find the stolen spirit of *Elémpe*!

"Our Almighty has brought it home, from the fools who failed to understand, that no external or internal thief, can forever have the spirit of Ila locked up!

"Now, I, with Chief Victor Dancemaster, shall unveil the recovered *Elémpe*, and escort him to our Almighty to resume his age long guarding duties!"

The announcement brought the new Chief Victor Dancemaster into official view for the first time in Eagle Square. Slowly he unveiled the covered statue in the middle of his float. Then both he and Fire Spirit followed *Elémpe* as two junior masquerades pushed its wheels to the front position between King Jap and his two queens. After two long decades, *Elémpe* was finally back at his sentry duties.

Another announcement of Fire Spirit took Victor and the entire Glaswegian contingent by surprise. It followed immediately after the four big kingdom masquerades had danced but were still waiting in the Square instead of retiring to the Main Shrine. Sese had now called Victor's group to start its dance parade.

"The announcement must have been made in error," Victor was quick to note. He communicated his conviction to other Glaswegian floats. They should wait till after the four big masquerades would have left for the shrine to disrobe – as Sese had told them in the palace before King Jap. Victor believed Fire Spirit would correct himself.

491

But it turned out that Sese, inside his Fire Spirit costume, had not erred. He had suspected there would be certain trouble from Victor to prevent at best, or contain at worst; and that he would need the joint strength of the big four kingdom masquerades to contain it. He had successfully deceived Victor and his group with the dancing arrangement he told them of earlier.

The Glaswegians were still struggling to assimilate Sese's trickery when Sese, through Silas, pulled the next fast one on them. Silas brought out ten machete-armed junior masquerades and put them into five pairs. Then he posted a pair each to lead each of the five Glaswegian floats including the Dancemaster's.

"But they are not our members," Ben challenged Silas. "Why do you send them to us, and why are they armed?"

"Not your members?" Silas derided. "So are hundreds of other people who are here now to dance with you and give you gifts.

"The junior masquerades are armed to hurt any person who would dare bring mayhem to your procession."

"They can't even dance," Ben, not satisfied with Silas' explanation, protested.

"They have been trained to try. Nothing is born with dancing – not even the larva!"

From where she hid herself, Jacq felt worried as she watched the delay and sensed the argument. She communicated her fears to Victor, prompting Victor to go to Ben and Silas, now joined by Fire Spirit. Though the argument was suspended, Silas and Fire Spirit conceded nothing to the Glaswegians. And so roared the music boxes mounted with each of Victor's five floats – and with the roar the forward march of the floats. The unimaginable spectacle for Ilas had taken off, the dream of Jacq started to be realised.

At a height of about ten feet, the magnificent white dove, the main depiction of the leading float, towered above the horse that pulled its wheeled platform. The dove was of a special mould complete with olive branch it held in its beak.

Ahead of the horse but behind the pair of junior masquerades Sese and Silas jointly posted to lead it was the first set of Glaswegian masquerades. Their dancing and beauty were special, rendering the dirty, leading junior masquerades stupidly odd. More groups of women and children of the Quarters, all distinct in their dresses, headwear, armbands and body decorations, danced round the float.

The masquerades of Ben Mackinnon and Mrs Dotti, Alfredo's wife, jointly captained the Dove float. With grandeur and handsomeness that marked their smooth-face masks, they strolled and danced to the calypso sound of the float, the two of them depicting an identical pair of male Scottish Highlanders, complete with long and flamboyant tartan kilts, bonnet caps, sporrans and sheathed *skean-dhus*.

In the dignitaries' zone, before the king, the float stopped to do its special dance, the throw dance. With mad generosity, all the masquerades turned to the dignitaries and threw presents at them. Beads, watches, fire-lighters, soaps, jewelleries, shirts, socks, vests and toys were freely given to mark the first ever 'throw' by a masquerade in Ila. King Jap and Fire Spirit were excited watching members of their families and the dignitaries sitting around the king, and competing almost to rioting to catch the articles that were being thrown. With frenzy the king waved his horse-tail whisk at the group, its dove and the olive branch in its beak. He exhibited so much happiness that the Glaswegians believed that the throw was already softening his heart – and that further throws would soften it even more on Jacq when she eventually showed up in the following float. That was the throw's principal objective and the Glaswegians were confident it was achieving just that.

The following float was a huge *Lepidoptera* of swallowtail stock with colourful spots glowing on its wings. A fully masked Yeoman Smith representing its abdomen walked along with the wings opened to the back.

The Masquerade

The Butterfly was planned to be the most crucial float of the mission. It masked the largest number of women. Among them was Patrizia in her full Viking Venetian costume, paired with Peacock, the costume other Glaswegians believed Jacq was in. Significantly, both women were planned to dance and unveil before the king, to reveal the first ever women masquerades in Ila! The Butterfly was thus assigned the unenviable tasks of detonating a double shock on the leaders of Ila and be the first to absorb Ila's peace or war reactions.

Yeoman on walking his float before the king stopped and ordered a throw more intensive than the Dove's. Then he sent out another signal – of crucial alert – that the moment had come. That all Glaswegians must be ready to defend the cultural abomination they were ready to commit before the Ilas in Eagle Square.

Sese appeared to sense the moment too. Suddenly he abandoned watching the throwing going on around the king and walked hurriedly across to the four senior masquerades for a brief chat. The aftermath saw about a dozen more junior masquerades rolled out to watch immediate surroundings of High Chief Victor Dancemaster and his spirit, and up to the Shepherd float that was next to Dancemaster. Sese, in Fire Spirit, was sure Victor had a terror he was ready to unleash if not on the kingdom, then on his chiefdom of Fire Spirit.

"Now, time for the ladies to go," Yeoman communicated to every float leader. "Now, before Fire Spirit returns to Jap." He followed it with a direct instruction which, starting with the Viking and the Peacock, simultaneously made all the women masquerades in the Butterfly float unveil.

"Here, Fire Spirit, come over and help!" Queen Azzanaite screamed. She just saw how the women's disrobing had turned her husband into a speechless shaking jelly on his throne. King Jap looked drowsy, as if about to pass out. "Help! Women masquerade in Eagle Square!!"

Azzanaite's call met Sese midway between where he and Silas had just posted some junior masquerades and the throne of the king. Automatically it added speed to his pacing.

"So this is it – yes, it is!" Sese croaked at the empty air between him and the women masquers standing before him, their masks and costume parts in their hands. He recovered quickly and blew his whistle, summoning Silas and the junior masquerades to join him by the king and the Butterfly.

"Where is she?" other Glaswegians could hear Yeoman asking as he discovered that Jacq wasn't the one who wore the Peacock. "For God's sake, where?"

"Safe," Patrizia answered him before Silas and his 'troop' of junior masquerades could reach the Butterfly.

"Now, guards, attack and arrest them!" King Jap yelled on recovering from his shock. Cleverly, he meant to use the instruction to escape the scene into the safety of his palace complex.

"Arrest them," he repeated, "and strike down any of them that resists!"

The four guards by him moved forward to comply with the royal order. In doing so they left behind the fifth 'guard', the legendary *Elémpe*!

Elémpe ably moved itself – turned round on its own axis. Then its back split along its lockable suture, hatching out an Amazon, Jacqensica Nek! The emergence, though split-second late to block King Japeedoe's escape, was in time to put Jacq face to face with Azzanaite and block her from fleeing with the king. Azzanaite looked into Jacq's face with horror and screamed "ghost! ghost!" fainting and falling with the scream. In no time disappeared the Glaswegians' expectation of peace, replaced by that of war between two different cultures.

Between Silas and Sese commanding the junior masquerades, Azzanaite, with Musli, was evacuated into the palace – moments after Jap who had long fled. Silas and Sese's Fire Spirit were so much disarrayed that in the evacuating process they left

495

behind the elite children who were seated with the dignitaries. Patrizia obtained the assistance of other Glaswegians to hold them together and safe.

Yeoman and Jacq made an effort to stop the fleeing royals but Jacq's pursuit was stopped by two arrows some junior masquerades shot at her back, felling her. That left only Yeoman who continued the chase into the palace he didn't know.

"Now, you witch will die for the final time," Fire Spirit mocked Jacq as Jacq stabilised herself from the fall. He was standing almost over Jacq, his execution sword drawn. "However many your lives may be, you will die now and be buried for the final time." He was calm and cold, ready for the kill.

"And so will you, Sese," Jacq, still remaining on the floor, told him. "You will die with the selfishness and corruption that drives your wicked soul."

Jacq made the sizing up a brief one. With flashing rapidity she fired the jet from the flamethrower she was carrying at the Fire Spirit masquerade. Sese in his Fire Spirit outfit had no chance: the hot force of the thrower lifted and dropped him in flames, staring him on his short, painful but irreversible journey to permanent hell. The scene rendered the third float, the Elephant, ready for its objective.

The mammoth elephant was moulded in light armour, with holes big enough to shoot from the inside. It was the mission's armoury cum ordinance, complete with its 'army personnel and reserves'. Inside its belly Alfredo Dotti, the missions Quartermaster and the floats captain, was on alert with twelve trained fighters.

Swiftly, Alfredo deployed his 'army' to reinforce the floats and secure every square inch of all grounds. He specifically deployed Latief and an elder from Dancemaster's Quarters to block Aroso and Worshipper from advancing to the dignitaries' area. Then Alfredo joined and took over the control of the blockade, pointing his gun at the two spirits and demanding that they surrender the swords they drew. Kaka read the scenario from behind and refused to make the advance with his fellow two senior masquerades. Instead, he went over to Victor, pledged his loyalty and disappeared to disrobe voluntarily.

"So, you, our elder, led the abomination and betrayal; and you, the manager, housed it," Aroso angrily addressed the two men who first blocked him and Worshipper. He wished both men didn't have the deadly pistols pointed at him and Worshipper. He knew it would be suicidal to confront head-on, a firepower that was practically superior to any of Ila's incantations or arms.

"What you term abomination is nothing but our resistance – against your corruption," replied the armed elder. "If there has been a betrayal it is yours – of the kingdom, of the people of Dancemaster Quarters, of Nek family...!"

Just then two poisoned arrows flew in and pierced the neck of the speaking elder. They struck precisely as Aroso himself broke out and headed towards the Butterfly float. While the shooter was identified and summarily shot, Aroso was instantly immobilised by a gunshot from Alfredo to his leg.

"We couldn't find Chief Priest to treat you, and no one could. You shall receive no treatment until you have disrobed yourself – here!" Alfredo told Aroso. "And you, Worshipper, the two of you must unmask now and let the people see your faces."

The argument lasted, but Alfredo prevailed. He showed no mercy in exposing the faces of the two senior corrupt masquerades to public ridicule. Another first in Ila.

"You are killing me, you know that don't you," Aroso groaned to Alfredo.

"Funny. Does a spirit ever die?" Alfredo mocked Aroso further.

"Please, call Chief Priest; don't let me bleed to death!" Aroso pleaded directly with Latief. "You know him. Please go for him."

"Very well," Alfredo agreed. He told Latief to go for Chief Priest among the standing Ila masquerades. But the manager could not find the Chief Priest. He had fled unnoticed – perhaps with the influence of *àféèrí* magic!

"Anyway, we shall search further for him to come and treat your wound," Alfredo assured Aroso. "Meanwhile you are under arrest and will be taken away.

"As for you Worshipper, for disrobing first, without giving us much problem, you can go, but with a warning never to venture again into any mask or cultural costume." Alfredo appointed two of the unveiled junior masquerades escorted by a Glaswegian, to accompany Worshipper in carrying his mask and costumes to deposit at the Main Shrine. As soon as the Glaswegian escort to the three men was on his way back to the Square, Worshipper commandeered his helpers to come with him to Bilitie Inn. There he had his first sweet revenge by burning down the hotel under the chant of hate songs.

"For sure now, they won't have a place to hide and plan again," one of the three arsonists said.

"Yeah," Worshipper agreed. "But not until their headquarter itself is removed. The new Dancemaster compound has to go, re-burnt and re-levelled to what it was a while ago!" And so the three men marched to the compound.

At Dancemaster Compound there was no one in sight. Even the Quarters were largely desolate. "Idiots," Worshipper jubilated at the prospect of an easy operation, "if only they realised that they are at their last carnival as a free people!" Then he led the assault on the main door while one of his helpers smashed his way in through the window next to the door. Their objective: arson started from within was always difficult to put out, more difficult to reach. He and the helpers set the compound on an unquenchable fire!

And with that burning eagerness to destroy, Worshipper closed his mind against analysing how a defence must have been put in place inside a moated castle. Four shots rang from inside the building, one at the first accomplice who went in through the window, and three at the door being assaulted. Two of the shots hit

Worshipper, one piercing the chest with which he braved corruption and the other his brain that once thought of nothing but how to steal. They gave him no chance to scream at the blood that streamed from his body. He was dead, instantly dead. The second accomplice fled, hoping no one had witnessed his role.

* * *

Meanwhile the fighting and stalking continued inside the palace. With Queen Azzanaite fully recovered, it was the king, his queens and Silas, all familiar with the palace layout against Yeoman Smith, a total stranger to the palace. Jacq therefore felt the urgent need for herself, Victor and Uggi to join up with Yeoman. She wanted no further blood split: Killing Silas or any of the royals could deprive her of ever knowing where her daughter and her husband were held; the death of Yeoman or anyone from Glasgow would rob her of a great friendship.

"Stop stalking them and tell us your exact position," Jacq spoke to Yeoman from her handset.

Yeoman only explained where he was as far as his unfamiliarity could get him. It wasn't very helpful.

"Speak with Glawanu then," she re-directed Yeoman. "He is here, and will understand the position better."

From their hidden position the king, his queens and Silas could hear Yeoman mention Glawanu and speak with him.

"So, Glawanu is with them; no wonder," lamented the king, regretfully.

"But Sese warned you, my Almighty," Silas responded. "I discovered it and told him to tell you. You ignored him."

Then they heard Yeoman repeating where in the near-total darkness of the palace he was – in a large hall, under a gourd covered with snakeskin and cowries. They also knew Glawanu would come up and lead Yeoman out of danger.

"I know where that is, where the Glaswegian is," Silas told the king, "and I am going out to finish him."

"No, not yet," the king disagreed. "Start with the traitor within first. I know he will attempt to come and lead him out. Cross him at the door and take him out first. That shall make us safer to fight from here."

Silas, now armed with a sword wouldn't miss his chance. He rushed out into the dark and took a position of ambush against Glawanu. As soon as Glawanu passed him he delivered a fatal blow from behind on his 'un-armoured' head, deep into his skull. By the time Silas finished with Glawanu, Yeoman had found the safe room and locked himself in it.

When Silas returned to the king and queens, he met Queen Azzanaite particularly angry at Musli. "If Glawanu was all that deep in it, so also must you, Musli," Azzanaite accused the junior queen. "You have become so friendly with Glawanu. I have seen many strange gifts with you; they must have come from Victor. Gifts you didn't let my Almighty know about!"

"That too we have always suspected," Silas corroborated to Jap. "We were waiting for proof to convince you that something existed between them and her."

"Now it could be too late for me," the king regretted, biting his teeth. "Musli, it means you actually carried the product farther than the market stall I designated for it. But before we perish you will have to make your confession. I will kill you first if you don't."

The argument and allegation raged on while Jacq, Victor and Uggi closed in. They now knew the exact position of Silas, Jap and his queens. They could hear Musli screaming and protesting against her beatings. They took position close to Silas and the royals.

"I will close my eyes and ears and let Silas make you confess," they could hear King Jap threaten Musli. "You can't be another Bambo here. If you are, Silas has my permission to purge you."

There were sounds of more beatings, followed by Jap's instruction to Silas to go for a rope, and telling Silas of its proximity to the covered gourd.

Promptly, Victor seized Silas, forcing Silas to lead them to Yeoman, and eventually, to Glawanu's lifeless body. Three pistols were then pointed at Silas as he was marched to the room holding Jap and his queens.

"Leave her alone," Victor yelled. Musli was on the floor, badly bruised and bleeding from her mouth, ears and nose.

"Everyone, keep still!" Jacq commanded, her flamethrower on her shoulder, pistol in one hand.

"I am sorry I trusted you, Victor," the king said.

"I am happy I knew you – for what you are," Victor responded. "Brainlessly you bastardised the masks, the costumes and masquerading. Shame, real shame, on you."

"We heard what you told Musli," Jacq said next. "It is all of you here who have confession to make before our people in the Square. Not her."

Jap, the queens and Silas could not believe what was unfolding. They watched prisoner Jacq become 'Empress' Jacq. But it was Silas who first found an answer, a desperate one. He drew out a small axe from his body, raised it and destined it for Victor's unprotected head.

"Victor, move!" Jacq shouted, and rained two shots at Silas' hand and chest, ending Silas' life of treachery and corruption.

"You are disgusting, Jacq," Azzanaite confronted her, looking straight into her eyes.

"So you know disgust and what is disgusting," Jacq responded. "I don't believe you do." Then Jacq drew nearer her and pointed her pistol at her head. But instead of pulling the trigger for a close range execution she landed a stunning slap on Azzanaite's face. "Where is Nek; and where is Sariya?" she demanded to know. "Where are they, before I take you out to confess, before I deal

501

similarly with you and your husband. It is then you will see proper ghosts!"

"I challenge you, use any power you have," Jap in agonising helplessness said to Jacq. "No one will tell you a thing about them. At this stage nothing can move us."

"Okay then," Jacq acknowledged. "May be nothing can, until something proves to you how one child is basically as valuable to her mother as another is to another mother. Same applies to husbands and wives.

"Wait, and it shall be proved to you."

Jacq went out of the room. She returned in just two minutes – with a five year old prince and a seven year old princess of Jap and Azzanaite, from the group the Glaswegians had separated out to safety in the Square.

"Take a good look at these two," Jacq called Jap and Azzanaite. "You will not see them again if you don't talk.

"How much have you used Sariya so that these ones here would grow? What have you done to Nek so that you would prosper?"

Jap and his queen though frightened, maintained their stand, uttered nothing. They stared on, at Jacq as she went out again.

Jacq re-entered with two of her group's masquerades. Each of them wore a 'death mask' and, strangely, a belt of cutlass and leather whip. The two kids, most scared, attempted to run to their parents but were stopped. "Where are my daughter and my husband?" she asked Jap and Azzanaite again. She could not wait to add another slap to Azzanaite and two fresh ones to Jap.

"You are slapping the Crown, you know that?" Jap reacted pitifully.

"No, yours is not a Crown," Jacq told him. "It is but a bloody mask that has drenched itself and the people it is supposed to protect!

"Take the children away – to where they must permanently belong," she ordered the death-mask masquerades.

"You are heartless, Jacq," Azzanaite broke her silence. "What would you say my children have done to you?"

"Other mothers have asked you similar questions, Azzanaite," Jacq responded, "and you offered no answers.

"Take them away!"

As the masquerades did, the parents looked, resigned to their helplessness before the guns of 'Goddess' Jacquensica.

Immediately after the door, the kids' screams became gradually drowned by the sound of lashing – until the king and the queens could hear only the lashing.

"How can you do this to small children?" Musli, disgusted, broke the silence and challenged Jacq. Like Azzanaite and Jap, she feared the kids were being beaten to death. "How can you? Are you correcting the evil or taking revenge?"

"Just shut up, you," Jacq cut her short. She was not ready to give away her tricks about the two kids.

"I won't, because I won't. Glawanu told me Nek, Sariya – and Bambo were being moved between the cell blocks of Sese and the palace here. He said they have been doing it for the past three days to make any rescue attempt impossible." Neither Jap nor Azzanaite confirmed or denied what parental concern had pushed Musli to reveal.

"Now, please hold them while I go to Sese's," Jacq enjoined Uggi, Victor and Yeoman. "I want to finish the rest by myself."

"You want one of us to follow you just in case?" Victor asked.

"Don't worry, I will arrange all that. I still remember the approach Glawanu took me through on the night these idiots saw my ghost."

Jacq, accompanied by four armed Glaswegians, speedily arrived in a van at a safe distance from Sese's compound. Then they entered the prison area by the back alley Jacq took the night Sese's guards claimed they saw the ghost of Jacq. They were able to surprise the two guards they met before any of them could pick his bow or use his machete. Totally, they were unaware of what the Carnival inside Eagle Square had turned out to be.

"Where are your prisoners, and your keys?" Jacq yelled at the two guards, covering them with her pistol.

"Ask my boss," one said, pointing to the other.

"Stop wasting time, before I shoot you," Jacq yelled again, this time at the second guard. Then she further ordered the senior guard's wife and her small boy, both with him, arrested in order to force his cooperation.

When the cells were opened for Jacq's platoon to see, they were all empty, their walls and floors heavily bloodied.

"Can't you see I am no more a ghost?" she asked in anger and desperation by the last cell, the most bloodied. "Where are my innocent daughter and husband before I shoot you all here!?

"Are these bloods theirs!?"

"They were moved to the palace, the Cell Block, early this morning. One of them was wounded."

"Alright then," Jacq said with confusing irrationality. "Alright, put the wife, husband and boy in separate cells and come with the keys," she ordered her men. "Let them have the taste! All of them!"

"Please, Jacq, don't do this to us," the senior guard begged as his son was being separated from him and his wife. "Please, don't; I will follow you to point out the cells."

"If you have not been talking voluntarily, then you won't show us willingly. We don't need people like you. You, your mate, and your family will rot here unless Nek, Sariya and Bambo are found alive."

"They are held in the palace's Cell Block," Jacq put a hurried call to Ben and Rev Ali Jaiye before her men could finish putting the guards away. "One of them is wounded; I don't know who. We are on our way but please organise the search now," she pleaded with great anxiety.

And with the same anxiety – and ruthless precision – a 'commando' led by Uggi took the Cell Block, inflicting heavy casualties on its guards. The rescue team met Sariya already cried to sleep inside the first cell. Bambo was pitiful inside the bare-floored cell that used to hold Jacq. Nek was in the last, too wounded to find any comfort in the single, mattress-less bed that was left in the cell. Out of resentment and rivalry, Sese, on the night of the ghost, had ordered extra beatings on him, leaving his head a bloody pulp.

"Thank you, Uggi," Bambo said on leaping out from her cell. "Remember me?"

"Yes, I do. So do I remember your cell. Two years ago it was your friend's."

"Is Victor alive – and Jacquensica?"

"We shall talk about that later. But many things have changed; many are changing; many we can't change."

Bambo felt worsened by Uggi's evasion of specifics to her questions. To her it meant Victor and Jacq who she asked for were dead. The assumption turned her stomach. "Can I use a toilet please?" she begged Uggi while at the same time pointing to the guards' house she knew had one.

Inside the guards' house, Bambo's mood changed on seeing the 'tools' the guards she believed to have been killed or arrested, left abandoned. So on her way out she helped herself to a small dagger and tucked it in her skirt, full of vengeance. Then with Nek and Sariya, the rescuers took her to the Lion Hall.

* * *

More than the little Sariya, the two big adults could not immediately understand the positions they met King Jap, his queens and Aroso inside the hall. A king and his queens in ropes – inside Lion Hall where the eyes of the same arrestees were once fed with people in ropes! A roped Jap bleeding on his left leg – and nobody cared! A wounded High Chief Aroso, also on the ropes!

"Oh my God," Bambo breathed, loosely covering her mouth with her hand. She could not sit. She looked again at Jap's bleed and knew what must have inflicted it. Again she looked across the faces of her sister, Azzanaite, and the junior queen, Musli, and could detect some elements of a mix-up and miscarriage of justice. "She is innocent, please. Musli is. Please cut her loose" Bambo pleaded for Musli. It was at that point Jacq entered the Lion, and she heard the plea of her old friend.

Jacq now had a wider area to stare through. She stood still and stared wildly at all who were before her: Musli she had never met before; Aroso demystified and held in disgrace; a shot king and his queen band in ropes; Sariya, still with the similar but bigger face; Nek with more head than body, seated delicately in a chair and feebly waving to her behind a most painful smile as if showing her everything was fine. Jacq recognised her husband, High Chief Nek Dancemaster, and ran to him. She bent over him, hugged him and sobbed. The embrace triggered in Sariya, the photographic memory of a distant parentage, and she joined her parents to share the moment.

Bambo moved to add her own hug on her family friends but she stopped on the second thought in order to allow the close family more time to hugging after such a long, forced separation. It was a sweet, tight hug, and it went sweeter and tighter until Jacq, in its middle, felt the sudden loosening of her husband's arms from her body. When she looked at Nek she saw a man gathering his last strength and breath under the same feebleness of a smile. Nek died. Jacq's scream was big, her tears hot. She bent on her husband, held on to him and rocked his chair. For minutes she was terribly shocked.

"Both of you king and queen, you see what you have done, don't you?" Bambo turned to the royal couple as the paramedics among the Glaswegian were going out with Nek's body being followed by Jacq and Sariya.

"You should be ashamed of yourself for this day," Bambo addressed all the captives under ropes. She was quite mad at them.

"And you, my sister, did I not warn you at the cemetery before the spirits of our parents?" she went on, drifting nearer to her sister, staring and pointing angrily at her. "Azzanaite, did my warnings then make sense to you now? I warned you to stop betraying your friend and your family didn't I, Azzanaite?"

"Don't you ever mention my name again, Bambo," Azzanaite shouted at her sister. "Better you mention the name of your witch friend who brought us to this and who has just openly muscled life out of her husband.

"Don't you ever mention my name or talk to me again!"

"Very well, I shall do neither anymore," Bambo said as she moved even closer to Azzanaite and looked her in the eyes. Then before anyone could note it, she sank her knife deeply into her sister's stomach and watched her fall fatally, in defiance.

* * *

For a moment the death of Nek threatened to stop the carnival. If there had to be other activities for that day, most Glaswegians in Ila thought they must be about executing some revenge on all the Ilas involved in the maltreatment of Jacq's family, the maltreatment that had just ended in Nek's brave but painful death. Whatever would happen, they believed Jacq, being the central figure in all this, must be allowed to have a final say. It was such a delicate issue; and delicately did they leave it in the wise and mature hands of Ali Jaiye and Ben Mackinnon to sort out with Jacq.

Both men invited Jacq to a part of the palace and consoled her. Then they put their suggestions to her: Perhaps they should suspend all further activities and do a burial for Nek instead. Perhaps they should continue with certain aspects of the carnival while excusing her to have time to grieve with her daughter. Perhaps they should call it the end of the Ila Carnival for the year. From her they wanted words that would recognise and honour Nek the best.

"Only one thing will make Nek happy wherever he may be now," Jacq responded to Ali and Ben. "This is that the carnival should go on."

"So, you want the carnival to continue?" Ali asked her.

"Yes, sir, and with my full, participation."

"And you will be in a good frame of mind for it?" Ben asked.

"Yes, sir. Sad, but in better frame of mind," she assured them. She went on to explain why continuing with it that day was more important than anything else:

The carnival wasn't just for her or for Nek's family. It was for everybody, by everybody, and to everybody. Since ages past it had existed that way.

Also, she was in that special time she had dreamt of, waited for, and feared might never come.

Nek actually saw it arrive and acknowledged it with a smile. He died smiling that it arrived without consuming his wife or his daughter.

Concluding it would restore the dignity, humanity and civilisation that Ila Kingdom was, and would be henceforth.

It would mean the complete restoration of the stolen dignity of the citizens including Nek and Tantalo, by the thieving generations of 'modern' cultists led by King Jap of the *Eagle*, and his father of the *Cobra*.

It would add value and honour to the business sacrifices Ben had made by stopping the Mackinnons' hereditary line of business.

The time, expenses, interests and aspirations of Yeoman and his wife, of the Cerianis, of the Dottis, and of others who came from far and near would not be a waste.

Lastly, if it ended well, Jacq was confident it would make a unique history of true cultural restoration.

Ali and Ben admired the high spirits in Jacq. Her strong mood would be helpful to the team. In no time its members were selectively re-deployed to convince everyone at the Square that the great procession would soon start. And within the hour, the stage was reset.

* * *

The arrest of King Jap, Aroso and Queen Azzanaite, with Queen Musli's release, eased the burdens of security when the processions were ready to start. So were the death of Sese, Silas and Worshipper. Chief Priest, the only corrupt titled man yet unaccounted for could not be found – not even to treat the wounds on Jap and Aroso, or to perform the death rites on High Chiefs Sese, Worshipper and Nek. As for Kaka and his followers, they stood shoulder to shoulder with Victor, helping and taking dictations.

Victor, as the most senior chief inside the Square led with a short address to the masquerades and the spectators. He told them that the floats still remained five, and in the same order of dancing as was in place hours ago before the troubles broke out: Dove, Butterfly, Elephant, Shepherd and Dancemaster. But Dancemaster's had now been massively expanded through the influx of Kaka and his followers as well as by some permitted sympathisers of Nek whose casket would be paraded simultaneously with the float of Dancemaster masquerade. "Consequently," he announced, "Jacq, with Sariya, had left the Cerianis to the Butterfly and moved to the Dancemaster's."

He told them it was a day of incredibility for the peoples' support and patient, for all that occurred in and outside the palace within the short spate of time, and how it would be for what next he had to do before the people. Because the day's victory and liberation over the loss and tragedy was spearheaded by Jacq he would relinquish the title of Dancemaster to Nek. And because Nek was no more, he hoped Jacq would assume the title. He prayed the blood of Nek would wash away that stupid aspect of Ila life that allowed women and children to be led perpetually by the kingdom's foolish, greedy and thieving male masquerades. He would voluntarily abdicate after others from Glasgow led by his father, Ben Mackinnon, had given their short testimonies.

"But we love you," Kaka shouted from the sides. "You are a great chief. Stay on as our chief!" Then he led the crowded indigenes in a chant:

We love you, baba; we love you –

We love you, baba; we love you!

"I love you too, and I will always, whether I am a chief or not, whether this chief or another chief.

"One thing I have learnt here is that the title is in one's acts – not in one's look or paraphernalia. Haven't we seen them with round cheeks and big mouths chewing what they stole and passing them into their sinful bellies? Haven't we seen many with nice human smiles that were pretended to you while actually rejoicing at what they had stolen from you for themselves and their children? Haven't we seen them in their big paraphernalia with staffs of authority, pamphlets of authority, shrines of authority, and scripture books of authority, and yet refusing to lead a fight for justice on the streets? Silly, pretentious thieves, not chiefs; cheaters, not preachers; looters, not leaders – of terrible dimensions!

"They should not waste more of our time; they have already wasted more of the life here. So let's hear my father, then your son and grandson Rev Ali Jaiye and Uggi, Mark and Patrizia Ceriani, Mr and Mrs Alfredo Dotti, and Mr and Mrs Yeoman Smith. After them Jacq will speak and take over the control."

Ben thanked the people and Jacq for the day. He told them he and Victor were of direct ancestry of Collin Mackinnon who was the first white man to visit Ila with a priest in 1760. Since then his family had maintained a close link with the kingdom.

"You've all heard of Tantalo, who stories mystified to have disappeared, haven't you?" he asked the crowd. "Actually, the then Japeedoe had him murdered and fed to his crocodile so he would disappear forever without trace. My great grandfather's camera captured the croc eating him."

Next he talked about *Elémpe*, how regrettably, his grandfather had paid the then Japeedoe and some of his chiefs to steal it for him. It was due to the guilt in the family that he had released the statue and paid to have it returned to Ila. He also had other artefacts that were stolen by past Ila kings and individuals. They were already handed over to Jacq who would ship them back as soon as the current thieving rulers were safely rid of.

Ben added that it was to atone for the family's sins to Ila that he had co-sponsored the carnival with Ali Jaiye. "It's a costly mission, but thank God we have achieved," he concluded.

"Next, Ali unveiled from the Shepherd with a small Bible in one hand, to talk. He walked towards the centre, stopped, knelt down and kissed the ground with a shout of "Thank Jesus; Ila, here returns Ologbonjaiye!" When he rose, he expressed his sad thoughts about Ila. He was sad that in this modern world the same linage of kings, chiefs and cultists who used the masks to sell off their children, feed their children to crocs, dominate women and children, and steal the treasures were still left to roam and plunder the kingdom.

"They were strong and brutal," one elder from Dancemaster's float shouted. "We were weak and hungry, so we couldn't attack them or do anything!"

"You could! Now you see you can! Unite and hold them tight. Did the junior masquerades they use to torture you not live among you? They are still on your streets, in your compounds, shrines, churches and mosques as leaders and friends. Next time start with them morally but firmly and persistently – without commercialising it. It will make them to 'junior-masquerade' fairly. Once they police fairly, their senders will have no option but to change. Neither the king nor his chiefs, nor his masquerades can police all that they have. Only their good behaviours can. From now change the masquerading forever."

Yeoman Smith came out next to address the crowd. He was accompanied by two masquerades who unveiled to reveal his wife and eight-year old son both of who he contentedly introduced. He confessed that he, at first, misjudged Jacq as being culturally vain and primitive for coming from Ila, a kingdom that dispersed and was still dispersing its own children all over through one type of primitively wicked masquerading or the other. Soon he discovered Jacq was modest and culturally progressive. Above all, he concluded that both he and Jacq were equal victims of the masked culture of Ila. He was happy that Jacq inspired him and his family to witness the end of the un-cultural and roguish rule. He was optimistic that with the looters dislodged, many diaspora families like his would feel safe to come to Ila not only to learn its true culture but also to live their lives with pride in the kingdom of their roots.

Then he announced what would be his contribution to the kingdom: an Arts School he would inspire and supervise. The school would offer modern studies in music, dance, juju, masks and costumes. It would be free to children, young men and women to start with... Then Yeoman twisted and fell to two poisoned arrows that fatally pierced his neck and face, narrowly missing his wife and his son.

"It won't happen – you won't defile our shrine and culture!" of Chief Priest, leading another bowman, accompanied the shots. Then the bowmen fled – angrily pursued by Jacq.

The chase ended inside the Main Shrine the Chief Priest fled into, jumping over his accomplice who had tripped and fallen outside by its door.

"Forgive me Jacq, please," the accomplice pleaded for mercy with Jacq now standing over him on catching up with him. "He made me do it – please!"

"No, he didn't. Your idiocy did, and never again." It was all Jacq could yell back as she discharged two bullets into his skull and proceeded inside to hunt for Chief Priest.

When Jacq discovered him it was from his back and he was kneeling, sandwiched among the falling bales of cannabis the *Eagles* had ready for export. Jacq shot at one of his soles and the shot evicted him from position. In pain he stood face to face with Jacq mumbling his last saviour, some incantations he desperately believed would save him.

"No way!" Jacq disputed, pointing her pistol at him. "Take your incantations with you from this shrine to hell!" Angrily, she quietened him forever with a series of volley shots into his mouth. Executed.

* * *

Inside the palace where Jacq, Ben, Ali, Victor and the two surviving Smiths retired to after Jacq's retaliatory execution of Chief Priest, Mrs Yeoman Smith with her son did not wait for long consoling to overcome the shock from her husband's murder by the Chief Priest. In fact, like other members of her group from Glasgow, she had anticipated a possible calamity befalling any, some, or all of them in Ila. They all knew they were going on a war mission, disguised as a carnival.

Mrs Smith was quick to remember a sealed envelope Yeoman gave to her two days to the team's departure from Glasgow. Yeoman's instruction then was that his wife should carry it with her to Ila, and possibly back to Glasgow unopened. She could only open it at a point, if any, when she was sure of returning from Ila earlier than, or without him. She took it out of her pocket and opened it: "IF THE LIBERATION SUCCEEDS AND I SHOULD DIE IN IT, PLEASE HAVE ME BURIED IN ILA A FREE MAN, IN THE PURIFIED LAND OF MY ANCESTORS," the note read.

For the first time Mrs Yeoman Smith cried, cuddling her son while Jacq took the note from her hand to enable its lines shared with others in the group.

"What shall we do now with all this devastation?" Ben asked the members present. "Do we go on still with the carnival – as planned?"

Ali's 'yes' was gloomy but emphatic, ahead of nods from Jacq and Mrs Smith. "Now that we've at last brought in the right festival to displace the old one that had caused so much backwardness within and outside the kingdom, we mustn't create a vacuum. Cancelling or postponing it will mean we've yielded with fear, to the system that had for long devastated the generations."

"It has also corrupted generations," Jacq added, "– many generations with only the possible exception of our kids, Jap's and the chiefs' including? Let us do it for them, the kids."

"Yes," Victor agreed, "with you taking the title and leading the floats to the cemetery. No doubt, Nek and Yeoman would love being buried side by side inside Ila's Main Cemetery."

And so Jacq led the masquerading and the burial from the evening through the night – for once under the lights. Jacq's Ila had found for all, a new masquerading form in the norm.

~The End~

Glossary

abbattoir-ed: (local slang, verb) matcheted or axed to death

ad hoc: (adjectival phrase) just for the purpose

àféèrí: (Yoruba noun) magic of disappearance and resurfacing

agley: (Scottish adjective) askew

agbádá: (Yoruba noun) men's large gown

àjé: (Yoruba noun) witch

allemande: a type of English dance

banjo: (Scottish verb) hit or strike

basket: a type of English dance

bàtá: (Yoruba noun) a double-headed drum that is beaten with palm on one head and with leather strap on the other at the same time

batucada: (Portuguese noun) Rio de Janeiro's type of samba music based on percussion instruments

Bell's: blend of Scottish whisky first produced by Arthur Bell and Sons, Perth

besom: (Scottish noun) derogatory term for a girl or woman

bianco: (Italian adjective) white

bloco (Portuguese noun) local or neighbourhood street band or troupe

Brahma: (Sanskrit noun) Hindu God of creation

Buon giorno: (Italian greeting) Good morning

bùrùkùtù: (Hausa noun) local alcohol from fermented guinea corn

cannabis sativa: (Greek) annual plant that is a source of cannabis drug

cantrips: (Scottish noun) magic charms

Certo, signori: (Italian response to a couple of man and woman) Certainly

Circles: a type of English dance

City: wealthy east Glasgow consisting of big commercial

and residential areas

Cliodna: (Celtic) Goddess of the sea

collishangie: (Scottish noun) loud quarrel or commotion

Comitato di arti di Venezia: (Italian noun) Venice Arts Committee

destaques: (Portuguese) main, distinctive carnival floats

Deus omnipotens : (Latin) The Almighty God... A general prayer

dinger: (Scottish verb) to lose one's temper

doots: (Scottish noun) doubts

Dip and Dive: a type of English dance

dramatis personae: (Latin phrase) main actors in an event

ẹdá: (Yoruba noun) a type of clever forest rat

èèwọ òrìshà: (Yoruba command) Never shall it happen or be possible

ẹ́ẹwẹ: (Yoruba noun) special acrobatic, praise-singing masquerade

ẹmẹ́sẹ: (Yoruba noun) male palace servant

en route: (French) along the way

erste: (German adjective) first

Escola de Samba: (Portuguese) School of Samba

esclusivo: (Italian adjective) exclusive

espectadores: (Portuguese noun) spectators

Èsù: (Yoruba noun) Devil, the trickster god

Exorcizo vos, numismata: (Latin) I exorcise you, medal...A special prayer for sacraments and exorcism

fair: (Scottish adverb) very

fairm: (Scottish noun) farm

fermata: (Italian noun) a bus shelter

figure 8: a type of English dance

fingers and hands: local means of weights and measure

ganja: (Sanskrit noun) marijuana

gied: (Scottish verb) gave

Glesga: (Scottish noun) Glasgow

golden-oldie: a hit of favourite of the past

gossypium: a genus of shrubs that produces cotton fibre

Grace: short prayer imparting a blessing

Grant's: Scottish whisky first blended in 1890 by William Grant and Sons, North Lanarkshire

haggis: (Scottish noun) dish of peppered minced liver, heart and lungs of a sheep mixed with suet and oatmeal

hallirackit: (Scottish adjective) wild and irresponsible person

hap: (Scottish verb) wrap up

harmonia: (Portuguese noun) a steward of Rio's carnival float

hems: (Scottish verb) controls or checks

hodden: (Scottish noun) old type heavy cloth woven of home spun wool

humba: (Brazilian slang, verb) bow for respect

humiliores ad bestias: (Latin) old game where Roman nobles sat and watched common citizens torn apart and eaten by lions in an amphitheatre

Ifá: (Yoruba): Oracle of divination

Il Carnevale: (Italian festival) The Carnival

Il mio zio: (Italian phrase) My uncle

Inghiltera Fantastica: (Italian expression) Fantastic England

jinn: creatures believed to be supernatural

julgadores: (Portuguese) judges sitting in the booths along Samba Avenue to judge floats of Rio's carnival

Kabbalistic Saphiroth: (Hebrew) Ten mystic attributes of God in Kabbalah

Kharma-phala: (Sanskrit noun) God of retribution and fruit of action

kissing: Type of English dance

Kú àbò: (Yoruba phrase) Welcome back!

La Domenica Veneziana: (Italian newspaper) Venice on

Sunday

La Notizia Venezia: (Italian newspaper) Venice News

latinus: (Latin adjective) of Latin

Lepidoptera: Order of butterfly and other scale-winged insects

Lion Rampat: (Scottish noun) Scottish national flag

locus standi: (Latin phrase) leg to stand on or appear before a court

lookery: (local slang, noun) an offence through looking at something or someone

Madre Teresa: (Italian) Mother Theresa

mestre-sala: (Portuguese) a male guard or leader to both the float and the flag bearer

monoblocos: (Portuguese noun) more famous street bands that can play all year round

mooth: (Scottish verb) mouth

Mr Objection: local term for a man who constantly disagrees with others

Mr Too-Know: local term for a man who is self-conceited

numero uno: (Italian phrase) number one

ògógóró: (Yoruba noun) locally brewed alcohol from palm-wine

Ògún: (Yoruba noun) God of war, iron and hunting

ògùr̩o: (Yoruba noun) white wine tapped from palm trees

olè: (Yoruba noun) thief

Olókun: (Yoruba noun) Goddess of the sea

Order of The Cobra: local cultic association, shortened to Cobra

Order of The Eagle: local cultic association, shortened to Eagle

Orò: (Yoruba noun) Executioner of criminals deity, usually unleashed during the night

Oya: (Yoruba noun) Goddess of River Niger

Papa-pox: (Yoruba noun) slang for a more devastating

small-pox

parola: (Italian noun) word

passaggi: (Italian noun) walk-ways

passistas: (Portuguese): marching dancers of the float

piazze: (Italian noun) squares or open areas

pitó: (Yoruba noun) strong local alcohol from fermented and doubly boiled guinea corn

planctus: song or poem of lamentation

porta-bandeira: (Portuguese noun) lady-flagbearer leading a float

primo e il megliore: (Italian phrase) first and best

primus inter pares: (Latin phrase) first among equals

robber-talking: (Trinidad slang) sweet talking

Sancte Micheal Archangele, defende nos in proelio: (Latin) Special prayer for self-defence against the devil to Archangel Michael

Sàngó: (Yoruba noun) also pronounced Shango, God of thunder, lightning and fire

signora: (Italian noun) lady

signore: (Italian noun) gentleman

signori e signore: (Italian) ladies and gentlemen

skean-dhus: (Scottish noun) a type of black dagger

smeddum: (Scottish noun) a person with resourcefulness

tomato-ed: (local slang, verb) food prepared with tomato

umqombothi: (Xhosa noun) beer from maize

White and Mackay: Scottish whisky produced by Whyte and Mackay Limited, Glasgow

White Horse: Scottish whisky produced in Edinburgh

Yemoja: (Yoruba noun) Goddess of small rivers and creeks

Yajna: (Hindu) Ritual of sacrifice

zoo-ed: (local slang, verb) to cage.

About Brotherly Shackles

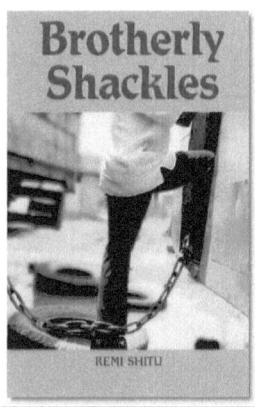

Brotherly Shackles is serious but light, true and current. It is a presentation and an analysis of the life of a gullible people who, though not blind, are unable to see beyond destiny, which they ignorantly worship. More importantly, it is about how brothers' cruelty to brothers perpetually seeks to present that destiny only in its negative form. And this community takes the destiny as every man's actual journey through life.

For Daniel Daniels, a way of embarking on such a journey of life is through establishing a successful public transport company in New Angel. But then, each of the three sets of unseen monsters waiting to devour him outright has its own uncompromising way of embarking on the same journey. The monsters are the Carlos Retfilled gang of indigenes he employs, the Olga-led gullible passengers, and the mistrusting townspeople under the wings of Johnson Dorman. With one group colonising along, another re-colonising and a third resisting; only the gods can predict the end of the journey for "the mass and single idiots" of New Angel.

ISBN 978-0-957-1140-1-2

About the Author

Remi Shitu was born in Nigeria. He studied Textile Technology and Design in Leicester (UK), and Industrial Engineering in Pordenone (Italy). As his working experiences took him round Africa and Europe, he could see many great stories begging to be written. He took the challenge with his first novel, *Brotherly Shackles* (2007). *The Masquerade* is his second. He lives with his family in the UK.

www.ingramcontent.com/pod-product-compliance
Lightning Source LLC
Chambersburg PA
CBHW031050260626
47172CB00001B/2